If I could I'd Wish it all away

by Lisa Helen Gray

Copyright © Lisa Helen Gray 2014/2016
All rights reserved
Edited by Hot Tree Editing

No part of this publication may be reproduced or transmitted in any form or by any means, electronic or mechanical, including photocopy, recording, or any information storage and retrieval system without the prior written consent off the publisher, except in the instance of quotes for reviews. No part of this book may be scanned, uploaded, or distrusted via the internet without the publishers permission and is a violation of the international copyright law, which subjects the violator to severe fines and imprisonment.

This book is licensed for your enjoyment. E-book/paperback copies may not be resold or given away to other people. If you would like to share with a friend, please buy an extra copy, and thank you for respecting the author's work.

Dedication

To the men who made me who I am today

Prologue

People always say that once you've hit rock bottom, the only way to go is up.

Now here I am, having officially hit rock bottom. Only I don't think there is any coming back from all of this for me.

I have been in a relationship with Patrick Holmes—we call him Rick—for five long years, and when I say long, I mean extremely long. The kind of long where you wished you'd have bitten off your own arm and beaten yourself over the head with it because it would have been so much easier than this.

At the beginning of our relationship, I always wondered what Rick saw in little ol' me. He'd say I was perfect and that I was beautiful. I, on the other hand, never saw the appeal. I was boring. Yes, I loved going out and having fun with Rick, but I was always at my happiest when I'd be sat down on the sofa, cuddled up and reading one of my favourite romance novels by myself. I could live my life reading, relaxing and getting lost in another world.

When I met Rick at my grandpa's law firm, I was finishing my final year at university, on my way to a business degree. I also had a work placement at one of the biggest editing companies. I was a bit hesitant to date him as he was eight years older than me, but after some persuasion from Rick, I didn't let it bother me.

We weren't even a year into our relationship when the strain began to show at home. It started with him working long hours, which I understood, as my father and grandfather both worked in a law firm. In fact, they owned it.

Rick would always come home giving me grief on how my grandfather had treated him unfairly and how it was my fault, accusing me of going to my grandfather and telling him what a useless boyfriend he was to me. This of course wasn't true, even though he really was a useless boyfriend; it just took me a while to figure that out. He changed, turning into someone I didn't recognise, someone who made me wonder if I had ever loved him to begin with.

When my parents died, I felt like a part of my soul died along with them. I just wanted someone to love me the way they did, but letting my emotions rule my heart gave Rick the power he needed to control me.

I wished I had never met him.

After long years of arguments and violence, I lost who I was, slowly and painfully. I questioned everything I did, calculated every move I made within the house and out. It was like he had taken hold of my soul, my mind, my body and had the means to break them all in two. I knew what he was doing to me was wrong, but for some reason, I still stayed.

And now? It's worse. I'm sitting here on our en-suite bathroom floor, shaking, bleeding and scared beyond anything I have ever felt before and Rick has a tendency to scare me.

Moving forward, I grab the sink for support, directing my eyes to the long mirror behind the bathroom door. Gasping at the sight in front of me, my tears flow freely as I take in my bruised eye, swollen lip and the blood that pours down my nose and over my mouth as well as from the gash at the top of my head. I inspect the rest of my body as I stand naked in front of the mirror, trembling from head to toe. The fresh bruises are scattered around my arms, stomach and legs. I think he may have done some serious damage to my ribs; either that or the bruising just feels worse than it looks. Though, from the angry blue bruises, there's no denying that I've taken a beating.

Blood gathers between my legs, running down from where Rick forced himself into me. My mind travels back to an hour ago, but before I can conjure up the painful memory, I shake my head, clearing my thoughts. I don't want to think about what happened, what he did or how it felt.

I can't.

I don't have the luxury of breaking, not yet.

Focus! I need to get out of this house and away from him. I turn to grab a towel to cover myself and freeze at the sight of my back. A pained noise escapes my throat as I eye the red welts cutting into my skin. The memory of the belt Rick used to create the thick, swollen lines across my back and backside has me flinching.

I hate him!

No, I *loathe* him!

Up until this moment, I really believed I could get him to change, get him to love me. I believed that because I didn't work—not that he would let me, of course—that it caused more stress on him somehow and I shouldered that blame for a long time, using it as an excuse for his behaviour. Not that I needed to work financially; I'd inherited my parents' millions when they died. I'd never spent the money, not until Rick had asked me for some towards the apartment we bought together last year. I only agreed because I honestly believed that without having to worry about rent he'd relax, but I was wrong.

God, I was so naive.

Banging on the door startles me from my thoughts. When Rick's loud voice booms through the wood, I begin to panic, hoping he doesn't try to get in. Tears run down my face as I shakily watch the door, my eyes never leaving the handle.

"What the fuck are you doing in there, Lola? Finishing yourself off?" he says with an evil snigger. My breath hitches painfully.

Deep down I know I can't be here anymore, that I need to get as far away from him as possible. But I'm afraid he'll just chase me down again and that this time, he'll kill me.

The few times I did manage to escape in the past, he found me, and it never ended well. The last time I escaped, he nearly killed me. My hands automatically go to my throat, remembering the feel of his fingers tightening around my neck and hearing his cruel laughter in my ear.

"I'll be out soon. I'm just grabbing a shower," I lie, shuddering.

There's no way I'm going out there until I know for a fact that he's passed out on the sofa. And with all the whisky he's consumed tonight, I predict that won't take too long.

Jumping in the shower, something inside me breaks, and I end up on the tub floor, sobbing with everything I have left inside me, ignoring my pain.

An hour later I make my way downstairs quietly, finding Rick passed out on the sofa as I'd predicted. The nearly empty bottle of whisky is on the floor, having slipped from his fingers.

This is my chance to decide whether I should stay.

The next time Rick gets angry could mean my death, so I know I no longer have a choice. I have to go. Looking at him on the sofa, my stomach curls with disgust and all my doubts fly away.

It takes me a while to get back upstairs because of my ribs, but I grab my suitcase from under my bed, feeling the adrenaline pumping through my veins.

Not really caring what I pack, I grab whatever I can reach and throw it in my suitcase. Finally having packed most of my clothes, I walk over to my dressing table, unlocking the bottom drawer that has all my private documents, contact numbers, bank cards and driver's license hidden inside.

IF I COULD WISH IT ALL AWAY

Grabbing the brown envelope out of the pile, I inhale deeply. It's the last and crucial part of this plan, one I've had set up for a while but have been too scared to carry out. I pull out two sets of keys, a small, shaky smile reaching my lips.

The first set of keys is for Cabin Lake. My parents were close friends with the owners there and we were always visiting, mostly during the summer holidays when we could stay as long as we wanted. I haven't seen the Salvatore's since my parents' funeral, but I hope they'll still remember and welcome me. I don't think I could handle them pushing me away right now, even though it's nothing short of what I deserve.

At the time, they reminded me too much of what I had lost, and my heart couldn't handle it, especially knowing I'd never be able to visit there without my parents again. I miss them though, all the time. I miss Dean too. He was my best friend growing up, but because of me, we didn't keep in touch. Like I said, everything at the time was hard for me.

Going back there will hurt me, but it's better than dealing with the physical pain I endure here. That's what I tell myself when I grab the second set of keys, the ones to the cheap vehicle I had the doorman help me buy a few months ago. Keeping it from Rick was surprisingly easy.

I never even told him about the Salvatore family. It was easier to just ignore that they existed, and at the time, I didn't want Rick to see me as a coward for cutting them out of my life so easily.

Looking around the room one last time, I make sure I have everything, grabbing a few personal pictures on the way out. He can keep the rest for all I care.

Rick is still passed out and snoring when I make it back downstairs, for which I'm thankful. The thought of him waking up when I'm so close to freedom terrifies me, and I remind myself that this is a solid plan.

Glancing at him I notice that he appears to have aged ten years in the five that I've known him. The drinking has made him look haggard, tired and old.

I thought I'd feel something, like regret or sorrow, but all I feel is relief. As I look down at his drunk, motionless body, I realise I'm saving myself. I walk out the door without a backwards glance.

This is for me.

Chapter One

It's been two weeks since I left Rick passed out in his front room, and I've finally made it to my destination, Cabin Lake.

Driving up to the front cabin, where the reception area is located, I park the car and make my way to the front entrance. Once inside, I'm surprised by how big it looks. It's the main cabin on the site, and I can clearly see why they've used the spacious area for the reception, but I don't remember it ever being so large.

There's a huge seating area, with gorgeous brown leather sofas set in front of a dimly lit fireplace. It looks warm and inviting, especially the chair in the corner by the floor-to-ceiling window looking out into the garden.

When I was little, the Salvatore's lived in the back portion of the cabin, in an extension they had built over twenty years ago.

I remember coming here every other weekend and for the summer holidays with my mom and dad. They were the best times of my life. Even though we weren't blood related, we were still a family. Mom and Lily made sure of it since they grew up together as best friends.

Mark's father passed away years before my parents and left all the land surrounding Cabin Lake to Mark and his wife, Lily. I figured they would expand on the property, but I never expected it to look so different yet somehow still be the same.

Now that I'm standing here, I feel stupid. What if they don't own it anymore? No! There's absolutely no way they don't own it. My mom and dad had their own cabin here for starters, not to mention the land has been in the Salvatore family for generations.

Surely I would know if they sold the place. Plus, my grandpa would have mentioned it to me. He, unlike me, kept in touch with the Salvatore's and learnt pretty quickly after my parents' passing not to mention them in front of me. Now I'm beginning to wish I'd asked questions or let him tell me what they were up to. At least then I'd have a clue as to what I've just walked in on.

I ring the bell on the front desk, crossing my fingers that it's Mark who greets me.

After a few seconds a man comes out of the office, grabbing my attention. I watch him walk down the wooden stairs and a memory hits me of all the times Dean, their son, and I would run up and down them or play in the office. We were inseparable, even though he was two years older than me. He was the most handsome boy I'd ever seen. He had an easy charm to him, was funny and caring and had a boy-next-door kind of personality. He's the main reason I loved coming here. Without him, I think I would've gotten bored.

The man walks towards me, keeping his head down. I don't think he's noticed me yet because he seems preoccupied and somewhat irritated.

"Hello, miss. Can I help you?" he asks, his face hard, staring at me in apparent frustration.

He may look pissed, but he's certainly polite and professional. Studying his features closely, I'm surprised at how shockingly handsome he is, and then at the fact that the thought popped into my head at all. The man could easily be a model.

He's wearing a black T-shirt that stretches tightly over his broad chest and a pair of worn jeans. He looks good; I'd have to be blind not to notice. He has a strong jaw; dark, piercing blue eyes; and short, dark hair. His skin is tanned from the summer sun and he towers over me. I'm only five-foot-four, so he must be going on six-foot-two if I were to take a guess.

Oddly enough, he looks familiar to me. In fact, he looks a lot like Dean. But if so, he would have remembered me, right?

I'm still lost in thought when he clears his throat. I need to talk to Mark, not ogle some stranger who is clearly having a bad day. Snapping out of it, I give him an apologetic smile.

"Hi, I, um… I was wondering if Mark Salvatore were here for me to talk to?" I ask, my voice hoarse from nerves and weeks of having no one to talk to. He looks taken aback for a second by my question and it has me wondering why. Then I see the flick of anger shining in his eyes. I automatically take a step back, my body starting to shake, knowing too well when someone is going to be aggressive.

"Have they sent you? Did those assholes send you? You can go back and tell them that they can stick their offer up their ass!" he roars, banging his fists on the front desk.

I'm ready to run out the door in fear, but then Mark comes storming out of the back room to see what all the commotion is about. Seeing him has me freezing in place, my legs, weighted to the floor.

"What on earth is going on?" he lectures, his jaw dropping when he sees me. He also seems to be frozen, but only for a second before he manages to snap out of it. The frown he wore when he first walked out turns into a huge-ass grin and I begin to relax somewhat. The other man, who I somehow forgot about, is looking at us, confusion written across his face. When he glances back at me, he gives me a sharp look, and I can't help the smirk that lifts at the corner of my mouth.

Turning my attention back to Mark, I'm shocked that he's exactly as I remember—built like a giant, eyes soft and warm, with a smile that would make anyone feel relaxed and welcome.

God, I've missed them. And up until now, I didn't realise quite how much. My eyes begin to water as a pang of regret and sadness hits me.

"Well, look who we have here. Damn, Lola, you look so much like your mother," Mark says, making me blush.

Coming around the reception desk, he walks over to me, pulling me in for a hug. I tense in his embrace, not used to the gentle affection he's showing. He must sense my unease because he steps back, keeping his hands on my shoulders as he studies me from head to toe. I know he can see the slight bruising that I couldn't manage to cover on my eye and cheek. It's another reason why it took me so long to get here; I didn't want to answer all their questions, so I waited it out until the visible bruises faded a little. Apart from the split lip and a slightly bruised eye, everything else is hidden by clothes and make-up. The gash on the top of my head needed stitches, but thankfully my hair covers the majority of it.

"Doll, have you been eating? Is everything okay? Oh God, it's so good to see you. It's been too long. We tried to get in touch, you know. We wrote to you so many times, but in the end, we agreed you would come back to us when you were ready," he rushes out, still flabbergasted at my arrival.

He doesn't mention the marks on my face but I know he's noticed them. The emotions are clear in his eyes, going from concern, to anger and then back to curious and confused. Before I can answer him, the handsome, muscled man interrupts me.

"Dad? Care to explain?" he questions, and I store that bit of information away for later. His eyes never leave mine, making me fidget back and forth on the balls of my feet.

He's looking at me like he's trying to figure out who I am, just like I've been doing with him.

"This is Lola Lawson. How the hell didn't you recognise her, son?"

I gasp, my eyes going back to the man. It *is* Dean! I haven't seen him since I was twelve years old.

Now that it's confirmed, I can't keep my eyes off him.

He sure has grown into his body. He is definitely all man.

IF I COULD WISH IT ALL AWAY

He turns back to me, his expression softening, and my heart starts to beat erratically. His eyes change to a lighter blue somehow, making him look more approachable and a lot like the Dean I remember. It's not until Mark speaks that I finally tear my gaze away from Dean and his captivating eyes.

"Lola, this is my son, Dean. I thought I'd introduce you just in case you hit your head and forgot who he is too. Jesus! You two used to be attached at the hip. I guess time really has changed you kids," he says sarcastically, his smile never wavering.

I smile, feeling lighter than I did when I first arrived. "Mr Salvatore, we haven't seen each other in sixteen years. I didn't exactly recognize him either," I admit, forcing a giggle.

I can feel Dean's gaze on me. Shivers run down my spine and my face flushes red for reasons I can't explain.

I'm going to be honest. When I was younger, I had a major crush on Dean. My mom would always tease me and say, "One day, you two will get married and have children of your own."

"To what do we owe the pleasure, my dear? I really am glad to see you. We've all missed you, doll," he says, emotion filling his voice.

This is what I didn't want. The sadness in his eyes as I look up at him is clear as day. I force a smile, trying to ease his worries. I wish I could explain why I did what I did, but after all this time, there is really no excuse.

I was twelve when I lost my mother and father in a car accident, and moving in with my grandma and grandpa had been an adjustment in itself. They lived farther away from my childhood home, so not only did I have to leave all my friends but the life I had with my parents as well. Losing both of them was so hard, and I found that once I moved into my grandparents' house it was easier to block out my old life and the pain caused by bringing it up. Still, I should've been in contact before now, keeping them in my life like my mother and father would have wanted for me,

"I was wondering if our cabin was free to stay in," I tell him sheepishly before just going for it, blurting out what I want to say before I chicken out. "I'm so sorry for not replying to any of your calls or your letters. With everything that happened with my parents' passing, it was too hard. I should never have ignored you though, and for that, I am truly sorry." Tears stream down my cheeks.

"Hey, it's okay, doll," he says soothingly. "Your cabin is always free. I've never allowed it to be rented out like it had been before. Aside from the cleaners I have in there on the odd occasion, nothing has changed from the last time you and your parents were here. Apart from the bed, anyway. We thought we should change it for when you came home." A smile lights up his face. "You know, Cece and Owen wanted to give it to you when you finished university. I swear those two had everything planned out. Your mother was the worst. She even had your wedding organised, and you were only ten at the time." He laughs and my heart swells with love.

"Really? I didn't know that." My chest tightens. "Is it... um.... Would you mind if I go on out there? I need to have a lie down. I drove down here and I haven't been sleeping well," I rush out, not having the heart to tell them I need some space, some time to process everything. Talking about my parents is causing old emotions to stir, and I don't want to lose it in front of Dean and Mark.

Dean is the one to answer, startling me. "You drove down here, all the way from your grandpa's? Why would you drive for that long?" he asks me. I don't tell him I drove from Kent and now Carlisle; it would raise too many questions.

After driving for hours, I had to admit that Rick did more damage than I could handle on my own. I'd been self-medicating on pain pills and changing bandages. I knew Rick couldn't have followed me because one, he was out cold when I left, and two, the doorman, Gavin, said he would tell Rick I left with a woman for a spa weekend. I completely trusted Gavin, as he'd worked in that building over forty years and knew everything that went on, including what Rick did to me. But even with his promise, I made sure to keep an eye out. So I went to the hospital, giving the name of a girl I once knew at uni.

It should only have been a day trip down here from Carlisle, a six-hour drive max. However, I made stops at Norwich, Herefordshire and then the detour I took going to my parents' old house in Kent, staying there for a few days to recover alone. The whole house was void of furniture when I arrived, although that didn't bother me so much. I was just grateful not having so many reminders of what I lost surrounding me.

When I arrived, I went out and purchased a sleeping bag and camped out in my old room. I don't bother telling Mark or Dean any of that though; like I said, it would raise too many questions.

For a minute there, Dean seemed to be worried about me. I push it aside, not deserving any of their concern. He probably doesn't even remember me—or hell, even care about me anymore. Why would he? It's been sixteen years; he's moved on.

"Yes, it was a long drive. I had a few things that I needed to do and a few other stops to make before I came here," I tell them while shrugging. It technically isn't a lie. I don't want to have to lie about too much though. Knowing me, I'll end up forgetting what I've told them and get myself caught up in one.

Lies always have a way of revealing themselves.

"It's dangerous. You should have called one of us. We would've happily come and got you," Mark says, looking a little hurt that I didn't.

Dean turns to face me again. This time his irritation is written all over his face, but I just don't know why. *What the fuck is his problem? What did I ever do to deserve his hostility?*

Snorting, Dean turns to his father.

"Dad, just let her go and rest. The poor girl looks like she just crawled out of a car crash," he mutters, wincing when he realises his choice of words have hit a sore spot.

Just remembering the way my parents died brings a whole new level of sadness over me, tiring me out completely. I don't even have the energy to flinch at his harsh words; instead, I just stare at him, showing him no emotion.

"Son, enough," Mark snaps, glaring at his son.

"Okay, maybe I should just go," I mumble, not wanting them to argue over me. I'm not worth it.

I hear Mark and Dean call my name as I rush out of the room but I ignore them, carrying on to my car, needing some fresh air.

I have no idea what to do now. Should I stay or should I go? I don't want to cause arguments between them; they're family, and I out of all people know just how precious family is. I never want to be the person who comes between that.

Letting out a deep breath, I notice my hands are shaking uncontrollably. Trying to calm myself, I sit in the front seat of my crappy car, taking in deep breaths, but it doesn't work.

A loud knock on the window has me jumping and screaming in fear. I bang my head on the roof of the car and wince, gasping in pain.

A noise to my right has another sharp squeal escaping me, and I turn just in time for the door to open. My heart beats wildly in my chest and I swear I could see it beating through my tank top.

I'm surprised that it's Dean opening the door and not his dad. I flinch when he bends down, kneeling in front of me as he pushes his head into the car and invades my personal space. I jump, trying to move back, but it's no use; there's nowhere to go. A sharp gasp escapes when Dean takes a loose strand of my wavy golden blonde hair, and tucks it behind my ear. He leans back once he's satisfied that it's not going to fall free again, giving me back some of my personal space, and I start to breathe evenly once more.

Curiosity, sympathy and concern reflect back at me when I look into his eyes, but the worst one, the one I hate, is the pity that's written all over his face.

I narrow my eyes at him. I don't want or need his pity.

"I'm sorry. I didn't mean to scare you," he says softly, like he thinks if he talks any louder he might startle me or bring on a panic attack.

I raise my eyebrows with more confidence than I feel. Yes, I'm being rude, for no reason whatsoever. He grins at my expression, which only infuriates me more.

"Honestly, I don't bite." He smirks, holding his hands up in surrender. "The reason I snapped at you earlier is because my dad is having some trouble with some folks who moved in across the lake. They've been trying to get us shut down for a while now and want us to sell them a piece of our land. As you can tell, we don't want to sell, and they don't like that. Still, I apologise for my behaviour. I was being rude and inconsiderate," he admits before shaking his head. "I still can't believe it's you. I didn't even recognise you. You're more beautiful than I remember. Your hair is longer, the blonde a lot lighter." He's using that soft, dreamy voice of his again, a small smile playing on his lips.

As he takes in a long breath, I take a minute to go over everything he's just said. Yes, I may have been naive when it came to Rick and his apologies, but with Dean his expression shows me how truly sorry he is. It's either that or his dad threatened to kick his ass. Then again, even as a kid Dean had this way about him, and he always had a kind heart.

I wish he'd piss off.

The second the thought hits me I sigh, knowing I'm being irrational and bitchy because of my lack of sleep.

Dean would pick on me as a kid, but in a teasing kind of way. He was never hurtful, which is the only reason I'm still here, giving him a chance.

We were always together, so we never really fell out over anything—not over something serious, anyway. Plus, I secretly liked his teasing and the attention he paid me. It felt like we had this strong connection and bond between the two of us, much like the one I felt back in the reception area.

As a young girl with a crush, I always found myself telling him all of my secrets, no matter how embarrassing they were.

Knowing I'm doing my spaced-out thing, I shake my head, turning to answer him. "Honestly, it's long forgotten, so you don't need to be sorry. I really just want to get to the cabin and crash, if you don't mind."

He looks surprised by my admission and maybe even a little curious, most likely wondering if I'm being sincere or not.

"Yes, sorry to keep you. Are you sure you're okay? Your lip and head, they don't look so good," he mentions sheepishly, looking wary about how I'll react.

"Yeah, it was just a minor accident. Still clumsy Lola," I lie dryly, forcing a chuckle and trying to make light of my injuries.

"So, before you go," he starts, looking nervous. I inwardly groan, just wanting to go to bed. "I know you probably have one of those dongles, but Dad said to take you out to apologise for the way I reacted and well, it made me wonder if you minded catching up tomorrow and going to the local bookshop? Maybe grab some breakfast beforehand?

"Mom isn't going to be back until the day after tomorrow. She went to some wine tasting event this morning, so it's only me and Dad here and he's busy. So, I, um… do you? I mean, you can say no, but the boat trip over there is amazing and you'll love the bookshop they have. What am I saying? You probably hate reading now," he finally finishes, looking flustered.

As much as I think he's cute when he's nervous, I can't help but start getting impatient with him. It's the cranky bitch I mentioned earlier coming out. It's the first time I've felt safe enough to even want to sleep and I'm not going to pass up the chance, knowing I need it. The energy I did have left just seems to be pouring out of me; it's why I'm so desperate to get out of here, not wanting to pass out in front of him.

I have to admit though, the fact he still reads intrigues me. I honestly believed he'd grow out of that once he hit puberty. I guess it's hard for me to picture him reading, especially someone as good-looking as he is. It seems unfair that he has both qualities to him.

Needing to wrap this up, I sigh, knowing I don't have a choice. Plus, I still haven't started reading *Fifty Shades Freed* yet, so a trip to the book store is tempting. I also have a feeling he won't stop until I relent.

"Dongle, Dean? Really? It's called a Kindle." A smile crosses my face and I chuckle when he blushes. *He's such a goof.* "I would love to come. Sorry for snapping at you. I'm just really tired and want to get some sleep. How about I meet you down at the dock around, say… nine o'clock?"

He gives me the biggest smile I have ever seen, like I just gave him the secret to world peace and my breath hitches. His smile makes my heart beat faster, and I know I'm the one who's blushing now. The feeling is so foreign to me that it has me pausing for a moment. A part of me wants to just push him away and speed off; the foreign feeling scares me that much.

"See, I'm thirty years old, and I have no idea what the thing is called. What I know is it puts bookshops out of business," he rants, looking like he's about to continue.

I nod, agreeing. "Goodbye, old man." I force him away with my hand, a grin on my face.

I laugh whilst driving off, my eyes focused in the rear-view mirror, watching as Dean's face lights up with a shit-eating grin.

I feel the tension coming off me the closer I get to the cabin. I didn't even realise just how much I missed him or this place until coming here. It feels like I'm back with my parents and telling him I can meet him after I unpack, like old times. A sad smile reaches my lips at all the memories swimming in my mind as everything passes me by.

Finally, I pull up outside my parents' cabin. Mark was right; the place hasn't changed. It's still the same as it was when I left all those years ago. Even the same flowers are growing in the pots my mom kept outside the cabin doors.

Leaving the safety of the car, I make my way inside. Tears sting my eyes when I notice my dad's slippers and boots by the front door, my mom's coat still hanging up on the coat rack. I lean in, breathing in her scent. God, I miss her smell. Even though it's faint, my mom's scent is there.

I never had the heart to come down here to sort through their personal belongings. Grandpa offered to do it himself after I refused to talk to Lily and Mark, but I declined on his offer, wanting this place to remain the same. I guess in a way I knew I'd be coming back.

Speaking of that, I never even went through our family home in Kent. I left my grandpa to sort through it all and left my grandma to box all my stuff up for me, so I didn't need to return here. I know my grandpa has kept some personal items that belonged to my parents in a storage unit, which I am truly grateful for. When I'm ready to, I'll ask him to take me so I can go through it myself.

Moving farther into the cabin, I remember how Dad loved coming here. I was an only child, so I think that played a big part in the reason he would regularly bring us down for mini vacations. I think he wanted to give me a bigger family, someone to grow up with, and the Salvatores gave me that.

Mom couldn't have any more children after complications whilst giving birth to me. It's why I inherited everything when they passed away. Bu none of the money meant anything to me when I couldn't have them. I miss them so much; every single day is a struggle, more so when I was a teenager, a young woman needing her mom.

Exhausted, I quickly run back out to the car, grabbing the first bag I can reach out of the boot. I drag it in, not even caring if it has anything I need in it. I'm too tired to go back out and grab the other case.

Walking towards the master bedroom, I stop at the door, not knowing whether to sleep in there or not.

Fighting back the tears, I take in a much-needed breath before pushing the door open. When it's open, my earlier question about sleeping in here or not is answered. The bed is brand spanking new and is freaking huge. It's bigger than any bed I have ever seen. Plus, I feel somewhat closer to my parents being in here, in a non-creepy way.

IF I COULD WISH IT ALL AWAY

When I was ill, I would always sleep in my parents' bed. There was something about being surrounded by their scent that relaxed and calmed me, always making me feel somewhat better. And although the bed is new, that scent still lingers in the cabin. It makes no sense, since they've been gone years, yet part of me feels like they're here.

Losing them when I did broke me in a way that made me believe I would never recover. When people came to the funeral and hugged me, telling me they were sorry for my loss, I just wanted to scream, "If they were lost, I would go and find them" at them.

But they were gone, and they were never coming back.

I would hate it more when people would sit me down, telling me it would get easier in time, when they all knew it wouldn't, not really. You just find a better way of masking the pain that consumes you.

I remember the day they died like it was yesterday; after all, it's one of my worst nightmares.

Grandpa had turned up in the middle of a dance class and pulled me out, taking me to the hospital. He tried to explain, but nothing reached my ears after he told me they were in an accident.

The minute a doctor reached us at the hospital, they told us that my dad had died on impact and my mom passed away during surgery.

They were sorry for our loss.

I didn't believe the doctor and I started hitting him, demanding he took me to them. I remember not being able to see through my tears and that my throat felt so raw, like a ball was stuck in my throat. I even told my grandpa that I hated him for believing them but after that, everything went black.

I was told later from Grandma that because I was so out of control, demanding they take me to my parents and fighting anyone who tried to stop me from searching for them, they had to heavily sedate me. It was probably for the best, but at the time I couldn't forgive them for letting the doctors do that to me.

The funeral was just as bad. Seeing their coffins, knowing they were there, made me want to jump down, scream at them to wake up, to stop playing games so we could go home, beg them to come back to me. But I didn't do any of that. I just sat there feeling numb.

My silent pleas went unanswered.

I close my eyes, letting my tears fall freely as I think about my parents, about Rick and about how my life used to be so normal.

I wish I could have that again.

Chapter Two

Waking up, I'm sore all over and still tired, even though I slept most of the night. My body is covered in sweat from the nightmare I had. I must have been seriously out of it because I don't even remember waking up once. For the past two weeks, I haven't slept well, too anxious and on edge since the night I fled from Rick. Most of the time the nightmares have kept me up, so last night's sleep was welcomed and much needed.

I've suffered from night terrors ever since my parents died, but they eased off after a year. When Rick began to abuse me, they came back and were much worse. The most painful ones were the ones where my mom and dad would appear, both disappointed and ashamed of me. But since I ran away, they've all been of the last night I spent with Rick, the images of what he did on repeat.

Rolling over, I look at the clock. When I see the time, I jump out of bed, snagging my toe on the chest of drawers.

"Fuck!" I wince, hopping on one foot.

Fuck! Shit! Fuck! Shit! Ouch! That really hurt. Goddammit, my poor toe.

It's eight in the morning. I promised Dean I'd be out on the dock in an hour. I'm going to be late. Rick is going to be seriously pissed. I shake my head, realising I'm not meeting Rick, that I'm meeting Dean. I need to remember that Dean isn't Rick and that Rick can't hurt me anymore.

Although I've just come out of a brutal relationship, I still can't help but think of what my life would have been like had I stayed here and ended up in a relationship with Dean, like my mother dreamed of. Even at five years old I had a crush on him. How much different my life would be if I had been with him or someone like him instead of Rick. Who am I kidding? A man like Dean doesn't go for girls like me. I'm not ugly, but I'm not pretty by any standard. Even if he did find me attractive now, there would be no point. I'm broken, completely shattered from who I once was. I'm not even half the person I used to be, and for that, I'll forever be a lost cause.

I always thought he was beautiful, but now his looks have amplified. He is more than hot. He is magnificent.

I loved how he looked at me yesterday when I was in the car, his bright blue eyes shining, looking right through to the deepest parts of me. It's something I've not felt in a long time. Rick tended to look through me, like I didn't exist.

I have to admit, Dean puts Taylor Lautner to shame, and that boy has a body I want to lick. And yes, just like a true Twihard, I can never resist Jacob Black topless. Come to think of it, even as a kid I wondered what Dean hid underneath his clothes. Now that he's a fully-grown man, the urge is much stronger since he seems to be packing more than he's showing.

Sighing, I turn to the suitcase I dragged in last night and grab some clothes. I need to meet the new, older Dean and get to know him. I want to see if he's anything like the boy I once knew.

It's nine, and I'm at the docks, surprised to find that I'm the only one here. Go me! I'm terrible with time, always have been. I'm one of those people who would be late for her own funeral. I think it's only the cinema I've never been late for and that's only because I can't miss the trailers. They're my favourite part. I'm a movie geek through and through.

"Good morning, sunshine," Dean greets. His voice startles me, making me jump. I hadn't even heard him approach.

Spinning around, I clutch my chest, trying to even my breathing but when I take in his appearance, I freeze. He's wearing a white linen shirt with a few buttons undone at the top and has it untucked, hanging over a pair of denim jeans.

Oh my good God! The man looks like he's heading to a modelling shoot and not to a bookshop. He looks… wow! Okay, I may be drooling a little.

Taylor Lautner has some serious competition.

Fully aware of my ogling, Dean wears the biggest smug grin ever. Heat creeps up my neck to my cheeks. Lowering my eyes, I take a step back, ashamed of my behaviour.

"Like what you see, huh?" he asks, cockily.

I shake my head, my cheeks heating further. "Morning. Sorry, I, uh… I was just…just trying to picture you as the boy I once knew. You seem to have grown a few inches." I inwardly roll my eyes at how ridiculous I sound.

"Of course you were," he says, wearing that shit-eating grin which kind of annoys me. "So, are you ready?"

"Yes. Um, Dean? Is there somewhere we could go to get some coffee? I didn't have time to hit an off-licence on the way over here yesterday, so there's nothing in."

I fidget as he takes a step towards me, stepping right into my personal space again. My body reacts *again*, shaking. I'm not comfortable with his close proximity and I don't think I ever will be. It's not because I think he'll hurt me, but because of other reasons.

When he dips his head so he's eye level with me, it brings him closer, making me nervous. Taking another step back, I repeat, *I'm not scared of Dean,* over and over in my head. Because I'm *not* afraid of him; I never have been. The only logical answer I have for why I'm so wary of him is because I haven't seen him in sixteen years. I don't know if he's the same boy I once knew.

I loved the boy he was back then. I trusted him with my life. We told each other everything, and even now, I have the urge to tell him about Rick and what he did to me.

I've spent so long not being able to confide in anyone that I'm ready to burst at the seams. Back *there,* I never had any friends to talk to, and it was one of the hardest things I had to adapt to. It's also one of the many reasons why Rick managed to control and manipulate me so easily.

I've always been a loner, and it's never bothered me. Not even now. When it comes to the same sex, I've always found it hard to get past the bitchiness they have towards other girls. It's why I never made any female friends during school or when I was at uni.

Dean had always been enough of a friend for me growing up that I never needed to seek out any female friendship. Plus, he was the one I went to when I needed someone to talk to. He helped me through some of the hardest times of my life. He was my anchor. I'll always remember the good times we shared and how young and carefree we once were.

When I feel the time is right, I'll more than likely confide in him. I already want to. Hell, I think I need to, if only for my sanity's sake.

Gavin, the doorman, had his suspicions. He told me he would help me leave Rick, but I never confirmed the beatings, nor did I want to. I'd been too ashamed and scared of people finding out, but more worried about what Rick would do to me if they *did* find out. Having Gavin suspect wasn't the same as being able to talk to someone about it.

Blinking rapidly, I clear my thoughts before looking back at Dean. I notice he's taken a step back, eyeing me warily. He looks like he's trying to figure me out, to find out what's wrong, but I don't let any emotion show on my face. I've had so many years of practice hiding them from everyone that it comes as second nature to me now.

"I'm sorry, what did you say?" I ask, embarrassed for spacing out.

"I said there's a place we can go to for coffee across the lake. It's actually not far from the bookshop I'll be taking you to. If you haven't had coffee, then I'm taking it you haven't eaten either. We can stop for breakfast too. I'll take you food shopping tomorrow if you want since I'll be going for Mom anyway."

"No, it's okay. I'm not hungry," I say, waving off his offer. "I just need to get some caffeine in me. Shopping sounds good though." I sigh, relieved since I have no idea where the nearest food shop is. "I can't wait to see your mom. I miss her, and I feel really bad for pushing you all away. You all meant a great deal to me.

"I've known all along that coming here would hurt some way, but seeing your father yesterday brought back some happy memories for me. It was nice to remember a happier time. I know now I was wrong to handle it the way I did." I take a deep breath, looking to the ground.

"You were just a kid, Lola. Mom and Dad understand why you did it. They've missed you too. They always talk about you, and not a day has gone by where they don't. They don't hold anything against you, Lola. I promise." A sheepish expression crosses his face, seeming uncomfortable before he continues. "I wrote to you a few times to see how you were, but you didn't reply. Mom and Dad told me to give you some time and I did. I guess over the years I just gave up hope that I would see you again."

I smile sadly, feeling the pain in his voice when he confesses that last part to me. A wave of respect for him hits me, and I'm grateful for him telling me the truth instead of sugar-coating everything.

"Come on. Let's go get some coffee." He grins, taking my hand in his and leading me towards the boat.

The boat trip over is the most freeing thing I've ever experienced apart from leaving Rick. Dean is obviously in no rush to get over the lake. The boat purrs smoothly across the water as we talk mindlessly.

I'm still grinning like a fool when we enter the café ten minutes later. But as soon as the shop door closes behind us, I lose my smile, seeing everyone's eyes on me. The notion that they could be staring at Dean doesn't even cross my mind; my anxiety is too far gone to even consider it.

My hands start to shake, my palms sweating. When the first customer greets Dean with a warm hello, my body begins to relax, and the shaking eases up.

Guiding me through the sea of tables, Dean sits us down at one near the window. He orders us a coffee straight away, seeming to know the staff well.

We talk about the boat trip over, Dean asking if I liked it. Before I know it, the waitress is setting our mugs of coffee down on the table and taking Dean's food order. I tune them out, turning to look out at the lake. It's beautiful with the morning sun glinting over the dark water.

Turning back to face Dean, I watch as he takes a sip of his coffee, a serious expression on his face. One that clearly says I'm not going to like what he has to say.

Oh boy, I think I'm in trouble.

"So, what brings you back to Cabin Lake?" he questions, reaching for another sash of sugar.

I pause, taking a deep breath. I've known from the beginning I'd be asked this question, even thought of all the different lies I could tell them, but there was one problem with that—I hate lying. It will only lead to more lies, and I know I'll never be able to stomach doing it to Dean and his family.

"I needed to escape my life for a bit, so I decided to come here, where it felt like home." I shrug like it's no big deal, when really it is. "Being here with you guys and my parents had been the happiest days of my life. I missed it, missed feeling at home." A forced laugh escapes me as I swirl my coffee around with my spoon. "Everyone says your home is where you make it, but for me, this has always been my home. It's where I grew up. It's where my parents and I would come together. They looked at this place like home. I just… I missed home," I whisper, a lump forming in my throat.

"Wow! I hadn't expected you to be *that* honest." He seems lost in thought, his face a mixture of emotions. "So… escaping? Are you on the run from something or do you have a murderous ex-boyfriend coming after you?" he teases, trying to lighten the tension, but his words suck all the air from my lungs, causing me to panic.

Breathe, Lola.

I know he's only teasing me—he couldn't possibly know the real reason—but it frightens me all the same. I freeze, my entire body locking up painfully from trying to block out the dark memories wanting to surface. It's no use. With each sharp pain in my skull they come, knocking the breath out of me.

"Lola, are you seriously going to fucking wear that outfit in public? We have a fucking meal to get to. We're not going to the red light district," Rick thunders, his face red with anger.

IF I COULD WISH IT ALL AWAY

I want to scream that he was the one who bought me the dress to wear, that it was he who demanded I wear it to impress his partners. I don't dare open my mouth and tell him that though, knowing it would only make him angrier. Instead, I bow my head, looking to the floor.

"I'll go change," *I whisper, close to tears from his harsh words. When he doesn't say anything, I dare to take a look at him. My breath hitches when I see the veins in his neck bulge, his hands clenching into fists at his side and his body turning rigid. He looks like he's trying to restrain himself, but I know better. Nothing can tame the monster inside him.*

I know what's coming. His posture and expression show it all.

I guess I knew the second he told me to change that this would happen. I should have known he wasn't going to allow me to relax and have a bruise-free night.

Before I can blink, his fist shoots out, knocking me to the floor. He kicks me once, twice, in the ribs. The pain becomes too much to handle as I curl into myself, shaking uncontrollably. A wave of terror hits me when I have no idea what he's going to do to me next. He's unpredictable at the moment, unstable to a frightening degree.

His large frame blocks the sharp light coming from overhead. I watch, fearing for my life as he kneels before me, his face red and pinched with anger. I start to sob harder when I catch the hollow, vacant look in his eyes. They're completely black, void of any emotion. More proof of how evil he is. I feel stupid for never seeing it before.

The second our eyes connect something snaps inside him, and he lunges for me, filled with rage. A scream tries to bubble out, but it is cut short when he wraps his hands around my throat, stopping the sound from escaping.

I can't breathe.

I'm going to die.

I try to plead with him to let me go, but no sound escapes when I open my mouth. Tears fall faster as I fight for air. I claw and slap at his arms, trying to get him to loosen his grip, but all it does is make him squeeze tighter. My throat burns, small gasps of air falling from my lips as my vision blurs.

"I'm going to squeeze the fucking life out of you, Lola. Yet again, we're fucking late, and it's all your fucking fault. You'll regret putting on that whore outfit. Mark my words, you're going to regret it. I can't believe it took you so long to get dressed like this. You're a fucking disgrace.

"Did you really think saying you'll go and change would make this better? Are you that fucking stupid?" *He laughs, and it sounds bitter and hollow.* "Fuck! When will you learn that you are nothing? It doesn't matter how hard you try to look good, you'll always be ugly. Always be unattractive," he sneers. Leaning in closer, the alcohol rolls off his breath, making me want to gag. "You're fucking lucky I put up with you because otherwise, you'd have no one. No one else wants you."

"Lola, are you okay? Lola! Lola! Please answer me. You're scaring me," Dean calls out, sounding panicked. My vision comes into focus, back to the present.

The realisation of what happened dawns on me, and I feel the colour drain from my face. My hands shake and my neck feels raw, just how it did in the memory when Rick wrapped his hands around my throat.

Coming to, I find Dean kneeling in front of me with one hand on the back of my chair, the other cupping my cheek, lovingly. His touch has my pulse skyrocketing. My heart is thumping, chest rising and falling heavily.

He's looking at me with so much concern, and I hate that I put that look there. I'm devastated he just witnessed what I call my freak-outs. I've spaced out a few times like this since I left Rick, putting it down to high stress levels. On the drive over here I was worried it would happen while I was driving and I'd cause an accident. I'd been lucky for the first time in my life because I managed not to have one.

"Sorry, I zoned out," I tell him, forcing a smile and hoping he believes me. But from the look on his face, he doesn't seem all that convinced. If I knew he'd mention an ex-boyfriend during a conversation, I would have prepared myself. Then again, I don't think it would have mattered; nothing could have prepared me mentally.

"Honestly, Dean, I'm fine. I just zoned out."

"It's where you zoned out to that's worrying me. Your eyes were completely blank. It looked like you weren't even in the room. You looked terrified." He runs a hand through his hair, pausing. "It fucking scared me, Lola. Where did you go in that head of yours? Did I say something to upset you?"

"Dean, please! Everything is fine. I just zoned out." Having to lie to him again has the fight leaving me.

Reluctantly he sits back down, at the same time the waitress walks over with his food. My eyes bug out of their sockets when I see the tray. There's a lot of food loaded on those plates, and I mean *loaded*. There's enough to feed a family of six, I swear.

My stomach rumbles from the delicious smell, but since I didn't order any food I ignore it, hoping Dean didn't hear it.

"Are you seriously going to eat all of that?" My voice comes out high, my expression shocked. "How can you eat all of this and be so buff?"

If he eats everything, I'll eat my pants.

Pausing, I remember when we were younger, and I take back what I just said. He could eat a lot back then too. He was constantly pinching food off my plate or grabbing seconds.

Wondering why he hasn't answered me, I look up, realisation dawning on me when I realise what I just said to him. I called him buff.

To his face.

I think I'm more annoyed at the fact I said the word 'buff' instead of something manly than I am about the fact I basically just called him hot.

His lips spread into a wide grin, his expression amused and knowing, like he can read my thoughts.

God, when he smiles like that, it makes his dimples pop out. My breath hitches, finding his grin panty dropping.

Shit! I'm so going to hell thinking like this, especially when I just managed to escape the last man I was with.

"Buff, huh?" He's still grinning, an amused glint in his eyes, and I blush.

Holy crap! I'm totally going to hell.

"Yes, buff. So… food… That hungry, huh?" I ramble, trying to hide the fact I feel like I'm dying with embarrassment right now.

"Nah, I don't feel comfortable with you not eating, especially when I know you haven't eaten since you arrived, so I ordered food for you too. I wasn't sure what you liked so I ordered a bunch of shit."

He chuckles, eyeing the plates of food.

Wow!

My throat tightens, a lump forming at the incredibly sweet gesture.

"Oh, okay."

He stares at me, still grinning, before snapping out of it and ordering me to eat something. Not needing to be told twice, I dig in and find myself enjoying a hot meal for the first time in over a week.

After a few minutes of eating in silence, we start chatting, mostly about his parents and the cabin. He stays clear of asking me anything personal, for which I'm thankful. Once I know for sure he isn't going to surprise me again, I begin to relax, enjoying his company.

We've been walking through the little town for five minutes. As we round the next corner, we come to a narrow street filled with cobbled stones.

Staring down at the cobbles, I don't notice that Dean has stopped walking until I bump into him.

"Sorry." I chuckle, turning to take in my surroundings. The shop we've stopped outside brightens the whole street. Most of the buildings surrounding it are vacant, except for a cancer research charity shop and a music shop across the road.

Looking back at the beautiful store, I smile and find myself falling in love with it, even though I haven't even stepped inside.

The panels on the building are a light purple, the door a slightly darker shade. It helps the shop stand out. Above the door is a huge sign in bold cursive, spelling out 'Brooke's Books' in different-coloured letters.

Giddy, I take a step inside, giggling when the wind chime echoes around the shop. The melody is relaxing.

My fingers run along the shelves, and I smile at how unique they are. They're all painted in brightly lit colours.

I find myself breathing in the scent of lavender as I walk farther into the bookshop. I can honestly say I've never seen anything like this. It's out of this world. If libraries or bookshops were to all look like this, then I'm willing to bet more people would start reading.

The shelves aren't the only bright-coloured fixtures in the shop. My favourites so far are the massive beanbags in every colour under the rainbow. There is no way I'll be able to leave here until I know where she ordered them from. I want one so bad. They look really comfy, and that's not the only thing that does. In the far corner is a green sofa, big enough to use as a double bed and has cushions piled on top in every colour I can run off my tongue.

The place is incredible, and I can't stop myself from taking in every little detail.

"Wow! This is mind-blowing," I whisper in awe.

"Thanks. I designed it myself," a sweet voice says, and I turn to the sound. "Hi, I'm Brooke."

A petite woman steps down into the room. She's so tiny and looks to be in her early thirties. She's dressed in bright, radiant colours, just like her shop, and is naturally pretty with her mid-length, brown wavy hair, and big brown eyes. No wonder the place lights up your mood when you walk in; it reflects its owner.

I already feel drawn to the woman, not only because of her shop but the aura that surrounds her. You can instantly tell from being with her for the shortest amount of time that she's a good person, that she's kind and would do anything for anyone. For that, I already like her and have a feeling we'll become fast friends.

"You designed this?" I ask, stunned. But looking at the strong, independent woman, I wonder why I'm so surprised.

"Yes. I designed everything from the beanbags to the hanging butterflies in the children's section back there." She smiles proudly, pointing to where she had just walked out from.

"Wow! It's all beautiful. Well done, you did a good job. It's left me speechless," I admit, smiling.

The place is truly amazing. I'm dying to go check out the children's section she just mentioned. It's like a world of magic, and definitely every kid's dream come true in here. Hell, this is *my* childhood dream come true. I was, and still am, proud to say that I am the biggest book geek ever known.

My father's passion was law, my mother's her music and reading. She chose to teach underprivileged children how to play the piano as a career.

Ever since I can remember, I've always wanted to become an editor. I loved the placement I was given from the university. I even had a good job after uni at an editing firm, but because of Rick and his old-fashioned ways, I had to leave so he could look after me. It wasn't until later on in our relationship that I figured out it was all just another way to get me where he wanted. Until now, I never realised it was his way of controlling me, a way of taking full power of our relationship, and over me.

Shaking the unwanted thoughts away, I remind myself that not all men are the same as Rick. My dad and grandpa are proof of that.

"Make yourself at home…?"

"Lola," I finish.

She smiles back at me. "Lola, please make yourself at home," she tells me before turning to Dean. "Dean, you didn't tell me that you finally met a beautiful girl. You've been in and out of this joint for years, listening to me prattle on, and you didn't think to return the favour?" She tuts at him before turning back to me with a huge smile. "His last girlfriend was a B.I.T.C.H. Honestly, if there was money involved she was there, but if there wasn't, well, you wouldn't be worth her time. I disliked her from the moment that spunk of a man brought her here. You know what the first thing she said when she walked in was?" she asks, never taking a breath. "She said, and I quote, 'Dean baby, I think we're lost. What is this place? I mean, seriously, 'What is this place?' C'mon," Brooke scoffs, laughing as she gestures to the books around her. "It's a bookshop. What else could this place possibly be?" She takes a deep breath, rolling her eyes. I giggle, loving her little outburst. She really gets going once she's started. Poor Dean looks seconds away from turning around and walking out of the shop, his cheeks flushed with embarrassment. He's so cute at the moment that I can't resist teasing him.

"Peroxide Barbie? You date those, really?" I raise my eyebrow, and I can't help the snort that escapes. I remember a time when he used to hate girls like that; girls that would wear next to nothing, act fake and full on flirt. He'd always tell me I was the only girl that he could stand to be around; that all those girls made him sick. The memory makes me laugh harder, and Dean narrows his eyes, playfully.

"Sweetheart, I think you should go look in the mirror. 'Peroxide Barbie' was what you said, wasn't it?" He winks, eyeing my hair, and my stomach flutters. He turns his attention back to Brooke. "And no, she isn't my girlfriend. Lola is a friend of the family who we haven't seen in years. We've known each other since we were babies."

I chuckle at his obvious discomfort, but then what he said clicks and I turn around, narrowing my eyes at him.

"Did you really just call *me* a peroxide Barbie?" I snap.

"Err, yes?" It comes out as a question, his bravado fading.

"One, Mister 'I don't know the difference between real and fake,' my hair has never and *will* never be near hair dye, bleach or any other hair chemical known to woman or man. The only time I even go near the hairdresser is if I want to get my hair cut.

"Two, my hair was blonder than this as a kid. You should know that since you said it shined brighter than the sun.

"And three, I didn't need to go to university to know what this store is. I knew before I even took a step inside. It's on the pissing sign above the door. So never, *ever*, get me confused with those bimbos." I finish my rant, taking a deep breath. God, it feels good to let off some steam. When I finally look up, Brooke and Dean are both staring at me, their mouths hanging wide open, catching flies.

"Okay, sweetheart, say what you really mean." Dean chuckles, teasing me, and I growl. "Grab your book so I can get you another coffee, preferably before you turn green. I want to get home safely." Leaning closer, his breath tickles my ear, sending a shiver down my spine. "I really want to say I'm sorry for upsetting you, but then I wouldn't have seen you all mad and riled up. It makes you look sexier, by the way. Welcome home, Lola."

"God, you're such a pig," I lie, my face heating. As I look away, my gaze meets Brooke's and she grins, sending me a wink.

"Find a book, Lola." He smirks, shaking his head.

I stomp off, looking for the book in mind as a small smile plays on my lips, his earlier words playing in my head.

Sexier. He thinks I'm sexy.

Hopefully when we get back, I can persuade Dean to take me out in the wooden rowboat I saw on the stones down by the docks this morning.

I don't know why but after experiencing this morning's ride on the boat, I want more.

Maybe I can take my book with me and read while he rows us far out onto the lake. I have to admit, the thought of watching Dean's biceps straining and bulging while he rows excites me. It also sickens me to feel

IF I COULD WISH IT ALL AWAY

something so soon after Rick.

Any feelings Dean may or may not return seems like a trick, an illusion. It's like Rick is still punishing me. His cruel words play over and over and remind me that no one will want me. Plus, even if I did have a chance, I lost it the minute Rick violated me.

Nobody wants something tainted and ugly.

Chapter Three

Dean stops rowing under some willow trees, and I can't help but glance around my surroundings, admiring how beautiful it is out here. The water is still, the sun is shining brightly, reflecting off the water, and the sound of the birds chirping in the sky is blissful. It's the most relaxing sound in the world.

"Why are we stopping?" I ask curiously. I thought we would be heading towards the south side of the lake where it's more open.

"This is my favourite spot to read. It's the scenery, the sound of the birds. Everything about being out on the water helps me relax," he admits, looking embarrassed.

"Yeah. It's really beautiful here."

With nothing left to do, I grab the third instalment of *Fifty Shades* out of my bag. Dean is right; the scenery, the sounds of the water lapping against the boat and the sound of the birds chirping makes this place the perfect spot for reading.

Opening the book, I chuckle to myself remembering how Brooke and I got into a heated conversation back at the store over it. We talked about how Ana gave herself so easily to Christian and how willing she was to play a part in his desires, desires that weren't even hers. All to make *him* happy.

That's when the conversation turned heated for *other* reasons, although I didn't really add much when she started talking about how hot the sex scenes were and her own sexual experiences. I've only ever slept with one person and haven't even experienced an orgasm, so I had no opinion over whether the book was realistic or not. I did read somewhere that it's common for women not to have an orgasm during sex, but after listening to Brooke go on about her conquests, I began to wonder if something is actually wrong with me. Don't get me wrong, reading the first two books had me so hot and bothered that I started to feel twinges in places I never knew I existed, but that's as far as I've ever gotten to feeling pleasure.

I was glad when Brooke changed the subject over to the topic of their relationship, but even talking about their relationship still had me feeling uncomfortable. The thought of giving myself—not just my body, but my trust—over to a man who wants the power over me sexually and emotionally too reminds me too much of what Rick happily took without permission. I couldn't do it, not again. But then, I do hope that one day I'll meet someone where giving him my mind, my body, and my soul, is done freely and willingly.

We left Brooke dealing with another customer and headed out, but not before I went and looked at the children's reading area.

It was exactly how I imagined it to be, and I'm willing to bet the kids have a blast when they visit. The same beanbags were there, only they were smaller. She even had a mini version of the sofa that she had out front with 'Twinkle, Twinkle, Little Star' written above it in italics, and there were star-shaped twinkle lights everywhere on the ceiling.

It was breathtaking, and the only change I would make if it were mine to do so would be to add a play gym with small ball pits. Maybe even add some fun picture slides or a baby sensory machine.

I think the reason I thought of all of that was because it's something I hope to give my children one day. I wanted to give them a place where they can lose themselves. I love kids, always have, and hope that one day I'll have some of my own.

Returning my attention back to the book, I turn the page and start to lose myself in the world of Christian Grey.

I think an hour has passed since I started reading. I'm already a quarter of the way through the book, with no intention of stopping. I'm so completely sucked into the story that I don't notice Dean has stopped reading his book, not until he knocks my leg off the side of the boat with his, startling me.

Seriously, how rude? How dare he take me away from my Christian Grey? Doesn't he care that it could get a man cut?

"I thought you zoned out again for a minute there," he says, grinning mischievously. "I see Mr Grey has you all hot and bothered and transfixed into the world of BDSM. You didn't even hear me call your name, did you? And I called you a few times."

He doesn't even finish his sentence before I feel heat rise in my cheeks. Knowing the fact that my face is glowing bright red only makes this more embarrassing.

"Sorry. It's a habit of mine. Whenever I read a good book, I get so lost in the story. It's like watching a movie inside my mind and everything around me is still. Nothing else exists," I tell him, flushing.

His grin grows bigger. "So you picture him doing that naughty stuff to his woman and giving her mind-blowing orgasms?" I know he's teasing me, but it doesn't stop my cheeks turning redder.

I cannot believe he just said that to me.

I choke on air, not knowing what to say or do. My belly turns like a washing machine, my stomach full of nerves.

"You've read the book?" I ask, stunned. It both surprises and embarrasses me at the same time. I just can't picture him reading this book, or any other male reading it for that matter. But having him mention anything about it makes me wish the world would swallow me up. I hate that he knows exactly what I'm reading, and what I'm most likely thinking whilst reading it.

"Um, yes." He doesn't even pause to think about it or come across as embarrassed. *Oh my God! This isn't happening to me.* "I'm actually shocked I even read it after hearing all the mixed reviews, but I couldn't help myself. I needed to know what all the fuss was about. Those books are seriously hot. I had to get off after reading each and every one of them. Sometimes during." He smirks, eyeing me up, and I flush once again. "Speaking of, you're looking kind of hot and bothered. Do you need me to take you back to the cabin?"

Seriously, what is he doing?

His expression is serious, so I can't tell if he's joking or not. This is so embarrassing, and if I thought my face couldn't get any hotter, I was wrong. I wish I couldn't swim so I could drown myself in the lake. I look anywhere other than at him.

Only this could happen to me.

"I am *not* hot and bothered," I screech at him. "If I look like I'm hot and bothered then it's because of how hot it is out here. And the fact you keep talking about orgasms and masturbation—which, by the way, I don't do, or wish to go and do, thank you very much." Everything just bursts out of my mouth, and I curse myself for getting so worked up. What is it about this place that brings out the sass in me? I blame Dean. Yeah, I blame him. It's all his fault I'm not acting like myself.

After letting him stare at me for over a minute without speaking, I finally snap. "What?"

"You've never touched yourself?" He looks completely shocked, like I've just told him I've found the cure to world hunger. I shake my head at him, frustrated at the deeper hole I keep digging myself into. I'm also pissed at him for teasing me in the first place. "Never?"

Ugh, why can't he just believe me?

"For fucks sake. It's none of your business, but if you *must* know, no, I don't touch myself. I never have. God! I've never even had an orgasm." I blurt out my most embarrassing secret before my mouth snaps shut, my teeth grinding together. I really need to learn how to keep shut around him. Not that becoming a mute is going to help me become a new and improved, stronger person.

"Never?"

I swear if he asks me again I'm pushing him overboard, right after I throttle him. It's the confusion and heat pooling in his eyes that has me pausing long enough not to harm him.

I look down at where my feet are crossed, shaking my head. "No," I whisper, barely audible.

"You're not a virgin, are you? I mean, not that being a virgin is a bad thing because it's not. In fact, it's kind of hot," he rushes out.

My eyes bug out of their sockets, trying to find out how we ended up talking about this. I'm also a little pissed off and shocked at his presumption, my temper rising.

"What? Am I that ugly you'd think I can't get a boyfriend to have sex with me? Do you believe all women should spread their legs or touch themselves just so they can get off? Life doesn't revolve around sex, you know," I fume. And because I feel like I'm on a roll, I carry on. "No, I'm not a virgin, but I'm not very experienced either. But I do know sex isn't pleasurable, with orgasms and romance like it's written in this book." I'm waving the book in his face, feeling angry tears pool in my eyes. "I also know when you give a man your virginity it doesn't go all fucking sweet and peaches like Ana's did. Some men abuse your trust. They manipulate you and hurt you just so they can get what they want," I croak out. "Can you take me home?" I whisper, drained and deflated.

"No," he growls sharply, and my head snaps up at the sound. I'm surprised to see that he's angry. Like really bloody angry.

I stand so fast that the boat starts rocking from side to side, causing me to lose my balance. Dean's quick, reaching me in time before I fall overboard.

I automatically react when I feel his hands on me, raising my arms out of instinct to shield my face.

Dean visibly flinches, the pain filling his deep blue eyes making me wince. I didn't do it because I thought he'd actually hurt me. I did it because I'm so used to shielding the hits Rick would dish out, wanting to make sure they wouldn't be visible. It occurred so much it's become second nature to me.

My throat closes up, a lump forming in the back and making it hard for me to take a deep breath. Dean stays frozen, so much pain and anger in the depths of his eyes I have to look away, hating that I've made him feel this way. Before I do, there's no hiding the fact he's worried and concerned for me. Seeing that after my reaction surprises me.

"Shit."

"A man hurt you, didn't he? Did he force you to sleep with him? Jesus, Lola, look at me. I will *never* hurt you, ever. I promise you that. Even if you stuck a knife in my gut or ruined my *C.S.I. Miami* box sets, I'd never raise my hand to you, or any other woman for that matter. Shit, I wouldn't even get mad at you if you told Mom it was me who set the hay on fire from trying cigarettes."

His breathing is hard, his face filled with so much emotion that I have to sit back. I try to keep myself steady, but it's hard when I'm shaking so badly.

The minute I glance at Dean, I wish I hadn't. He looks so torn up, and it's breaking my heart. I can't bring myself to say the words I know he needs to hear, especially after he just reminded me how much I can trust him.

"I…," I start, but shake my head, frustrated when nothing else comes out.

"Please, Lola. Talk to me. I knew there was something wrong when you first turned up. I saw the faint bruising on your eye, and I knew make-up was covering a lot of it." He looks so sad as he eyes where I've covered my bruises. Instinctively, I reach up, touching my bruise. "Hell, I might have believed you about your clumsiness, but I know *you*, Lo, and I know when you're hiding something. If that lie didn't tell me everything I needed to know, then the fact you looked petrified, too scared to even run when I raised my voice, would have. You did it again just now, thinking I was going to hurt you. You should know me enough to know I'd never hurt anyone defenceless."

I know I can't lie to him any longer. His voice is breaking through the walls that I've built around my heart to protect myself from being hurt again.

If I ever want to change, this is a good time to take the first step. The only thing that could go wrong is Dean not believing me, but he said he knows me. He knows I was raised right and that I wouldn't lie to him about something like this.

I know deep in my heart that I can trust him. Even with years of distance between us I know that much is true; I feel it in my soul. It's just finding the courage to tell him.

Needing to start off somewhere, I look into his eyes, showing him how hard this is for me to admit.

"Yes."

As soon as the three-letter word escapes my mouth, my shoulders sag with relief, the heavy load I've been carrying finally easing off me somehow. All that shame, all that guilt, feels like it's been washed away with just that one word.

I can do this!

I wish I had done this sooner.

Chapter Four

We both sit staring at each other for a few minutes. The only sounds I can hear are our harsh breathing and the birds chirping in the whistling trees above.

I'm just about to open my mouth to break the uncomfortable silence when Dean speaks, his voice hollow, filled with hurt and pain.

"Why didn't you say anything?" He doesn't give me a chance to answer. "Tell me. Tell me everything. I know it's going to be hard for you, but you need to know that I'm here for you no matter what.

"I've worked on a few domestic violence cases and seen situations like this before. There's nothing you can tell me that would make me see you any differently. I'd never judge you. The only person I'll be judging is the fucking prick who did this to you. If your dad was still here, he would kill him, Lola. Fuck, *I* want to kill him," he bites out.

"I've never told anyone before. I don't think I can. You don't understand how long I've let him do those things to me or what I let him get away with," I state honestly, my voice shaky.

"You *can* do this, Lola. I can help you, but you have to help yourself first by getting it all out and letting someone in. You're not on your own anymore.

"Remember when my granddad died and you told me that nothing could change what I'd seen or felt, but that telling someone would help set all of it free? It worked, and I know if you do the same thing, you'll be free," he tells me fiercely.

I remember when Dean's granddad died. He'd been there with him when it happened. It had been hard for him seeing that, and he ended up pulling away from everyone but me. He wouldn't talk to anyone about it, so I took him to our favourite spot at the meadow down by the lake one afternoon. I told him he needed to set it free, to tell if not me then the meadow everything he was feeling. I didn't realise how much that helped him until now.

IF I COULD WISH IT ALL AWAY

Looking back at him, I know I need to do this. My parents didn't raise me like this; they raised me to be honest and upfront. But it's harder to talk about than I thought it would be. The only thing that's helping is the fact that Dean was always the person I went to when I needed to get something off my chest. Hell, even if I'd done something wrong I was upfront and honest about it to my parents, but talking about this? It's different.

Knowing I have nothing left to lose at this point, I take a deep breath, preparing myself to reveal my hidden past, my living nightmare. But first, I need Dean to promise me something.

"First, you've got to promise that you won't interrupt me until I've finished. I just… I need to get it all out. I need to do it before I chicken out." My throat tightens again, almost painfully, as I gulp.

"I promise."

"Oh, and one more thing. You can't tell your mom or dad. I don't want them treating me any differently or looking at me with pity."

My eyes plead with him to agree when he doesn't say anything. I begin to worry he can't make that promise, but then he jerks his head in a tight nod. He might not be happy about keeping this to himself, but he'll respect my wishes, for which I'm thankful.

"I met Rick at my grandpa's law firm. He was different compared to all the other boys I knew. He took the time to get to know me, to pursue me, and I liked that. He didn't give up on me when I had doubts about him being eight years older than me and when I finally did get over the age issue, we started dating. Not long after, I fell in love with him. Well, I thought it was love, anyway. Looking back, I think it had more to do with the fact I'd been lonely and I used him to fill that void inside me.

"Everything was perfect in the beginning. *He* was perfect. He never gave me any reasons to question who he was or what he was capable of. I never thought I should be scared of him. Why would I? I loved him, but I should have known something wasn't right with him when we first broke up. It's clear to me now, but back then," I shake my head, willing my shaky voice to still.

"The first time we broke up—well, he broke up with me—was because I wouldn't sleep with him. I'd been a virgin. I was scared of the unknown, and I guess a huge part of me wasn't ready to give him something so sacred. He broke it off, telling me that I didn't love him and if I believed we had any kind of future together then I'd just… do it.

"The week during the breakup was horrible. I missed him. I missed not having anyone to talk to or fill my time with. There was no one there to care if I had a bad day at uni or failed an exam, and it got to the point I would tell myself he made my life better. So I slept with him. He wasn't gentle. He wasn't loving. And he didn't care that I wasn't comfortable. I spent the whole time crying. I cried for days after too. Every time I would move the wrong way and feel the sharp sting between my legs, it was a reminder of how badly it hurt."

I clench my thighs together as I remember the horrific experience. With a shaky voice, I continue, twiddling my fingers together.

"He used the same manipulation to get me to move in with him. It was always the same kind of manipulation, and it wasn't long after moving in together that he started getting possessive, not letting me out. He isolated me from everything."

I take a deep breath, thinking of everything I missed out on because of him. I glance over to Dean, trying to gauge his reaction, but his expression is blank. The only way I can tell he's affected is from his clenched jaw.

Giving me a tight nod, he signals for me to carry on. My throat dries up, my body tense.

"After that, the possessiveness and controlling got worse, much worse. Like one time, when I was on placement at the editing company the university assigned me to, and the boss invited us to a last-minute celebratory dinner and drinks. We had just landed a major client, so I was really excited about being asked to go and celebrate. I went, fully intending to text Rick, but I left my phone at the office. It turned out that Rick called, and my archenemy at the company answered the phone.

"You have to understand, it was rare for our boss to even pick female placements, let alone work alongside them. It was an honour and I didn't want to ruin that by telling him no, that my boyfriend wouldn't like it. This other girl on placement didn't like that she was with all the other students, so when Rick called she made sure to stir the pot. From what Rick told me after, she had basically convinced him I was cheating on him. She told him it wasn't the first 'dinner date' I'd gone on with our boss.

"We were finishing our dessert when he showed up. God, Dean, he was so mad. Sam, another student on placement, got in the middle of us when Rick grabbed me and everything went from bad to worse. Rick punched him, and when my boss got involved, Rick just went wild. He hit him too, screaming and accusing him of taking advantage of me. I remember screaming, begging for Rick to stop, but he wouldn't listen. He got us out of there before the cops were called.

"That night, not only did I lose my placement but I also lost everything else that made me who I was. It was the first time he hit me. God, it had been the worst night of my life, but when he woke up, he was different. He was like the old Rick, the one I first met. He kept saying he was sorry over and over and that he'd never do it again. There were so many excuses for why he got so angry, so many tears, and I couldn't take it, so I forgave him.

IF I COULD WISH IT ALL AWAY

"After that, it was a vicious circle—the beatings, the controlling, everything. But... but it was when he used sex to punish me that would break me." I start crying, my throat raw when I reveal the hardest part of everything that Rick did to me. "He would tell me over and over that I was his, that no one would want me and that I needed to be taught a lesson. He'd scream at me to stop being such a dirty whore.

"I'm so scared, Dean. So fucking scared. I'm scared of the constant fear of bumping into him. I hate I was weak. I was so weak I wished that the next time he hit me, he'd do it just right so he'd kill me. I just wanted all the pain to stop."

My chest heaves with weighty sobs and Dean sits next to me, pulling me into his arms. Leaning my head against his chest, I can hear his heart beating erratically. I lean into him, crying for everything I lost, for the person I once was before I met *him*.

"It's okay, Lola, I've got you. I'll never let him hurt you ever again," he promises, holding me a little tighter. "Does this Rick know about this place, about us?" he asks. I look up to find his eyes shadowed, darkening with anger, and although I'd usually be scared, I know his anger isn't directed at me.

"Unless he followed me here, he wouldn't know where I am. The first half of the drive was a blur. Plus, I never spoke about this place to anyone, not even my grandpa."

"How did you get away? How didn't anyone know what he was doing and report him?"

I know he isn't asking because he doesn't believe, but because he's trying to understand how Rick got away with it for so long.

"You really want to know?" Tears build in my eyes as I recall the night I left. Out of everything he did to punish me, that night was by far the worst.

"I don't want to push you into telling me anything you don't want to. I can tell you're holding back and what you've said isn't the worst he's done to you, but please, don't hesitate to tell me anything. I'm only asking because I want to be prepared. If he ever turns up, I want to know everything I can about him. God, I want to go find him now and give him a taste of his own medicine," he growls.

My head snaps up, my eyes widening. "You cannot be serious? He'll kill you. Like not breathing kill you. He's gotten away with this for years, Dean. You don't understand." I close my eyes, breathing through the panic.

"Then explain that to me, Lo," he begs. "Explain how he got away with it."

"He has friends in high places," I shrug, wishing I could explain just how high. "The first time he raped me, I reported him to the police. They took me out back for questioning while they arrested him, and it was the most humiliating experience of my life. He wasn't with them for ten minutes before they were bringing him into the room they were holding me in, like *I* was the criminal. He told them I liked it rough and that I tend to get carried away with the whole rape fantasy," I bite out, remembering the lingering stare from the one officer, clear lust in his eyes. "I couldn't afford to go to the police again after that. What he did to me after… God, it was horrible, and I'd have done anything not to go through that again."

"I'm so fucking sorry this has happened to you. I can't even begin to imagine what you're going through. But I think you need to go to the police," he says, and before I can open my mouth in protest, he holds his hand up, stopping me. "Just listen to me. I might not be a cop anymore, but it doesn't mean I don't know the right people. Good people. I could get someone I trust, someone not willing to be influenced, to take the case." His voice softens, his eyes pleading with me to listen to him.

"I don't know if I can talk about this to someone else," I whisper, fiddling with the edge of my top.

"So start with me. Tell me what made you leave."

"He came in late from work, drunk. I'd tried waiting up to have dinner with him, but it got too late, and I was already so tired, so I went to bed. I didn't hear him come back or walk up the stairs. I remember jumping up in bed, startled from the door slamming against the wall. When I realised it was him, I panicked. I knew it was going to be bad, but before I could ask what was wrong or tell him I was sorry, he threw his cold dinner at me. The plate smashed against my head," I tell him quietly, running my fingers along the scar on my forehead as visions of what happened play in front of my eyes. "I couldn't see with the blood running into my eyes, but I could hear him. He was shouting so loudly it was piercing my eardrums. I couldn't make out what he said because the buzzing in my ears and my blurred vision made it hard to concentrate.

"He hated being ignored so when I didn't answer the question I didn't even hear, he swung at me, hitting the side of my head once, maybe twice before dragging me off the bed by my hair. I could feel it being pulled out, the pain becoming too much for me to handle. I was in such a state I didn't get a chance to block the worst of the blows like I normally did when he got mad. He kicked me repeatedly in the ribs until he tired out. But he just decided on a better punishment," I choke out, not wanting to tell him the next part.

Dean, for the most part, hasn't said anything, but I can feel the anger rolling off him. I know it must be taking everything inside him to keep himself in check.

"He… he… he…. Fuck, I couldn't stop him," I shout, my voice

IF I COULD WISH IT ALL AWAY

hoarse. "I tried everything to stop him. I begged and pleaded, but he didn't care. He threw me across the bed, and I landed on my stomach. He ripped my knickers down my legs and all I remember is hearing his belt unbuckle. I tried everything, *everything* for him to stop, but no matter how hard I tried to kick him away or crawl across the bed, it was no use. He was too strong.

"The first hit from his belt knocked the wind out of me. The pain was excruciating, the worst I've ever experienced. The second hit hurt the most. I remember wishing he'd just kill me, but I passed out before I could beg him.

"I woke up to him taking me from behind. I couldn't even tell you which hurt the most, him hitting me with his belt or him taking me *there*." I sob, my heart squeezing painfully. "All the other times he raped me he never went that far. I don't remember much, just the pain because I kept coming in and out of consciousness. It was only when he finished that I finally managed to move off the bed and into the bathroom.

"I couldn't go to the police, I couldn't go to Grandpa, and I knew I couldn't stay. I cleaned myself up and I left. I'd been planning it for months since none of my other attempts of leaving him were successful. I knew if I was to succeed I needed to be smart.

"I left him on the sofa passed out and didn't look back. I got in my car and made it as far as I could before exhaustion overtook me. The following days were bad. I couldn't drive for more than an hour before I needed to rest, the pain too much for me to handle. When I got halfway, I knew I needed to go to the hospital, so I checked in under a girl's name I went to school with. The doctor tried to get me to stay and report what happened, but I knew if I did he'd find me. She gave up and discharged me, giving me some leaflets that had helpline numbers. After a few more stops I ended up here. I won't risk doing anything for him to find me." My whole body sags with exhaustion as I cry into my hands. I can't even look at Dean, not wanting to see his reaction. If I see disgust in his eyes, I don't know what I'll do. He hasn't spoken a word yet; hell, I don't think he's taken a breath since I finished telling him everything that happened. I can't help the broken sob that falls from my lips.

"I'm going to kill that fucking son of a bitch!" he roars suddenly before standing up in the boat, causing it to rock from side to side.

I jump up, startled and scared, gasping when I take in Dean's murderous expression. His eyes are full of tears, his jaw clenched, his face pinched with pain and sorrow.

But before I can comfort him, the realisation of what he's said hits me, and I panic. "No, Dean, no! He'll find me! He can't find me, Dean. I came here to be safe. Please don't take that away from me. Please, I can't go back there. I won't. I'd rather kill myself than endure another second with him. You hear me? I can't go back there. *I can't*! I can't, I can't, I can't," I chant, falling back down on the seat. My whole body trembles as painful sobs escape, causing my chest to tighten.

I hear Dean move before I feel his presence in front of me. I look up through watery eyes, pleading with him not to do anything, as hard as it may be for him. His eyes are red and glassy. I'm unsure of what he's going to do, but when he pulls me to his chest, I fall into his arms easily, sobbing uncontrollably. I didn't know how much I needed to be held until this moment.

He rubs my back soothingly, kissing the top of my head. "I will keep you safe, Lola. It's okay. Everything is okay. Shush, baby. I promise nobody is going to hurt you," he coos, rocking me from side to side. "I've missed you so damn much it hurt, but the notion that you were living a good life was the only thing that helped the pain go away. Knowing you were going through this? It fucking kills me, Lola. It really fucking pains me. You didn't deserve that life, no one does, and I promise you until my dying breath that he will never hurt you again. No one fucking will. I'd die making sure of it."

Chapter Five

It hasn't been long since I spilled my guts to Dean back on the boat. Once he calmed me down enough to move away, he rowed us to the docks and drove the short drive back to my cabin.

I'm exhausted, emotionally and physically. We haven't spoken since my confession, and I'm grateful. I'm still trying to process everything going on in my head. Dean has tried asking if I'm okay a few times, but in my zombie state I've not been able to answer, opting to stay mute.

He drops the keys on the mahogany coffee table before turning to me with a worried expression.

"Go lie down on the sofa. I'll make you a cuppa," he says, but when he reaches the open kitchen, he notices I only have hot chocolate sachets. I guess he forgot I haven't been able to go to a shop yet.

While he moves around the kitchen, I lie down on the sofa, relaxing to the sound of him opening and closing cupboards. As soon as the smell of hot chocolate hits my senses, it lures me to sleep.

I wake up to the sound of my own screams. My breathing is heavy and deep as I recall the nightmare I just endured. Rick had come for me, squeezing the life out of me. The nightmare felt so real, so raw, that I can still feel the pressure of his hands around my neck.

Dean startles me when he comes rushing to my side, sitting down next to my curled-up knees. "Fuck! What's happened? Are you okay?" His words are rushed, panicked as he looks over me for any signs of injury.

"I'm sorry. I had a bad dream," I explain, feeling bad for scaring him.

"Do you want to talk about it?" He takes a deep breath, relaxing somewhat. His expression is softer now, but concern still fills his features, and I'm beginning to wonder if that is the only way he'll look at me from now on. For some reason, that worries me, but I'm unsure why.

Seeing the deep concern in his intense expression, I know he won't rest easy until he knows, so I explain the nightmare and what happened. I tell him how Rick had turned up here looking for me, about the beating he gave me and how the second I knew I was going to die I screamed myself awake.

Throughout it all he remained there, still as a statue, but the minute I finish he tenses, his face becoming hard.

"He's not coming here, and if he does, I'll kill him. That's a promise. I hate that this is happening to you," he tells me, giving me the comfort I've needed for so long but never knew I wanted.

But it doesn't matter how sincere he sounds or how much I believe him. When he says he'll kill him, there's still this nagging feeling in the back of my mind that tells me this is only going to end one way—badly.

A part of me wonders if coming here was a good idea. Did I get myself out just to put someone else in danger? Is this what I want, for Dean to be involved? No, it's not! I know how strong Rick is, know it first-hand. And even though my beatings were bad, a part of me knows he held back; if he really lost control, I would have been dead a long time ago.

My stomach rumbles, reminding me I haven't eaten since breakfast. Dean looks at my stomach with wide eyes before a small chuckle escapes his lips.

"I need to tell you something. Mom called when you were asleep. It's why I was outside before." I realise that's where he had come from when he rushed in to see if I was okay. "Dad called her last night, letting her know you were here, and she rushed back this morning to see you. I think she would have come back last night, but Dad told her not to drive tired." He chuckles, speaking fondly of his mom. "She wants to see you, but I've held her off. I told her you weren't feeling too good and were asleep. If you want, we can go round for some dinner."

I wince, knowing I can't handle seeing her right now. "I… I don't think I can see anyone right now. I can't pretend I'm okay, not after today, and I don't think I can handle their questions. I know they'll have plenty to ask." I feel bad for brushing off his parents, but he seems to understand. "But if you want to go, it's fine. I'll be okay on my own. I think I'm just gonna go to bed anyway."

"No, I'd rather stay with you. Mom will understand. She sounded worried on the phone, so I'll let her know you're okay and just want to rest. That will give us until tomorrow, but eventually you're going to have to face her," he warns, and I nod, understanding. "Let me go to mine and grab some food. I'll cook us some dinner. You're not going to bed until you've eaten." I open my mouth, ready to protest and decline his offer, but he interrupts me before I can say anything. "Nope, I'm not listening to your excuses. I'm going to get some food and cook us some dinner. I'll be back in fifteen minutes, so no falling asleep."

He grabs his coat and keys before heading to the door. As soon as it shuts behind him, the dread of being alone seeps into my bones, and I begin to shake.

A shiver runs down my spine, and I'm suddenly cold. I start rubbing my hands up and down my arms to warn off the sudden chill. When it doesn't work, I go out to the car, grabbing my other suitcase which I know has my cashmere jumper inside.

I'm fidgeting and restless, my nerves all over the place as I wait idly for Dean to get back. I just hope he keeps his promise and doesn't take too long.

Sitting back on the sofa, I sigh, my stomach full with masala. God, just thinking about it has my mouth watering. It was the nicest dinner I've ever eaten, and I've eaten at some fancy restaurants in my time.

Who knew Dean could cook? When he walked in fifteen minutes after leaving, I'd been surprised by the amount of food he brought over. I honestly believed he would throw a sandwich together, not cook us a five-star meal that would put Gordon Ramsey to shame. The pork tenderloin masala topped with mushrooms and onions tasted exquisite with the fried rice he made. It had a hint of spice to it, adding to the divine taste. I wish my stomach wasn't full because I could seriously eat that all over again.

"That was amazing. Where did you learn to cook like that?" I ask him, genuinely interested.

"I don't know. I must take after my mom because my dad still can't cook for shit. He set the bread on fire in a toaster once when Mom was holed up in bed with the flu. Never, if he offers, eat his beans on toast—you'll get black bread and cold beans. The man doesn't even know how to heat them up." We both start to laugh and when the memory of Mark cooking pasta for us when we were younger surfaces, I laugh harder.

My dad was working, and Mom and Lily had gone on a spa day, which left Mark to babysit. He tried to cook us pasta, but it didn't turn out so well. He never filled the pan with water, and it ended up on fire, the pasta burnt to a black crisp at the bottom of the pan. We laughed so hard at the poor man who was still trying to salvage the dinner, adding water, milk, and butter. It was a disaster, that's for sure.

"That's beautiful." Dean sudden comment has my laugh fading to a chuckle. My eyes pinch together in confusion as I meet his eyes.

"What is?" I ask, and although I'm confused by what he means, my cheeks flush.

"Your laughter. It's more beautiful than I remember. You should do it more often. I've missed it."

I jump up from the sofa avoiding his eyes as I make my way into the kitchen to swill my plate off. I've been told most of my life how beautiful my laugh is and how I should do it more often, but I've had no reason *to* laugh lately.

"Don't get used to it," I mumble under my breath, startled to find out he heard me.

"Oh, I plan on it. I'm going to make it my personal mission to make sure you're always laughing and smiling from now on." He grins at me, a twinkle in his eye.

For a second I'm too stunned to move. My mouth hangs open in shock, and the heaviness of what he said hits my heart. I can't help but think how incredibly sweet he is. I know he's only doing it because of what's happened to me, but still, it's really nice of him.

I don't really have a response, so I busy myself and finish cleaning the dishes before heading back over to the sofa with a fresh glass of orange juice in my hands.

Dean switches the channel on the TV, opting for a movie they have playing on channel five. As he sits down, a phone starts ringing throughout the cabin. At first, I think it's Dean's, but then I see his phone on the coffee table, the screen blank. Realisation dawns on me, my eyes widening when I realise it's mine.

"Shit! I thought I switched that off." I panic as I rush over to my bag near the door.

Grandpa hasn't stopped texting me since the day after I left Carlisle. We were meant to be meeting for lunch, and in the haste of everything happening, I totally forgot to cancel. Now he's worried sick about where I am since Rick obviously hasn't said anything to him. I texted him this morning before I left to meet Dean, telling him I was okay and was having a spa weekend with an old friend. He obviously hasn't taken my evasive message well if he's still ringing me.

Grandpa doesn't like Rick, but I still can't bring myself to tell him what's been going on. Knowing my grandpa, he'd get fired up over it and end up blurting out where I am.

The phone stops ringing just as I grab it out of my bag. My eyes glance quickly at grandpa's name on the screen before it disappears. An alert saying I have fifteen missed calls flashes on the screen and I sigh. I'm about to send another message when it rings again. Without thinking, I end up accepting the call instead of ending it.

"Hi Grandpa. I'm sorry I—" I start.

"Lola ... Where the *fuck* are you?" Rick roars down the phone. All the air leaves my lungs as the phone falls limply from between my fingers, the blood draining from my face as my eyes widen in horror.

Dean, hearing the phone smash to the floor, jumps up from the sofa. His face pales when he sees me. I look at him, my mouth opening and closing as I try to tell him what's happened, but no sound escapes, not even a gasp of breath.

My eyes widen even more, the fear of not being able to breathe making me panic, my heart racing. *Oh God, what if he knows where I am? What if he's here? Oh no, I'm going to be sick.*

I run down the hall to the bathroom connected to my room. My knees hit the tiled floor with a sickening crunch, and I violently throw up the dinner Dean just cooked. My chest heaves as I try to catch my breath.

"Fuck! Hold on, let me get you some water," Dean blurts before leaving the room. I hadn't even heard him following me. When he returns, I want to protest, not wanting him to see me more vulnerable. "Fuck, Lola. What happened? Who was on the phone? Is your grandpa okay?" he asks, the questions flying off his tongue.

"I... I..." I gasp for air, my lungs burning as I try to swallow down the rising bile. "Rick." I manage to get his name out before heaving into the toilet once more.

The air in the small bathroom shrinks, the anger radiating off Dean in waves making the room seem much smaller.

His face hardens before he rushes out the room with a determined expression on his face. It scares me, and I begin to worry about what he's going to do.

Wiping my face with the towel, I take a sip of water, swishing it around my mouth before spitting it back out. Once I feel sure I'm not going to spew again, I make my way back down the hall, my breathing evening out.

Back in the main room, Dean is fixing my phone back together, and a surge of panic hits me. I run over, snatching the phone from him.

"Please, don't do this. I can't let him find me," I plead, looking back down at the phone, sagging a little when I see it's still turned off. "I thought I turned it off this morning after I texted Grandpa," I explain. Dean is standing stock still, his anger palpable. "How did he even get my grandpa's phone? He doesn't go to the bloody loo without it." I'm rambling, panic rising again as I wonder if he's done something to hurt my grandpa. And he could have. I wouldn't even know if he did because he's the only family or friend I have in Carlisle. There'd be no one to contact me, not really.

Snapping out of whatever trance he was in, Dean moves forwards, pulling me into his arms and holding me tightly.

"It's going to be fine. I will fix this. I wasn't going to pressure you, not today because you've already been through enough," he says, running a hand down my back. "But Lola, you have to go to the police station. You need to report him. You need to tell them what you told me. And before you tell me no, just think about it, for me, please. They have medical records now, and we can take pictures of the welts on your back."

My breath hitches painfully when he mentions them. *How the hell did he see them?* My mind races and I begin to feel dizzy, my mind not able to process all of this.

As if he can read my thoughts, Dean bends down, his eyes level with mine. "I didn't touch you. I promise. Your top rose up when you were sleeping, and I saw them. Fuck, Lola, you should still be in hospital with injuries like that," he hisses, his breathing coming in deep pants as he tries to control his anger.

"Dean—" I start, shaking my head but he squeezes me tighter, stopping the next words from flowing out.

"No! Please just think about it. He could have done this before or do it again. He needs to be stopped, but most importantly you deserve justice. He should be behind bars for what he's done to you. You know I'm right." He sighs, and I drop my head to his chest, closing my eyes tightly. "I've got a friend who can help you. He's one of the best men I know, and he deals with these cases all the time. He's brilliant at what he does. You don't deserve this life, Lo. You shouldn't have to hide away in fear. Not you. Not someone so pure, so kind."

He lifts my chin with his fist so I have to look at him. "You have a light inside you that shines so bright it lights up the lives of those closest to you. I think that's why I didn't recognise you yesterday. The girl I remembered wasn't in there. Her eyes were dead, void of emotion, but then today… today I saw it in you at times, and it took my breath away. You're better than this. *My* Lola would take her life back. She would get back up on her feet fighting, and today you did that. You took that first step by telling me everything. Now you need to take the next one."

I can do nothing but stare at him in awe, completely struck by his statement of, *my Lola*. I can see in his eyes that he isn't trying to manipulate me into doing something he wants. He has no reason to, not really. Plus, what he's saying is true. I do need to step up and take my life back. I need to fight for it.

"Okay, I'll think about it," I whisper, knowing that's all I can give him right now.

IF I COULD WISH IT ALL AWAY

His lips tilt up at the corners as he squeezes me against him. "I'm so fucking proud of you," he tells me, and my heart lurches, a small smile on my lips as a thank you.

His fingers run smoothly down my arm and my breath hitches, completely freezing as a tingling sensation runs down my arm. Lost in that feeling, I don't notice his hand close around my phone until it's too late. Snatching it away, he gives me a look as if to say 'trust me'—and for some reason, I do. It's why I don't argue for him to give me the phone back.

I'm surprised when he takes the back of the phone off, slipping the SIM card out before putting it back together. He throws the phone, and I watch as it goes sailing through the air, landing softly and intact on the sofa.

The second I turn back though, he's holding the SIM card between his thumb and index finger, snapping it in half. My body relaxes instantly, and a wave of tranquillity eases through my body.

Knowing I'm no longer alone is something I can't put into words.

I wish I had done this sooner. Wish I hadn't waited so long to find my way back home.

Chapter Six

Waking up, I hear Dean in the living area moving around. He stayed with me last night after refusing to leave me in the state I was in. I still feel ashamed he saw me like that, and that he knows every little detail about my life. It's hard to think of him seeing me differently.

From arriving the day before last to waking up right now, it's been a whirlwind of emotions. Not only have I seen family friends who I haven't seen in years, but I've also emotionally expelled myself in front of Dean. I never expected to tell him, or anyone, but waking up without all that suffering on my shoulders has me feeling a little better.

The only thing that's really troubling me now is how Rick got my grandpa's phone. I've been desperate to ring Grandpa but I couldn't because one, Dean broke my SIM card and two, I don't want to risk Rick still having it. I can only hope he secretly took the phone and put it back because the different scenarios running through my head sickens me.

It's also pushing me a little more towards the idea of going to the police. I'd do anything for him not to hurt the ones I love. The only thing stopping me is the thought of him getting away with it and coming after me harder. Which he will, no doubt. I guess it's what other women worry about in the same situation because it's all I can think about. If I didn't think he was capable of hurting someone else, I would have left him long ago.

There's a small knock on my door before it opens slightly, giving me time to pull the sheets up to my chest.

"Morning," Dean greets, his voice raspy with sleep. His hair is tousled, his clothes wrinkled from sleeping in them, yet he still manages to look sexy as hell.

"Morning," I reply shyly, my cheeks heating.

"I brought you some coffee," he says as he walks farther into the room, and for the first time I see the steaming cup of coffee in his hand.

"Oh God, we're BFFs for life. Thank you." I take the cup from him, yawning. I'm still tired from waking up every so often due to my nightmares.

"How are you doing?"

He seems to be looking me over for any signs of emotional trauma, and I find myself giving him a small smile, finding his caring attributes adoring.

"I'm fine, thank you. And thank you for staying. I know that settee mustn't have been comfy." I wince, thinking of his large frame lying on that uncomfortable sofa. It's not the best but it makes do. It's just not suitable for sleeping on.

"It's fine," he tells me, waving me off. "I need to get going. I've got to meet up with some workmen, but after, I'm taking Dolly and Hunter out for a ride. Do you want to come?" My eyes fill with tears as I sit up, a big grin spreading across my face.

"Dolly is still here?" I gasp, smiling so wide it hurts. I was so sure they'd have given her away. It's so expensive to keep one, especially for this long.

"Of course. She's yours. I've been looking after them all my life, but they're getting on a bit." He winces, seeming saddened by that and I can understand. I was gutted leaving her behind, and I dread to think what I would have been like had she died. They're going on seventeen years old, and I have no idea how old that is in horse years. "So, would you like to come?"

"Of course I would." I grin, excited to see her again and if I get to ride her, even better.

"All right, then. I'll meet you at the main cabin around eleven. Is that okay?" he asks while I yawn, trying to cover it with my hand. He chuckles, shaking his head.

I nod. "Sorry," I say through another yawn. "Yeah, I'll meet you there." I wave goodbye, and he leaves, walking himself out. I should have followed him. I know just sitting here is rude, but there's no way I'm moving from this bed when I'm only wearing a thin top without a bra on.

Falling back onto my pillow, I start kicking my legs, an excited squeal escaping my lips over seeing Dolly again.

My God, I haven't seen her since a few weeks before my parents died. I'd received her on my eleventh birthday, Dean getting Hunter for his thirteenth. Our birthdays were only a few days apart, so they decided to surprise us both with the horses together. Getting a foal for my birthday is still the best present I've ever received. That was the best birthday I've ever had, not just because I got my horse but because it was the last one I spent with my parents, all of us together. On my twelfth birthday I'd been away on a school trip, so I never got to see them.

I also remember giving Dean a detective board game and a framed picture of me, him and the twins—his brother and sister.

We played a lot of pranks on the two youngest and in the picture, just as it was snapped, Dean and I pricked a pin on their necks. Their reaction was priceless. It's safe to say the picture turned out perfect, and although it was taken years ago, I can still see mine and Dean's faces. We're laughing our heads off while the twins look horrified, both of their expressions filled with pain.

Shaking away old memories, I drag myself out of the bed before I fall back asleep. Today I have an extra bounce in my step, and I know it's because I'll be seeing Dolly.

Arriving at the reception, I step inside. The place is quiet until a sweet voice starts shouting orders at someone. My face splits into a grin because I'd know that voice anywhere. Lily had always had a way about her. One minute she could be the sweetest woman you'd ever meet and the next, she could be in mother mode, threatening to bulldoze her way right over you.

Stepping forwards, I ring the reception bell and wait for someone to notice my presence. It feels weird waiting here since I'd always run wild around the place like it was my second home when I was younger. For some reason, treating the place like home feels wrong, rude, like I don't belong here anymore or have the right to just waltz around. It's been so long that we're practically strangers.

Lily steps out from the back, and my eyes take her in while she's preoccupied with her tablet, seeming frustrated. Her hair is shorter than she used to wear it, the colour greying somewhat at the roots. Even her skin has aged, making her look completely different. Her fashion choices have changed too, opting to wear casual instead of the usual summer dresses she wore all year round. The only thing that's remained the same is her eyes. They're as blue as the sky and look so warm, filled with love.

Tears fill my eyes the second I take in the woman I saw as a second mom. She may have changed appearance-wise, but I can tell the woman I once knew is still in there, for which I'm thankful.

She looks up from her tablet, ready to greet who I presume she thinks is another customer. When her eyes reach mine, her face turns a deathly pale, and her eyes begin to water.

My body freezes, wondering if I had heard Dean right last night when he said his mom was thrilled to see me. It doesn't seem that way right now. But then she opens her mouth, clutching her chest like she's struggling.

IF I COULD WISH IT ALL AWAY

"Oh my," she breathes out. "My baby. Doll. It's really you," she cries, staring at me in awe.

I do the same, but we both seem to snap out of it at the same time. We rush across the room, meeting each other halfway before pulling into each other for a tight hug. My arms go around her, and my breath hitches at the familiar scent. My sobs echo around the reception area, but I don't care.

"Oh Lola, I have missed you so very much," she whispers, pulling back to take my face in her hands. "Look at you, all grown up. You're so beautiful. I always knew you'd grow up to be a stunning woman, just like your mother." She says the last part like a broken plea, tears falling.

"Lily," I choke out, shaking my head as more tears run down my cheeks.

It hurts sometimes looking like my mom. Having to see that pain in other people's eyes is gut-wrenching. It was worse when my grandpa and grandma would look at me like they saw a ghost. I knew I was just a reminder of what they'd lost.

I see my mom every time I look in the mirror, so I know their pain, to some level. We both had long, wavy, sandy blonde hair; slim figures; round backsides; and we were both blessed in the breast department. We also shared our bow-shaped lips and small button nose. The only thing I had in common with my dad was my eyes. Whereas my mum's were blue with specks of green, mine and my dad's were emerald green. They were so bright that people always took another second to look.

"Let's go sit down in the dining room," she tells me, pulling me towards their part of the cabin. I follow, still trying to swallow the lump in my throat. "Would you like some breakfast? How about a cup of tea? We can catch up. I want to know how you are and what you've been up to,"

We walk into the dining room and instead of taking a seat Lily turns around, focusing her attention on me. "I heard about your grandma. I'm so very sorry for your loss."

I nod, not trusting myself to speak.

When she takes my hands in hers, more tears fall, and I sniffle lamely before looking back up at her. "What did I do? I'm so sorry for leaving. So very sorry," I cry and, out of nowhere, I'm pulling her in for another hug. "I've missed you so much. So, so much. I just couldn't cope, Lily. I couldn't come here without them, not then," I choke out, and she makes a pained noise in the back of her throat.

Pulling back, she wipes under my eyes with her thumbs, giving me a sad smile while shaking her head. "You have nothing to worry about, my sweet girl. We understood, and your parents would have too. Do we wish we could have been there for you? Yes. But at the cost of hurting you more? No. We never wanted you to be in pain, ever. But you're home now, and we couldn't be happier," she gushes through a watery smile.

I can hear the pain in her voice and how much she missed me, and misses my parents. Out of everyone, Lily is the only one who understands my pain. She also lost her mom at a young age, but at the time I didn't see anything other than my own pain. It was selfish of me.

"Don't you dare apologise again," she tells me before taking a closer look at my face, her brows pinching together. "Oh my! What on earth has happened to your beautiful face?" She gasps, her face full of horror. I'm glad I'm covered up because I dread to think what she'd do if she saw what the rest of me looked like.

Having her worry—hell, having Dean worrying about me yesterday—is a weird concept to me. But it's a welcomed one after living years with so much abuse.

"I'm fine," I tell her, waving her off, even though my heart is beating way too fast. "I had an accident a few weeks back. It was nothing major, just me being clumsy." I force a laugh, and it sounds unconvincing to my own ears.

Her brows are still pinched together, and I can see her mind working behind her eyes, clearly not believing me. I'm grateful when she doesn't press for anymore, and I love her for that.

My already broken heart breaks a little more. I miss my mom terribly now that I'm seeing Lily and having her worry about me. I want to ask for her advice, to ask what she would do if she were in my situation, but she's not here, and I don't think I could stomach Lily knowing about everything.

"Sit down," she tells me, seeming to snap out of it. I sit in the nearest seat, turning to watch Lily take the one next to me. "Dean said you were meeting this morning. He's not back yet though. He's out on the field showing some construction men where to set up," she informs me, and I remember Dean mentioning the same thing this morning. My cheeks heat from her knowing he stayed over, even though she doesn't look like she minds. "Would you like something to eat? Drink?"

"I'm fine, thank you. I've already eaten," I lie, not having the heart to tell her I'm too unsettled to eat something right now.

"I think I'm in shock." She giggles, not taking her eyes off me. "When Mark called and told me you were here, I didn't believe him. I had to see you for myself. I've waited so long for this day, for you to come home. Everyday I've prayed for you to find your way back."

God, I don't think I've cried so much in my life—and I've had a lot to cry about. What makes it worse is seeing Lily's face. I hate seeing her so upset.

"Well, I'm here, and I'll be staying for as long as you'll have me." I smile. "I've missed you all so much."

"I'll always want you here."

Her tablet beeps and a frown forms above her eyes from whatever she's reading. "I swear they do this on purpose. Everyone's trying to get tonight perfect, and we're down a few staff members," she grumbles, typing away.

"Tonight?" I ask, wondering what tonight is about and really hoping it has nothing to do with me.

"We cleaned up one of the side fields, needing to use it for something, so we gave Pagan the task of coming up with something for the guests and for the people who live here to enjoy."

"For months she's had that field under construction, laying new grass, new flowers, and whatnot. Now we have one side being set up with an outdoor movie theatre. It's what Dean is helping with right now. We'll be hiring the equipment for the first few months just to see how it goes.

"I'm so proud of her, of all of them, but what she's done will bring in a lot more people. We'll have one side of the field for events. We've got a gazebo that's attached to the new building that's been built. It's small, but we needed a bar for the events, and we can't exactly leave the tents up all year round…. Look at me, getting all carried away." She sighs, shaking her head as Dean walks in.

"No, it's fine. That sounds really amazing," I tell her, earning a bright smile in return.

"Well, hello. I didn't think I'd see you again after I left this morning. You looked like you were ready to go back to sleep," Dean teases, making me blush.

"Nope." I grin. "Sorry to disappoint you, old man," I tease back.

"Look at you two," Lily gushes, glancing between us with a beaming smile.

I blush, and Dean just shakes his head, looking amused. "Do you want some breakfast? I can make you an omelette."

Before I can open my mouth, Lily interrupts. "Dean, boy, stop hassling the poor girl," she scolds, still smiling. "And do you think I've got no manners? I've already asked Lola if she wanted anything and she said she's already eaten."

"Sorry," he mumbles, looking like a little boy, which makes me smile. "Are you ready, then?"

"Yeah." I smile, standing. Lily stands too, moving in front of me. When she pulls me in for another hug, I can't help but hug her back, breathing in her vanilla scent.

"Please come by and see me again. Don't leave without saying goodbye either," she tells me, choking up.

"I won't," I promise.

"It's like I can feel your parents presence with you here. It's beautiful. I can't thank you enough for bringing them back to me too." Her voice is barely a whisper, bringing tears to my eyes.

I forgot Lily was spiritual. She believes in ghosts, in the afterlife and that we all have the one spirit connected to us. One we are destined to spend eternity with. She believes she can sense them, and she most likely can but honestly, I don't know what to believe. But that doesn't matter because if Lily says she can sense them, then I believe her.

"Really?"

"My, yes. I've been in and out of your cabin for years and, years and apart from a faint scent of your mother's perfume, I could never sense either of them. It broke my heart. But now you're here, and they're back. They've always been with you." She smiles, and I can't help the tears that run down my cheeks. I promised myself I wouldn't cry again, show any kind of weakness, but then this happens.

"Mom," Dean groans.

"I think you're wrong. I've never really felt at home, like they've been with me. But the minute I stepped inside that cabin, it was like I was finally home. I've not felt this close to them since they were alive," I admit, my voice hoarse.

Suddenly, I'm back in her arms. She's hugging me so tight that I can't help but wheeze, nor can I contain the painful sob that breaks out.

Neither of us moves. It's only when Dean walks up behind me, gently pulling me away from his mom, that I let go. His arms move around my waist, supporting my body against his front. I stiffen at the intimate position, but once I feel the tips of his fingers rubbing soothing circles on my hip, I begin to relax into him, needing that support.

We're both a crying mess, me more so since my head is hidden a little in Dean's chest. I see Mark walk in from the front, his eyes moving from me to Lily, and then back to me, a slow grin forming on his lips as he takes us in.

He nods at Dean, a silent communication going on, and I file it away, wanting to ask Dean about it later. I watch as Mark walks over to Lily, wrapping her up in his arms as she cries into his shoulder, her words breaking my heart.

"My girl is back home."

"Come on, love. Let's get a cup of tea and then settle down. We can let the kids catch up, okay?" he says, holding her with loving care as he steers her through the dining room, towards the kitchen.

"Come on, let's get you out of here and cheer you up. I promised you laughter and smiles, not tears and heartbreak," Dean says in a light teasing tone.

"What are you waiting for, then?"

His grin broadens. He takes my hand, pulling me out of the cabin, and I giggle, loving this playful side to him.

Dean made true on his promise, making me laugh the whole way to the barns. I don't know why I ever thought coming here would be so bad because all it's done is bring me happy memories. Memories I could have done with when I was younger.

Everywhere I turn there is somewhere I can point out and say I did such and such with my parents. It's a thrilling feeling, and I can't help the smile that crosses my face.

Most people presumed because I grew up with rich parents that it meant I was spoiled. They thought I was taken to different countries every week and lavished with outrageous gifts, but the truth is my parents never really spent money on anything extravagant. My horse was as flashy as they got.

But I wouldn't have had them any other way because they gave me Cabin Lake. They gave me a home and brought me up to cherish everything I was blessed with. I wasn't spoiled. I was given minimal pocket money just like any other kid my age. They showered me with love and affection, not material things.

I guess being back here, back to my roots as such, has brought back those memories for me. And as hard as they are, I'm blessed with every single one of them. My parents gave me them, gave me that treasure, and I'll be forever grateful.

I'm in complete bliss by the time I'm jumping off Dolly. There is nothing like having the wind blowing in your hair, your mind free of thought and being surrounded by fresh air, the smell of trees and cut grass. I'm so out of it I don't realise we've been out here for hours; I've been having too much fun and reminiscing. I'm surprised I remembered how to ride her, but once I was up, it was just like riding a bike.

I grin, rubbing my hand down Dolly's neck before turning back to Dean. "That was amazing."

"It never gets old, does it?" His grin is infectious, and I can't help my own. "She loved having you," he says as he strokes down her muzzle.

"I can't believe she even remembered me." I'm still in awe of how she reacted when I first walked up to her. She was going mad in her stall, and as soon as I reached her, she was shoving her nose in my face, demanding fuss. "Who takes her out?" I ask him, something I've wondered a couple of times before now.

"I do." He shrugs it off, acting like it's not a big deal. My heart beats wildly and melts. "I take Hunter out for a good run, clean him down and then come back and do the same with Dolly."

"Well, thank you. I think I blocked out so much of my life back then that a lot of stuff didn't even register. I feel so selfish for leaving everyone, and Dolly." I sigh. "Thank you. Thank you for looking after her."

"You really need to stop apologising to me. You don't need to. Plus, I was only looking after her until you got back. Now it's your turn to clean up horse manure." He grins, winking.

I giggle, throwing my head back before taking Dolly's reins and leading her into the stable, ready to clean her up. I grab the brush and start grooming her down, but my attention focuses on Dean. From the corner of my eye, I watch his muscles flex in his grey T-shirt as he brushes down Hunter. I can't help the heat that creeps up my neck at how strikingly handsome he is.

Before he can catch me staring, I turn away, concentrating on Dolly and not Dean. But not before promising myself that I won't look again.

I'm not even five minutes in before my head turns, my eyes catching Dean's as he knowingly glances back at me, his eyes hypnotising.

God, I wish I could take it all back. I wish I never ran away from my problems sixteen years ago.

Chapter Seven

After spending two hours without Dean, I'm beginning to feel antsy. He dropped me off after promising to be back later to take me shopping, but I feel like climbing the walls, and I've still got an hour until he said he'd arrive.

Pacing the floor, a silent gasp leaves my mouth as a loud continuous pounding rattles the front door. Frozen with fear, I do the only thing I can manage—I run to the guest bathroom off from the living area, closing the door behind me and locking it. Someone continues to bang on the door, seeming frustrated with each knock, and a whimper escapes my mouth. I slide down the door, my legs feeling like jelly.

It's him!

When I hear a familiar voice, a tear slips free, and I wipe it away, angry with myself. Dean told me earlier I shouldn't have to live in fear or keep looking over my shoulder, and he's right. No matter how safe I feel here, someone only has to knock on the door, and I'm hiding away in a bathroom, shaking like a leaf.

Feeling stupid and rather embarrassed, I stand on shaky legs, opening the bathroom door. I hear Mark talking, disagreeing with someone I can't hear. When he tells the other person I'm not answering and that he's on his way, I rush over to the door, flinging it open and startling him.

"Hey." I wave, feeling lame.

"Oh wait, she's here. I'll be there in two," he says to whoever is on the other side of the phone before flipping it shut.

"Sorry, Mark. I was in the bathroom and didn't hear you," I lie, wincing and willing my stupid hands to stop shaking.

"It's okay, doll. Are you okay? You look really pale." He takes a step closer, his arms up like he's ready to catch me if I faint and I force a smile.

"I'm fine. I'm just a little tired. What can I do for you?" I ask him, trying to change the subject, hoping he doesn't push or demand I get some sleep. That is the last thing I need right now.

"Dean called me to come pick you up. He said he's taking you shopping, and since I was already nearby he told me to come get you."

"Okay." I smile and I am about to turn back inside the cabin when he stops me, his warm hand reaching out for mine. I try hard not to flinch, I really do, but my body still protests. If he notices, he doesn't say anything. Instead, he slowly removes his hand and looks up at me.

"Lily and I have a dinner reservation tonight, but we were hoping we would see you later at the movie?" he asks, looking hopeful.

I give him a small smile. "Can I let you know how I feel later?"

"Of course you can." He smiles lovingly, reminding me of Dean at that moment. "Are you ready?" he asks, looking at my hands.

I shake my head. "Let me just get my purse."

Running back into the cabin, I grab my bag from the floor, along with my keys from the hook near the door.

"C'mon then, let's get you to Dean before he sends out a search party," he says, grinning. He places one hand at the bottom of my back, guiding me to the front seat of his car before shutting the door behind me.

I smile, glad to finally spend a little more time with him, but more excited about hanging out with Dean.

As promised, Dean takes me food shopping. Both of us chatter mindlessly, arguing over which radio station to listen to when he pulls into the car park.

"Heart is so much better," I mutter, needing the last word. As we get out, Dean grabs the stash of 'bags for life' bags his mom lumped him with out of the boot. He mutters something under his breath, grinning, so I shove him with my shoulder playfully.

"So, where to first?" he asks, handing me the shopping list Lily wrote while he gets a trolley.

I scan through the list, noting we pretty much need the same items. That is until I come across tampons, with '*Don't forget my size, honey*' in brackets next to it.

Choking on a laugh, I try to smother it with a cough. My eyes are already watering from trying to hold it in.

"What's wrong?" Dean asks, and I cough again, looking away to hide my wide smile.

"Got a tickly throat," I lie, my voice sounding off since I'm dying to laugh.

"Ah, sucks when you have one of those," he tells me, having no idea

IF I COULD WISH IT ALL AWAY

what's really wrong with me. "What aisle next?"

"Toiletries and beauty," I choke out, walking past several aisles until we get there.

I try to keep a straight face, and it quickly becomes one of the hardest things I've ever had to do.

Lily has clearly done this for her own amusement because there is no way she could still have her menstrual cycle, not at her age. Plus, I know from when I started my own period that Lily uses sanitary pads, not tampons.

She and Mom were the ones who gave me 'the talk' since I started earlier than most girls. At the ripe old age of eleven, Mom sat me down and gave me all the pros and cons of using tampons. Lily did the same about sanitary pads, since that's what they both knew and used. It was all kinds of awkward and mortifying, that's for sure.

Shaking the memory away, I hand Dean the list back, pretending to look through the shelves. Really I'm watching him from the corner of my eye, waiting for the exact moment he realises what he needs to get. I can't wait to see if he freaks out.

But to my surprise, he just stands there looking at the variety of tampons in concentration. He seems confused as he reads the note she left on the list before checking back over the different brands and sizes.

"What size do I get Mom, Lo?"

He looks so embarrassed that it takes everything in me not to burst out laughing. It's becoming painful to hold back and before I can answer, I have to take a deep breath, swallowing down the laughter.

"I'm not sure," I tell him, trying to appear as confused as he seems to be. Then I see an older lady just down the aisle, standing next to the deodorants, and an idea forms. "How about you ask that lady? They seem to be the same size and age."

He turns to the woman in question, eyeing her up and down. He nods in agreement, and I bite my lip. I have to look away, pretending to have another coughing fit. He doesn't seem suspicious of my behaviour; if anything, he's concentrating more on whether or not he should approach the woman. Bless him, he looks redder and more torn up than ever as he glances between the note and boxes.

"Will you go and ask her for me, please? It's women shit, and I haven't got any business asking her about *this*," he says, pleading now.

I shake my head viciously, all the laughter dying from my mouth. Here I am, laughing at the poor man when it's the one thing I've never liked to buy myself.

After my first period, my mom kept supplies for me in my bathroom. But when she passed away, she was no longer there to help me through that period of my life—excuse the pun.

It happened when I was at school, and because I didn't have any girlfriends, I had no one to turn to. I was too embarrassed to go to the teachers and ask them for help.

I tried everything to make sure I didn't bleed through, but I did. I ended up leaving school a little early, so I could get to the shop. I emptied my money tin to get supplies, but by the time I got to the shop, most of the school was already in there, spending what they had left over from lunch.

I had to buy them because there was no way I couldn't. I tried to wait, even tried to dodge other kids, but when I saw one of the boys who had always picked on me at school, I hid the packet of sanitary pads in my school blazer to hide them from him. The security guard stopped me, thinking I was stealing. He made a huge production of getting me to empty my pockets. By that time, a bunch of kids were gaping and laughing, holding their phones up to record my shame.

I'm still unsure who was more embarrassed, me or the security guard, because once he saw what I had and why I hid them, he had turned bright red. I didn't end up getting them either, I just ran out of the shop as soon as I explained and he let me go.

After that, Grandma made sure to supply me with everything a girl would need for those seven days a month, and I was grateful.

Now, looking at Dean, I actually start to feel a little guilty, but if he couldn't handle it, his mom wouldn't have done it.

"I can't, Dean. I'm not good with strangers," I tell him, which is the truth.

The puppy-dog look he gives me almost makes me give in and tell him that it's all a joke. But then he turns to the woman and I know I have to watch this play out, a small smile tugging at my lips when indecision crosses his face.

He takes in a deep breath whilst rolling his shoulders. Once he seems to be ready, he takes a step towards the woman with a determined expression.

I can't help but watch with amusement, moving closer to the shelves, so it doesn't look obvious.

As he approaches the woman, she turns, as if noticing his large presence for the first time. She seems a little confused, clear wonder in her eyes.

Cougar!

Dean greets her with a wide smile on his face. I can't hear exactly what they're saying, but I do hear the word, 'size' and 'tampon'. I giggle behind my hand.

Dean's face is redder than a tomato. In a blink of an eye, the woman's confusion turns into anger. She curses before slapping Dean with her handbag, hitting him straight in the face.

I do nothing but stand there and watch in complete horror, even as he tries to explain to her that his mom sent him and he just needed some help. She's not listening; I can tell by the way her face gets redder every time he opens his mouth. I'm mortified on his behalf, but I can't control the laughter bubbling inside me. I know I should probably go over there and intervene before she kills him, but my goodness, I've not had this much fun in a long time.

Her voice rises as she shouts at him, gaining the attention of other shoppers and the shop floor assistants.

"Get some manners, young man," she hisses, her voice so loud it comes out more as a screech, making my ears bleed. "You people today are rude, all of you. Diabolically rude. Would you like it if I asked you what size your private area was?" A few people burst out laughing as do I, when she reveals this trivial bit of information. At least I don't have to smother my laughter any longer.

The verbal abuse goes on for a while and becomes funnier the madder she gets at him. I'm howling with laughter when she asks if he wants an ultra-absorbency shoved up his rear end. Dean stands there like a statue, his eyes wide in fear. He hasn't tried to console her again, not since she smacked him with her bag, and I don't blame him. She's actually quite violent.

As he walks back over to me, his steps are slow and unsure. He's holding a box of ultra-absorbency tampons, his face pale, and I burst out laughing all over again, doubling over in the middle of the store with tears streaming down my face. It's so bad I have to place my hands on my knees to keep myself from tipping over and going Tickle Me Elmo on the shop floor.

Dean finally reaches me with a deadpan look, his eyebrows raised, not looking at all impressed with me. It just fuels my laughter, and I soon find it hard to catch my breath once again.

"What's funny, Miss Lola? Is the fact I just got attacked by Queen B over there funny to you?" he asks, trying to sound mad but failing.

My laughter subsides, although I'm still finding it hard to concentrate on anything else since all I want to do is laugh. My side is killing me because of it, but I ignore the pain.

"Mr Salvatore, how old is your mom?" I ask him through a chuckle as I stand up straight.

"Fifty-six. Why?" he asks, his eyes scrunched together. I realise then that he still hasn't caught on. I grin at him knowingly. This is going to be so much fun.

"Dean? A woman your mom's age doesn't *get* periods."

My confession has him looking at me with a dire expression, and another burst of laughter escapes me. His face is priceless, worth more than seeing someone knock Kanye West down a peg or two. Once everything begins to click into place, I wish I had a phone to record him. This is definitely a Kodak moment.

"She played me again?" he asks, like this has happened before, which doesn't surprise me. She was the kind of mom to play pranks on all of us when we were little, complaining about how she needed to keep herself cool.

I nod at Dean, chuckling. He sobers, and I know what's just clicked for him. "Oh my God. You… you knew, didn't you? Of course you did. I bet you two were in on this together."

He starts to ramble as we move quickly out of the beauty aisle, passing the fuming woman who is still ranting to a staff member.

"I didn't know until I read the note." I giggle.

"And you didn't tell me?" he asks, already knowing the answer.

"Nope," I say, letting the '*p*' pop from my lips.

"I'm so getting you both back for this," he promises.

I'm too late to mask my fallen expression because Dean grins, a mischievous glint in his eyes.

With that look, I stomp—yes, stomp—my feet and push away from him, taking the trolley with me. On the way round the store, I tease Dean continuously about what happened, laughing when someone would point over to him and begin to whisper.

Who knew word would have gotten around so quickly.

Dean and I ended up going to the movie night together later that evening. Dean wanted to go to support his sister, who I still haven't had a chance to see. I went along because I honestly didn't want to go back to the empty cabin, where I knew I'd only toss and turn from nightmares.

We spent an hour speaking to Lily and Mark, all of us getting to know each other again. I found myself having more fun, realising that my time here so far has been good for me.

I honestly believed the horse riding was the best part of the day, but the minute Dean settled us down on a picnic blanket, away from the large crowd, I knew then and there that would be the best night of my life. In fact, not only was it the best night, but it was also the best moment of my life too.

IF I COULD WISH IT ALL AWAY

He had gently tucked me against his hard chest, covering us both with a fleece blanket. It was all incredibly sweet, especially since we were sitting under the bright twinkly stars. All of it felt intimate, giving off a romantic atmosphere to the night, and I couldn't help but feel blissfully happy.

The last thing I remember is leaning back, watching *Grease* up on the screen before falling into a deep, peaceful sleep.

I just wish I could have stayed awake long enough to savour what it was like to be in his arms.

Chapter Eight

"Please, Rick. No!" I plead, screaming in pain as he drags me from the bed roughly.

I've been in bed for two days straight with what I can only presume are broken ribs, since he refuses to take me to the hospital.

"Get the fuck out of bed." The smell of whisky from his breath when he shouts makes me gag. "I don't work all goddamn day so you can lie in bed on your fat fucking ass," he yells, throwing his hands in the air.

I whimper, trying to shuffle back on my arse. A slap to the face knocks my head to the side, sending me dizzy.

"Please stop," I beg, tears running down my cheeks. I wrap my arms around my sore ribs, trying to prevent him making them worse. But somehow I know before he even raises his hand that he's going to punch me again in the ribs. Only nothing could have prepared me for the agonising pain that shoots through my whole body when he does.

"Get the fuck up! Get yourself together and go make yourself useful. Dinner needs making," he shouts over my whimpering cries. When I don't move, he raises his leg in the air, and it's the last thing I see before passing out.

I wake up gasping, fighting for air as a strangled scream rises from deep in my chest. I clutch at my chest, trying to control my breathing, and hear quick footsteps heading towards me. Still in the clutches of my nightmare, I stumble off the bed in a frightened panic, gathering myself into the corner and trying to hide as much as possible.

The door opens, and the hallway light shines behind a large male figure. I can feel my pulse beating heavily, ready to burst through my skin.

As the fogginess from the nightmare wears off, I notice it's not Rick but Dean. Another whimper escapes as I begin to shake with relief. I open my mouth—to say what, I don't know. He walks into the room, bending down in front of me, and I try to blink back tears.

"Jesus, Lola! It's me. It's Dean. Everything is okay. It was just a bad dream," he says, his words rushed as he tries to calm me. My mouth opens again to try and tell I'm okay, but only a gasp of air comes out, frustrating me. I'm still shaking and can't help but huddle closer to the wall to ward off the chill. "Talk to me! Are you okay?"

His arms come around me, helping me up off the floor and back over to the bed, where he lays me down against the pillows.

Once he pulls away, I give him a small smile. "Yes," I croak before clearing my throat. "Yes, I'm okay. Just another nightmare."

As I tell him, something occurs to me, and I look up at him, my cheeks heating. The last thing I remember is Dean and me cuddled together while John Travolta sang. "Did I fall asleep on you again?"

"Yes, you were really out of it, so I brought you back here. I didn't want to leave for you to wake up and wonder where you were, so I stayed on the sofa. Do you want to talk about your nightmare?"

My mind goes back to the nightmare, the pain I felt and endured. I don't think I'll ever be able to forget my time with *him*, although I wish to every day. It's starting to become impossible to forget. Most people's nightmares are of monsters under the bed; mine just so happen to be someone I had *in* my bed.

I cast a quick glance at Dean, seeing the emotion written on his face, but I can't talk about my nightmares, not now. Maybe one day.

I shake my head. "I don't want to talk about it. I just want to forget," I whisper.

"Okay." He sighs sadly. "I'll go and turn everything off, and then I'll leave you to get some rest," he tells me as he starts to stand. Without thinking, I grab his hand, holding it tightly.

"Would you, um... I... I...," I start, too embarrassed to ask him to stay with me. I shake my head and lower it, focusing on the edge of my T-shirt.

"What is it?" he asks, sitting back down on the bed.

Taking a deep breath, I glance back at him, a shiver running down my spine. "Can you stay with me? I don't want to be alone."

"Of course," he answers immediately. "I'll grab the spare blankets for the sofa. Do you want anything?"

I don't let go of his hand, even as I feel my cheeks warming once again. Fortunately for me, it's dark, so he can't see the dark shade of my cheeks or the level of my discomfort.

"No... I mean... I want you to lie here, with me," I tell him quietly, staring to feel unsure.

He hesitates for only a moment before nodding. Walking to the end of the bed, he picks up the bed sheets I managed to kick off during my nightmare and pull them back up, covering my cold body.

I watch as he leaves the room, the lights turning off in the living area before he walks back in. He moves straight to the lamp on the other side of the bed, flicking it off.

He moves around the room effortlessly, and an old memory resurfaces of the time Dean and I had set up a tent in the Salvatore garden. Before we settled down for the night, I had gone back to mine to have dinner with my parents. But on the way back to the cabin, a few other kids who were on holiday started giving me a hard time. They had been there two weeks, and in those two weeks, they were always mean to me. And they always did it when Dean wasn't around.

Anyway, they ended up calling me names and pushing me over. My hands and knees scraped on the stone ground, leaving me a bloody mess.

I didn't think anyone had seen and because I was that embarrassed and upset, I had rushed home, not bothering to look around. The twins had seen the whole thing and apparently, after they spoke to one of the other kids there, found out it had happened to me before. They told Dean and, as you can imagine, he wasn't happy. He got upset with me for not telling him and he stormed out of the tent, leaving me alone. At first I thought it was because he didn't want to be my friend anymore, but later when he came back, he told me he'd dealt with them and that they wouldn't be picking on me again.

That night I cried until we both fell asleep. I also think that was when I told myself I was in love with Dean Salvatore.

"I'm sorry I woke you up," I whisper, turning to face him in the dark.

"I'm just glad I can be here for you. I hate what this is doing to you. I know I can't erase your nightmares or your past, but I'll help you through it any way I can. You're a strong woman, and I believe you'll get through this."

"Yeah," I whisper back, feeling my eyes water.

"Good." He runs his fingers down the side of my cheek. My breath hitches from the sudden, warm touch.

Feeling sleepy, I roll over, giving him my back. He doesn't waste any time in comforting me the way he used to. Only this time it feels different.

His hand glides across my hips to the front of my stomach, and I stiffen from the intimate touch. I can't breathe, my body frozen as he presses my back against his hard chest. It doesn't take me long to relax against him, butterflies in my stomach.

His breath against my ear sends delicious shivers down my spine. Even as relaxed as I am, I still feel like my body is coiled up tight.

"Breathe, Lola. I'm only going to hold you. That's all I'm going to do. Okay?" he promises me, and I sigh, relaxing.

My heart melts at his sweet, caring gesture and I can't help but enjoy the feel of him wrapped around me, making me feel safe and comforted.

With that as my last thought, I fall into a dreamless sleep.

The sun streaming through the cabin window wakes me up. The first thing I notice is that my pillow feels hard.

My eyes widen when I realise it's not a hard pillow, but instead a hard body, a body belonging to Dean. I peep down through my lashes, checking out the cut ridges of his abdomen and I'm struck again by the beauty of him.

Somehow through the night, I've managed to wrap my body around his. One leg is shoved between his thighs, and one of my arms is wrapped around his chest as my head lies in the nook of his shoulder.

My eyes take in every inch of him, memorising just how good he feels and how soft his skin is. God, the view is seriously hot. He has a body only books can describe, and only computers can air brush. This man is pure muscle, pure beauty, and pure man.

I can smell his scent clearly, his natural masculinity, dark and musky. It reminds me of being in the woods after a storm has hit.

His scent makes me dizzy, my blood rushing to places I've never felt before. I'm so fixated on how he's making me feel that I failed to notice his impressive morning wood, which is thick and long and pressed against my thigh. A new wave of dizziness hits me, and my body burns like it's on fire.

I'm about to sneak out of bed when he moves. My whole body freezes, wondering how I'll escape this position, but his hand tightens on my hip. He moves fast, turning me quickly so we're both on our sides. I squeal in surprise.

"Morning, beautiful," he rasps, his voice husky with sleep.

Hearing him call me 'beautiful' has my breath hitching. No one has ever called me beautiful before. Not unless they're blood related, but they don't count; they're meant to give you compliments.

He feels sorry for you, Lola, nothing more. You're just a charity case. I frown at my inner thoughts, the negativity causing me to hesitate. Dean is everything I'm not, and everything a girl could wish for.

"Are you okay?" he asks, looking at me with concern, and I realise I've spaced out.

Blinking, I force a smile, pushing my darkened thoughts aside. "Yeah, sorry. Good morning! Did you sleep okay?" I ask, trying hard not to check out his body again.

"Yes, I did, thank you. Best night's sleep I've had in ages," he says as the hand still on my hip gives me a gentle squeeze, causing a jolt of electricity to shoot down my spine. He must know what he's doing to me because his smile turns into an arrogant grin.

I go to get up, but his firm grip keeps me pinned to the bed. "What's the matter, Lo? You're acting funny. Is it about your nightmare?" he asks, and I wince, wishing he hadn't mentioned it. I *was* finally managing to forget.

"I'm fine. C'mon, I'll make you some breakfast. After, maybe we can go out for another ride with Dolly and Hunter? We can go up Liza Mountain and make a proper day of it. What do you think?" I ask him.

Now that I've thought about it, I'm excited about riding up the mountain. I loved it when we would go camping out there.

His smile widens as he rolls me so he's half on me and half on the bed. His face comes close enough to mine that if I were to take a deep breath, we would be touching. I freeze, thinking he's about to kiss me, yet he doesn't move any closer.

The butterflies are back in full force from being under his scrutiny, and I feel a little dizzy from it. My skin begins to burn as his thumb starts moving in a light circular movement on my hip, driving me wild.

"Okay, Lola, Liza Mountain it is. But if we take the horses, babe, it will mean staying up there overnight. There's a cabin up on the mountain now, one the rangers use. I use it when I need a break from this place. It's basically mine since I helped build it. We still have the occasional camper up there, but other than that it will be just us. Is that okay? I'll pack some supplies if you still want to go."

Thinking it over, I surprise myself by still wanting to go, giddy and excited. "Yeah, it sounds like fun."

I have to admit this has to be one of my better ideas. Getting away from civilisation and any responsibility sounds like heaven right about now.

The only conflict I have is being alone with Dean for another night. For some reason it doesn't feel right after last night. Something changed on that field, and I can't quite explain what. All I know is that my childhood crush no longer feels like a crush. It's become something much more.

I know my attraction to Dean is too soon after Rick and it's making me question what's real and what's not. For all I know, my feelings for Dean are only there because of his gentle affection towards me and his caring nature. Even still, thinking that makes my stomach coil. I don't want to think of Dean as a rebound, not when he means so much more to me than that. I loved him before I even knew Rick existed.

I guess the only way to find out if our friendship means more is for me

IF I COULD WISH IT ALL AWAY

to spend more time with him and get to know him better.
    I just wish I could predict the future and find out what I'm destined for.

Chapter Nine

We decided to take the scenic route to the cabin, which added another twenty minutes to our journey.

Dolly and Hunter loved the ride. According to Dean they really dislike being cooped up in the stables, so it was nice giving them that freedom. Apparently, there are more renters around now, so they can't let them run wild in the fields.

We've just finished our ten-minute hike after getting the horses settled in for the night at the stables.

The cabin doesn't look like much from the outside. Two rocking chairs creak back and forth as we step onto the wooden front porch and I can't help but admire their antique beauty.

Walking inside, I gasp in surprise. The whole bottom floor is one room. The kitchen is in the far-left corner, with an L-shaped breakfast bar separating it from the other areas of the room. There are a couple of old brown sofas that have seen better days to my right, but their cushions look plump and soft.

There's a huge HD TV on the wall with a large selection of DVDs, CDs and a few old videos stacked on some shelves on either side.

In the back left of the room, there are a few camp beds folded up and maps of the area taped to the wall, along with other paper clippings and articles. The desk is old and worn, just like its rickety chair. The desk doesn't look very organized. It's covered with plastic cups of old stale tea and wrappers of chocolate bars and crisp packets.

In the centre of the room is a set of stairs that leads up to an open-plan bedroom. As I walk up the stairs, the first thing I notice is the bed. I mean, you can't miss it—it's huge, as in two king-size beds stuck together huge. It looks soft with thick fluffy pillows on it and a blanket clearly made for winter.

To the left of the room is a door, the first I've seen in the cabin, which must mean it's the bathroom. *Thank God that isn't open-spaced too.*

IF I COULD WISH IT ALL AWAY

The only other furniture in the room is an old TV stand with an older-looking television sitting on it. If I was to guess, I would say it once belonged downstairs until someone—I'm guessing Dean—bought the big-ass plasma instead.

The place is beautiful. It needs some work done on the outside and a clean-up downstairs but other than that, I love it here. They must have had this built after my parents died; there was no way my parents knew about this place and didn't bring me. This is the kind of place my dad loved because of the potential hunting game.

"This is amazing. I was kind of worried that it would fall down on us in our sleep," I admit, chuckling at Dean's expression.

He bursts out laughing at my remark. "Lo, the place is stronger than it looks, I swear. The only reason the outside doesn't look like much is because it hasn't been painted in a few years.

"We had a few bad storms a while back, and it caused the paint to start chipping away. The cabin managed to stay standing through it, which is more than I can say for the stables. They were originally built by the gates, the ones we first entered. The storm completely destroyed them."

"Oh, I wondered why the horses were so far away," I murmur, hoping none of the horses got hurt.

"We didn't want to risk re-building them in case we had another storm. We were lucky none of the horses were up here. One of the blokes who worked for my granddad warned us it wouldn't be safe when dad first built the barn, especially since we were so high up and all, so we built another one lower down. We needed to. Not only did some of the rangers sleep here but so did I. I basically lived here at one point, building it up. I was going to move in permanently, but it's a pain in the ass coming up and down all the time."

"Well, I think the place looks great. I *was* wondering why there was a bed and stuff here," I tell him truthfully, still eyeing its characteristics. "No wonder you like it here, it's great."

The place is beautiful. Yes, it's old and looks like it needs some TLC, but Dean has done a great job. That's if you turn a blind eye to the junk wrappers on the desk downstairs.

"C'mon back downstairs. I'll make us some dinner," he says, heading for the stairs before stopping and turning to eye me. "Do you want to watch a movie? It's getting too late to go explore."

I ponder the question as he looks on at me amused. I tap at my chin dramatically. I mean, do I want to put Dean through a chick flick, comedy, or a sappy romance? Decisions, decisions.

"Hmmm," I hum, my expression straight faced.

"If you're even thinking about watching a chick flick, you can think again. There aren't any here." He grins like he can read my blooming mind.

I burst out laughing as the memory of making him sit through the movies *Bring it On*, *Ghost* and, of course, *The Lion King* pops into my head. Dean was not a happy camper, not just because of my DVD choice but because I sang to all the cheerleading chants in *Bring It On*. Although, he never even criticised my singing or dancing skills, which weren't really *that* bad. I think I made the night worse for him when I put on *The Lion King*. We had just got to the part when the dad lion dies when his parents and a few of his mates, walked in. By that time, Dean was a sobbing mess. He never lived crying at the cartoon movie down. He ignored me for weeks after that. God, his face when he realised he had been caught… It was epic.

"What's so funny?" he asks, lifting his eyebrow in confusion when I start to chuckle out loud.

"Oh, you know, nothing much." I shrug, staring at him mischievously. It's hard to keep a straight face. "Just thinking about that time you cried like a baby at *The Lion King*."

"Is that so?" he asks, grinning as he takes a step forward. God, the look in his eyes. I know that look; he's up to something. "You do realise I had something in my eye, and that I wasn't actually crying, right? It had nothing to do with that damn movie."

Sheesh, he's even good-looking when he sulks.

"What? Can't handle the truth, Dean?" I tease, giggling. I think back then he told himself that he had something in his eyes so much he actually started to believe the lie himself.

I take a step back as he takes another towards me. He has that mischievous grin on his face which can only mean trouble.

"Oh, you are so going to pay for that, Lola Bear." He takes another step towards me, but that's not why I step back; it's the old nickname he used to call me. He'd only ever use it when he was about to torture me by tickling me to death. Before I can run or take another step, I'm airborne, landing on the bed with a bounce.

He jumps on top of me, pinning my arms above my head with one hand while the other begins to tickle me. I start to laugh uncontrollably.

Squirming under him in a fit of giggles, I try everything I can to buck him off. His strong hold falls when I knock his elbow with my hand, but it only causes his arm to bend, bringing his face closer to mine. Time stops, along with my breath, as I lie there staring into the most hypnotising, beautiful blue eyes.

My breathing comes in huge pants, along with Dean's. We're both lost in each other's gaze for a few minutes before his eyes flicker down to my lips. My tongue snakes out, licking the bottom one, and his eyes dilate.

IF I COULD WISH IT ALL AWAY

I wish he would just kiss me.

I don't know where that thought comes from, or what it means. Since arriving here at Cabin Lake, I've felt like I'm living another life. My head is all over the place. One thing I'm sure of—I'm happy here. I finally feel like I belong.

I'm too busy with wishing he'd kiss me and thinking of running away when the door downstairs flings open, interrupting us. At the sound, we both pull apart, our locked gaze breaking. I flush, embarrassed.

"Hello?" a man shouts from downstairs, sounding frighteningly scary.

I hear Dean mutter a curse under his breath, along with something else. And although I've not fully heard what he's said, I nod, totally agreeing with him. Whoever has disturbed us better have a good excuse because for once, I was about to do something I wanted to do and not what someone else wanted me to do.

When the man shouts up the stairs again, this time sounding weary, it's familiar, like I've heard him before.

Intrigued and a little curious, I follow Dean downstairs, wanting to put a face to that voice.

Chapter Ten

Half way down the stairs, I stop, letting Dean walk ahead to where the man is standing at the front door with a big grin on his face. It takes me all but a few seconds to realise who it is—Jeff, the caretaker, who by now is easily in his late seventies.

His grin fades when he sees me on the stairs. I wave lamely, not knowing what else to do.

Jeff doesn't clean and sweep floors as a caretaker. His job is to maintain the cabins' security as well as their upkeep.

He doesn't look happy to see me, and I don't blame him. Dean and I used to make his life hell, and he hated us. We were always removing his ladders, leaving him stranded on roofs, and once we even went as far as to put a laxative in his drink. At the time, we didn't know what it was; we just knew it made our dad stay on the toilet longer than necessary.

I laugh out loud when the memory of the time we swapped his chair out for a broken one at one of the BBQs the Salvatores put on once a year. He went flying backwards, holding onto the table cloth, and all of the food, including the glasses of red wine that were on the table, went all over him as they both crashed to the floor.

It was funny as hell, and so worth the telling off and the grounding we were given for the whole week after.

"You, Mr Salvatore, I can deal with," Jeff says, pointing his finger at Dean before turning back to me. His beady eyes narrow and I gulp. "Even you, Miss Lawson, I could deal with on my own, but the two of you together? No! It's going to cause my heart to play up."

He shakes his head, cursing, and I can't help but laugh at his horrified expression. His face is flaming fifty shades of red, just like it normally does any time he's around Dean and me. His temples pulse as he grits his teeth, looking at us.

"What's so funny, Miss Lola?" Jeff asks, sounding snotty.

"Nothing much, Mr Jeffery. I was just thinking back to the good old days," I answer, smiling sweetly.

"Amusing, I'm sure," he mutters dryly. "Well, I best be off. Mrs Salvatore asked that I check in on the place and I have." He shakes his head, seeming amused now. "When I walked up the path and heard a commotion, I thought some damsel was in distress. *Clearly* I was wrong. Of course, now I know it was you, Miss Lola, I doubt you needed to be rescued. I pray for the man you end up marrying if you haven't already cursed a poor soul."

He laughs, but it sounds distant through my ears. I know Jeff couldn't possibly know what's happened to me, yet his words hurt me all the same.

My vision begins to blur as my breathing picks up, heavy and quick. My hands shoot out, gripping the banister as I slowly bend down to sit on the step, but with shaky legs and sweaty palms, it becomes nearly impossible. My head is swimming, my vision completely blurred, and I think I'm crying. I'm about to have a massive panic attack, and I'll most likely pass out from the pressure on my chest.

No! This cannot be happening, not now, not in front of Dean and Jeff. Not when I'm in such a vulnerable position.

Jeff's words play over in my head, and it has me questioning whether that's what people see when they look at me. Would they think it was Rick who needed rescuing from *me*?

He's charming, knows how to work a crowd and manipulate them into doing his bidding, and they don't even realise he's doing it. Whenever we were out for a work function, I was constantly reminded by everyone we greeted that I was lucky to have him and I wouldn't find a better man.

It actually makes me wonder if they would care that he hit me, *if* they believed me. He'd probably charm his way out of it, giving them a legitimate excuse as to why he did what he did.

Hell, I've lost count of the amount of excuses he used on me, and when those didn't work, he switched to domination, using his strength and manipulation against me.

My lungs squeeze painfully, and it seems like I'm surrounded by smoke as I try to focus, but with each passing second that I can't catch my breath, my panic increases, and a loud buzzing sound ringing in my ears.

Dean's talking to me from somewhere in the room. Maybe shouting? I don't know. When I feel his warm hands on my shoulders, I know he's close, and my breathing starts to steady at the same time the ringing in my ears begin to fade.

"Lola, baby, he's gone. It's okay," he says soothingly. "What just happened? Are you okay? Talk to me. Please!"

I'm still struggling to catch my breath, even though the panic has started to subside. I feel Dean shift closer, and before I know it, I'm up and in his arms. With a shaky breath, I fall limply into his arms. He starts to move, and I wonder where he's taking me. It's only when he bends down with me still in his arms that I realise he's moved us to the sofa.

His scent and his hard, warm body surround me, and I sigh contently as I move my face into the crook of his neck, breathing him in.

It takes me a few more minutes—but it feels like hours—before I fully calm myself down. I stay in his lap, needing his comfort. It feels good, right, and I can finally breathe again.

"No one would believe me," I blurt out. "Even old man Jeff thinks Rick would need rescuing from me. I know he has no idea how much his words affected me, but they did." I breathe in and out for a few minutes, trying to catch my breath again as more tears fall. "Don't you see? No one is going to believe me. Hell, not even the police believed me, and it's their job to. Everyone in our town considers him a good man, a gentleman. On the outside and on paper, he is, but behind closed doors, he's another man altogether. They'll take his side. They'll believe him because I'm just a nobody," I say incredulously, wiping at my eyes.

He lets out a string of curses whilst turning me to face him, grasping my face in his palms.

"You listen here, Lo, and listen good," he says, a hard edge to his tone. "If Jeff knew what that fucking sick fuck did to you, he would kill him, just like I want to.

"When you started to panic, he knew something was going on. He knew he said something to make you lose it like you did. I watched his jaw tense, his hands lock into tight fists because he was worried about you. Hell, I was worried he was ready to feed me to the bears," he tells me, trying to lighten the mood. He leans in closer, his nose touching mine as his grip tightens at my waist. Then, in barely a whisper, he carries on, making my heart pound.

"Lola, you're wrong about no one believing you. *I* believe you! *I do*! Not one cell in my body or brain has ever doubted you. Anyone who doesn't ever know you personally will only have to take one look at you, *one look,* and will know that you're telling the truth.

"That saying, *'Never judge a book by its cover'*? Well, people do. They can't help it. They see a man with tattoos, piercings, and a motorcycle, and they see a bad guy, a dangerous guy. But when they see a person who is clean cut, a bloke with no tattoos, no piercings, they see a good guy. What they don't see is the person beyond that appearance. They don't see how wrong their judgment truly is. So babe, even knowing that, and looking at you, looking into your eyes, you can see there is only honesty and good in you.

"No one will ever judge you, but they will envy you. You're strong,

strong enough to get through all of this. You need to own what's happened, believe you can do it and then move on from it because I believe you can," he concludes, taking my breath away and causing tears to run down my cheeks.

After a few minutes, I look up into Dean's eyes and see nothing but the truth. He does believe me, and he truly believes that other people will too. Not only that but he thinks I'm strong enough.

If only I felt the same way.

I open my mouth, but nothing comes out, too overwhelmed by his brutal honesty to find the right words.

"Lola, can you remember Jeff's daughter, Blaire?" he asks slowly. When I nod, confused at the sudden conversation change, he continues. "Well, five years ago, Jeff left here without a word or a goodbye. It was just out of the blue," he tells me and that shocks me. From what little I can remember, Jeff has never left this little town. "We found out a few days later when he brought his Blair home *why* he left. She was badly beaten and raped. She had been tortured to the point she couldn't form a sentence, and all because of her ex-husband.

"Although Mom and Dad were worried, they didn't press Jeff for details. It got to the point they were worried about what he was going to do because he was angry all the time, unpredictable. So they sat him down to talk.

"Blaire took a shining to Mom, and only Mom. She wouldn't even communicate with her own father and panicked whenever another male was in the room. It was hard to watch her go from being so outgoing and talkative to a woman who would simply jump at her own shadow. Anyway, Dad took Jeff into the back garden, and I heard them talking. I know I shouldn't have eavesdropped, but I did. I was so worried about her, and we weren't even close. She wasn't the girl I remembered. I just wished I could do something, so I listened, figuring if I knew what was wrong I could help.

"She divorced her husband when he started to become overbearing and controlling. His behaviour changed out of the blue. There was clearly more to the story, but I don't think Jeff knew, or maybe he didn't want to divulge her personal business to other people. Her visits to Jeff became infrequent, and she was distant the whole time she was there. Before that though, Jeff said the couple was always so happy and in love. He never doubted she had been mistreated, and I think it killed him to know there was something so sadistic going on behind closed doors.

"He had started giving her trouble, wanting her back. When she didn't go running back, he would cause a scene. I guess it got bad enough for a work colleague of hers to be worried about her not coming into work and ringing her next of kin. When the colleague explained to Jeff why she was so worried and how bad everything had gotten, he was furious. He made her explain everything about Blaire's ex-husband and what he had been doing. From what I could make out, he was already concerned and had planned to visit her to corner her over it all.

"That's when Blaire called him from the hospital…"

I'm thankful when he trails off because I don't need to hear what happened to her. My stomach is already turning, and my heart aches for her.

"When Jeff got there, I guess Blaire filled him in on the rest because I heard him telling Dad that her ex was stalking her and threatening her. The police, yet again, couldn't do anything since there wasn't any proof and he wasn't breaking any laws by turning up in public places.

"Blaire didn't think he was ever capable of doing what he did. She also admitted he hit her before, but that it never went farther than a few punches and kicks. Like that made it okay. She came here and was completely broken, always staring off into space and never speaking a word. She wouldn't leave the cabin for a while, so I never got to see her the first few weeks, but when she finally came out to visit Mom with Jeff the day Dad had a talk with him, she was still in a really bad condition. She had a broken arm and a fractured bone in her left leg. I can't even describe her cuts and bruises because they were… God, they were everywhere." He shudders, shaking his head. "I remember thinking of joining Jeff and finding the fucker who hurt her.

"I guess what I'm trying to say is abuse happens to different people, in different ways. It's the same with the coping stage—everyone does it differently. No one ever heals the same way. But Blaire started attending a Women's Aid group. It's a support aid that helps women and children who are affected by domestic violence. They can provide support in so many ways, whether it's talking to someone on a helpline, attending one of their drop-in meetings and so on. I know from an incident I was called out on that they can provide safety in a refuge too. Blaire chose the helpline first, not ready to talk to someone face-to-face and she said it helped her when I last talked to her. She's actually running some meetings now and helping other people. I think she still has her moments where it affects her, but she's like you, she's strong.

"Maybe when you're ready you can talk to Blaire about it, about attending a meeting or something. What do you think?" he asks, taking in a deep breath as if he's preparing himself.

Comparing the Blaire I remember to the Blaire he's just described is hard. I can't picture her, but I do feel her strength in his words. I'm in awe of how brave she sounds, how strong she is. If I'm honest I'm a little envious.

A part of me wants to meet her, but the other part is scared that I won't be able to find the courage and strength like she did.

I also feel myself melt towards Dean and his obvious protectiveness of a girl he barely knew. He got to know her, help her, and that's honourable.

"Can I think about it? I don't want to bring back her nightmares by talking about mine," I tell him honestly. My mind goes over the possibility of talking about it to someone other than Dean, but fear stops me.

"Of course. Let me know when you're ready."

I burst into tears, my heart aching as I think about what Blaire went through, what I went through. Sheesh, what thousands of other women go through daily. I cry until my throat is dry and my voice is hoarse.

My eyes close. I'm emotionally exhausted.

Chapter Eleven

My eyes open as I hear gunfire and explosions coming from the TV. My head is on Dean's lap, my body curled up on the sofa.

Yep! I totally feel like a dick.

First, I go and cry on him like the weak little girl he probably thinks I am—that I know I am—and now he most likely thinks I'm clingy.

Determined to be stronger, I go to get up from his lap, but the hand he has pressed on my shoulder stops me from going anywhere.

"Lie down, love. The film's nearly finished, but we can watch another one after if you like," he offers softly, his thumb making sweet circles on my bare shoulder.

Reluctantly, my head turns, and I lie on my back, facing him. "I don't think this film counts as the first one since I fell asleep and all. How long have I been out? I'm sorry for breaking down on you and for crying. Oh, *and* for falling asleep on you, *again*."

"First, I knew you wouldn't like this movie, and it was already in the DVD player since I didn't get to finish it the last time I was up here. I would have changed it, but I didn't want to wake you." He shrugs. "Secondly, I'll always be here to catch and hold you when you fall. Don't ever feel like you can't come to me for comfort, *ever*. I was going to go with a third, but I think my second pretty much nailed what I wanted to say. Plus, you didn't drool on me, so we're cool," he teases, smirking at me.

I giggle, loving the way he seems to always know what to say to make me feel better. When his belly rumbles, loudly, I can't help but laugh.

Sitting up, I swing my legs off the sofa and grab the two empty glasses off the coffee table.

"Right, mister, let's get you fed. What do you have here? I can cook us something if you like?"

"I've never had a woman cook for me... except for Mom of course. It would be an honour to let you cook for me," he says, in a mocking superior voice. He sounds so serious that I laugh again, which feels good. "Although, I don't know what we have. I did bring some stuff, so it's what you can make out of it, I suppose."

With that, he gets up and follows me into the kitchen. The mood is lighter, our earlier conversation no longer lingering in the air. Although, I won't lie and say it isn't at the back of my mind.

It's just under an hour later when we finally sit down to eat our food, Cajun chicken salad with cheesy pasta. The dinner is so random that we decided to make it more spontaneous by adding garlic bread and some onion rings that were left at the bottom of the freezer. We eat our dinner while making small talk. I feel like I'm a different person when I'm around him. I'm finally free to say what I want, when I want, and how I want, without having to worry about retribution. He doesn't judge me or patronise me, just listens and talks. It feels like I can finally be the Lola I was born to be.

After dinner, we both decide to watch another movie since it's still fairly early, there's not much else to do around here when it's dark. We sit back on the sofa, both at different ends after Dean pops a movie in. I feel like we're sitting too far away, but I don't want to presume he wants to be closer to me and make a fool of myself.

The rain starts to pour heavily outside, and I mean, really pour, hitting the roof hard and loud. It echoes around the cabin, making the place feel like one of those spas that play raindrops in the background. It's actually relaxing. At the first sound of the thunder, I shiver, and Dean looks over at me, grinning like an idiot. I've always hated thunder and lightning, but it's the lightning that scares me the most. It's only a matter of seconds before the area outside the cabin lights up, the sky bright.

I hate not knowing where the shot of electricity comes from or where it will land, singeing whatever it touches to a crisp. I suppose I could Google it, to help ease my mind, but sometimes, as sad as it is, it's better not knowing. When the lightning flashes, making the whole room light up, I don't think, jumping out of my seat and into Dean's lap, ignoring his amused expression. His body shakes and I realise too late that the little shit is laughing at me.

"Hey," I snap. "This isn't funny. I hate lightning," I remind him, narrowing his eyes.

"Lola, it's outside, not inside. Come on." He chuckles, holding his arm open for me after grabbing the fleece blanket from off the back of the sofa. I shuffle off his lap, snuggling into his open arm. I sigh when his arm wraps around my waist, and he covers us both with the blanket with his other hand.

We agreed over dinner to watch the new GI Joe film. Obviously, my reasons were because of the gorgeous Channing Tatum and Dwayne Johnson, but his reasons were boring. He only wanted to watch it for the action and fighting.

I snuggle deeply against Dean, jumping every now and then from the storm. It hasn't shown any signs of slowing down, which isn't helping my anxiety. But with Dean's arm wrapped protectively around me, it doesn't seem so bad.

Not long into the film, Channing Tatum dies, much to my disappointment. Seriously? Why tease us with that gorgeous man and then take him away before we even get to see him in any real action? I'm actually enjoying myself watching the film, so I don't sulk about losing him for too long. I hate watching violence, but thankfully this isn't really violence, more like a martial arts kind of thing.

Lightning strikes once again, lighting up the whole damn cabin. I scream and jump in Dean's lap, moving closer to him. I wiggle my backside in his lap, wanting to get more comfortable, but I still, and gasp at the feel of Dean's erection. I'm more surprised by my own reaction, my arousal evident in my expression and body language.

Placing a firm grip on my waist, he leans forward, his breath blowing against my ear and sending delicious shivers down my spine.

"Lola, please, for the love of God, stop pressing that sweet ass of yours against my dick. I feel like I'm going to explode in my pants like a teenager if you move again," he rasps, and a breathy sound escapes me. Knowing I'm the reason he has an erection turns me on more than I've ever been in my life. I can't stop the moan that escapes me as I move again, his erection pressing into my ass.

"Lola, you're killing me. I really want to turn you around and fuck you until you're screaming my name and coming all over my dick. I can't though. I won't take advantage of you like that. Even if it hurts this fucking badly." His words hold promise, and a shiver of anticipation runs through me. "I want you. More than you'll ever know. I don't want you to think I don't. Okay?" he rasps, stilling my movements with his strong hands. I hadn't even realised I was still moving.

He wants me. He really does want me.

No! my brain screams. *He doesn't. You heard him. He wants to fuck you, not marry you and have his babies.*

I shake my head, not knowing what to think. I know he'll never hurt me, not emotionally nor physically.

IF I COULD WISH IT ALL AWAY

It's Dean, I've had a huge crush on him since we were children, one that clearly hasn't gone away.

But a small voice in the back of my mind is telling me to go for this, to take what I need and want. There's nothing stopping me, and I really do want him. All of this may be new to me, as well as the sensations running through my body, but I know I can trust him.

With that last thought, I turn around so my front is pressed against his chest, my legs straddling his thighs so my sex is directly above his erection.

Pressing my weight down, a deep moan escapes both our mouths. When I look up into his eyes, I find him watching me, his pupils dilated and darker, and a small gasp escapes past my lips.

"Yeah, okay," I answer, my voice wavering as I speak. Finding my confidence, I move a little closer. My eyes flicker from his deep blue eyes to his soft, full, plump lips.

He draws closer, and I don't think he means to. Our lips are now a breath away, and my chest rises and falls heavily, rubbing against his. My sex burns and aches from the friction and I want more.

"Lola," he rasps, sounding breathless. "Can I... can I kiss you? Please say it's okay to kiss you," he growls, his eyes searching mine for an answer.

Without thought, I press down harder on his erection, both of us moaning when my core rubs against his heat.

"Okay," I whisper, nerves pooling in the pit of my stomach. I manage to get the word out before he moves, his lips crashing against mine as he pulls me closer.

The kiss is hard, demanding, yet he still manages such softness and care. Every fibre in my body is on fire from his assault.

His hands move down to my back, pressing me even closer than before. I moan as he slides his tongue into my mouth, massaging it against mine, giving me my first taste. He's driving me crazy with his kiss and touch. I've never felt so powerful or sexy, or found a kiss so seductive before.

I move my hands into his hair, one at the nape of his neck and pull it softly as the kiss becomes more heated.

I've never been kissed like this. Yikes, I never knew a kiss *could* feel like this. I feel like I'm on the biggest high of my life and it's all because of him. My hips start moving of their own volition, rocking faster as I rub my sex along his erection, chasing a sensation I've never felt before. It's like my body is gearing up for something big, something explosive, and with each tightening of my core, I know I'm one step closer.

The friction of our bodies rubbing together is exotic and naughty, but oh so good. I can't get enough of him, and when Dean slides forward and lies back on the sofa, I nearly scream with the amount of pleasure coursing through my body. His sudden change in position gives me better access, and I can feel every delicious inch of him. *Every. Delicious. Inch.*

The unexpected urgency to move quicker, to find more friction, is a shock to my system, but instead of thinking about it, I let go.

A hidden part of me, deep in my subconscious, is waiting for the pain. I've only ever been able to associate sex with pain, and what I'm feeling right now is anything but painful.

Dean runs his hand under my top, moving to cup my breast. I gasp when he squeezes my nipple, tugging at the sensitive bud, and a new kind of fire burns through my body. Everything in my lower body tightens, a million volts of pleasurable electricity shooting off in every direction, making it hard for me to pinpoint exactly where I'm feeling it from. It seems to spread across my body and my back arches as a scream tears from my mouth, wave after wave of pleasure coursing through me.

When everything becomes less fuzzy, I realise the significance of what just happened.

I just had my first orgasm.

Holy shitballs.

I lay limp in Dean's arms, willing my erratic breathing to slow down. It doesn't, of course. My body is too hyper aware of Dean beneath me, my body seeking out more of the pleasure only he can bring me.

What do I say to him? 'Thank you' doesn't really seem appropriate or adequate for what we just did.

My face starts burning, a blush surely spreading up my neck to my cheeks as I think of how he touched me and how I went wild on his lap.

Rick's taunts are like a slap in the face, the cruel words ringing in my ear. *"You're disgusting, Lola." "No one will ever want you. It's bad enough I have to force myself to finish." "You're nothing." "You're worthless."*

"Wow!" Dean whispers and I glance down at him, my eyes watering when I see that his eyes are pinched shut, his jaw clenched.

Oh no! He must be mortified. No! No, no, no, no! I'm never going to be able to live this down. I can't believe I just had my first orgasm after practically attacking him and humping him like a dog does a tree.

God, what he must think of me.

I shoot out of his lap so quickly I'm surprised I don't fall flat on my face. Dean's eyes fly open in shock, but before he can open his mouth, I move, running up the stairs in shame.

Locking myself in the bathroom, tears fill my eyes. Then slowly, one by one, they fall, coming faster by the second.

IF I COULD WISH IT ALL AWAY

Dean's footsteps are rushed as I hear him climb the stairs. I rush over to the shower and turn the water on, hoping to drown out his voice. I don't waste any time standing around, stepping into the shower fully clothed, needing to wash away the shame.

He knocks on the door a few times, but I ignore him. He pleads with me to open the door, his voice soft like he's talking to a child.

The shame of what I've just done weighs down on me. It's the only thing keeping me in the shower instead of obeying Dean's orders.

I still can't believe that I got off by rubbing myself on him.

Shaking my head, I try to push thoughts of him aside, focusing my attention on my present predicament. Wet clothes cling to me, so I start to peel them off, grateful the water was quick to heat up because my teeth were beginning to chatter.

Having the hot steamy water hitting my aching body makes me almost enjoy it, but thoughts of what awaits me on the other side of the door plagues me. I can't help but wonder what will happen now. Will he still want to talk to me, or will he be too disgusted with me? Even if by chance he's not, I still can't picture someone as handsome as Dean wanting to be with someone like me. I'm damaged goods, after all.

He kissed you back.

But God, the way he made my skin burn, the way he touched me, it was… it was powerful, intense. I can still feel his touch everywhere, even in places he didn't touch.

I don't need to know a lot about sex to know that Dean didn't enjoy it, not like I did. I made a complete and utter fool out of myself. I would be lying if I said it doesn't hurt or that washing his touch away from my skin or his taste out of my mouth doesn't bother me. My heart aches, a strange pull inside my chest causing me to rub at the pain.

Knowing I must leave the shower at some point, I step out. Wrapping a towel around me, I grab the robe for extra coverage, all my clothes on the other side of the door. Where Dean is.

Taking a deep breath, I open the door, embarrassed to be stepping out practically naked. He'll most likely think I'm going to jump him again. The whole situation is mortifying.

Dean is lying on the bed with his ankles crossed, his hands relaxed behind his head with his eyes closed. I must have been in the shower longer than I thought because he seems to be asleep. I sigh, feeling grateful because I don't want to have this talk with him right now—or in the near future. I know deep down that he'll want to talk about it, but if I can avoid it, I will. He probably wants to set some boundaries and ground rules.

His eyes snap open when I take another step into the room. He jumps up to his knees at the end of the bed and kneels in front of me. My hands are sweating, knowing what's about to come. I don't think I'm ready to hear him reject me, yet for some reason I stay standing in front of him, frozen. A cold shiver runs down my spine, so I grab at the belt attached to my robe and pull it tighter around my waist.

"Lola, what happened downstairs was entirely my fault. I started that, and I shouldn't have. I shouldn't have abused your trust the way I did. I'm so fucking sorry," he says hoarsely, his eyes filled with pain.

I shake my head at his words, wondering why the hell he's blaming himself when it was me who did this. I have to look away before I break down. The shame inside me is overwhelming. I know he only said what he did because he feels obligated to. He just feels sorry for me, and I think that hurts more.

"Dean, it's fine. It's not your fault. I don't know what came over me downstairs, but I'm so sorry for pouncing on you. I shouldn't have done that. You've been nothing but great and supportive towards me, and then I went and read more into it like an idiot. You didn't need me embarrassing you like that, forcing myself on you—"

My words are cut off when he rises from the bed. At first, I think he's going to leave and my heart clenches. Instead, he walks over to stand in front of me. He's so close that I can feel the heat radiating off his chest and my breath hitches. My eyes water as I stand there, scared sick over what he's going to say.

"No, Lola. That's where you're wrong. What happened… fuck! It was… it was *perfect*. I've never felt a connection like that with anyone before. I've never been so turned on in my life, not even as a teenager."

My heart pounds inside my chest as he takes another step, coming closer and running his fingers through the wet strands of my hair.

"What happened between us was the best thing to ever happen to me. I don't even think you realise just how long I've wanted this, wanted *you*. I don't think I've ever been so bent out of shape over a woman before. Then again, I never really got over losing you. So please don't regret what happened between us. Don't turn something beautiful into something twisted and seedy. If anyone should feel bad, it should be me. I'm the one who betrayed your trust, and I'm sorry for that," he says sincerely, his eyes dilating.

My eyes water at his admission, feeling so many emotions swirling in the pit of my stomach. All of it is beginning to overwhelm me.

"I just had my first orgasm, straddling you, humping you like a dog," I say, embarrassed. "I don't have any experience when it comes to sex, not really, but what happened downstairs has never happened to me before. You didn't betray anything. I just feel like such a fool." I sigh, tilting my head back to get a better look at him.

IF I COULD WISH IT ALL AWAY

"You deserve someone so much better than me, someone who isn't broken and has more baggage than an airport. I pushed myself onto you, not giving you a choice. I guess it just made me realise that Rick has been right all along." Admitting what's actually nagging at me is hard, and I have to ignore his confused expression and the way his jaw tenses when I say *his* name to keep going. "I really am a disgusting whore," I whisper, tears rushing from my eyes.

"What?" Dean snaps, eyes blazing so wildly I take a step back. "You are not a fucking whore! What happened downstairs was between two consenting adults. You haven't slept with a bunch of random guys, and you certainly don't go through them like you change your underwear. I can see what happened between us has your emotions all over the place and I can understand that, especially after everything that jerk has done to you, but don't ever believe a word of what he's told you. I love the way you trusted me down there. You trusted me enough to let go, to share that moment with me, so don't let him taint that because I wouldn't change what we did for the world," he says, fiercely.

I stare in awe, my heart melting at his words. His emotions are clear to see and even though he's angry right now, I know it's not aimed at me. He's angry at Rick and what he did.

God, the way he looks at me, the way his voice softens when he speaks to me, shows me just how much he cares for me. And I love him for that. I love that I can trust him with my life and know he'll never physically hurt me.

"It's not *just* that. It's… it's also the fact I just got out of a relationship, an abusive one at that. To rush into something else so soon feels shameful. I was out of control down there, and I can't handle you thinking badly of me. Because… like I said, I've just broken it off with Rick."

Dean pulls me closer. "You and that prick were finished the first day he laid his hands on you, Lola. He has nothing to do with us. He didn't deserve you. He had the whole world in his hands, and he mistreated you in the biggest way. Wherever this is going between us, we'll be in it together. He doesn't exist for you anymore. Do you understand what I'm saying?"

"Yeah, sort of. You're right. We did break up long before now. It's just hard to get my head around it all. I know I shouldn't care, but I do. But you should know that whenever I'm around you, that life, that nightmare, it all fades into the background. You make me feel things I've never felt before, not with anyone. You make me crazy… crazy for you."

He groans, pressing our foreheads together and running his nose along mine before cupping my cheeks in his warm hands. He pulls back a breath, locking our gazes.

"You have no idea what you do to me," he says huskily. "Even when we were kids I admired you. I loved how you always made me laugh, helped get me out of trouble a time or two, and even took the blame for me on occasion. But it was more than that. It was who you were, how easy we fitted together. You were the best part of my childhood, Lola and now I want more. I want a future with you. Since you came back, I feel like I'm whole again, and that's because of *you*," he admits, kissing the tip of my nose.

A shudder rolls through me. That's exactly how I feel. God, the whole conversation feels surreal, like I'm going to wake up any moment to find out that this was all a dream. I don't know what the future holds for us, but I don't want this—whatever this is—to end. I've missed him too much.

It feels like my whole life has revolved around missing someone. I miss my parents and my grandma every day. Hell, I even miss my grandpa when I don't see him, but until now, I never realised just how much I missed Dean and his family. And I don't want to risk losing that.

"You don't think all this is happening too soon? I mean, I've only been here a few days, Dean, and already we've spent every night but one together."

"No," he answers immediately, shaking his head. "No, I don't, not when it comes to us."

"You make me feel stronger. I no longer feel like the worthless, weak, scared person who let him do those things to me. I should have fought him and ran away, never looking back. I know you disagree, but a part of me blames myself. After all, I did stay with him. I chose to carry on living alongside him," I whisper, taking a deep breath. Before he can interrupt, I place my finger over his lips, shutting him up. I need him to hear this, to listen to what I have to say. He needs to know what he's getting himself into.

"I've been so lost since I lost Mom and Dad. I've literally been living in hell since but you, Mr Salvatore, have brought me back to life. I thought it was the cabin that brought me here, but now I know it wasn't even about the cabin. It was about you. I've always thought about you, whether it was memories of us playing together or just wondering what you were doing at that second. It helped me get through so many bad days. I guess you were the best part of my childhood too, and I'm so glad I found my way back home. I'm just scared I'm going to lose it all," I admit, wiping a lone tear away.

Taking my hand, Dean pulls me down to sit on the bed, keeping our fingers laced together. He pulls in a steady breath before facing me.

"You don't need to be scared. You'll never lose any of us, especially me. I'll never do anything that will hurt you. Ever. You can trust that I will never change who you are or betray that trust. I hate knowing what you've been through and that I didn't do a damn thing to track you down or come see you. I wanted to so many times," he says and then shakes away the pained look on his face. "You might have been lost, but you're found now, and you did that by yourself. I'm proud of you, and awestruck at your incredible strength."

Tears are streaming down my face but ignore them as I push myself into Dean's arms, hugging him tightly. He's right, I did do it. And no matter what I endured, it brought me here. It brought me to Dean, and for that, I'll be forever thankful.

He picks me up off the edge of the bed and carries me to the top, placing me down gently on the mountain of luxury pillows.

I blush furiously when I realise I'm still only in a towel and robe, my hair slightly damp.

"I'm just going to get another movie from downstairs. There's a horror in the DVD player up here, and I know you hate them," he says, ending our earlier conversation.

"Does that thing even work?" I tease, looking at the old box sitting on the television stand.

"Yeah." Dean laughs, shaking his head at me before leaving to go downstairs.

Sitting up, I make quick work of putting on a pair of knickers and some pyjamas. I've just finished pulling on my top when Dean walks up.

He has the DVD in, and the television switched on in record time. He jumps into bed with a bounce, making me giggle.

Big kid!

"C'mon," he says, tapping his chest.

I give him a puzzled expression, wondering what he's up to, but I still place my head on his chest. It's only a few seconds later that I get my answer. He runs his fingers through my hair, and it feels *amazing*. A shiver races down my spine, causing the hairs on my arms to stand on edge. He really has no idea what his touch does to me. As he strokes, he manages to catch the sensitive spot between my neck and collarbone, and I moan. Immediately, Dean becomes hard beneath me, and a small smile touches my lips. I love the fact I'm the one who aroused him. It's also a relief to know that I don't disgust him and that he feels the same as I do. I turn my head to look up at him, and his eyes blaze with fire and passion. Bringing my hand up to his face, I run my thumb along his strong, masculine jaw line. He leans in to my touch, his eyes closing and my heart melts.

A few seconds pass in silence before his eyes finally open, those deep blues looking down at me with such intensity that my heart picks up. He gives my shoulder a gentle squeeze before turning his attention back to the movie. My eyes stay focused on him a while longer before I reluctantly turn back to the movie as well.

The storm hasn't gotten any better since it started; the thunder seems closer, the lightning brighter. The sound of the rain relaxes me though, soothing my tense muscles as it hits the skylight window.

Dean gets back into bed after switching the television off, shivering as he positions himself so he's facing me. He brings his hand to my jaw before leaning in closer, his breath fanning my face.

"Lola, I really want to kiss you again. Right now," he says, his voice low and husky.

My body reacts instantly, heating up at the memory of his lips on mine, how he tasted. But my mind and heart aren't ready for anything else sexually, or a repeat performance of earlier, no matter how good he made me feel.

It's not that I don't want Dean that way, but when we do have sex, I want my mind to be free of my past experiences. I want to be sure that when Dean is inside me for the first that it won't be tainted with memories of Rick.

"Just a kiss?" I ask, my voice a whisper as it shakes slightly.

"Just a kiss," he agrees, before moving forward, his lips pressing against mine. Everything around me is drowned out as he kisses me passionately with wild abandon. Nothing else exists; there is only us at that moment.

He starts the kiss off slow, nipping at the corners of my mouth and along my jaw before moving his way down my neck. When his lips return to mine, I'm a pile of mush, and the second his intoxicating taste hits my tongue, I arch my back in bliss. The same shock of electricity runs through me, pulsing almost painfully at my sex.

In the back of my mind, my subconscious screams at me to stop, even though my body wants it *badly*.

I grip the back of his neck as he devours my mouth. I tell myself I'm going to stop in just a minute, but I never do.

Having Dean kissing me this way reminds me of a book I read not so long ago. The woman in the book says that he 'fucks her mouth' when she's describing their heated kiss. It isn't until now that I understand what she meant. It's like making love to my mouth, lovingly and thoroughly. I'm completely drunk on him, addicted as I pull him in for more.

IF I COULD WISH IT ALL AWAY

So many sensations course through my veins that I feel like I'm going to pass out, overdose on my all-time high.

I never knew my body could react this way over a kiss. It makes me wonder what it will feel like when we make love for the first time.

The dirty thoughts have my cheeks heating as I duck my gaze, settling in closer for the night.

When we finally break apart we're both breathing heavily, our chests rising and falling in unison. I can still feel his arousal pressed again my stomach and I have to squeeze my thighs together to ease the pulsing ache between my legs.

When our breathing finally calms down, we both gaze at each other, neither of us wavering. The only light in the room is coming from the storm, but it lets me see his features clearly. I'm giddy when his face splits into a smile, and I smile back, blushing.

"Why are you smiling?" I ask, my voice husky and sounding strange, even to me.

"You make me smile," he states, grinning now. "Your beauty is breathtaking. You make me crumble under the slightest touch, and you can make me feel like I could explode into a million pieces from just that touch. It makes me smile because I've never had that, never *felt* like that."

"Oh." Nothing I say will ever compete with that.

God, his words make me feel invincible. It's hard not to fall for the man in front of me.

"Yeah, *oh*," he repeats, clearly amused by my dumbstruck expression.

He pulls me against him, my head falling to his chest again. I listen to his heart beating, the sound fast and strong. My eyes close; it's like a lullaby, ready to poof me into the land of fairies.

At the sound of the rain and wind, my mouth stretches into a yawn making Dean chuckle.

"Sleep, love," he says gently, running his fingers up and down my arm.

"Night, Dean," I whisper back, my mind and body shutting down with exhaustion.

Just before I'm lured into the deep sleep, I swear I hear Dean whisper "I think I may love you more than I did as a youngster." But with the day's events, I can't be sure. Only time will tell.

Chapter Twelve

I wake up alone, snuggled into my pillow. I can still smell Dean's muscular scent on the sheets. The scent is strong, so I know he hasn't been out of bed long. Just thinking about him puts a giddy smile on my face.

He oozes masculinity and with his seductive personality, he can easily make anyone become addicted to him.

Have you ever read a book where they describe the male hero, and he's everything you ever wanted? Well, Dean fits their descriptions perfectly. He has the perfect muscled physique, along with his chiselled good looks. Hell, even his personality is perfect—perfect to me anyway. He has the muscles of a man who goes to the gym seven days a week with four hours of training, except he doesn't go to the gym. Not that I've seen since I've been here anyway.

Those broad shoulders and bulging arms—obviously not too big, but still—had me wrapped up tightly all night, making me feel safe. And God, feeling safe is something I've not been able to enjoy in a very long time. Yet, he only has to be around me to evoke those feelings inside me.

Having Dean hold me and take care of me is something I didn't think I'd be able to grant another man. I've given him my heart, something I never truly gave Rick, and I did it happily. Unlike with Rick, I know that giving Dean my body won't lead to him beating it. I know giving him my time, my love, that he won't abuse it. I also know he'll do everything to keep me safe, treasure me like a princess.

Rick manipulated me; used my vulnerability and need for love to get what he wanted. He controlled every aspect of my life. Dean doesn't want to control me, doesn't want to manipulate me; he just wants me for me. He could have used my vulnerability to manipulate me into bed last night, but Dean wouldn't do that to me. I know that in my soul.

Needing to see him, I head downstairs, stopping at the bottom when I see the work of art in front of me. Dean is standing at the stove, frying eggs and bacon, his broad shoulders and back on full display, making my mouth water.

He looks hot.

Even the way his back muscles flex as he moves elegantly around the kitchen is sexy as hell. I can't help the smile that spreads across my face when I see the two dimples in his lower back, becoming more pronounced as he bends over, giving me a delicious view of his tight arse.

I watch him for a while longer, liking the fact I can get my fill without him knowing. It's nice to see him without any guards up—not that I think he has any since he looks pretty much the same, but there's just something about watching someone when they don't know. It's like you get a real chance to *see* them, not just look at them. You get to see inside their soul, deep within themselves.

He moves effortlessly around the kitchen, each move strong and precise. He looks like he doesn't have a care in the world at that moment and I smile, seeing a new side to him. Dean's a contradiction; he looks rough and a little intimidating but would never use it against people weaker than him. He also has a heart of gold, but I've known that for a long time, even with years of separation. I don't think that could have ever changed. But after knowing how some men can be, it's nice seeing a man who isn't, a man who has morals and honour.

Knowing I can't stand around forever ogling him, I take a step down, my bare feet slapping against the wooden flooring.

"Morning," I call out, taking the last few steps into the kitchen.

Dean jumps, startled, and I giggle. I never once thought I'd scare him. He turns around facing me, a huge smile spreading across his face as he eyes my outfit. I'd put his shirt over my pyjamas and from the look on his face, he doesn't seem to mind. The way he's looking at me, you'd think I just made his day. Maybe I have.

"Morning, beautiful," he greets, and my breath hitches at his sweet endearment. I can't help but feel vain, loving it when he calls me beautiful. It's what every girl wants to hear but for me, it's more than that. I feel ugly on the inside, not just ugly from the scars that I bear on the outside, but somehow he still makes me feel sexy, beautiful.

My belly flutters when he walks over to me, pulling me into his arms and kissing the tip of my nose.

"Breakfast, huh? A woman could get used to this you know," I say as I pull away to sit down on the breakfast stool.

"Me cooking you breakfast, huh? Well, that doesn't really seem much of a duty if it means I get to wake up to you." He smiles.

Realising the hidden meaning behind his words, my lips part and I look at him shock. He steps closer so his groin meets my knees and leans forwards, kissing the corner of my mouth. The touch is only brief, and a part of me wants to groan with displeasure, but he only pulls away to tuck a loose strand of hair behind my ear. The gesture is sweet, and it melts my heart. A blush rises up my neck to my cheeks, and I try to look away before he can see, but it's too late.

"Aww, did I make you blush? C'mon, we used to share a bed and have baths together all the time as babies," he teases, a small smirk playing on those devilish lips. "Surely waking up to me isn't as bad as that. I mean, I know you have bad bed hair and everything, but at least your morning breath isn't *that* bad." He chuckles at my expression.

"Hey, I do not have bad morning breath," I snap, my hand unconsciously covering my mouth, making him laugh. "Shut up and make me breakfast, wench." I smack his firm backside, snorting out a giggle.

He laughs, leaning down to kiss me once again before turning back to the oven. And just like that, I give another piece of my heart to the man in front of me.

My cheeks hurt from smiling so much. It feels good, really good, and I can't help but feel like another piece of the old me is returning.

I just hope I can keep putting these pieces back together.

As I walk along the beaten path, I think over yesterday and the day I spent with Dean. We decided it would be a good idea to spend another night up here since it carried on raining throughout the day again yesterday, pretty much keeping us inside. The only time we left was to check on the horses to make sure they had enough food and water. I would've liked to have taken them out, but with the weather so bad it wasn't a good idea, especially since Hunter is afraid of storms.

After that we pretty much just snuggled up on the sofa, switching between watching movies and talking. I don't think I've spoken so much to anyone in my life. We talked about everything, including Dean filling me in on the fact he was a police officer. He had mentioned something before, but because of everything being so fresh in my head with Rick the comment blew right over my head.

I wanted to question him more about his old job, but the way he locked up over it had me keep quiet. He asked me what I wanted to do now that I was free. It's such a loaded question, so much so that I hadn't really thought about it until then. In the end, I told him to ask me in a week or so when I finally get a chance to sort through everything in my head.

I'd like to say that sorting things out through my head is going great, but it would be a lie. Instead of thinking of what to do next, where I'll go, how I'll work, I'm thinking of Dean and all the stolen kisses and small touches he's been giving me. He's driving me crazy.

In a good way of course.

"C'mon slow poke," Dean calls out, making me puff at the hair that's fallen in front of my face.

That last comment about him driving me crazy? I take back the good part.

Who knew Dean was such a serious hiker. I swear, with his long legs and eager attitude he's going to kill me with exhaustion. Although, and I will not admit this out loud, I'm actually enjoying the brisk walk, seeing all the trees surrounding us as birds tweet and the smell of the forest fills the air. It's unbelievable.

"I'm coming," I pant, balancing on a tree as I take a huge swig of my bottled water.

Okay, I gulp down the whole bottle but sue me, I'm not athletic. I'm seriously unfit, and five minutes into the hike should have been enough to clue me in to the fact that this was going to kill me.

"We're nearly there," he calls back, and I look up, narrowing my eyes at him. There's no sign of exhaustion; he's not even sweating. I want to push him over a fallen tree trunk for it because I look a hot mess.

I'm starting to wonder if we made the right decision last night when we agreed to do the half-hour hike to the edge of the mountain forest, where the trees end and it opens up to a huge clearing. The only reason I said yes was because I missed the place and the rain had finally stopped sometime through the night. The weather forecast said it was going to be dry, hence the reason we're taking a picnic up a mountain.

Walking forward, Dean takes off, leaving me to follow behind at a slower pace, his laughter only egging me to move faster on my feet.

A gasp sticks in my throat as I clear the trees, pausing momentarily as I take in the magnificent view. It's as beautiful and breathtaking as I remember.

The view from here looks all over Cabin Lake and the rest of the Salvatore land, plus more surrounding land. It goes on for miles. It's phenomenal, the view breathtaking, the atmosphere incredible.

"Are you ready for something to eat?" Dean calls, snapping me out of my trance. I nod and look over at him, watching him take off his rucksack. I take a step forward, breathing in the fresh air as I make my way over.

Since the ground is still damp from all the rain, we had to bring some plastic tarp to put down before the blanket. I watch, twiddling my thumbs and still trying to catch my breath as he lays it all out before looking up at me. His eyes are questioning, and that's when I realise he's asked me a something.

"Yes, please." I smile, looking around at the spot he chose for us. Dandelions cover the ground, millions of them scattered all over the place.

I look around, finding one that hasn't been destroyed by the rain, and mindlessly pick it up before moving closer to the edge of the mountain, the drop high enough to turn my stomach inside out.

Twirling the dandelion between my forefinger and thumb, I think of the last time I'd seen one of these. I'm pretty sure it was as a kid. My mom loved them. She would always make me pick one whenever we saw them, no matter where we were, telling me to close my eyes, blow, and make a wish, that all my dreams would come true.

My eyes water as I bring the dandelion closer to my face, taking in the beautiful fuzzy ball, each seed looking umbrella-like. Closing my eyes, I take in a deep breath before blowing out. "I wish it all away," I whisper before opening my eyes and watch dozens and dozens of fluffy white seeds floating off into the sky, carrying my wish into the wind.

Wiping my eyes before Dean can catch me, I turn around, shocked for a second to find him already staring at me intently. I give him what I hope is a reassuring smile before walking over to where he has everything laid out on the carpets.

"Are you okay?" he asks, before I get a chance to sit down.

"Yeah, just... just memories," I tell him, not wanting to divulge too much, or sound like a dork.

Knowing I'm hiding something, he pulls me against him, his lips coming down on mine and kissing me until I can hardly breathe. By the time we pull apart, he's gazing down at me with such care and desire that my body sags into him. Before I chicken out, I reach up for another kiss, shocking him.

"Thank you," I whisper breathlessly, and I don't mean for the kiss. For distracting me, knowing I needed a moment to myself and letting me have it and then not pushing me to explain.

"C'mon, sit down." He smiles, tucking another loose strand of hair behind my ear even though it's a lost cause. I've stopped bothering to tie it back whenever a piece gets loose because seconds later a new strand will fall.

I sit on the blanket next to Dean, grinning when he hands me a lunchbox tub of pasta salad that his mom clearly made. She sent Jeff back up with a picnic full of food this morning, which was good considering we didn't really have anything.

"Mmm, this is so good," I moan, taking another mouthful.

"Careful," he rasps, and I blink my eyes open, bending my head down shyly when I find him staring at me, his eyes filled with lust.

"Sorry," I say, biting my bottom lip.

He groans and leans forward, capturing my lips with his. I fall back onto the blanket, my pasta long forgotten as he moves on top of me, the kiss becoming more heated.

I lose track of time, so I have no idea how long we were kissing each other breathless. I just know time may have stopped for us, but still gone round for the rest of the world. I love it when we get into our little bubble. It's like only Dean and I matter; no one else exists.

"What are you thinking?" he whispers as he lies on his side above me.

"Everything." I grin.

"About me then?" He smirks, kissing the tip of my nose.

I melt, giddy at his affection. I don't think I'll ever get enough of that, of him being so openly affectionate and for saying the most romantic things to me. But mostly for how protective he is of me.

"What about you? What are you thinking?" I sigh, tilting my head to the side.

"You. Always you, Lola," he tells me, all teasing gone from his tone.

"Oh," I whisper, a little overwhelmed. "Thank you."

"For what?" he asks, his eyes scrunched together.

"For everything," I tell him, not looking away. "For bringing me here. It's like heaven. For giving me peace and for giving me you, but most of all, for giving me everything I didn't feel I'd have."

He lies on his back, like my words knocked the wind out of him. His chest rises and falls heavily. I stare dumbly, not knowing what to do with myself, but then he speaks, his voice gruff and raw.

"C'mon, lie with me," he says, pulling me against his chest. I don't bother hiding my soft smile or the excitement in my eyes. His arms have become my favourite place to be. I don't know what it is about having him hold me, or for me to just lie there on him, but it makes me feel all kinds of things.

"I wish we could stay like this forever," I whisper before closing my eyes, knowing it ends tomorrow morning when we have to go back down to the real world.

Chapter Thirteen

It is early afternoon by the time we arrive back at Cabin Lake. The mood between us changed the second we woke up, neither of us ready to leave our sanctuary yet. I wish we could've had more time up the mountain, away from all my worries and fears. It's selfish of me, I know, but I like keeping him all to myself. The routine between us is easy and comfortable, and it's going to be hard to move on from that.

We're just leaving the stables when we hear a loud, high-pitched squeal coming from across the field. We both jump and I turn to see a young woman who looks like a younger version of Lily, waving at us with so much enthusiasm. Guessing this must be Pagan, I smile, waving back. She was nine the last time I saw her, maybe eight, but she looks so much like her mother now that it's hard not to recognise her.

"Well hello there, bro. How ya doing?" she says sweetly as she bounces up next to us.

"Pagan," Dean grumbles in a greeting, looking like he wants to avoid his sister and wishing she'd disappear. It makes me giggle.

Pagan ignores his indifferent behaviour, clearly used to it by now, and turns to me. A bright smile lights up her entire face, and she looks beautiful.

"You must be Lola," she says, holding her hand to me and I take it, nodding. "Mom and Dad have told me so much about you. I only remember little bits of you from when we were younger. Sid doesn't know much about yesterday, let alone sixteen years ago. Plus, big bro over there has always talked about you. I remember him pining over you as a child. How are you, anyway?" she rambles, not taking a breath.

Wow! She's full of energy.

I laugh at the comment about Sid. He was always so quiet, keeping to himself, while little Pagan here was nearly as bad as Dean and me, always getting herself into mischief.

"I'm good, thank you. I know, it's been such a long time. So *this* brother is old and grey, and Sid has dementia. You all grow up so quickly around here," I tease, shrugging off the comment about Dean pining over me, not wanting to address it.

Pagan laughs, and as my eyes catch Dean's, his are dancing with humour before a glimmer of something else flashes in them. Mine widen.

Uh-oh!

I know that look, and it means trouble. Before I can apologise about the 'old man' comment he's moving towards me, bent at the waist as he softly lifts me over his shoulder and a high-pitched squeal leaving my mouth.

Dean begins to laugh, his shoulders shaking beneath me. Instead of being angry, I find myself laughing along with him.

"Old, huh. You sure about that? Could an old man do this?" he says, but before I can question what he means he lands a sharp slap to my arse. Bursting into hysterical laughter, I try to tell him to put me down, only I can't catch my breath long enough to get a word out.

As we arrive outside Lily and Mark's home, they're both standing in the doorway grinning, clearly having seen the show Dean just put on.

He slides me down his body painfully slow as laughter shines in his eyes. I almost sway from the look, nearly pleading in front of everyone for him to kiss me. Even though we've kissed a lot since that first night, Dean has made no more moves since we woke up this morning. He stands close to me at all times, always touching me somehow, which is really sweet of him. But I just want him to kiss me again. I know I shouldn't want to, but I do. I can't help the way he makes me feel when his lips touch mine. But I'm starting to worry that our time up the mountain was just a fluke, a dream, and now he's going to regret it.

After hanging around the cabin all day, helping out with some chores that needed doing, we're finally sitting down together for dinner.

We all take our seats—Sid and Pagan joining us which—according to Dean, is rare. They're normally all too busy to be here at the same time, which is really sad if I'm honest.

I notice that Pagan is right about Sid; he looks confused as to why he's here, and he's been that way all day. It's only when Lily walks out with the food that his face shows any recognition as to what he's doing. I want to laugh desperately, as it looks like he's stoned, but then I would have to tell everyone why and I don't want to draw attention to myself.

"Have you spoken to your grandpa, dear? I tried calling him to tell him what a wonderful surprise it was seeing you, but he never answered," Lily asks as she takes a bite of her food.

The blood rushes from my face. I never thought about them calling him and now I'm kicking myself for it. It's not like I could prevent it, not unless I directly told them not to, but then that would have raised more questions.

"He never answers," Mark scoffs lightly.

"He's away," Dean says quickly.

Lily's eyes scrunch together, eyeing her son. "Since when? We spoke to him a few weeks ago, and he never mentioned anything about going away."

Thinking quickly, I chime in. "It's a business meeting," I tell her, forcing a smile.

"That explains it. Your father was just as bad going on those trips." Mark chuckles, making me relax.

They bought my story, but it doesn't make it any better. I still feel like crap for lying.

"We'll have to go for coffee sometime. I know a great little place we can go to that's twenty minutes from here. There are some great clothes shops around there too," Pagan offers.

"Oh, you'll have to take her to that Pink's Boutique," Lily gushes before facing me. "They sell the best clothes. They do an older clothes line, so I get most of my clothes there too, but it's mostly for the younger generation."

"Sounds good. I'd love to." I smile at Pagan.

"I'll drive you," Dean says.

Pagan scowls at him, narrowing her eyes. "No, you won't. It will be a girls day, so no boys are allowed," she snaps.

"We're not twelve, Pagan. I'll drive. At least then I'll know you got there safely," he tells her, not giving in.

"I passed my test years ago, Dean, I'm capable of driving. It's a girls day, end of. If you think you're coming, then you can think again. I'll make your life hell. I'll drag you into every lingerie shop I see and try on every—"

"Okay, I get it," he snaps, scowling at her.

I giggle, loving the banter between the two, but mostly because Sid has been watching them, his head ping-ponging side to side as they argue back and forth.

"What do you do, Sid?" I ask, already knowing Pagan's an event planner. She's new at her job and apparently already one of the best.

"I'm a musician as well as a music teacher," he tells me, before scarfing down the rest of his dinner.

IF I COULD WISH IT ALL AWAY

He's a teacher? But he's so... he looks so....

How can I put this without sounding like a complete bitch? Irresponsible—that's the only way I can describe him. Christ, I'm still ninety-nine percent certain he's stoned as hell.

"You're in a band or something?" I ask, interested.

"Yeah, we do some gigs here and there." He nods, smiling.

"He's brilliant. A few of my clients have hired them before." Pagan smiles, sounding proud of her twin.

He looks over at her, shaking his head, but still smiling.

"What about you? What do you do?" Sid asks.

Shyly, I look down at my plate, moving my food around with my fork. "I... I don't work at the moment. It's been awhile, actually," I whisper, really feeling the expanse of the life I've missed out on. Instead of being able to fill them in on the different types of jobs I've had or do, I have nothing, and it makes me feel like a lesser person.

"Cool. I'd love that. My kids drive me crazy." He grins, and I frown, wondering why no one mentioned he had kids. "Not *my* kids. Well, they are, but they're my class kids." He chuckles.

My face relaxes, and I giggle at his expression, like he's horrified at the thought of having kids.

"Well, that's good. I was worried you had thirty-some-odd kids for a minute there," I joke, and the table erupts in laughter. Only Pagan remains quiet, her expression thoughtful and deep in thought as she studies me.

"So what are you going to do now?"

Ah, the big question. One Dean has already asked me. Knowing I can't give them the same answer, I try to be as honest as I can possibly be, hating all the lies I'm telling.

"I don't honestly know. I guess I'll look for a job somewhere along the line, but I don't know what's next for me yet," I admit, and that's the truth. Dean tenses beside me, and I wonder what I said to upset him. I try to give him a questioning look, but he just smiles, concentrating on his food.

"Have you managed to see anything whilst you've been here?" Lily asks, picking up her glass of wine.

"I've seen the bookshop in town." The bookshop was the first thing that popped in my mind. I think it's because I can't wait to go back there, not even to get a book but just to hang out.

Pagan starts gushing about the bookshop and telling me about all the empty shops on the street that really need filling. She hates that their small town is getting smaller because of no jobs available. She seems to feel strongly about it, and it warms my heart to see someone as young as her so dedicated to making the world a better place.

We walk in silence back to the cabin after dinner, and for some reason it feels awkward, which makes me nervous.

Needing to make conversation, I ask Dean what I've wanted to ask him all night. When everyone told me about their jobs, I noticed Dean kept quiet, and no one else brought up his time as an officer. It just intrigued me more.

"Dean? I want to ask you something, and I don't know if it's okay for me to ask. If it's not, then please feel free to tell me to mind my own business. Okay?" I say, biting my bottom lip.

I glance at him from the corner of my eye to find him staring at me curiously, a wary look crossing his face.

"Yeah, go on, you can ask me anything," he tells me softly, and I give him a small smile, surprised he agreed so easily when he looked so conflicted.

"You mentioned you were a cop but never said why you left or anything. I presumed you did because you mentioned owning a P.I company. I guess I wanted to know if you were following your dreams still," I admit, knowing how much he wanted to become an officer. As a kid, he'd always have me playing cops and robbers with him or one of his detective board games. To find out he's not a cop anymore is surprising and worrying because something must have happened for him to leave the job he loved.

He looks at me nervously, and I can see him trying to relax his breathing. He looks like he wants to deflect the question, but I'm thankful when he doesn't and lets me in.

"No, I'm not a cop anymore," he states, confirming what I already knew.

"Can I ask why?" I ask softly, been careful not to overstep.

"It's a long story, and it's really gritty." The look in his eyes reflects how relieved he is to be able to talk to someone about it.

"We've got all night," I tell him. "I'm here to listen, but if you don't want to talk to me about it, I'll understand," I offer, just in case I read his expression wrong.

He sucks in a deep breath before taking my hand in his, looking straight ahead.

"A co-worker—my girlfriend at the time—and I were undercover. We were working a huge drug case and were forced into doing shit we weren't comfortable with by the head of our department. Becca… she hadn't been undercover for very long, and she was new to our team. I'd vouched for her when a vacancy opened up, so she got hired right away.

"I'd been working the case for years trying to take this high-profile gang down. Years of my life were invested, and I hated what I had to become to achieve getting into their inner circle. But I needed to protect my identity and to do that, I had to do shit I wasn't comfortable with.

"The last six months of the case, Becca was selected to come in. They needed the job finished. The gang was getting ruthless and out of control, but we needed to know who the leader was, the man behind it all, before we could do anything. It wasn't until a few months before Becca started that I finally met him. All we had to do was tie evidence to him. He kept himself private, low-key and was anonymous to most members for a long time. It's why the job took so long. If we arrested everyone else, then he would've just hired more members and started all over again. And trust me, it had happened before. Officers had died trying to take this gang down. No one was ever able to get enough evidence or get far enough into the gang to find out who their leader was.

"Our boss made Becca and me use our relationship as an advantage to get her into the inner circle quicker. There was no way for us to get another male officer prepped and taken on as a member. The leader didn't trust any of the new recruits, so he stopped taking new people on. Our only option was Becca. She was good at first, staying quiet and by my side most of the time.

"One night they threw a huge party, and he turned up. That night, the leader met Becca for the first time and took a liking to her, not caring we were together. I think he actually enjoyed the fact that she was taken. It gave him a challenge and boosted his ego thinking he could take what he wanted," he says bitterly and my stomach rolls, hating where this is going.

"Are you okay?" I ask softly, squeezing his hand.

"Yeah, I just… This is hard." He looks so sad, so lost. I reach out, taking his hand in mine.

"If you need to stop, you can," I tell him, and he nods, clearing his throat.

"After that night he became infatuated with her. He'd always find a way to be near her, to get her away from me just so he could make her feel uncomfortable. She admitted she didn't feel safe, that she felt like her position was compromised, but didn't bother telling us from the very beginning. She kept it hidden well, and although I had an inkling of what was going on, I trusted her to tell me she was having trouble. But because it had taken her so long to get where she was in her job, she didn't want to jeopardise her position. It was already hard for her as a female cop, and I guess that's why she held back.

"Our boss told her to use his obsession against him, for her to get close to him so she could get some critical information out of him," he says, taking in a forced breath. "I still can't believe he thought she could manipulate him by seducing him. The bloke was smart. Hell, he'd kept himself from heading to prison for years.

"The boss got his wish. Becca did everything he suggested. Only trouble was she struggled to keep the bastard at arm's length. He just kept pushing and pushing her. He took her refusal to sleep with him as disobedience, so he spiked her drink with a new drug to make her compliant. It was similar to a date-rape drug, only it made the victim a willing participant, even though they had no control over what was happening to them or their body's reaction. And that's what happened to her when he raped her," he whispers, his voice filled with so much pain my heart bleeds.

My gasp is loud and clear, tears filling my eyes. I can't believe what he's telling me, what they both went through, what *she* went through. It's heartbreaking. I don't even know what to do or what to say to make this better, to take away his pain.

It's also clear from how gruff and raw his voice is that this is the first time he's speaking to someone about it.

"What happened?" I whisper, wiping my tears.

"The day it happened, we were all out on the docks waiting for a huge shipment to come in. God, we were so close to getting what we needed to put those bastards away for good. It was what we were all waiting for. The leader was in attendance due to the amount of shit they were importing. We had everything planned.

"Becca wasn't even supposed to be working that night since she wasn't a part of the inner gang. I told her to stay at home instead of helping the others who were making the arrests. We couldn't chance one of them seeing her and them ordering a hit on her or something. But our boss had other plans and went behind everyone's back, telling her to stay close to the leader and to inform him if anything changed or if she thought the leader knew something was happening. We weren't sure if he had people working for him in the department who gave him a heads-up about our busts, but even still, he shouldn't have asked that of her, especially without warning any of us first and having someone at her back.

"She went in unknown to anyone but him. No one was listening in on her because she wasn't even fucking wired. It was a fucking mess. She was raped and then brought to the beat, thrown into the centre of us all, naked, bruised and bleeding, pleading for her life," he chokes out, his eyes watering. "I stood there frozen, and did nothing. I guess a part of me knew it was a test and that he wanted to see who would step up and help her. I just stood there and did fuck all, nothing as she lay there naked and bleeding!" he shouts, fisting his hair. I stand in front of him, placing my hands around his neck and hugging him to me.

"It's okay! It's okay," I repeat, needing him to know I'm there.

"He shot her in the chest, right in front of me, and I had to watch from a distance as the life drained out of her. I just stood there," he repeats, his voice hollow. "I was a fucking coward, worse than those monsters. I should have fucking done something." He starts to cry, and I let him, rubbing his arm. "And the worst part about it is the fact that my team moved in five minutes later making arrests. If the shipment had been a couple minutes early or our team moved in when they saw her. She'd be alive. She would've had a chance. God, I try to change that day in my head all the time, and with every scenario I come up with, she walks out of there alive."

It breaks my heart listening to his voice crack talking about it. I can't believe what I'm hearing. I'm completely speechless. It feels like a horrific scene out of a movie, not something that happened in real life.

"Dean, you didn't know what was going to happen. Your boss should have protected her, and you. You did what you had to do, and if you had gone to her, they would have killed you too. And as hard as this is to say, Becca would have died whether you had gone to her or not. Think about it. She was already bleeding and beaten, and with a gunshot wound to the chest, she would have died before an ambulance arrived. And that's only if they had let you live long enough to call one," I tell him, trying my best to get him to understand that he isn't at fault, that he couldn't have prevented her death. The only ones who had the power to do that were her boss and Becca herself.

"When I vouched for her, I was under the impression that she would just be there with me as a second set of eyes. I didn't think she would get in so deep. She stayed on the case because she honestly believed she had to prove herself to everyone that a female officer can rank high in a job. I should have tried harder to get her to quit when I found out about the leader's obsession. But she was so stubborn. She kept telling me over and over that, if she quit every time someone made her feel uncomfortable, she'd be out of a job. I'd have understood, I really would've, had it not been for how obsessed he was with her. It was unhealthy the way he was with her, and she knew that. I should have made her see sense, got her fired or something. It would have saved her life if I did."

"Don't think like that. She knew what she was getting into. She knew going in without backup was a risk. Why didn't she leave?"

"Because when she started to get cold feet, our boss pulled her aside and said something to her that convinced her to stay. It's what made her go back to that psycho and act like she enjoyed being around him." He scoffs, shaking his head as he runs his palms over his face. "I hated seeing her with him. I could tell she was still scared and that he was making her life hell, but there was nothing I could say to convince her.

"You know, our boss had the whole fucking team in the conference room the day after, congratulating everyone on their hard work. He even organised a celebratory dinner and drinks. Not one word was mentioned about Becca. Fuck all! Not even an apology," he cries, and my heart clenches. I hate that her life was dismissed like that. "After he mentioned the dinner and drinks I lost it. I got up in his face and punched him. I remember saying, 'It doesn't matter how many times you wash those hands, sir. You will never be able wash away her blood. What happened is on you.' I hated him for the part he played in her death. He gave me a speech in front of everyone, saying how Becca knew what she was getting herself into, that she knew all the risks when she signed up for the job. It was more than that, and he knew it. He knew putting her in that position would get her killed.

"He told me I needed to get used to losing teammates in my line of work and, if I couldn't, I was in the wrong occupation. So I left, and I never looked back. I worked years training to bring down the bad guys, but they didn't train me to lose someone, to lose a fellow officer, a friend. They also didn't prepare me that sometimes I'll be working for wankers and that some people are worse than the actual criminals."

"So that's why you don't do it," I say, more to myself than him. I feel bad that he left something he loved because of someone else's incompetence and careless attitude for other people's lives.

"I do P.I work every now and then, but mostly I help out around here. I've got a business down in Courtney Springs that I've hired someone to run. I only take jobs that he can't at the moment because Dad needs help around the cabins. Since they had the extensions done they've had their hands full, so I offered to take time out from work to help them. I'll go back to it once everything here settles down," he says, before the both of us fall silent. "Fuck! Lo, I shouldn't have gone into that much detail. I'm so fucking sorry," he suddenly bursts out, making me jump and a little confused for a second until it hits me.

I will admit that listening to what both he and Becca went through makes my stomach sink and my skin crawl. I'm pretty sure I'll be having a nightmare over it too, but as gritty as it was, I'm glad he confided in me. No one should have to go through that and suffer alone in silence.

It's also nice to be there for him for a change. I feel like I'm finally giving back instead of taking.

"No, Dean, I'm the one who's sorry. I'm sorry you went through that, and that Becca went through it." I stop on the path and turn so I'm facing him. "You have to know that none of this is your fault. You didn't force her to do anything. It was *her* career choice, *her* choice to join up with your team and *her* choice not to leave. I know it doesn't make what happened any easier and it's an awful thing to happen to someone, but you can't carry that blame, Dean. Her death isn't on you. Your boss should have taken care of you better. He shouldn't have let her go in alone, and he shouldn't have jeopardised your lives like that. I'm so sorry, for all of it, and I can understand why you left and don't talk about it."

He holds onto my wrists as I cup his jaw, leaning in to my touch. "I couldn't look at them anymore, especially *him*. We're supposed to protect people, not...." He shakes his head, taking my hand again as we walk closer towards my cabin. "Let's not think about it any longer."

"Okay," I whisper, giving his hand a slight squeeze as we walk the rest of the way back in silence, soaking in the chilled night air.

When we arrive outside the cabin, I reach into my handbag to try and find the keys and a sudden knot forms in my stomach at the thought of being alone. We've been inseparable since the day after I arrived and have slept in the same bed every night since then. I'm not ready for that to end or to be alone again. In fact, just thinking about it has my insides twisting.

I feel selfish for taking so much of his time up. He probably wants his space back. A part of me wants him to stay just so I can comfort him, knowing everything he just laid bare is hurting him, the memories haunting him. But the other part of me, the selfish part, just wants him near me, needing his touch, his company and the comfort he brings me.

"Would you like to stay? I can make you a cup of coffee or tea," I offer, hoping I can steer the conversation somehow into him staying over again.

"Sure, why not. Tea sounds good. The night's still young, even if I'm not," he teases, but there's still a dark shadow clouding his eyes.

I laugh before turning to go into the kitchen to make a fresh pot of tea. It's amazing how we've just gone from having this intense conversation to light, easy banter.

He's most likely putting on a brave face for my benefit, and I admire him for that, but I need him to know he doesn't have to hide his emotions from me. I want him to be open about everything, the good *and* the bad.

Hopefully, I can get him to forget the conversation altogether.

The old grandfather clock chimes, signalling midnight. Dean sighs, his eyes on the clock as he stands with a grunt, stretching the kinks out of his back and neck. The minute he does, a spark of panic surfaces, causing my heart to race.

"Right, I'd best be going. You need to get some serious beauty sleep," he teases, winking at me.

My stomach flutters and I playfully smack his arm, laughing when he fakes being hurt, rubbing the spot I hit.

"Are you saying I'm ugly, Mr Salvatore?" I joke right back, narrowing my eyes.

His intense gaze bores into me, heating my skin all over. He looks so serious as he steps into my personal space.

"No, I'm most definitely not. I think you're the most beautiful woman I've ever met by far," he says, his eyes never once leaving mine as he palms my cheeks. I lean in to his touch, loving the feel of his hands on me.

I don't want him to go. I'm not ready, and the feeling is foreign to me. Uneasiness twists inside my stomach at the thought of him walking out that door. When he's around me, I feel so safe, but it's more than that. I find myself craving his company, enjoying it and not feeling alone anymore. My eyes pool with frustrated tears from wishing I had the courage to ask him to stay the night, to ask him not to leave me. I feel like I'm constantly taking from him and never giving him anything in return. I worry that I'm becoming too needy and clingy and that soon he's going to have enough of me and resent me for taking up all of his time.

"Hey, what's wrong?" he asks, noticing my sudden mood change.

"I don't want you to go. I'm not ready for you to leave me. I feel safe when I'm with you," I blurt out, closing my eyes in embarrassment.

"Can't resist this *old* man, can you? It's because I'm irresistibly hot, isn't it?" he teases, making me laugh, my embarrassment long forgotten. Although, he still hasn't answered the question.

"Who said you were hot?" I ask him, sounding serious and not giving him time to answer. "They must be blind or something, unless you paid them. Or was it Sid? Because he's the only one to say something that crazy." I giggle, not able to keep a straight face as I cling to his shirt for support.

He laughs too, grabbing me by my ass as he lifts me into his arms, leaving me no-other option than to swing my legs firmly around his waist.

I take that as a yes, and that he's staying.

Giddy, I wrap my arms around his neck, leaning in as I run my nose up towards his jaw, breathing in his scent and quickly getting high from it. God, being surrounded by all that is Dean is intoxicating, addictive. I've never felt this pull, this comfort around anyone else, ever.

"C'mon, sleeping beauty, let's get you to bed. You're starting to think you're funny," he jokes as he walks us down to my room with an extra bounce in his step.

Dean drops my feet to the floor but leaves no room between us as we enter the bedroom. My breath comes out in tiny gasps, a yelp leaving my lips as he gives my arse a playful smack.

"Go get ready," he orders and I nod, grinning as I salute him.

We both do our thing, working around each other to get ready for bed. Dean still has his bag from our stay at the cabin, so I leave him shifting through that before grabbing some clean pyjamas for myself.

Heading into the adjoining bathroom, I close the door behind me, going about my business. By the time I've cleaned my teeth, washed my face and moisturised my face and body, I'm pulling my pyjamas on and walking back out the door.

Entering the bedroom, I gasp. Dean is lying on the bed wearing only his boxers. I don't think I'll ever grow tired of the sight of him half naked. His tanned skin looks flawless against his white boxer shorts, making it seem darker. The rippled muscles on his abdomen flex, leaving me breathless as each ab becomes more pronounced, each muscle well cut. My eyes struggle to look away from his six-pack, but they do and I become even more breathless.

Even his legs are impressive, the calf muscles looking strong and powerful as he uncrosses his ankles, his legs tensing for a second before relaxing. My eyes rake up his body, covering every muscle in his legs before reaching his boxers. All the blood rushes from my face when I find the thick, long outline of his erection standing at attention. And boy, does it have my attention.

Dean clears his throat, and my eyes snap to his. My cheeks heat when I find him staring back at me, an amused smirk on his face.

"Sorry, what did you say?" I ask, shaking my head.

He chuckles. "C'mon, get into bed. You can ogle me all you want from here."

I groan, tilting back and staring up at the ceiling at his teasing. "Shut up," I pout, looking back at him as I cross my arms over my chest, stomping over to my side of the bed.

God, listen to me. *My side* of the bed. Meaning he has a side too.

Once we're both in bed, he leans over and switches the bedside lamp off, blanketing us in complete darkness.

I'm disappointed for a second that he hasn't touched me, but then I hear his hands shift under the blanket before feeling them wrap around my waist, pulling me into his body. I go willingly, placing my head on his chest as I snuggle into him.

"Did you have a good time the past few days?" he asks softly.

"It's been the best few days of my life, and I have you to thank for that. So thank you! What about you? Did you have a good time?"

"Believe it or not, these past few days have been the best days of my entire life. You have no reason to be thankful. I'm the one who is thankful. I'm thankful every day that you weren't in the car the night of your parents' accident. I'm thankful that our parents were as tight as our grandparents were. But most of all, I'm thankful to your mom and dad for bringing you into this world and giving you to me," he says, raw emotion pouring out with each word.

Silent tears fall from hearing his beautifully honest admission, the powerful speech causing my heart to skip a beat.

"I don't know what to say," I whisper, choked up with emotion.

"You don't need to say anything," he says softly, kissing my head as he begins running his fingers through the ponytail. "Now sleep."

"Goodnight, Dean," I murmur, snuggling closer.

"Night, love," he replies, giving me a light squeeze before he relaxes into the bed, keeping his arm wrapped around me.

As I begin to drift off, his words play over and over in my head, and I know there'll never be another Dean for me. I find myself okay with that, wanting my life to be with him and only him.

My last thought is that I may just be falling for Dean Salvatore.

Chapter Fourteen

The weeks progress, bringing Dean and me even closer, more so than when we were kids. I've done nothing but fantasise about kissing him, wanting to feel his mouth on mine and to taste him. I've never wanted a man's touch the way I want his, but since the morning we left the mountains, he still hasn't made a move to kiss me.

Whatever is stopping him from kissing me is something only he can sort through himself. And I know for a fact he wants me too; his erection pressing against my stomach whenever we're close is evidence of that. I've wanted to make the first move so many times, but my insecurities and fear of rejection stop me from making a complete fool of myself.

We've spent so much time together over the past few weeks, including time with Lily, Mark, and the twins.

Lily and Mark have taken us out to dinner a few times or invited us over for dinner. It was nice getting out of Cabin Lake, but I still felt like I was constantly looking over my shoulder, wondering when Rick would turn up. Thankfully Mark and Lily have kept me busy, letting me help with the cabins, even if most of it has involved cleaning. Not that I minded, as cleaning helps me relax.

Dean has also kept me busy, always finding something for us to do. He even took me to Brooke's Books, where Brooke and I got to know each other well. We've become fast friends.

My first impression of the sweet woman was correct because she's everything you could possibly need and want in a friend. We spoke for so long and found ourselves finding more and more in common with each other.

Even our upbringings, although under different circumstances, were the same. We were both raised by our grandparents, but whereas I lost my parents tragically, Brooke had been taken away from hers after social services found them physically abusing her. Her story, although heartbreaking, was really inspiring. She grew up with very little, coming from nothing—her words, not mine—but still managed to make something of herself. She's worked hard every single day of her life to achieve her dreams, proving to herself that she's nothing like her parents.

It was also good to be filled in on things I missed about Dean, stuff he hadn't shared. And now I can see why. Apparently, Dean has a string of ex-girlfriends, none lasting more than a couple of weeks before it ended. Hearing this would normally put me off any male, but for some reason, I can't help but be thankful he never settled down with any of them. That thought alone shocked the hell out of me, but I've found thoughts like that one have surfaced quite a lot lately. Because let's face it—I have the hots for Dean and not even coming from an abused relationship is stopping me from wanting to explore that.

I know a lot of people will judge me and wonder what the hell I'm thinking, but I've tasted the hate and evil, been subjected to live with it for years. Dean is pure and good, someone I already treasured and love, and I'm going to snatch that up. Any woman would, and if they understood what it's like, they'd understand my want and need for Dean. He's good, caring, kind and generous. He sees the real me and hasn't judged me once.

However, the main thing to happen over the past few weeks was that Jeff's daughter agreed to meet up with me. When Dean got in touch with Jeff, explaining my situation, he was more than willing to help. He also made Jeff agree not to talk to anyone about me or my situation because I didn't want Lily or Mark finding out.

Blaire arranged to meet me at Brooke's Books after Dean suggested being in familiar place, one that was calm. His choice was perfect. Although I was still nervous, I felt more at ease there than if we had been in a cafe. I'd have spent the whole time wondering if people could overhear us and get paranoid, thinking people were staring.

Blaire told me everything about her ex-relationship. Some things she said surprised me, while others I already knew through Dean. I was shocked and happy to hear that she's now happily married. They're also expecting their first baby, due in August.

She told me she didn't think she'd ever trust another man again, but her dad helped her see that not all men were the same. He was a walking advertisement that there are good ones in the world, and I really have to agree. My dad and granddad were—*are*—good men. They never treated a woman badly.

She spoke briefly about how badly she first handled getting into her relationship, and how it wasn't till her dad sat her down and told her to stop looking for signs that he was bad that she began to relax with her partner.

The first thing she did after their talk was speak to her partner, telling him why she was behaving the way she was. He never knew the full extent of her previous relationship, not until then, having presumed she was just cheated on and had trust issues.

She gave me her number, as well as another number I could call for someone to talk to, someone professional. It was a relief when she said I could keep my identity anonymous. She gave me guidance on what to expect, letting me know I could call the helpline any time I wanted to talk until I felt I was ready to take the next step. She told me none of them would ever judge me or make me *feel* like I was being judged.

Calling the helpline was easier than I thought it would be. Dean had given me his phone to use for every time I felt like I needed to talk someone. He'd give me privacy during the phone calls, but as soon as they were over, he was there for me.

After a week of phone calls, I made the choice to meet up with someone from Women's Aid, which is why I'm sitting in Brooke's Books.

After filling Brooke in the other day about my past, she kindly offered to let me use the bookshop. She's been really understanding about the whole situation, becoming one of the bestest friends I've ever had. In fact, she's the only female friend I've ever really had.

The knock on the door startles me from my thoughts. As I turn, I find a woman standing in the doorway, smiling. I motion for her to come in and I stand to greet her.

"Hello, I'm looking for Miss Lawson. Is she here?" she asks, softly spoken as she eyes the store in awe, the same expression I wore a few weeks ago when I first entered.

"I'm Miss Lawson, but please, call me Lola." My palms begin to sweat from nerves so I wipe them down my jeans.

"Hi, Lola, I'm Julie Franklin from Women's Aid. I've come for the assessment as to how we can help you. Please don't feel nervous." Her voice is soothing, and I'm not surprised she can see how terrified I am. "I've been where you are now and know how scary it can seem at first, but I promise you that you have no reason to be scared or nervous. You don't have to answer anything you're not comfortable with and can pass to another question at any time. There isn't a right or wrong answer, okay?"

I feel myself relax at her reassurance. Julie is a larger-framed woman with dark brown hair and a beautiful heart-shaped face.

She eases my mind with each question she asks, never pressuring me into answering any of them. She does ask a lot of random questions and some downright disturbing ones, but assures me that it's all for the procedure.

After explaining to me that she and another colleague will be going over my answers to establish what sort of help I'll need, she moves onto more personal questions.

Some are hard to hear but even harder to answer. Thankfully she's patient, assuring me that I'm in a safe place and if I wasn't ready, we could move on.

Going into detail about what happened in my relationship feels weird, as not even Dean knows the full extent of my abuse, but talking to a stranger who knows nothing about me has made the whole process a lot easier.

It also feels great taking this first step, and there's no denying the fact that this has done me some good. It's given me back some confidence and control.

She tells me the different types of help she can offer me, and I choose to go to an open group that starts in November, thinking it could be beneficial to have a group of women to talk to who have been through the same.

"After hearing everything you've had to say I would recommend having a panic button installed," she tells me, and when I go to interrupt, she holds up her hand. "Let me explain first. We offer up a large range of help to survivors. We can arrange to have regular uniformed police officers and community work officers knock on your door for safety checks, but you're already in a safe place with no immediate danger. You've taken the biggest step of all Lola, and you should be really proud of yourself. But a panic button will be wired up to dispatch police officers to you once that button is pressed. It's a safety measure most survivors who are in immediate danger take. It can be near your bed, near a phone or by a door, and it doesn't have to be visible. But I can also understand why some don't take the option." She smiles as I think it over but no matter the pros and cons, one thing remains the same.

"I can't. I won't feel safe with them there. I know it sounds stupid, but having that button will just be a constant reminder of why it's there, that I'm not safe. I'm fed up of feeling frightened, and as scary as it is to know that you feel I need one, I'm going to have to kindly decline," I tell her, feeling my cheeks heat. I don't want her to think I'm not taking this seriously, that I don't want her help when I do.

"It's fine, Lola. You can decide which precautions you would like to take. We're here to listen, to help in any way we can and make sure you stay safe. I do advise that you have your phone on you at all times, and recommend strongly that you talk to the police about getting a restraining order against him, but if you're not ready, we can talk about it later," she tells me, writing something down on her pad.

"I've got to get a new phone, but I promise to keep it on me at all times. I'm not sure about the police yet. It might give him an indication as to where I am," I explain, and I know she can tell I'm thinking of the main reason. Rick is friends with some of the police officers in our town; one favour and he could find out everything.

"I'm going to leave these with you." She hands me a little gift bag full of leaflets and other items. "There's a key ring inside that has a barcode on it. Make sure you attach it to your keys as soon as possible. It has our emergency line number on it. It's an easier way of keeping our number without someone knowing you're in touch with us," she explains, finishing her cup of coffee.

"Do you have any questions?"

I think about it for a second or two when a thought occurs to me. "Do you think I'm safe enough to use my bank cards? I mean, I have a little cash on me, but I want to know if I'm safe withdrawing it from my account."

"Lola, I'm not certain what connections your ex has to establish whether or not you're okay to withdraw you're money. In my opinion, do what you feel is best. Don't let that man rule your life anymore. My ex-husband was the same until I ran away, just like you did. I had no one to run to and no one to help me get myself better, emotionally or physically. I couldn't sleep because I was so scared.

"I lived in a women's shelter for a while, and they helped me so much. I can't describe the strength of some of the women I met. They inspired me so much that I went to the police. Granted, it took me a while to go, but I did, and it was the best day of my life. I'm not going to lie and say it's as simple as going to the police. They're just the first steps, but I had an amazing group of women at my back. After months of court he was sentenced to prison," she tells me, smiling sadly. "You've done the hardest part by leaving him. Most women can't bring themselves to get that far because they're too frightened. Everyone's relationship and story are different, so it's only natural that we all cope in different ways too. You can only do what you think is best."

I run over everything she's said, understanding that, if I can't move forward, Rick is still winning, still having that control over me. He wants to keep me isolated, scared and lonely, which he's still managing to do even though he's miles away. I can't let him take anymore away from me. I need to take control of my own life.

"Thank you," I tell her, feeling a lot lighter now that I have a goal. My eyes water, not because I'm sad but because I'm happy, elated that I've taken this step.

"The first meeting can always be overwhelming." She hands me a tissue, giving me a small smile.

"It certainly is." I chuckle through my tears, wiping them away. "Thank you again, for everything. I'd been so worried and scared, but it's helped, more than you know."

"It's my pleasure, Lola. I need to get going, but you've got my number. You can call me any time you like."

"I will," I promise as we stand, walking to the entrance of the store. "Goodbye." I wave as she steps outside.

"Speak to you soon, Lola. Take care," she says before leaving.

"Hey, Lola, are you in here?" Brooke shouts, stepping into the store.

It's a few hours after Julie left. I've been watching the store for Brooke, which I've done a few times since we become friends. I love it here, love being surrounded by the smell of old and new books and the silence. There's nothing else like it.

I've never really thought about what I would do once I left Rick, but helping out Brooke has become one of my anchors, one of my new favourite things to do. I love how lost I get in my work, and the peace and calmness. It's my new safe haven, along with Dean and the rest of the Salvatores.

"Hey, I'm in the back," I shout back as I hear the door shutting behind her.

She smiles as she walks in, laughing when she sees me surrounded by piles of books. She had a bunch donated and brought into the store, which she sells to raise money for the community school or church, so I offered to help her sort through them. I didn't know at the time that she hadn't had the time to empty any of the bins, so when I got a look at the hundreds and hundreds of books, I nearly passed out. I've been sorting them out into genres, and it's taken longer than I had originally thought it would. I've been at it for hours, yet I'm still shocked at how much progress I've made. I didn't even think I made a dent in them.

"Hey, look at you, Miss Book-worm. I didn't expect you to get this far," she says, eyeing the piles I've stacked around me, taking up every available space I could find. I laugh, having just thought the same thing. "I'm sorry Lola, but I'm going to have to kick your ass out of here. There's a sexy-looking dude waiting out front, and I think he's here for you," she teases with a fake pout, and I know she's talking about Dean.

"Sexy-looking, huh?" I ask, tapping my chin like I'm thinking that over. "Well, it can't be for me. It must be for you Brookey." I smirk, using the nickname I heard Dean call her. "It could be your Prince Charming coming to whisk you away. Plus, from what you said, he's no Shrek." I wink, using the term she used to describe the bloke that asked her out on a date last week.

Shaking her head, she laughs, stepping over a pile of books to get to the table.

"Nope," she says, popping the *P*. "He's definitely not Shrek, and you, sweetie, sure aren't Fiona. So get your sexy ass outta my shop before I bar you," she scolds playfully.

"This isn't a pub, ya lush." I giggle. She goes to order me out again, but I wave her off, standing up and stretching my sore, aching muscles. "Fine, I'll go. I know where I'm not wanted," I pout. "I'll go and never, ever return. Well, until tomorrow. I've still got a ton of books to get through."

She laughs at my serious expression, throwing her head back. "Lola, who wouldn't want you around? Seriously, I've known you, what, four weeks? Three?" she asks, and I nod, holding up four fingers. "See, and I already feel like I've known you forever. Guess who else I've known forever?" I shrug as I grab my bag off the table. "Dean! And you know what Dean looks like outside?" I shake my head. "He looks nervous as hell, so go put that poor man out of his misery."

I giggle, knowing what she's referring to. She seems to think I need to be the one to make the first move. She's been pestering me about it ever since I opened my mouth and told her everything about Dean and me. Now she's got it in her head that I need to be the one to… well, in her words, "jump him."

"Goodbye, Brooke. See you tomorrow," I call out, ignoring her comment with a heavy heart when all I want to do is kiss and hold him again.

"Goodbye," she hollers back.

I smile, giving her one last wave before stepping outside. I find Dean leaning against the shop window next door. He's wearing denim jeans, ankles crossed, with a crisp white shirt that fits his muscled physique perfectly. The muscles in his arms flex in just the right way under the thin material, showing off what I think are his best features. They're big and strong and sure know how to make me feel safe and cocooned.

"Hey," I greet, feeling nervous, especially since I can't read his expression, due to the pair of mirrored Ray-Bans he has on. God, he's mouth-watering. I can't help but fantasise about leaning into his body, tracing my tongue across his neck, exploring and tasting every inch.

"Hey, beautiful," he calls back, a huge smile on his face. Even with his eyes covered I can still feel them running over my body, my skin heating. He must read the need and lust I feel for him in my eyes because he gives me one of his knowing smirks, making me blush.

That smirk has me squirming, my thighs clenching together, but it's the look in his eyes as he pushes his sunglasses on top of his head that has my throat drying as dangerous, dirty thoughts run through my mind.

"You look good," I croak out. "Real good."

His smirk and wink make me blush harder. "Well, thank you, my lady. So do you. I've prepared a beautiful dinner out on the lake for us. I know it's getting late, but Brooke said you hadn't eaten since she went out on her errands this morning. I thought we could eat together," he offers, and my heart melts at his sweet gesture.

"Sounds amazing. It's a date," I grin, then realise what I just said and groan.

"C'mon," He chuckles, thankfully not mentioning my date comment—although his eyes say it all.

Night has fallen by the time Dean stops the boat, leaving us floating in the middle of the lake. I lean back onto the pillows he brought along for us and gaze up at the stars. They seem to be shining extra bright tonight.

My mind drifts to Dean and all the sweet gestures he does for me, sometimes without even realising it. Like the time he gently grabbed my arm, helping me down a rocky step, so I didn't face-plant to the ground, or when he bought me some flower seeds to plant in the front of the cabin after I mentioned it needing brightening up. The little things make me open my heart up for him more and more.

Dean hands me a baguette and lies back against the pillows next to me, getting lost in the stars. He's been uncharacteristically quiet tonight, and it's beginning to worry me.

As I chew on my baguette, I glance at him, gauging his reaction. He seems lost in thought, and I know something is deeply bothering him. It's written all over his face. His features are all scrunched up, and his body is incredibly tight.

"Dean, have I done something wrong? Or have I said something to upset you?" I ask him, so nervous my hands start to shake. I have to put down the last half of my baguette, my appetite gone.

Maybe he regrets our time together up at the mountain. I've been obsessing over it, the thought plaguing my mind.

He shakes his head at my question, giving me no words or answer. Pain fills his features, like whatever is bothering him is physically hurting him and either he doesn't know how to tell me, or he doesn't know how to approach the subject. Knowing him, he's most likely trying to protect me.

"What is it, Dean? You're scaring me."

IF I COULD WISH IT ALL AWAY

I will not cry!

Not when I need to be strong for him, for me, and for us. I need to show him I'm strong enough to handle whatever he's about to throw at me.

When he finally looks up at me, his eyes are filled with pain and despair. My heart breaks from seeing him like this, and I desperately wish there was something I could do to make this better. But I can't do anything to make this better if I don't even know what's wrong.

"There's something I need to tell you, and you're not going to like it. I just want you to know before I tell you that I'm sorting it all out. I promise you," he says, his eyes sad and haunted.

Why do I feel like my world is about to come tumbling down around me?

Chapter Fifteen

A million thoughts are running through my head at what he could possibly need to tell me. *What has he done? Did he contact Rick? Has he found me?* My breathing comes short and fast, leaving me gasping for air as a million and one negative scenarios run through my mind.

I feel his hands on my back, his soothing voice urging me to calm down. "Lola, take a deep breath, slowly. C'mon, breathe in through your nose, baby, and out through your mouth. That's it," he praises as he runs a hand up and down my back, helping me to calm down.

"Tell me," I demand. A conflicted look crosses his face before disappearing just as quickly. "Please, Dean. Whatever it is, you have to tell me. Please; please just tell me."

"Okay." He nods, gulping, and looks me square in the face. "You know when you first arrived and I told you we were having problems with some people over the land?" he asks.

"Yeah."

"Well, as you know we bought the land surrounding the field we had the outdoor cinema on. We paid double the amount the land is indeed worth, and to make the money back, my mom and Pagan had a bunch of ideas to bring in more visitors. Anyway, a woman came around three months after we bought the land, asking us to sell it to her for three times the amount we originally paid. Mom declined and so did Dad since the land is important to us. With the economy the way it is, we need all the help we can get, and the cabins are Mom and Dad's only income.

"Ever since they declined she's been trying to get us to sell the company as a whole. When she found out how much the place is actually worth, she started becoming relentless. We don't want to sell to her, so she's been making it difficult for us to obtain certain requirements we'll need to make this a success. She keeps finding clauses in the business contract we set up with the local council. It's made it difficult for us to get the go-ahead with our plans and the cabin expansions."

"Okay," I say slowly, not really sure if I'm following the bigger picture. As much as I hate that this woman is ruining their livelihood, I'm puzzled as to why he seemed scared to tell me about this. I don't understand why he would think I'd be upset.

"Dad texted me when we arrived back from the mountains. He said he's arranged a meeting with our lawyers to go over everything," he explains, but that only confuses me more, like having a puzzle with missing pieces.

Dean, seeing my confusion, gives me a regretful look, one filled with such sadness that the hairs on the back of my neck begin to rise.

"Lola, our lawyers are with Lawson Solicitors. Your father was originally Dad's attorney, but we were passed over to your granddad after... after your parents died." Pausing, he takes in a deep breath. "I found out today that your granddad has assigned our case to Patrick Holmes," he says and I pause, blocking everything out as I try to process what he's telling me.

He looks down at his hands, waiting for me to catch up and when I do, everything around me begins to blur. *How? Why? When? Oh God, when?*

When he sees my panicked look, he pulls me into his lap. I shove my face into the crook of his neck, letting out a strangled sob. I thought I was getting stronger, that I was ready for anything, but this? This just proves I'm nowhere near ready.

"Lola, please don't cry. It's breaking my heart. I'm going to ring your granddad when we get back and get him to give our case to someone else. I won't tell him anything if you don't want me to. I'll even tell Dad to go down there instead of them coming here, but if he does, then he'll definitely mention you being here. We need to tell someone, Lo. I think you granddad will be the best bet since he can stop Rick from working our case. At least if he does, then he'll know you're safe."

"When does he come?" I ask, my voice a hoarse whisper. I'm still in shock. I really believed I was free.

"In a week. He takes the twenty-minute flight on Wednesday, so that gives us eight days to arrange something else. Okay?"

"Okay," I agree, still trying to wrap my head around the whole thing. "What do I do, Dean? If I tell Grandpa what he's done to me, then he's going to fire him. He'll just end up bringing himself a lawsuit for an unfair dismissal. If I tell your dad then he'll tell your mom, and they'll both treat me differently, and I don't want them to think I'm weak, Dean. I don't think I can do it. I don't think I can burden them with this."

"Lola, no one could ever think you're weak. Will they worry about you? Yes. You need to realise that we love you, Lola. We always have. You're not alone anymore. I'll talk to Dad about it, and I promise not to go into too much detail. I'll just give him a brief rundown.

"Your granddad has been a lawyer for a long time, and his father was one too. I think he knows ways of firing someone without breaking their contact. I think you need to have more faith in him, in me, in us, and my parents. You need to believe that we will never let anyone hurt you or even treat you differently.

"Yes, I treat you with care, Lo, but that's because you've been through too much. I feel like when I talk to you, when Brooke talks to you, nothing we say registers. It's like you don't believe what we're telling you. What Rick drilled into your head is making it hard for you to trust us. Your mind has gotten used to all the negativity he threw at you. You need to let us remove the poison he injected in your mind by replacing it with our love and care. Are you with me?" he asks, holding me closely.

My belly flips when he says 'we love you.' I know it's not him saying he's in love with me, but still, the fact they love me is a gift all on its own. It's enough to help me through this, I hope.

"Okay, but I need to be the one to tell Lily and Grandpa. I understand everything you're telling me, Dean, but it's just so hard sometimes to process it. I can't explain how many times I've been put down or how deep his words cut me. It's hard to remove what is already imbedded. I felt his words more than his fist. The way he would say them, like it was a normal thing for a boyfriend to say, when in reality, none of what he said was okay. I didn't deserve those hateful words or his anger, I know that now.

"The way I dressed, what I slept in, what I did for a job, what I drove, what I spent money on, who I talked to, when I bathed—they're just a few of the things he had control over. But it's taken me until now to realise that. There are some things that never even registered in my mind because I couldn't see it. There was always something worse happening between us, so I never noticed the smaller things he was doing," I tell him, wiping under my eyes.

"Fuck, Lo. You need to get me and get me quick. You have all that back now. Look, I didn't want to say anything because I knew you'd be upset, but I've contacted an old colleague to dig up some dirt on Rick without it being traced back to us. I just can't sit back and do nothing, and every time you mention something new of what that fucker did to you, the stronger my urge is to kill him. I just want you to be happy. I'd do anything to protect you," he says fiercely, running his fingers through his hair.

I understand now why Dean was so worried about telling me. I always knew I would eventually see him again, one way or another, but I hadn't expected it to be so soon.

"Shit! I'm so fucking sorry for keeping this from you. I swear," he says and when I don't answer, my mind still going over everything, he takes my silence the wrong way. "I'll take you home," he says quietly, looking defeated.

I'm still sitting in his lap, so I turn, swinging my legs on either side of him to straddle him. His face is full of shock, and I'm pretty sure mine is just the same.

Then it hits me why he's been so distant intimately, when I've known he's wanted me.

He wanted to protect me.

He wanted to keep me from knowing until he thought I was ready to hear it without breaking down. And he knows I'm big on trust and if he had acted like nothing was going on and kissing and hugging me, I would be pissed. I can't even be mad at him because I'd have done the same if the roles were reversed.

But he also wanted to give me some control back, letting me initiate what we do. He's letting me be the one to make the decisions.

Finally having something figured out, something I know I can fix, I lean forward, letting my lips hover over his before giving him a soft, wet kiss, my arms snaking up his biceps before clinging to his shoulders.

He angles his head so he can deepen the kiss and I moan into his mouth, needing him closer.

"So, we're okay?" he asks, a hopeful look on his face.

"Yes, but Dean? Have you not kissed me because you wanted me to make the first move, or did you just not want to kiss me?" I ask, feigning being brave.

"I'll always want you to kiss me," he says, his eyes hooded as he reaches forward, sealing my lips with another kiss before moving back. "But I needed you to know you have complete control over this, that you have control over me and that there's nothing I wouldn't do for you," he mumbles against my lips.

"Stupid, stupid man." I chuckle. "It's not about control with you. You could give me that, and it wouldn't matter because we don't need it. We're equals,"

His eyes darken before he slams his lips back down on mine, stealing my breath away.

The kiss deepens, and I find myself moving closer, *needing* to be closer. I grind down on him, and the sensation of my sex rubbing along his thick, hard length has me moaning into his mouth and clinging to his broad shoulders. His hands slide down to my hips, and the pressure from the tips of his fingers sends delicious tingles shooting through my body. It feels so good it hurts.

When we pull away, we're both breathing heavily, and Dean gives me one of his sexy grins. I blush when he looks down, seeing the position we're in.

Asshole!

He gives me a dirty smirk.

Regardless of the awful conversation we've just had, I feel safe. I can relax easily despite knowing Rick might be coming because I trust Dean to protect me. There's no way he'd let anyone hurt me. They'd have to go through him first, and as much as I don't want Dean involved or to get hurt, he already is.

I shift in his lap and sparks of pleasure shoot to my clit, causing my eyes to roll back. Dropping my head and focusing on Dean, I giggle at his expression and the pained noise that escapes his mouth.

"What's so funny, Miss Lawson?" he whispers, his voice hoarse and scratchy.

"Just the position I have you in, Mr Salvatore," I tell him, surprised by my bold remark.

"Ahh, Miss Lawson. I believe you're blushing." He smirks, squeezing my hips with a dark chuckle.

"You would be correct, Mr Salvatore. After all, not everyone can have your confidence and arrogance," I tease.

"Oh, fighting talk. I love it when you talk dirty to me."

He smirks and winks, and I playfully smack his arm, which only makes him laugh. Before I know what's happening, I'm on my back with my arms pinned above me.

Then he does the unexpected, the one thing I can't cope with.

He tickles me.

I scream, laugh and snort, not even caring how unladylike I sound. Gah, I hate being tickled.

Have you ever been tickled so much that it hurts your sides and you can no longer control your body's reaction? Yep, that's what Dean's doing to me. I'm embarrassed to admit I'm seconds away from peeing myself too.

"Please, Dean, stop! I'm... I'm going to... wee... myself," I say through streams of laughter. My cheeks ache and my stomach hurts from laughing so hard. It feels good, really good, to finally let go.

He stops tickling me, yet keeps my arms pinned above my head. This position would normally cause a major panic attack, but I don't even freeze. There's nothing about Dean that scares me.

He presses his weight on top of me, making me feel warm and safe, amongst other things. Meeting his gaze, I see so many emotions flashing—love, lust, and desire.

When he brings his mouth back down to mine, I feel like magic is being passed through us. I feel light, like I'm floating on air.

IF I COULD WISH IT ALL AWAY

Unlike his previous kisses, this one is softer, more tender, and I cling to him like he's my lifeline. Something in the kiss feels different, stronger, and I don't know whether it's because my feelings for him have grown or something else. My emotions are all over the place, but I make sure to pour as much love into the kiss as I can, wanting to show Dean without words how I feel.

"Wow!" he rasps, licking his bottom lip.

You can say that again! I stare up at him, my hands still above my head. I wiggle my wrists and fingers, and immediately he loosens his grip.

"That's one word you could use," I say, nodding, breathless.

Dean grins down at me, his eyes shining. "Do you want to go home?"

I shake my head, grinning. "No."

Believe it or not, I'm feeling more alive than I have for a while. I actually feel like doing something I've never done before, never experienced. Dean makes me feel like I can do anything, and I want that to be true so desperately. I want to show him I'm not just some weak girl, that I can be much more, and I can have fun.

Before I even came to the cabins, I swore to myself I would never let another man near my mind, body or my soul. In fact, the thought of being with another man made me physically sick. But it was the fear of never falling in love or having children of my own that haunted me, made me want to change. With Dean, I don't have to worry about him *taking* anything from me because he consumes all of my waking thoughts. I'd also willingly give him my heart, my soul, and my body.

"What would you like to do?" He grins, and I grin back, tilting my head to the side. A thought occurs to me, and a wide smile spreads across my face.

"How about we go for a swim?" I ask, looking up through my dark, long eyelashes at him.

He cocks his eyebrow at me, making him even sexier—which I thought was impossible. I give him a daring grin, the one I'd give him as a child when I knew he wouldn't go through with something. He laughs, shaking his head at me before standing up and slowly peeling off his clothes. I can't help but ogle his muscled chest as he reaches behind his neck and lifts the shirt off in one fluid motion. My breath catches.

He catches me looking at his defined six-pack—or should I say eight-pack—and I blush. I don't bother looking away; I've already been caught, so I'm going to get my fill.

"Lola, my eyes are up here," he says, pointing to them, trying to act offended.

I laugh and stand up, stripping out of my clothes, Dean's hot gaze on my body. Everywhere he looks it leaves a burning sensation in its wake.

His eyes rake up my legs, over my stomach before reaching my breasts, lingering for a little longer there. A blush creeps up my cheeks, and I can't help but look away from his perusal, feeling shy and insecure.

His body is perfection, and seeing him looking all god-like only ignites the insecurity I have in me.

I'm damaged goods.

I find myself trying to cover up as I stand there in only a red lace bra and matching briefs. I feel stupid for even buying them now and for thinking I could pull them off.

Ann Summers was the place I'd normally get all my underwear from, but that all changed when Rick and I started having problems. I didn't feel comfortable wearing sexy underwear around him, choosing something far more plain and comfortable.

"Don't do that," he says, moving closer.

"Don't do what?" I ask him, confused, my arms wrapped around my bare midriff.

"Don't hide from me. *Never* hide your body from me. You're beautiful and should never hide a body that is alluring, artistic and heavenly. You're perfect inside and out." He moves my hands away from my stomach, and I let them fall limply to my side.

"I bet that's what you tell all the girls," I tease, trying not to show how uncomfortable I am with being the centre of attention. His words are sweet, and they melt my heart, but I've looked in the mirror. I've seen the ugly scars on the inside and out.

"No, Lola. Only you." He steps closer so we're chest to chest, his warmth pressing against my breasts causes a throb low in my stomach. My nipples tighten, the hard tips brushing against the lacy fabric of my bra and the sensation of the rough material rubbing against my already sensitive breasts has tingles pulsating all the way to my clit.

"No one is as beautiful as you, Lola," he whispers, his piercing blue eyes glistening with affection. When he looks at me like that, I only see the truth and the love he has for me. And as cliché as it sounds, he really does make me feel like I'm the only girl in the world whenever I'm around him. He's constantly paying attention to everything I do and say, and not many men do that.

I bite down on my bottom lip trying to be brave and sexy, although my whole body is shaking with nerves and excitement. I most likely look demented and crazed, instead of the seductress I was going for. I want to run and hide, but something inside me doesn't let me. Placing my hands on his bare chest, I run my finger across his defined, cut abs.

I'm so turned on, and it's all because of this man in front of me. The softness in his eyes turns into a fiery blaze. I squeeze my thighs together at the wetness seeping between them. I try to sound seductive enough to distract him, fighting a giggle.

"Dean, baby, is it cold?" I whisper, batting my eyelashes.

He seems confused, but before he has time to think or open his mouth, I push him over the edge of the boat. I stand, laughing, his shocked expression hilarious before he disappears under the water.

Too busy laughing, I don't hear Dean re-surface, and by the time I realise what's happening, he's grabbing my wrists, pulling me into the freezing water. I squeal as I fall head first, coming up spluttering water, whipping the hair out of my face. I start giggling, splashing Dean before swimming off farther into the lake.

The water has done very little to cool down the fire that is burning inside me. Even now, when my body is getting used to the temperature of the lake, I still feel like I'm in a furnace.

Dean swims over to me, pulling me against his body, and I immediately wrap my legs around his waist, rubbing my sex up his hard shaft, gasping at the sensation. I didn't even mean to do it; it was just a knee-jerk reaction. He growls in my ear, sending shivers up my spine, so I do it again. I love it when he makes that sound; it makes me feel powerful and sexy.

Lifting his head from my neck, his lips find mine, kissing me passionately. The kiss turns into something more, something deeper, and it's like something inside me shifts because I want him, like *really* want him.

It's not about sex; it's about Dean and the way he makes me feel. I know he would wait a lifetime for me, but I feel like we've already waited a lifetime to be with each other.

It's overwhelming, a mind whirl, but it also feels right, no matter how quickly it's happening.

"I want you," I tell him, fighting myself to not look away. I'm nervous he's going to turn me down; even though it's clear he wants me.

"I want you too, Lola, but we can wait for that. We have forever," he tells me sincerely, looking at me with adoration.

"No, I want you, Dean. I need you now," I plead, frustration lacing my tone. I've never been surer of anything. I just wish he could see that.

"Let's get you home." He smiles, and even though he hasn't answered, I can only be thankful that he hasn't said no.

Chapter Sixteen

All the way back to the cabin my nerves get the best of me. Whether it's due to excitement or the unknown, I'm not sure; all I know is that I desperately want this. Every time I glance at Dean, he looks deep in thought and those nerves inside me intensify, thinking he's changed his mind. The possibility that he's trying to think of a way to gently let me down also crosses my mind, and it's making me sick to my stomach.

"We don't have to do this if you don't want me like that," I assure him, my voice a whisper as I keep my gaze on the ground. I want to move forward, and the thought of him not wanting me tears something deep inside me.

Dean breaks through my thoughts as he grabs my hand, pulling me against him. Just his touch is sending sparks through me, but the moment I look up, I'm startled by the intensity in his eyes. The powerful look sends shivers racing through my body.

"I want you, Lola. I've *always* wanted you. I just don't want to rush you. I can wait as long as you need me to. I'm not going anywhere. Please don't push yourself to do something you aren't ready for," he says softly, taking care to not hurt my feelings.

"Dean, you're not forcing me into anything I don't want to do. I want this, and I want you. I've feared intimacy for so long and never thought I'd ever get to experience what every other woman out there has with their partners. They get the best parts of sex, whereas I've done nothing but fear it, dread the act. But whenever you touch or kiss me, I feel like my whole body is being set alight. You make me feel, make me want and need things I've never felt before. I want more," I say, taking another step closer to him and lifting my head.

He growls deep in the back of his throat before slamming his lips against mine, picking me up by the backs of my thighs. I grab his shoulders, swinging my legs around his waist, his mouth swallowing my moan.

IF I COULD WISH IT ALL AWAY

After a few attempts to open the door, Dean finally succeeds, stepping through and kicking it shut behind us. Leading us to the bedroom, he never once breaks apart from our kiss. My nerves have me shaking in anticipation, and I begin to worry if I'll be good enough. Will he enjoy it?

Dean deepens the kiss, and I forget all about my insecurities and fears. The kiss turns hotter, more passionate, and desperate. Clinging to his hair, I pull him to me, needing him closer. He slides me down his body, and as my feet hit the floor, I immediately reach for his T-shirt. I only manage to lift it so far before Dean has to help me out, pulling it the rest of the way off in one fluid movement.

Never getting tired of seeing his incredible body, I step forward, my finger moving over each ridge of muscles, before inching lower, over his happy trail and towards that defined V I so desperately want to lick.

He sucks in a breath, and I'm surprised I'm having such a strong effect on him. His eyes darken, and his hands move towards my top.

Lifting my arms, he pulls the top over my head. He bends down, placing sweet kisses across my stomach, trailing them up my chest, all the way to my favourite spot behind my ear. God, I love it when he kisses me there, nibbling at the sensitive skin. Goosebumps trail down my spine, causing me to shiver.

Needing to see more of his skin, I move to the zipper on his jeans, thankful he left the button undone after getting dressed on the boat.

He reaches behind me to the clasp of my bra and my heart pounds. When my breasts come free, I can't help the moan that slips out, my nipples puckering from the cool air. Another shiver runs through me as he slowly slides the straps of my bra down my arms until it falls to the floor. A pained groan escapes me. I just want him to rip it off and ravage me. I need him so fucking much, my stomach tightening in anticipation.

Even though he's causing me to lose my mind, I manage not to lose *all* my concentration and get the zipper down, revealing his boxers.

Dean pulls me against him, kissing me once again as he moves me backwards towards the bed. Laying me down, he presses kisses from my mouth, down my neck, nipping at my skin as he goes. When he reaches my breasts, he takes my erect nipple into his mouth, his fingers twisting and pulling the other, not wanting to leave it out. I don't even recognise the sound that comes out of my mouth. My whole body feels like it's on fire and I'm so overwhelmed with emotions that I could explode at any given moment. Static flows through me, the caress intoxicating.

Lying here half naked, pressed beneath Dean's hard body, is the most pleasurable moment I've ever had. As soon as I feel his thick, erection through his jeans, I move. It's like my body has a mind of its own, pushing and rubbing against him, seeking out the right amount of friction to give me what I need.

His touch seems to be everywhere at once, leaving sparks of electricity burning along my skin.. Grabbing the belt loops on my shorts, he pushes them down my legs, taking my red lace briefs with them. I can feel the cool air hit my hot, wet folds, and my breath catches, my chest swelling.

Dean lets out a ragged breath, his liquid gaze meeting mine. For minutes he just looks down at me, his gaze searing into mine, like he's searching my soul.

We both react at the same time; him brushing his knuckles gently down my cheek as I caress his cheek with my thumb, palming his strong jaw lovingly.

"Are you sure?" he asks, a tremor coursing through his body. I don't think I can speak with all the emotions knotting in my throat, so I just nod, watching his eyes flare with hunger.

Dean sits up, sliding off the bed and walking over to the dresser. At first, I think he's changed his mind and is going to leave, but my heart pounds when he reaches for his jeans. He pulls them down his legs, along with his boxers, and his erection springs free, slapping against his hard stomach.

Oh. My. God!

Dean's erection stands proud, and I lick my lips, wondering how he tastes. He rolls a condom along his length before walking back over to the bed, his eyes never leaving mine as he settles between my thighs. He spreads my legs using his large thighs, leaving me vulnerable and open, my naked body on full display.

My emotions are scattered all over the place, jumping from excitement to lust, and then to desire and nervousness. I'm a little scared and worried too, but nothing is going to stop me from having him, from making love to him tonight.

I trust my feelings towards Dean. I know this isn't me on the rebound or settling for the first person to be nice to me, what I feel for him is real and no one can tell me any different. I can't explain or think of words good enough to describe the intensity of my feelings and over analysing everything isn't going to help anything.

One of his hands reaches behind my neck, guiding my lips to his as he gives me another earth-shattering kiss. The tip of his erection slides through my folds, never once entering me, but the sensation is just as breathtaking. I moan at the same time he growls into the kiss. He reaches for my hips, stopping me from rocking against him. I growl in frustration, wanting him inside me, yet all he does is chuckle.

"Lola, I need to hear you say that this is okay, baby," he rasps out, his eyes darkening as he stares down at me.

"I've never wanted anything more or as desperately as I want you. I trust you with my life. I know if I need you to stop, you will. You'll do it without hesitation and be okay with it, not once making me feel guilty. So please, Dean, make love to me," I plead, trying to position my hips so he can enter me but he pulls back. I'm about to tear into him when the sight of him reaching between us stops me.

Dean circles his hand around his erection, pumping it once, twice before guiding himself into my wet heat, his eyes wild and filled with need. With shaky hands, I grip his shoulders, tears filling my eyes at how incredibly gentle he's being, how different this is from what I've been used to.

I feel full, his length stretching me like I've never been stretched before. A slight sting lingers, but it soon disappears as he thrusts all the way to the hilt. Our breathing comes out ragged and fast, panting against each other.

His hands roam my backside, palming the globes as he rocks deep with slow, torturous thrusts. Moaning, I lean up and sweep my tongue into his mouth before turning it into a kiss.

My back bows off the bed when he lowers his mouth to my nipple, sucking the tight bud till he has me in a withering mess.

"Yes! More," I beg, arching my breasts to his mouth again. My eyes close as his tongue circling my nipple, flicking it once, twice before circling all over again.

His pace is torturous, and I need more. I *want* more, and I know he's holding back on me.

Licking a path up his neck, I reach his ear, biting down on his earlobe before sucking the sting away. A growl rumbles from his chest, and I feel the sound down to my toes.

"Let go! God, please, let go. I need you, all of you," I moan. I move my hips in rhythm to his thrusts, and when I don't get the friction I need, a frustrated curse whispers from my lips.

A guttural growl rumbles from his chest, and whatever control he was holding onto snaps. He slams into me, hitting something deep inside me that causes an earthquake to erupt. My back arches and I scream out in pleasure, all the muscles in my body tightening. I scrape my fingers down his back, placing them on his firm, tight ass as I push up then slam back down onto his erection, meeting him thrust for thrust.

Dean throws his head back, his eyes closed as an animalistic sound erupts from his mouth. At first, I think I've hurt him, but when his eyes meet mine, they're full of passion, a searing hunger and if I'm not mistaken, love.

"Dean, please." I don't even know what I'm pleading for; I just know I need... something.

"Jesus, Lo. I'm not going to last long. God, you're so fucking tight, and so fucking beautiful. Fuck! You're sexy, and you feel so fucking incredible," he rasps out, and I smile up at him.

Feeling full and out of control, I drive my hips up before plunging down on him. The sounds of our flesh slapping together echoes around the room, our bodies slick with sweat as we move together.

His thrusts become punishing, and I wrap my legs around his waist, he goes deeper. I'm so overwhelmed that I don't know my left to my right.

My head is spinning, and with each thrust, he manages to unleash another cry from me. With each cry, my muscles tingle. God, my entire core is tightening, waves of pleasure coursing through. I don't think I'm going to last much longer.

My tongue snakes out, licking his nipples before biting down gently, causing his abdominal muscles to tighten.

My moans grow louder, as do Dean's, his thrusts deeper, harder. The intensity has my body heating all over.

He reaches down, rubbing his thumb against my clit in a circular motion. I scream out in pleasure, wanting to fall over the edge but I hold on, willing my body to last because I don't want this to ever to end between us.

"Let go, Lo. Come for me. I want to feel you come apart around my cock. I want to hear you scream my name," Dean rasps, his dick pulsing inside me at the same time his fingers press harder, moving faster on my clit.

With his dirty words and hard thrusts, I shatter, my core spasming as a million tiny volts shoot through it, a strangled cry echoing around the room.

I don't have time to come down before Dean's thrusts become harder, ragged. Even though I'm still shaking and sensitive from my first orgasm, he manages to bring me into another one, my voice hoarse from calling out his name.

Dean grunts into my neck as my body shakes with tremors. Seconds later he's throwing his head back, releasing his own sound of pleasure as he releases inside me, his dick twitching with each spurt of cum.

He pulls out slowly, and I gasp at the sudden twinge of soreness between my legs. A part of me wishes he could stay inside me forever. He takes in a deep ragged breath before throwing the condom into the bin by the side of my bed.

My sex stings a little, feeling raw, but I like knowing that Dean is the reason it's there, and it's caused by pleasure instead of the pain that I'm used to.

He rolls to his side, pulling me to his chest, his breathing unsteady and heavy just like mine. I feel like I've just run a marathon.

He lazily turns his head. "Lola, that was… fuck! I don't even know *what* that was, but it felt incredible."

I lean over to kiss his chest. "Yes, you were pretty incredible, Mr Salvatore," I tease, and he smiles against my head.

"No, Lola, you were amazing. Nothing can compare to what we just shared. Thank you. Thank you for trusting me with your body and letting me make love to you."

I inhale deeply, hearing him say those words doing funning things to my insides. I reach up to kiss his mouth quickly, not expecting him to deepen the kiss.

My eyes widen when he begins to stir, his erection pressing against my hip. I start laughing at how insatiable he is.

"What's so funny?" he asks, lifting one eyebrow questioningly. God, he's sexy when he does that. I can't help but stare, still amazed at what this man did to my body.

"Um…," I giggle, pointing down to his erection.

He laughs with me, rolling so he's on top of me. The movement causes his erection to rub against my sensitive sex, making me moan once more.

"When it comes to you, my dick is always hard. And now that I've see you naked it's going to a permanent fixture. You're the most beautiful woman I've ever seen. You're strong, passionate, caring, sexy, attractive, sensitive, funny, and most of all, you're just… you. I love everything about you," he says, a sexy grin tugging at his lips.

My heart starts beating rapidly against my chest as a realisation smacks me in the face. I'm in love with Dean Salvatore.

I can run from my past, but there's no running from my feelings for him. I don't want the only relationship I've ever had to be the one that defines my life. I won't let Rick ruin my chances at future happiness when he's already taken so much from me.

Dean makes me happy. Really happy.

Palming his jaw, I give his lips a light, soft kiss before lying back down, my eyes focusing on his chest so he can't see the terror on my face for what I'm about to do. Before I can say those three words, he brings his lips back down to mine, hovering over them with just a breath separating us.

"I love you, Lola. I think I always have, and I always will," Dean admits, and I gasp, my eyes shooting to his. My mind is spinning, screaming that he loves me. *Me*! I throw myself at him, not giving him a chance to blink before I'm kissing him, pouring everything inside me, all of my love, into that one kiss.

Pulling back, breathless, I look into his eyes, my own shining with unleashed tears. This night went from bad to unforgettable. It's a day I'll never forget.

"I love you too, Dean. I loved you as a child, but I love you more as an adult. It's more now, means more, and I understand it," I say through a watery smile. I watch as his face lights up, his eyes glowing with hunger as he grabs the back of my neck, pulling me in for a soul-shattering kiss.

His erection presses against my opening, and I hiss from the soreness. He quickly lifts his weight off me, worry and concern sketched into his features.

"What? Are you okay? Did I hurt you?" he asks quickly, looking down at me and checking me over. He lifts his chin so his eyes meet mine once again, I give him a shy smile.

"Just a bit sore is all," I tell him quietly, too embarrassed to say it's from the giant anaconda he's blessed with.

"Well, how about you take a shower and I'll grab you some water with a couple pain-killers? I'm sorry I hurt you, Lola. I should've been more careful and took things a little bit slower. I just... I couldn't control myself, not around you."

I run my fingers over his eyebrows, smoothing out his frown lines.

"Dean, I wouldn't change a thing that just happened between us. It was magical, everything I've ever dreamed of and more. Please don't say you're sorry, not when making love to you was... It was everything," I whisper, fluttering my eyelashes shyly as I look up at him. "And I'll only take a shower if you have one with me," I whisper seductively, running my hand down his body and palming his erection in my hand, pumping it lazily. "After all, it's you who got me all dirty, so it's only fair that it's you who cleans me down."

His grin is huge when he looks up from where I'm pumping him with lazy strokes.

It takes my breath away at how shockingly beautiful he is, and knowing that it's me he loves.

A squeal escapes me when I'm suddenly thrown over his shoulder, but it soon turns into a giggle when I smack his ass, and he growls, smacking my backside playfully as he carries me over to the bathroom.

Entering the bathroom, he immediately turns the shower head on. He doesn't bother to wait for the water to heat up before he pulls me under the cold spray. I squeal again as the cold water hits my back and Dean makes me suffer the agony for a few seconds before letting me down, my slick body sliding down his.

IF I COULD WISH IT ALL AWAY

Water runs down my breasts and Dean notices, leaning down to lick the droplets off my breast. Stepping closer and feeling him harden against my stomach, I moan as my body lights up, needing him again.

Tugging at his hair, I pull his head closer so our eyes are level, our lips a mere breath away.

"Please. I need you again," I say, staring into his deep penetrating eyes.

"You're going to be the death of me, baby, but I'd do anything for you. It will be my fucking pleasure." He leans in to kiss me again, but before his lips can touch mine he pulls away with a frown. "Shit! I don't have a condom. Wait here," he tells me—like I'm going to leave right now—before rushing out of the shower dripping wet. He heads into the bedroom on his tiptoes, careful not to slip, and I laugh while watching his fine ass bounce as he leaves the room.

Placing my head under the spray, I sigh, loving the feel of the water rushing down my body. My thoughts are overtaken by Dean and the way he felt when he was inside me, making love to me, and my core tingles. God, the way his kisses feel against my throat, across my breasts, but mostly the way they feel on my lips. I love how he'll entwine his tongue with mine. There's nothing in this world that feels better.

I'm so consumed with thoughts of us together that I don't hear him enter the bathroom. My eyes snap open when I feel him moving towards me in the shower, and I stand straighter, spellbound, his eyes hypnotising me. Lust, love, and pure hunger reflects back at me, and with just that one look, he has me wet and ready for him once again. My legs feel like jelly, and when he makes no move to step towards me, I make the decision myself, leaving no space between us.

Suddenly he snaps out of his daze and reaches for me. His movements are fast, and before I know it, I'm being pushed against the cool tiles in the shower.

Lifting me so I'm at the right angle, he enters me in one fluid motion, and we both cry out in ecstasy.

He thrusts into me repeatedly, and we're both screaming out our release. As he places me back down, we study one another lovingly before reaching around me for a washcloth. He takes his time washing me, cleaning every inch of my body and when it's my turn, I take my time exploring every delicious hard ridge of his body.

Neither of us talk, taking the time to just be with one another as we dry off. It's only when we get into bed that we exchange words, holding each other tightly.

"I love you, baby," he whispers, giving me a brief kiss.

I smile lazily, my body aching and sated in a good way. "I love you too," I whisper back, my words filled with so much emotion.

"Goodnight, love. Sweet dreams," he says, pulling me closer to his body, like he's afraid I'll run away during the night.

Fat chance of that. He's stuck with me now.

"Night, Dean." I yawn and close my eyes, exhausted from tonight's sexual activities.

Chapter Seventeen

I wake up blissfully happy, a wide smile spreading across my face. Stretching my body, I feel the soreness from last night's events between my legs. It's a good feeling, and I love knowing it was Dean who put it there. His hands felt like silk sliding across my skin. Just thinking about him and his touch is making me wet, more so now that I know what he can do with that body of his.

I never expected sex to be like that. Reading thousands of romance novels, I always thought mind-blowing, world-altering sex was a myth, fiction. Boy, was I wrong. Not that I have anything other than Rick to compare it to, but then I don't think he should be given the privilege. What he did to me wasn't sex or making love, it was... It was evil. It was degrading and...

Shaking my head, I rid myself of negative thoughts. I'm can't think of him right now, not when I finally have someone good in my life.

I was worried Dean wouldn't enjoy himself, or that I'd do something wrong that would put him off me, but I couldn't have been more wrong. What happened between us was worldly, absolutely incredible and something I'll forever treasure.

I turn around, feeling Dean's breathing shallow out, and I know he's stirring awake.

"Morning, beautiful," he greets, his voice raspy and filled with sleep. I have to bite back a moan when I feel his morning wood pressed against my backside.

"Morning." I turn to face him, a bright smile lighting up my entire face when I catch sight of him. His eyes are lazy with sleep, the colour a deep blue, and he's in need of a good shave, but I've never seen him sexier.

"What would you like to do today? I have the whole morning off, but I do have to pick up an order for Mom tonight. We can do something before I have to leave though, if you want?" he asks, and my mind runs wild. I can think of a million things, some including us naked, but there's something important I need to do. And I think I need to do it before I can talk myself out of it, so it needs to be today.

"Well, I've actually been thinking about what you said to me last night, and I think you're right," I tell him before meeting his eyes, seeing he doesn't understand.

"I said a lot of things last night," he says, raising his eyebrow at me.

I fidget nervously with my hands, not meeting his eyes. "I mean about telling someone, telling my grandpa and your parents about Rick. I'm not comfortable with telling them, but I know they'll only worry about me more if I don't. I'm so torn about it, but it's the right thing to do. I can't keep letting my grandpa worry. With my SIM card snapped up, I can't even call him to say I'm okay.

"Your parents have a lot going on too. I heard them going over the plans for the masquerade ball and the charity event coming up. I couldn't live with myself if I somehow messed that up because they're worried about me. But really, when is a good time to tell someone that kind of thing?" I ramble, my anxiety bubbling to the surface.

Lily and Mark have been throwing charity events for as long as I can remember. They take each one of them seriously, and although I was never old enough to attend one before, I knew how important they were to the couple. Back then they only ever rented the cabins out for attending guests, but this time they'll be doing more than accommodating. They'll be holding the event here, at Cabin Lake.

It's going to be a lot for them to deal with, especially if I tell them about my past and what happened to me. I don't want to be a burden to them. And since I'm excited to attend an event myself, I don't want to jeopardise anything and ruin it for them.

"Lola, they would never be too busy for you. You need to know you don't need to do this if you're not ready." He sighs, resting his cheek in the palm of his hand "If this is about last night and what I said about our case with your granddad, then I'll handle it. I'll handle *him*. I don't want you to worry over that. I only told you because I hated keeping things from you. It wasn't right, and it was killing me. We can talk to your granddad about changing lawyers. It's up to you though. Whatever you decide to do, I'll be beside you one-hundred percent.

"Personally, I think you're strong enough for anything. Also, if we tell your granddad, then he can keep an eye on Rick for us. We still don't know what he's up to or what connections he has. Hell, we don't even know if he's looking for you. If your granddad keeps an eye out, we'll have the upper hand. He can keep us one step ahead," he says, rubbing soothing circles on my hip.

He's right, and I'm kicking myself for not thinking of it first.

Maybe telling Grandpa won't be that bad.

I need to suck it up. I told Dean pretty much everything, and the relief made me feel lighter. It's helped to make dealing with it all easier. So if getting this out in the open will bring me one step closer to feeling like my old self again, or even a step towards the new me, I'll take it. It might help me breathe easier too, knowing it's all out there. Lying isn't one of my strong suits and every time I tell one, even if it's a little white lie, I feel sick to my stomach, a part of my soul chipping away.

"Okay, but will you stay with me when I call him? And can I use your phone, please?" I ask, my voice shaking slightly.

"Oh, crap! Wait, I forgot to give you something," he says, jumping off the bed. He runs to the bag he brought over with some fresh clothes and starts rummaging through it. Since he's stayed every night but one, it only seemed right he brought over some of his things. It also prevented him from having to keep going back and forth between cabins.

It's comforting to know that he's here when I wake up from one of my nightmares. He stays with me, always soothing me and calming me down. He makes me feel safe when all I see is Rick in my nightmare, reliving it all over again while I'm awake. He'll sit there for hours if need be saying it's not real, that's it's just a nightmare. It's nice to have that reassurance because some nights I need him like I need air to breathe.

I've lain in his arms wishing he would kiss me, secretly hoping he'll make a move. I'm just glad that isn't something I have to worry about anymore because I can kiss him whenever and wherever I want to. He's mine and I'm his.

Dean comes back to the bed holding a box in his hands, and I sit up, intrigued.

Opening it up, he pulls out a new iPhone from the box, and I gasp at the incredibly sweet and kind gesture. He simply is the best man I know.

"I got you this the other day, but I kept getting too distracted to give it to you. I knew you would refuse to let me get you one, so I went out and did it on my own. I've installed mine, Moms, Dads, Pagan's and Sid's phone numbers. Oh, and Brooke's. I've also saved my office number and my other work number just in case you can't get a hold of me on my normal phone. Is that okay?" he asks, looking unsure now that he's finished explaining.

I can't get over how thoughtful he's being. He went out of his way to get me a phone, and I didn't even ask for one. God, he's always finding things to make me love him that much more.

I wrap my arms around his neck and lean in, kissing him softly, moaning when he deepens the kiss. His hands move to my back, pressing me closer against his warm chest.

Reluctantly, I pull away breathing hard. If I don't, I'll never get around to making this phone call.

Swinging my legs off the bed, I glance over my shoulder at Dean, grinning. "Come on! I won't be able to concentrate knowing you're in here naked. We need to move into the front room."

Dean bursts out laughing, making me pause to admire his incredibly handsome features. I love his laugh. It sounds deep, husky, and carefree. I also find the way his eyes crinkle at the corners when he laughs incredibly fucking sexy.

I head into the living room as Dean makes us some coffee. He hands me the steamy cup of goodness, joining me on the sofa and placing a comforting hand on my thigh as I dial my grandpa's office in case Rick still has his mobile.

After the fourth ring, my hands begin to feel clammy. Sweat trickles down my back, between my breasts, and across my forehead. My throat is knotted up, and I hope that when he finally answers, I'll somehow manage to find my voice. My mouth is so dry, even with the sips of coffee I'm taking.

"Lawson Law. You have Sally Coyle speaking. How may I help you?" Sally greets, and I want to groan into the handset.

Sally was once my grandpa's personal assistant, but a few years ago he pretended to promote her to personal receptionist. Really it was a demotion. I honestly don't know how she didn't see the difference between the two jobs. She was happy with the 'promotion'.

When I questioned Grandpa on it, he simply said he couldn't handle her attending another meeting with him and that the next time he had to I'd be arranging his funeral because she was so annoying to work with. He still had to put up with her whining and lack of work ethics, but at least he didn't have to take her with him to meetings and business trips.

Once, we were on the phone to each other, and I laughed the whole time he bitched about her. Rick had watched the whole thing with a murderous and judgemental expression. He didn't like that my attention wasn't solely focused on him. It was another reason why he hated my grandpa. You see, my grandpa is a good, kind man, but he loves work gossip. When he was younger, nothing scandalous ever happened, so he loved to keep up with the office gossip, so he felt like he was somehow a part of their group. I guess men never really grow up; they're just big kids at heart.

When I got off the phone, Rick had turned the entire conversation I had with Grandpa to be about him. He accused me of keeping things from him just because I didn't want to tell him who the girl was that we were talking about. I didn't want to tell him it was about Sally because I knew he liked her and because I didn't particularly want to cause trouble for anyone in the office. I tried everything in my power not to mention her name, but then I slipped up in the heat of the moment.

I wasn't expecting the reaction I got.

He beat me that night, covering my body in bruises. I was just thankful he had enough control to avoid my face.

I wasn't one to be bitchy or mean, but there was something about Sally that got me angry and riled up.

The phone call was the first time I'd ever expressed how I really felt about her. I usually kept quiet, keeping my opinions to myself, but that night I had to say something. I called her a bitch. One word, that's it. And I think I deserved that outlet after all the times she'd bitched and was mean to me.

It didn't help that it was Sally who was rumoured to have slept with Rick. Grandpa overheard the rumour at work and told me about it, seeing truth in it and worrying for me.

I confronted Rick after and he immediately denied it, going as far as to cause a massive argument, accusing me of having trust issues. He turned it all around on me, saying I was only accusing him of cheating because I had a guilty conscience. In the end, I believed he was telling me the truth or maybe, deep down, I ignored it knowing there was nothing I could do if he *had* cheated. There was no way out for me. Stupid, I know.

When Grandpa confronted Rick the next day in his office, giving him a hard time over the rumours, Rick had come home, livid. It was the first time he broke my ribs—two of them, in fact.

I remember hating Sally more than I normally did after that. I blamed her, and I blamed him. Every time I struggled to breathe or winced in pain, I'd plan the perfect revenge in my head… on both of them.

"Hello," Sally's irritated, snotty voice says through the phone. It snaps me out of my daze, and I shake my head, annoyed with myself for getting lost in my own thoughts.

"Hi, may I speak with Dwayne Lawson, please?" I ask, clearing my throat. I don't bother introducing myself; she'd only have it announced on all floors in five minutes. Plus I don't want her to know it's me just in case Grandpa isn't in his office.

"I'm sorry, but he's with a client right now. If you can call back tomorrow, I'm sure he'll be free," she says, being brash, and I can feel myself getting worked up already. She has that effect on people.

He isn't in a meeting at all, she's just too lazy to lift her finger to the phone to buzz me through. She's probably at her desk painting her nails like she always is. The only reason she even answers the phone is so my grandpa doesn't hear the phone constantly ringing and fire her for being incompetent.

"No." My voice is firm and before she can speak, I interrupt her. "Please put Dwayne Lawson on the phone right now. Tell him it's an emergency and that his granddaughter is on the phone," I snap.

"Well, well, well. Look who's finally come out of the woodwork. Dwayne isn't very pleased with you, Lola. I don't think he'll want to talk to you at the moment. I always thought you were a whore, but to run out on darling Rick, and for no reason? Tut tut! He was going to propose and everything," she scolds, but doesn't sound all that bothered by it. "Don't worry though, I've been taking real good care of him." Her voice is sickeningly sweet, and it grates on my nerves.

I would love to say she can keep him, but I wouldn't wish him on my own worst enemy… including her.

Then it occurs to me. If Rick has moved on with Sally, then maybe he's over me and doesn't care where I am. I'm naive to even think that statement holds any truth, but a girl can only hope.

"Sally, stop thinking you know what happened because if you did, we'd be having an entirely different conversation right now. So, if you don't mind, could you actually do your job and transfer me to my grandpa. Or do I have to call his mobile and tell him you're refusing to put me through to him? I'm pretty certain he wouldn't be too pleased with that, now, would he?" I keep my voice firm, trying to sound as professional as I can get, even though I'm shaking uncontrollably.

Looking up, Dean is smiling at me. I shake my head, my lips twitching. I never noticed the amount of tension coiled tightly in my body until I saw his smile. I instantly relaxe.

Lost in each other's eyes, the heated look hits me between my legs. A blush creeps up my neck to my cheeks when an image of what we could be doing right now pops into my head.

"Hello? Lola, are you there?" My grandpa's voice is strained and panicked, and my eyes fill with tears. He sounds older, stressed and worn out, and a twinge of guilt slams into my stomach.

"I'm here," I whisper, willing the tears to stay at bay so I can get through this conversation without having to repeat it all over again.

"Where have you been, Lola? Where are you now? I've been worried sick, and I've had no way of getting in touch with you. I lost my phone at one of the conference meetings, and since I haven't got your mobile number stored anywhere else, I couldn't call. Rick said your phone was disconnected when I asked him for your number. He's accused you of leaving with another man. Is that true, Lola? I just don't believe it. He seems broken, destroyed. He isn't the same man he was before you left. I was hoping after I gave him a few days off work he'd be okay to return, but he's still losing his temper and drinking on the job. God, doll, I've had to give him two warnings already. He's got one more before he's out. The bloke is losing us too many clients. In all fairness, I'm just so happy you've finally left his sorry ass," he rambles.

I choke back a sob, gritting my teeth together whenever he mentions how bad *poor* Rick is doing. I can't stand to listen to another minute it. *He did this. Him, not me!* So if he's feeling the loss of our relationship or somehow found his heart whilst I've been gone and is feeling remorse for his actions… well, he can fuck off. I don't care what he has to say or what he's going through; he has no one to blame but himself, and I can't believe I've spent years and years blaming myself for his actions. Always telling myself I could have got dinner done quicker, or I didn't need to get that book or ask for new bed sheets.

Well, not anymore.

"Grandpa, there's something I need to tell you, and I need you to be alone for it to happen. Can you make sure Sally doesn't listen in? In fact, go take the phone off her until we end the call, please. It's really important," I explain, my voice barely a whisper as I try to hide my emotions. I want to ask him a million questions, like how he is, but I need to get this out.

"Lola, are you in trouble? Where are you?" he rushes out, sounding worried.

"I'm fine, but please go and take the phone off her. I'll explain everything then, I promise."

He agrees, and I hear the phone being dropped on his desk, followed by some mumbled words of what I expect is him talking to Sally. She doesn't sound too happy about the phone being removed, so I guess she was already listening in.

The bitch.

"It's done. Now tell me everything and start from the beginning," he says, sounding far too serious.

I take a deep breath to calm my nerves, but it doesn't work. Dean, noticing the sudden change, lifts me into his lap. I'm so nervous my hands are shaking, although cuddling up to Dean has eased some of my worry. He knows how hard this is for me and how hard it is for me to tell my grandpa, the man who raised me, about Rick. He must have guessed that telling Grandpa will be like reliving the whole ordeal all over again. Just thinking about all the abuse and torment I've encountered over the past five years has my stomach coiling.

"Grandpa, there's no easy way to tell you this, so I'm just going to come straight out and say it. Rick's been physically abusing me for years,"

I say, and then go on to tell him about the abuse, how he'd hit me. I tell him about the rapes in as little detail as I can muster.

I can't bring myself to tell him about all the times Rick used his reprimands at work as an excuse as to why he'd lose his temper. I know my grandpa would blame himself, and it's not his fault. None of it is.

Rick always managed to find someone to blame one way or another. No matter what instigated the argument in the first place, he'd find a way. It was *never his* fault. Whoever's fault it was, it always ended up being because of something I did. Whether it was because I'd breathe funny or woke him up if I went to the toilet during the night, he'd punish me for it.

I tell him about the night I left, about the hospital, and just as I'm about to reveal the rest, I pause, fear seeping in.

"I need you to keep my location a secret, Grandpa. You can't tell a soul."

"I promise," he chokes out hoarsely.

"I'm at Cabin Lake with Lily, Mark, Dean, and the twins. I had to get away from him and to a place I knew he couldn't find me and where I felt safe. I couldn't risk telling you because I knew you would fire him and he would have just had you sued for unfair dismissal. I'm so sorry, Grandpa. I really am," I say, choking up. "But there's also another reason I called you. I need you to take the Salvatore case off Rick. I can't have him here. Can you do this for me?" I ask him, my voice shaky.

He's stayed quiet during everything, being true to his word. But the silence is killing me. My breathing is heavy down the line, and more tears fall from my eyes, pooling on my knees.

A minute or so passes, and he still hasn't said anything, I begin to worry he's not there so I lift the phone to my face, checking to make sure we've got a signal or that I haven't somehow managed to cut him off. When I see we're still connected, I place the phone back against my ear, just in time to hear a faint sob coming through the line.

"Grandpa? Are you there? Are you okay?" I call out.

A few seconds later, the phone crackles and his ragged breathing sounds heavy. My heart breaks knowing he's upset enough to take that long to get himself together. I wish he was in front of me, that we were having this conversation face-to-face.

"Lola, I'm so sorry," he says, choked up. "You could have come to me. You *should* have come to me." He sounds so broken, and tears fall from my eyes. "I'm going to come down as scheduled and take Rick's place. While I'm down there, we can start gathering up a case to get that sick bastard sentenced. I know you want to keep it quiet and we will, but only until we have the evidence we need to send him to prison. I'll call in some favours so we can nail this sick fucker.

IF I COULD WISH IT ALL AWAY

"In the meantime, I'm going to fire this fucker. I know you don't want me to, but he's on his last warning, and with the way he's acting, he'll be gone by the end of the week anyway. I wouldn't be surprised if it's not by the end of the day. Legally too, so you won't have to worry about me."

I breathe a sigh of relief.

We talk for a while longer about Rick, Dean, the cabin, about himself and what he's been up to. He told me to say hello to everyone and to apologise to Lily and Mark about not returning their phone calls, work being too hectic.

We say our tearful goodbyes, promising to keep in touch. I blink through my tears, staring down at the phone clutched in my hands.

"Do you feel better?" Dean asks, and I stare blankly at the message from Grandpa, giving me his new mobile number. I'm glad Dean stayed with me through everything, lightly stroking my back. Without him, I don't think I'd have had the strength to do it.

"I do," I say, forcing a small smile.

"What did he say?"

I fill Dean in on everything Grandpa said, and about his plans to look further into Rick's background so he can start building a case.

Grandpa's business partner, Ted, isn't a fan of Rick either, so he's going to ask him for some advice and help since that's his area of expertise. My grandpa's law degree is mostly business.

I don't know how I got so lucky. I've lived in a nightmare for the past few years, never finding a way out, but here I am, less than a month of being free and I feel like I'm in heaven. It all seems surreal, like I could wake up at any moment to find out this is all a dream.

I'll never forgive or truly forget what Rick has done to me. It will always be there, rooted deep in the darkest parts of me. But I feel like I can finally breathe and that I can be me, the real me, and not have to worry about the repercussions. Although I have far to go, I'm going to try my damnedest to keep the other Lola buried, the Lola who was weak-minded and frail. I'm going to pretend I left that part of me back in Carlisle.

I'm so grateful for Dean being in my life again and for the nightmare he's helped pull me out of. His guidance and faith in me have given me the courage and strength to start over. It's given me a chance to be who I want to be without living in fear. I'll always love him for that, but mostly I'll love him for just being himself.

Since leaving, I've become a stronger person. I'd been merely a shadow, a shell of my former self, and I hated looking in the mirror each morning and seeing that person reflected back at me.

It's made me learn a valuable life lesson that looks can be deceiving. One thing is for certain—I'll never let myself be put in that position ever again.

"Now it's time to go and tell your parents. Do you think I'm doing the right thing? I don't want them to treat me differently," I question him, biting my bottom lip.

"Yes, you most certainly are. C'mon. If we hurry up, we'll have plenty of time to talk to them and let them absorb it all before Pagan and Sid arrive for lunch. Oh, and Lo?" he calls as I stand to get dressed.

I turn around, facing him. "Yeah?"

"I don't know if I've told you this lately, but I'm so fucking proud of you, baby," he says, stepping in front of me. He takes my face in his warm palms and brings it closer to his, kissing me breathless.

Chapter Eighteen

Walking into the kitchen, Lily greets us with a bright smile, her hands clearly full. She's prepping lunch whilst juggling her phone, letters, and other papers scattered about.

Putting down the phone and dropping a letter, she steps up to us. "It's so good to see you two," she beams, bringing me in for a hug. I tense but scold myself and relax into the hug.

"Hi." I smile and step away, letting Dean give his mom a hug and kiss on the cheek.

"I'm just going to feed the horses. I'll be back in five or ten minutes," Dean says, winking at me and making me blush before leaving.

"What's all this?" I ask, picking up a flyer.

"It's for the charity event we're throwing. These pompous arses said they sent over the charity details, but I can't find them anywhere. I've been on the phone to them all morning, but they keep mugging me about." She sighs. "They take life for granted, only caring how much money they have in their bank accounts. I wouldn't be surprised if they benefited somehow from doing this event. If your mom was here, she'd have them all up by their balls. She wouldn't take this shit," she rants, and I giggle. Hearing her get all worked up is funny. "Hold on," she says, holding her finger up as her phone rings.

She answers the phone, her voice changing to one I remember from when she'd tell Dean or the twins off. I tune her out, knowing she means business. I feel sorry for the poor soul on the other end of the phone.

She's right about my mom though; she would've had them by their balls. Both my parents gave a lot to charity, usually as an anonymous donation and sometimes through my dad's company. They never wanted the recognition or the publicity, wanting people to concentrate on the charity instead.

I think they also kept their donations quiet because no one knew how wealthy they were. They never wanted to risk the dangers of having money. They didn't like the saying 'money changes you,' strongly believing money actually changed the people around you. They didn't want people to be their friends just because they could get something from them. They couldn't stand fake people and didn't want to be associated with them.

I actually carried on donating to the charities my parents were involved with. It's another thing Rick didn't like me doing. He would say there were millions of people in the world who could donate and that it didn't have to be me. He hated the fact I *gave* my money away, yet never seemed to want it, if that makes sense. It's what always confused me about him. He didn't want my money yet always moaned about paying the bills. I even offered to pay for them, but he refused, saying I was rubbing it in his face about how much money I had.

He even went to my grandpa once, demanding he be given guardianship over my inheritance. There was no beating he could have given me to make me sign over my parents hard-earned money, so Grandpa was the last resort. Of course, he declined and was actually pissed at Rick for having the nerve to even ask such a thing.

Lily ends her phone call, immediately rushing over to a stack of folders. She grabs one and starts shifting through it before sighing with relief.

"Everything okay?" I ask, stepping forward, a worried frown on my face as I take in her dishevelled appearance.

"The charity is for McMillan Cancer," she says, sounding shocked as she reads through a letter.

"You seem surprised, Lily." It seems like a good cause to me. In fact, it's one of the charities I make monthly donations to.

"I am, doll. Last year they all stayed here whilst holding the benefit at the town hall, and they were so rude, impolite, snobby and arrogant. They didn't even know what charity they were raising money for and it irked me. They came across as selfish and spent the whole night talking business deals. They didn't take the night seriously. It was just a ruse to make deals," she tells me.

"That's bad," I whisper, appalled.

"It was. They were supposed to make a speech for the chosen charity, but the speaker spoke about a different one, and even then the facts weren't right. It was a shambles. It's the same group of people who are attending this year, but with the venue being bigger, we've involved some other local businesses."

"Maybe this year they could have their act together," I suggest, though Lily looks doubtful.

"Maybe, but they're still arses."

I giggle at her cussing. She doesn't do it much, but when she does it sounds like a foreign language. It's hilarious.

"Hey, what did I miss?" Dean interrupts, stepping into the room.

"Your mom cussed," I blab, and Lily shoots me a death glare, making me giggle.

"*Mom*," Dean scolds, narrowing his eyes though he's clearly amused.

"I'll put a quid in the swear jar," she mutters, shaking her head.

"Swear jar?" I ask, wondering how that happened.

"Yeah," Dean answers, chuckling. "Dad kept swearing in front of clients. Mom and Pagan told him it was unprofessional and that it reflected badly on their business, so she bought a swear jar."

I laugh, throwing my head back. They're simply a crazy bunch.

"Shall we call the twins to come back early?" Lily asks, and the laughter leaves me, suddenly nervous because I know what's about to happen.

"Actually, Mom, Lola has something she wants to tell you and Dad. It's important," Dean says, his voice serious. "I think it best she tells you without the twins here, okay?"

Lily looks between us, her expression curious and concerned, and I start to feel queasy.

"I'll just go get your father, then. We'll meet you in the dining room," she states before making her way out of the room to find Mark.

I take a deep breath, feeling like I'm going to be sick. I wasn't like this when I talked to Grandpa, but then again I was feeling all kinds of brave this morning. Now it seems to have worn off, nerves kicking in and bringing friends.

"Hey, it's going to be okay. I promise. I'll be with you all the way through it," Dean tells me as we walk hand in hand to the dining room. The place is spacious like the rest of the cabin, the dark wood glossy and brilliantly fitting with the rest of the room. It has a warm feeling, with thick white candles filling every available space. On the walls are canvas photos of the views around the land. Everything in here is inviting, and I can't help but be comforted by that.

Two minutes later, Mark and Lily walk in, both looking concerned as they take a seat at the mahogany table. My chest tightens.

Dean, sensing my unease, places a reassuring hand on my thigh, squeezing me gently.

"What did you need to talk about?" Lily asks, and Mark places his hand over hers, hearing the tremor in her voice.

"I need to tell you something, and it's going to be hard for me," I tell them, looking at both straight on and gulping. "By the end of it you'll understand why I can't tell you everything, but you deserve to know as much as possible. If my parents were still alive I'd have sat here a long time ago telling you, so please let me get it all out before you want to ask me anything, okay?" I ask gently.

"You can tell us anything, darling," Mark assures me, and I give him a sad smile.

"Thank you," I whisper, then start from the beginning—how I met Rick, how it all started and then to the beating.

I find myself going into more detail, not able to stop the words from leaving my mouth.

I share about this morning, telling Grandpa for the first time and what he has planned. The whole time my eyes focus on Lily, watching her as she silently cries yet never once interrupts me. It's so hard to watch and I want to stop so many times through everything just so I could comfort her.

My eyes sting from holding back tears. I feel like I'm going to split apart at any second. It doesn't feel the same as when I told Dean, Blaire, Brooke, or even Julie. It was hard telling Grandpa, but even after telling him, I felt the weight being lifted off me. But somehow, somewhere, I feel like I've let Lily and Mark down. It's the same feeling I get when I think of my parents knowing.

God, it's killing me knowing I've put them through so much pain.

After finishing I look down at the table, fighting tears. The dreaded silence begins to weigh me down. I feel like I'm paralysed, fearing the unknown of what they're thinking.

I honestly don't know what I'd do if they hated me or were disappointed in me. Just the thought leaves a bad taste in my mouth.

Lily clears her throat after what feels like hours of silence, when in reality it's only been a few minutes or so.

"Lola, baby. I'm so sorry. This is all our fault. We should have been there for you. We shouldn't have given you time or let you push us away. God, your mother will be turning in her grave knowing I let you get hurt." She sobs, clutching her chest as tears fall free.

"No," I deny, shaking my head as tears fall, blurring my vision. There's nothing she could do that would upset my mom and it's certainly not her fault.

"Yes, Lola. It's true. We should have protected you. If we were in your lives, then we would have seen the signs and helped you, my girl. We don't deserve your forgiveness, but I hope you can find it in your heart to. I'm so sorry this happened to you." She sobs into Mark's chest, clutching his shirt. "He hurt our girl. *Our* girl. What kind of monster would hurt her?" she cries and my nose stings, more tears falling as I choke back my own sob.

"Are you disappointed in me?" I ask quietly. "I knew what he was doing was wrong, and I tried. I really did try to leave him, but—"

"No! Don't think like that, *ever*. We could never be disappointed in you. You're such a strong woman, Lola, but no one, and I mean no one, should ever have to go through that," Mark says, his eyes watering.

"But I—"

"No, girl. No buts. We love you and never should have left you. It's breaking my heart to know you've been alone all these years with that monster," Lily chokes out.

Not being able to stand to see her in so much pain, I lift myself out of my chair and make my way over to her. She pulls away from Mark, watching me curiously, and when I pull her in for a hug, she returns it. Holding onto each other for dear life, we sob into one another's shoulders.

Two chairs scrape across the wooden floor, causing us to pull apart. Dean and Mark quietly exit the room, giving us some privacy.

"I'm so sorry we let you down," Lily says, more tears falling as her chin wobbles.

"No, Lily, you didn't let me down. I was too weak, but it was always this place that kept me strong. Every time he laid a hand on me, or I was recovering from one of his tempers, I'd close my eyes and revert back to my happier moments, back here. This place was my safe haven. Why I never thought to come here before is beyond me.

"Please don't blame yourself. Back then, I was grieving too much, and I couldn't deal with any reminders. As years went by, that hole in my heart just got bigger and bigger, but then I met Rick. I desperately wanted to be loved, and he filled a little of that hole, if only for a short while. But since I've been back here? It's like I'm whole again. So don't ever feel responsible, ever," I tell her, my voice choked up as I explain it to her.

"Oh, darling, you've always been loved. I love you like you're my own daughter. I always have. Your parents died loving you, and they'll be in heaven looking down on you, loving you more. When I look at you, I don't just see your mother, my best friend, my soul mate. I see your beauty, your strength, and your heart. It's pure and magical.

"Knowing someone tried to take all that away from you breaks my heart. I wish we could have been there for you and that you had come to us sooner. I understand why, but darling, there is only one person to blame in all of this and that's him. I know you haven't told us everything he did, and I hope one day you'll come to me and tell me. I know your mother would want that for you. She'd want there to be someone for you to talk to," she whispers, and I break. Falling into her arms, I sob so hard we end up on our knees on the floor, holding each other.

I can barely speak when we pull away, looking at her through blurry eyes.

"I will, Lily. I promise. I just need some time. I can't do this without any of you, and I was stupid to ever think I could. I was so scared you'd all be disappointed in me for staying with him for so long, or that you'd hate me for letting him do all those awful things to me," I choke out, exhausted.

"Never. And did you give him permission to hurt you?"

I look up at her sharply, confused and a little hurt by her question. Because of course I didn't give him permission. What kind of person would?

"What? No! Never," I tell her, shaking my head.

"Then you never let him do those things to you, doll. You couldn't be a disappointment if you tried. You're too loving, too caring, and so much like your mother it's uncanny," she says, running her fingers through my hair before cupping my cheek.

"I love you so much," I sob, trying to calm down. "I love you all and I didn't want to taint you with all of this, but I promise to tell you everything from now on. I'll never keep anything from you again."

"Take all the time you need." she whispers, pulling me into her lap and kissing my temple.

After a few minutes, my sobs subside. A few tears still fall, but I manage to pry myself out of her arms and look up at her.

"C'mon, let's go see where our men have gone. I don't want them messing in my kitchen and eating the food," she says, lightening the conversation.

She helps me to my feet, and we try to straighten our clothes, but when we look at our appearances, our eyes meet, and we burst out laughing.

"God, I look a mess." I giggle, my throat still raw from crying.

"You look beautiful." She tucks a strand of hair behind my ear before wiping under her eyes.

"Yeah, right." I chuckle, rolling my eyes.

We walk towards the door leading to the kitchen, but instead of opening it, Lily stops to look over her shoulder at me. She seems reluctant about something, and it has me shifting on my feet.

"Can I ask you something?" She turns to face me fully.

"Yeah, anything," I nod, although I feel a little nervous about what she's going to ask.

"It's nothing bad," she quickly assures me, waving me off. "It's just... well, you can tell me to mind my own business, but you and Dean... seem close. Like, really close," she says, and I blush. I can hide my reaction, she's jumping and squealing.

"What?" I ask, wondering what's going on.

"I knew it! I freaking knew it." She laughs, bouncing excitedly. "You know, your mother and I watched how close you were growing up, and we planned your future together. We said you'd end up married with children."

"I know. She'd always go on about it, making me blush." I giggle.

"Yeah, she'd say you were going to be what tied our family together as blood, but then, even if you didn't get together, we'd always be family." She smiles.

I don't know why but her words have me choking up again, as does Lily. But the second we meet each other's eyes we start giggling, a few tears falling free.

God, what are we like?

"C'mon, we need to get lunch ready for our men." She winks and I blush. There's no denying how my belly flutters at hearing her call them *our* men.

She never was good at giving a subtle hint.

Chapter Nineteen

"Bye," I call out, waving to everyone after spending ten minutes convincing Lily and Mark that I'd be okay walking home on my own.

They call back their goodbyes before heading back inside and shutting the door. I've had a good day, and I can't wipe the smile off my face as I make my way back home. The night air is cool, the stars bright and the full moon glowing brightly.

I've spent the afternoon getting to know everyone. Pagan held most of the conversation, filling me in on everything I'd missed over the years.

All my life I've felt alone, and even though I had my grandpa close by, that sense of loneliness never went away. Rick never filled the gaping hole my parents deaths left in my heart, not really. He only made it easier to live with. But over time our relationship sucked everything out of me and made that hole seem empty and hollow.

But then I spend one day with them all, and it's filled that void in my heart. I've never felt so full. I'm practically floating with happiness.

God, I learnt so many things about all of them today. I just wish I'd been there to see it for myself.

Apparently, Sid got into teaching when he was offered a job at the local school. A fan of the band, who was a teacher at the school, approached him at one of his gigs. They'd been watching him and were impressed with how he interacted with younger kids when he would give them guitar lessons in his spare time. It's incredibly sweet of him to do that, and I can't wait to see him play.

They offered him a job, telling him they'd keep it available whilst he got his degree in education. He immediately took to the idea, finally finding something he wanted to do and was passionate about. And Sid is passionate about music; you could tell by the way he spoke about it.

So he got his degree, working as a T.A at the school between classes. But because the school was having trouble finding a stand-in music teacher, he was basically teaching the class himself under the supervision

IF I COULD WISH IT ALL AWAY

of another teacher.

I'm happy for him.

Apparently Pagan can sing too, but even with all her confidence, she can't sing in public or even in front of her family. She gets stage fright. It surprised me, to be honest. She's so carefree and bubbly and always saying what's on her mind, no matter how rude or inappropriate it may be. Though, her being able to sing doesn't surprise me. She and Sid have always shared some of the same qualities. I guess singing is one of them.

But although singing wasn't her career choice, she still managed to find something she was passionate about. She's just finished her business and personal relations degree, passing at the top of her class. Secretly, I think she just loves the control the job entails. She seems like the 'take charge' kind of person.

At the moment though, she only helps out with Cabin Lake events for her father. She's slowly been building up her portfolio so that one day she an open up her own business, which is ultimately her end game. But at the moment she's hoping the work she does for her father gets her noticed, as the more recognition she gets, the more people will want to hire her. Personally, I don't think she's going to have a problem there.

She's organised the charity even for this Saturday. It shouldn't have come as a surprise, but from the way Lily spoke about it the other day, I presumed the 'pompous asses' were hiring people to do it.

The day had been a good distraction from my heart-to-heart conversation with Lily and Mark this morning. I can't even explain how good it felt not to be pulled down into a depressing mood, which is what I always get like when I'm feeling mentally exhausted.

Instead, they all kept me entertained for hours and hours and our lunch ended up rolling into dinner, hence the reason why I'm walking back so late.

Speaking of Dean, before he left earlier, he said he wouldn't be long, but the sun's long gone down and he still isn't back.

I'm at my cabin door when my phone rings. Pulling it out of my pocket, a wide grin stretches across my face when I see Dean's name flashing across the screen.

"Hello?" I answer excitedly. "I was just thinking about you."

"You were, huh?" He chuckles, sounding tired. "I just wanted to check in and say I'm sorry for not being back already. After I picked up the crap Mom needed me to get, the office called. There's been an urgent call from a client, and I need to go in. I need to get briefed so I won't know when I'll be back. It's most likely going to be late, so I'll understand if you want me to crash at mine tonight. You probably want your space back." He chuckles again, but it sounds forced. It's like the idea of not spending the night with me upsets him, and that thought makes me smile.

Plus the thought of being without him scares me, and as much as I know I need to be stronger, I can't. I just got him back in my life, and I'm not ready to let him go. I don't even think I could sleep without him anymore.

I rely on Dean a lot. I know I shouldn't, but I've dreamt of this moment for so long. When he looks at me, I feel loved, cherished and special. I could live off that feeling alone for the rest of my life and die a happy woman.

He loves me, and I love him. He shows me every day, and in every way a person can show someone they love them. I know people throw around the word love all willy-nilly—hell, Rick claimed he loved me, but for someone who claimed to have loved me, he had a funny way of showing it. If you love someone, you won't hurt them, strip away their existence or tear them down inch by inch, until they felt like nothing.

But when Dean tells me he loves me, it's real. The words ring true every time he says them. It's a love people dream of having, and I want to spend the rest of my life with him proving I love him back just as much.

"No, I want you to come home to me," I answer, smiling as I kick the bottom step, hovering outside in the cool air as we speak.

I hear him sigh down the phone and I smile. I can picture him now, his relaxed face and his shoulders sagging with relief.

Aww, he really didn't want to go home.

"I love the way you say *home*," he half whispers, and the sound sends a shiver down my spine.

"Yeah? Me too," I admit honestly, biting my bottom lip.

"Good, baby. I love you, Lo, and I promise I'll be home as quickly as I can. Go to bed. I'll grab the spare set of keys out of Dad's office and let myself in so I don't wake you up."

I nod, cursing inwardly when I realise he can't see me. "Okay, I'm going to relax for a bit and watch a film first. Hopefully, I'm still up when you come home."

"Hopefully," he whispers, sounding like he'd rather be here. "Get some rest. You've had a long day. I love you."

"I love you too." I grin as we both say our goodbyes and end the call.

A thought occurs to me when I get off the phone, and I bite my bottom lip worriedly. I know how important his job is to him; I don't want to distract him or keep him from doing his job.

Whatever he's got going on tonight, I just hope it's safe. After Pagan filled me in on his job and what it entails, I'll do nothing but worry about him whenever he has to go in.

She told me about the time he got badly beaten due to a case he'd been working on. He was beaten for information about what he knew and who he was working for, but he didn't know what they were talking about.

She told me he would've died if it weren't for the fact they ransacked his office, finding information that proved he was who he said he was and that he was spying on them.

It turned out that the case he was doing surveillance for happened to be at his attackers' restaurant. The bloke he was watching kept eating there, every day like clockwork, so Dean kept turning up, watching him.

His attackers were part of a local gang, and they were in the middle of a gang war at the time, so seeing Dean outside watching every day, they automatically assumed he was working for the other gang.

It scares me to know his job could get that bad. Just knowing there could be a chance I'll never see him again or hear him tell me he loves me, has my stomach sinking.

Shaking those thoughts away, I change into my pyjamas before heading into the kitchen to make a mug of hot chocolate.

After that, I head into the living room, finding Mom's favourite movie, *The Bodyguard,* and putting it on.

Settling down on the sofa, I grab the throw blanket and snuggle into the warmth, before sitting back to watch the film, feeling relaxed.

"Wakey, wakey, beautiful. I'm sorry I'm late," Dean whispers in my ear, waking me up.

My eyes open to find his handsome face staring down at me. He looks tired and stressed out. Reaching up, I cup his jaw, my fingers running through his two days' worth of stubble. I love it. It makes him look manly and sexy, and my pulse picks up at the smile he gives me.

I guide my lips to his, giving him a quick peck on his before pulling back, smiling.

"I've missed you," I whisper, my voice filled with sleep.

"I've missed you too, love." He grins, lifting me up like I weigh no more than a feather. He then carries me down the hall to the main bedroom, which I suppose is *our* bedroom now.

Gently and gracefully he lowers me onto the bed, and because I'm not ready to let him go, I tighten the hold I have around his neck.

He chuckles, and I use the distraction to my advantage, pulling him down. He lands on top of me, easily manoeuvring himself, so he's not squashing me before settling between my legs.

The moment he presses down on me, his erection hits me in the spot that has me gasping. That yearning I've been feeling for him all day heightens.

I push my hips up, grinding my sex over his hardness.

Dean groans so I do it again, this time harder, causing us both to moan.

"I want you," I whisper seductively. I clutch the ends of his shirt in my fists, pulling it over his head.

His eyes darken, and he moves, grabbing my thin tank top, lifting it over my head before throwing it across the room. My bare breasts fall free, heavy and begging for attention.

He captures my lips in a scorching kiss, his hands going to my hips and pulling my pyjama shorts down.

I don't know how it happened, it's a blur, but we're both naked in no time. Dean leans over me, his eyes burning with hunger as he rakes his eyes over my naked body, and I can feel the heat in his gaze.

I'm about to come undone with just one look from him. My whole body is building up with a fiery need.

"God, you're fucking stunning," he says. He kisses me passionately, leaving me completely breathless.

He takes a condom out from the bedside drawer, having put them there this morning after he left to get some more clean clothes.

All day I've been fantasising about being with him, and the more I thought about him, the needier I got. I also thought about going on the pill. I don't want anything between us when we make love. I want to feel all of him.

He slowly guides the tip of his erection into my sex, nudging my entrance teasingly. I can't stop the growing pleasure building inside me, driving me wild.

Feeling brave, I push down, his hardness stretching me, making me feel full and complete.

An animalistic growl erupts from his chest, smothering my own moan of pleasure. I'm so wet for him, so ready. He slowly pulls out before thrusting back in at a torturous pace, but nonetheless pleasurable. But I need more; I need him to lose control, to slam himself into me, and make me feel.

"Dean," I moan. "Faster… harder… I want you to own me. Make me yours," I beg, rocking my hips to try and speed up our movements.

His eyes meet mine for a split second, his eyes darkening as he devours me. He leans up on his knees, pushing my thighs against my chest as he thrusts inside me with hard, punishing stokes.

"Fuck!" I scream, throwing my head back.

Dean gasps, his eyes closed, clearly lost in the sensation.

"God, you're so fucking hot inside," he rumbles, looking between my legs where he's filling me. He lets my legs drop, his hands running up my waist to my breasts, squeezing and tugging at my nipples before leaning down and taking one into his mouth. His free hand moves down between us, his fingers rubbing my clit in slow circles, sending sweet waves of pleasure through my body.

"I need to come," I cry, rolling my hips to meet his thrusts.

I'm so close, so fucking close that I can barely keep it together.

"Oh, Lola," he growls, and I can feel his dick pulse inside me, letting me know he's close. "Come for me, baby. That's it, come all over my cock,"

With his dirty words, his fingers on my clit and his dick thrusting inside me, I'm thrown over the edge, my body soaring with pleasure. I scream his name over and over, my sex clenching around him as my orgasm tears through me.

Just when I think it's going to stop, the pleasure becoming too intense to handle, he prolongs my orgasm by slamming inside me at a new angle, roaring out his own release. Everything blurs, my vision completely vanishing, and for a second I wonder if I'm actually going to black out.

"I love you," I whisper, trying to gain control of my heavy breathing. My sex is trembling, still sensitive from my release as he pulls out of me, quickly disposing of the condom.

"Fuck." He sighs as he rolls onto his back panting, sweat covering his muscled chest. "You're amazing. That was…." He shakes his head, speechless.

"Breathtaking? Mind-blowing? Magnificent? Remarkable?" I chime in, finishing his sentence with a giggle.

He laughs, pulling me across his chest. "You really are the sexiest fucking woman I've ever met. I feel like I'm a teenager all over again, except my fantasies are actually coming true this time around. I'm so fucking lucky to have you, and I'll thank my lucky stars every day for you coming back to me. I'm going to spend the rest of my life making sure you're happy. I love you. I love you so fucking much," he rasps.

I'm so moved by his honesty that tears fill my eyes.

"Oh Dean, I love you too, but can't you see? It's me who's the lucky one. You have no idea what you do to me. Our relationship was destined to be, as cliché as it sounds. You fit me. You complete me."

"Oh, Lola," he whispers, cupping my jaw and turning my head to face him.

"It's true, Dean." I blush. "You know? At first, I felt like I was jumping from one relationship to another, but then we had that conversation about my relationship with Rick being over a long time ago, and it made me realise that it didn't matter when it ended or why. What matters is the here and now. If people want to keep wasting precious moments in their lives, waiting for what other people deem a suitable period of time to move on, then that's their prerogative. All they'll be doing is missing valuable time with who and what truly matters. And you truly matter, Dean. I love you and I always will," I tell him, my heart bursting with love for this man.

"Fuck! What you do to me," he chokes out, clearing his throat. "You mean the fucking world to me, and I'm never letting you go. I'm not going to become one of those people who wastes precious moments because I'm going to be spending all of them with you."

A few tears fall from my eyes as I snuggle up to him tighter, not caring that I'm still naked. An obnoxious yawn slips past my lips, making Dean chuckle.

"Sleep," he orders, sounding close to sleep himself.

"Night," I mumble, already closing my eyes, feeling like I've been given the world in just one day.

Chapter Twenty

My hands sweat from nerves as Dean and I make our way to Brooke's Books. We've left everyone else back at Cabin Lake setting everything up for the charity event tonight.

For the past few weeks, I've been thinking about my future and what I want to do with it. I think listening to Pagan go on about hers and Sid's accomplishments has helped my decision about doing something with my degree.

And because I've been spending more and more time with Brooke, helping her out at the store, I've thought about owning my own store. Not just any store, but one that coexists with Brooke's. I've been planning the perfect presentation for a few weeks, but the fear of her turning me down—or worse, falling out with me—has scared me from saying anything. But today, that's going to change.

I want us to work together without her thinking I'm treading on anyone's toes. I can't help but remember all the times she's mentioned her dream of expanding but never having the funds to do it. I can make that come true for her if she chooses to agree. Although, I'll help her even if she says no.

No one knows about my proposition, not even Dean. He didn't even question me when I said I was coming to visit Brooke, but I know he knows something is going on with me. I'd have told him everything, but I want to talk to Brooke first. I don't want Dean somehow persuading her to say yes. It's something I want to accomplish on my own. What I *need* to do on my own.

Pulling over not far from Brooke's Books, Dean shuts off the car. Turning, he pulls me in for a kiss, leaving me completely breathless. All the nerves I had when I woke up disappear, and I sigh into his mouth.

"I'll pick you up whenever you're ready. Just give me a call, and I'll come get you, okay?" he says, leaning in for another kiss. "I wish you'd tell me what's making you so nervous."

I grin, kissing his frown away. "I will later. I promise. I just need to go over some stuff with Brooke before I talk to you about it. Is that okay?" I ask, hoping he doesn't think I'm purposely keeping things from him.

"Baby, as long as you're okay and there's nothing wrong, you don't need to tell me anything if you don't want to."

"I'm nervous because…," I start, then shake my head and grin when I realise what he just did. "I'm not nervous in a bad way. What I need to talk to her about is a good thing," I tell him, and that piques his interest, his eyebrows rising.

"Okay." He chuckles. "I need to help Pagan out with a few things and then help Dad mend a broken fence. You do what you need to do. I'm only a phone call away."

"Have fun." I grin, leaning in and kissing him. "I love you." I smile and turn to open the door, but his arm shoots out, stopping me. I gasp, turning around to see what's wrong, but his eyes are filled with hunger. A hunger I know all too well.

"Always kiss me like this," he whispers from a breath away before pulling me in for a deep kiss. I lean in to him, pouring as much passion as I can into it.

His lips are soft, yet firm, and when his tongue massages against mine, I squirm in my seat, my thighs clenching together. The ache that's growing between my legs becomes unbearable, and I'm ready to cancel today just so I can go back to bed with him.

Dean reluctantly pulls back, dropping his forehead to mine as he stares into my eyes.

"Are you sure you have to see Brooke today?" he rasps.

I want to say no, but I know we both have busy days. "Yes, I do. Just like you have to help your dad and sister. Now go before I change my mind." I grin, opening the door.

"God, I fucking love you, woman. Don't forget to call me," he calls out, and I lean back into the car, kissing him once more before reaching into the back seat and grabbing my things.

"Bye, Dean. Have fun. Oh, and don't work too hard. I have a surprise for you later." I wink. "Love you." I slam the door shut behind me, leaving his mouth hanging wide open.

He beeps the horn, and I turn, and wave goodbye, grinning before walking into Brooke's. She's expecting me since I called her last night, telling her I needed to talk to her. We picked her lunch break for me to pop in; however, when I walk in, it's quiet.

"Hello," I call out as I step into the store, locking the door behind me like Brooke instructed me to do so we wouldn't be interrupted.

Loud footfalls come from the back hallway. "Lo? Hi," she says, coming towards me with a pinched expression. "Please spit it out. My brain has been doing somersaults all morning thinking about what you could possibly need to discuss with me."

I laugh at her expression and erratic behaviour. She's literally bouncing on her feet. It's nice knowing how much she cares though, and how close we've become for her to even worry about me. I love it. I love having a girlfriend, one I can trust and count on, and won't bitch about me behind my back.

"Calm down. I have something I want to run across you. A proposal as such, and I'm nervous as hell, so can you sit down? And will you please stop bouncing? It's making me worse. Oh, and don't speak until I finish." I chuckle, but it's forced because my nerves are back with friends.

"Okay, let me grab our coffees," she says, moving slower as she eyes me curiously. I'd giggle if I weren't so nervous. She looks afraid to move too quickly just in case I pass out or attack her.

"Okay, spill," she says, handing me a coffee.

"I've been thinking a lot lately about what I want to do with my future and where I see myself in a few years. I want to do something I can be proud of, that I can call mine, and say 'I did that.'" I hand over the papers that the estate agency emailed over to me. It has details and pictures of the shop.

"I want to buy the store next door. I want to fill it with books, up-to-date computers and offer snack foods, along with coffee. Here," I say, showing her the picture of a spiral staircase before moving it over to the page with the upstairs room. "This is the upstairs. I'm going to convert it into an office to start my own editing business for indie authors—"

"I know I said I wouldn't interrupt, but I have to say this. All of this sounds great, it really does, and I'm excited for you, but I'm wondering what this has to do with me," Brooke says politely, not wanting to come across as rude.

I shake my head, fighting a smile since I knew she wouldn't be able to wait until I finished. "If you'd let me finish...."

"Sorry," she mumbles, taking a sip of her coffee.

"Okay, so this is my proposition. I will give you fifty-thousand plus for you to make the renovations you want to the store. The changes you said you dreamed you could have made," I begin, and she goes ghostly pale.

"N-no...," she stutters, shaking her head.

"Wait! In exchange, I want all of your book stock, and to run the donation bank. I also want you to do my books. I went to business school, but I didn't enjoy it as much as I did my literate classes. And to be able to run a successful business I need someone who knows what they're doing,"

I explain, my words rushed.

"Lola, sweetie, you can do that without buying my books. You could get your own and get a business partner. I can't take that kind of money from you," she says, and my heart sinks.

"I need someone I can trust, someone I can rely on. I honestly need you. It might seem that you're getting a bigger deal out of this, but you're really not. I swear to you, you'll be doing me a huge favour. And if I have to use emotional blackmail, I will."

"You wouldn't," she warns, narrowing her eyes when I start to pout.

"Oh, I would." I giggle. "But seriously, I really want this, but I won't do it without your help. I've seen the way your eyes sparkle when you speak about what you wanted to do to the store, and it inspired me. I wanted to help you achieve that. You deserve it. This shop is amazing, and what you do raising money, it's just… It's honourable.

"You've become my best friend in such a short amount of time, and I want you to have this, but I also want to share my dream with you too. Please say you'll help me, because I need help going over all this," I say, gesturing to all the paperwork involved. "Please. I can't do this without you," I beg.

Brooke's eyes fill with tears, and one escapes, falling down her cheek and onto the table. A part of me hopes I haven't offended her. I know how hard she's worked on her own to get this far. With her upbringing she had to work harder, only having the previous owners of the store to help her. They saw her potential, and when she told them her dreams of owning her own shop one day, one where she'd have a fun place for kids to learn to read, they wanted to help her. She enjoys it and my God, I've seen her face on the days she does story time with the local kids. Her whole face lights up with love and excitement.

Slipping off my chair, I take the one next to her before pulling her in for a hug.

"If you don't want to, please just say. I didn't mean to upset you," I whisper.

"Lola, you don't know how much this means to me. No one has ever cared for me enough to even buy me a birthday present," she cries, wiping her eyes.

"Well, let me know when it is and I'll go wild." I wink, teasing her. Wiping some of her tears away, my own begin to water. How can anyone not care for this incredibly amazing woman? Each word she says about her past pierces my heart.

She laughs, grabbing a tissue from her pocket. "Are you sure though? It's a lot of money, Lola, and I honestly feel wrong taking it when I haven't earned it." Her voice is a whisper, and hope sparks inside my chest.

IF I COULD WISH IT ALL AWAY

"I've been thinking about this for weeks, Brooke. It's all I've thought about, and every time I do, I end up thinking of a new idea. It's always something new to add, but the one thing that hasn't changed is having you as a part of it. My mom and dad left me a hell of a lot of money, and until now, I've never touched it. I wanted to use it for something they'd be proud of, something I know they'd want for me, and Brooke, your business is worth investing in. But I am being selfish too. I want this for me as well, and although you're right that I could hire anyone to do what I need, I don't want to. I want you. So will you, please?"

She beams, more tears falling. "I'd love to work with you. I don't know anyone I'd rather work alongside than you."

"Yes! Yes!" I squeal, jumping out of the chair, tears filling my own eyes. "Oh my God! Thank you," I shout, pulling her out of her chair.

"It's me who should be thanking you." She grins. "I can't believe this is happening."

"Believe it," I tell her, hugging her again.

"You truly are amazing, Lola," she gushes, hugging me tighter.

"I'm going to do this. *We're* going to do this. God, Brooke, you don't even realise how happy you've made me," I cry. "I'm finally doing something for myself, something I decided to do, and it feels so good. Is this how you feel every time you walk in here?" I ask, feeling a knot form in my throat.

"Oh, Lola, you should be proud of yourself no matter what you have in life. You've been through so much and come out much, much stronger. You have no idea how truly amazing you are," she whispers. "And to answer your question, yes, I do feel like that every time I walk in here. This store is everything to me. It's my baby, and you'll never understand what the gift you just gave me means to me. I just wish there was a way to repay you."

"Silly woman," I scold playfully. "You repaid me the second you said yes. But… there is something," I say innocently.

"How? I'd do anything," she says, so eager, and my heart melts at that. She'd literally do anything to repay me and that, to me, is what friendship is all about. I love her for it.

"Well… you could let me edit that book you told me about. I've already set you up as an indie author, and I would be honoured to help self-publish it for you," I announce, grinning.

Her mouth gapes open, her eyes completely wide open. You could hear a pin drop.

"*Holy fucking shit!*" she screams, and I wince, laughing as I move my head away. "How the hell did you do this? Where's your fucking magical wand, woman?"

"My wand?" I ask, giggling.

"Yeah. You're like a fairy fucking godmother without the whole dress thingy," she says, her arms gesturing to my outfit.

I laugh harder, shaking my head. "Sorry to disappoint you, but I'm just Lola."

"Just Lola, my ass. You, Lola Lawson, are truly fucking amazing. You have the kindest heart I know. I've honestly never met anyone like you. You're not selfish, bitchy, mean or even self-centred. You're just you, who is kind, generous, caring, lovable and I could go on." She laughs.

"Thank you. Thank you so much. I don't even know what to say," she admits, sitting down in shock now that the excitement has worn off. "What did I do to deserve this?"

"Hey, you did everything to deserve this," I tell her, taking back my seat. "Now, c'mon, we need to go over these plans. I need to see what you agree and disagree with."

"Where do you want to start?" she asks, getting her shit together.

"Office equipment? I can't order anything just yet since I'm waiting to hear back about the keys next door."

"They've been trying to sell that place for years, hon. I'm so glad it's you moving in there," she tells me, and I smile wide.

"I can't wait to tell Dean," I tell her, clapping my hands.

"I still can't believe you managed to keep this from him," she says in awe. "That guy is so stellar, he can tell me what I had for breakfast."

I laugh with her, nodding in agreement. "He knows I'm here to talk to you about something, just not what it's about. But I'll tell him. I can't wait to surprise him."

"Let's get some of this done so you can go and fill him in on everything," she says, then stands up to get her laptop, coming back with a wide grin still on her face.

My phone rings, and when I go to answer, I notice two and a half hours have passed.

"Holy crap! We've been going through this for almost three hours." I giggle before answering the phone. "Hello?"

"Hey, baby. Is everything okay? You've not called yet, and I thought you wanted to go to dinner before getting ready for tonight."

I smile goofily down the phone. "I've been busy, but you can come pick me up now if you'd like," I tell him, still not able to wipe the smile off my face.

IF I COULD WISH IT ALL AWAY

God, I love this man.

"What has you so happy? Do I have to be jealous of Brooke?" he asks, and I start laughing, shaking my head in amusement.

"No. Brooke's not into me that way," I tease.

"Baby," he growls. "Everyone is into you."

"Shut up." I giggle, laughing when Brooke gives me 'what the hell' eyes. I just shrug at her.

"Okay, I'll stop. I'm on my way. We can go straight to the Lincoln Inn for dinner if you'd like, or would you rather go home and change?"

"No, I'm good. We can go straight there. We need to celebrate," I tell him, grinning when Brooke smiles wide at me, giving me a thumbs up.

"What are we celebrating?" he asks curiously.

"You'll have to wait until you get here."

"You little minx. I'll see you in a bit, love."

We say our goodbyes, and I turn to Brooke with a wide smile on my face.

"Do you think he'll be okay with all of this? I mean, I love him and he loves me, but what if he only said that because he thought I was only here temporarily?" I ramble, and now that the negative thought is there, I bite my lip worriedly.

"Are you kidding me? Even if you wanted to leave, that man would tie you to his bed. He's so in love with you. He doesn't want to let you go," she tells me, and I grin, sagging with relief.

"I know we rushed into everything, but it feels right. I do love him. I love him so much that any time I let myself truly feel it, I'm overcome with so much emotion that my heart can't take it. I feel like I'm going to burst from all the love I have stored inside me. It's like I've waited a lifetime to have him in my life like this," I admit, blushing when I realise how much detail I've gone into.

She gives me a goofy smile, her eyes all soft. "God, it's so sickening how much you two love each other. It's rare to find that love. Hold on tight to it."

"I plan to." I smile, feeling giddy.

"Let's put this all away. I've emailed those links to you, and on Monday we can go over contractors, if you want?"

"Yeah, that's perfect. My grandpa is coming later, and he's going to organise the paperwork for us so I can sign the funds over and all that jazz. You can have a lawyer look over it, but it basically says that you agree to hand over your books in return for blah, blah, blah," I giggle.

"I trust you."

"Wait, shouldn't we leave this out for Dean to see?" I ask, biting my bottom lip.

"Nah, just this one," she says, handing me the photos and description of the store next door, and I smile brightly. "He's going to have two surprises tonight."

"I think he's going to like my other one a lot better." I wink, and we both laugh.

We're just finishing off our mugs of coffee when Dean walks in, looking handsome as ever.

"Hello, ladies," he drawls, then gets a look at my face and frowns. "Why the hell have you been crying?" he asks, rushing over to me.

How the hell can he tell I've been crying?

"I'm fine." I smile, kissing his lips to shut him up.

"So *why* have you been crying?" he asks, his face scrunched up adorably.

"Well, you know when we were up in the mountain, and you asked me what I wanted to do with my life now that I was free?"

"Yeah," he says, still looking confused.

"Well, apart from the obvious, which is growing old with you—"

He stops me from continuing when he pulls me in for a kiss, a wide grin on his face.

"That's a given," he murmurs against my lips before pulling away. "So, what's next for you, love?"

"Well, I'm buying this," I tell him, stepping out of his embrace and grabbing the documents off the table.

"What's this?" he asks, reading it over. "Isn't this next door?" He looks at Brooke, who smiles and nods.

"Yep." I grin, bouncing on the balls of my feet. "And I'm going to be the proud new owner. Long story short, Brooke is going to give me all her pretties inside here, minus the furniture. She's going to concentrate on the children side of things. Although, we are planning on going with the same theme," I ramble, taking a deep breath. "She's also going to help me with the books and starting up, and all the other boring stuff. Oh, and she's going to let me edit her new book," I add.

"You wrote a book?" he asks her, looking surprised.

"Yeah, but keep listening," she whispers, amused.

"Go on," he smiles, shaking his head.

"So basically I'll be selling books now, with a mini snack bar that sells coffee because, well book people love coffee. They'll also have a selection of up-to-date computers to write on, or do homework or what have you. But the best part is that I'll be turning the upstairs into an office. I'm going to start my own editing company and work with indie authors."

"Holy fucking shit!" he yells, grinning, and I take a step back. My eyes are wide with surprise, but I'm still smiling as he rushes over to me, lifting me up in his arms. He spins me around, whooping loudly, and I laugh, like really laugh. I've not felt this happy since before my parents died, and I can't help but rejoice.

"Put me down." I giggle, feeling dizzy.

He stops spinning me around and slides me down his body, keeping me pinned against him.

"Holy fucking shit, love. I'm so fucking proud of you, Lola. *So fucking proud.*" He grins, his eyes shining with love. "This is… fuck! You're remarkable. God, I love you."

He leans down, capturing my lips, and I fall into the kiss. My arms go around his neck and when he pulls me against him, his hands at the bottom of my back, I moan into his mouth.

A throat clearing has us pulling away, and a blush reaches my cheeks. I'd completely forgotten Brooke was there.

"Get a room," she teases, and I start laughing again, sticking my tongue out at her.

"We're in one." I wink, the same time as Dean speaks.

"Oh, we will, later. First, though, we're going out to dinner to celebrate my girl becoming an editor and starting her own business." He grins proudly, and his eyes shine in awe as he stares down at me, so much love in that one gaze.

"Go have fun. I'll see you both later." She giggles.

"Do you need a lift to the party later?" I ask.

"No, I'll be driving tonight. I'm not going to stay long. I can't stand most of the people who attend them," she says, brutally honest.

I laugh. "You and Lily will get along fine. She can't stand them either."

"Aww, then we're already best friends in my book."

"I still can't believe you've only met a handful of times," I say, shaking my head. From what Dean and Brooke have said, they've been friends for years, ever since she took over from the previous owners, so it's surprising Lily hasn't made this place her regular stop-off. Lily, like my mom, loves books and spent most of our childhood taking us to libraries.

"Dean always carted her away, getting embarrassed," she teases him, winking at me.

"Shush," he warns her, and I giggle, knowing there's a story there.

"Go on before I tell her about the time your mom said she walked in on you losing your virginity."

My eyes widen before I burst out laughing. I turn to Dean who is staring at the ceiling, groaning.

"You just did," he growls, making me giggle harder.

"Oh my God, fill me in later," I call behind me as Dean starts pulling me towards the door.

"If she knows what's good for her, she'll keep it zipped!" he shouts, sounding amused.

"See you later," I yell, and she waves bye, laughing.

"Come on, baby. Let's go celebrate my brilliant-minded girlfriend," he says against my lips as we step outside.

"Girlfriend," I whisper, liking how it sounds rolling off my lips.

"Not forever." He winks, stunning me. Does he mean he's going to break up with me soon? Or does he mean I'll be… more? God, I can't even say it. My stomach is doing somersaults, butterflies fluttering in my stomach.

The whole way to the restaurant I'm grinning, floating with happiness.

Chapter Twenty-One

Standing in the bathroom, I look in the door full-length mirror and take in my appearance. The long strapless velvet gown falls down to the floor, clinging to my body in all the right places and highlighting every curve.

However, my favourite part of is what I have hidden underneath—a corset in a lighter shade of violet. It fits perfectly, enhancing my breasts and making them look rounder, fuller. I also have matching panties on with violet garters, going all out.

I twirl around in a circle, trying to keep my eyes on my reflection. I feel sexy, and I know Dean is going to lose his mind when he sees me. I plan to surprise him when we get back from the charity event with my sexy little number, wanting to render him speechless.

Brooke persuaded me to buy the dress even though I was unsure about the amount of cleavage I'd have on display. But it will be worth it to feel this good, all night long. I feel like an independent, strong, professional woman.

My hair is twisted into an up-do with a few loose strands falling around my face. But as sexy as I feel, there's a reason I'm hiding out in the bathroom. I'm worried about Dean's reaction. I know he's going to love it—he's a man after all—but a deeper part of me fears he'll make me change.

Reminding myself that he's not Rick, I leave the confinements of the bathroom and head out in search of Dean.

I find him leaning behind the sofa flicking through channels. Holy shit, my man looks even hotter in a suit. He's wearing black, trousers that match his black jacket, along with a white crisp shirt with a thin black tie.

Dean is hot in anything he wears, but seeing him looking like a model out of a magazine has my mouth hanging open. I'm pretty sure I've drooled a little.

Clearing my throat to gain his attention, he turns around slowly before snapping his head fully around when he sees me, his eyes widening. His slow appraisal has me shifting nervously, twiddling my thumbs.

A few minutes pass with him just staring and not saying a word. I want to tell him to say something, anything, but when I open my mouth, no words come out.

He stalks over to me, and for the first time since he took in my appearance, I look up into his eyes. I gasp when I see the desire burning in them.

I don't have time to think, move or even comprehend what is about to happen because Dean is on me within seconds. His hands reach around my waist, pushing me backwards until my back is slamming against the wall. Another gasp escapes my lips and my body tingles with awareness and lust.

Lifting my gown, he gently raises it slowly up my legs, the feel of the delicate silk sliding up my legs making me shiver. The sensation is oddly erotic. He picks me up, my legs going around his waist immediately, and I moan from the contact.

"You look so fucking beautiful, Lola. Every guy in that room is going to want what's mine," he says gently, his eyes transfixed on my chest.

My body is on fire as he starts raining kisses down my neck and over my swollen breasts that are begging for his attention.

No one has ever treated me this way, like they can't get enough of me; it's exotic and such a turn-on.

I gasp when he moves my knickers to the side with his one hand, his other keeping me steady against the wall.

"Oh God! More," I beg as he runs his fingers through my wet heat.

"My pleasure." He grins, before inserting two fingers inside me. I moan as my back arches from the sheer pleasure. His skilled fingers assault my sex, pumping in and out while he swipes his thumb over my clit. My stomach tightens and my hips strain, wanting to ride his fingers until I'm coming apart all over them.

"Yes," I breathe into his neck. My God, he feels so good.

My whole body is burning, more so when he increases his pace. I wither beneath him, bucking my hips as I meet each thrust with my own, pressing down on his fingers. I'm shaking with pleasure, my whole body heating up.

I'm so close!

"I want you to come, love. I want you to come all over my fingers," he growls.

The minute he uses that dirty mouth of his, I'm screaming his name. I begin to shake from the aftershocks of my orgasm, so lost in the sensation that I don't hear him undo the zipper on his trousers. Before I know it, he's inside me, slamming his hard shaft into my sex and pushing me against the wall. I lock my ankles behind his back for support as he drives into me over and over again, hitting the spot that drives me wild.

"God, you're so sexy. Never…." Thrust! "Been…." Thrust! "This…." Thrust! "Good," he rasps.

I shatter into a thousand pieces. The room spins, blurring around us as I cling to Dean's shoulders, waiting for my orgasm to subside.

We're both breathing heavily, trying to catch our breaths when I feel his arousal dripping down my legs.

"I love you," he says, distracting me, making me forget all about the mess between my thighs.

"I love you too," I tell him before kissing him. He slowly places me back down on my feet, and my legs shake. He holds me up with one hand while the other smooths out my dress. Once I'm presentable, he tucks himself in and zips up his trousers.

"I take it you like my dress?" I ask sweetly, fighting a grin.

"Yes, I do. You look perfect, baby. You're stunning and so beautiful it makes me want to take you again. Right here." He grins, taking a step forward.

"Oh no, you don't! We need to be at the marquee before the guests arrive. Let me go freshen up so we can get going," I tell him, fighting myself not to say 'fuck the event, let's just go back to bed and make love all night.'

"You spoiled my night," he pouts, making me giggle.

"Oh my God, this place looks amazing," I gush to Lily when we walk up to her. The marquee, which is attached to the bar toilets, and kitchen and so on, is lit up with fairy lights, elegant and magical.

Round tables are scattered everywhere with beautiful rose decorations. Silver and blue balloon arches and towers surround the room, giving it more of an edge. There's even a champagne fountain in the middle of the room, providing a sophisticated look. I can't believe they've transformed the place to look like this. This morning it was bare, plain, and I was worried they'd never make it charity-event worthy. I was wrong.

"It's all Pagan." Lily smiles, taking in Dean and me holding hands, a big grin on her face. "You look beautiful," she tells me, and I blush.

We're pretty late thanks to Dean. He couldn't keep his hands off me, and I ended up having to straighten my hair *and* make-up out.

"Thank you, so do you." In her black sequinned dress, she looks ten years younger.

"Oh, this old thing." She chuckles, waving to her dress.

"I can't believe there are so many people here already," I blurt out, then wince when I realise why. "Sorry we're late. It was Dean's fault."

"No worries." She grins, giving us a knowing look.

"Where's the DJ?" Dean asks his mom, looking around.

"He's setting up still. He got stuck in traffic," she explains, rolling her eyes. "We'll be starting the auctions soon."

My eyes are wide as I take in the room. There are business-men everywhere, some with elegant looking women on their arms and some prowling the room like they're searching for a woman for the night. Everyone looks beautiful, and I'm so proud of Pagan and Lily for pulling this off.

According to Lily, they've already raised thirty thousand from ticket sales. With the items being auctioned off, they'll raise a lot more.

"I'm going to show Lola around and introduce her to a few people," Dean says, pulling me away from his mom and dad. I give her a smile and a quick wave.

"That was rude," I playfully scold.

"I want to dance." He grins, and I'm about to mention there's no music when Ed Sheeran's "Thinking Out Loud" starts in the background.

When he pulls me into his arms, I throw my head back and laugh, wrapping my arms around his neck. "You're terrible." I smile up at him.

"I love you." He kisses the tip of my nose.

"I love you too." I blush, then place my head on his shoulder, swaying with him to the beautiful melody.

Throughout the evening I've managed to walk around the room a thousand times, Dean introducing me to a million people. Some are nice and polite, but then there are the few I've desperately wanted to kick in the balls.

The best part of the night so far has to be the auction. They raised thousands of pounds, more than I expected, and it was overwhelming to be a part of that.

Dean and I arrive at the group of men Lily referred to as pompous asses. They're also the men who are the main beneficiaries for tonight's event. It's the only reason Dean is going over to say hello; otherwise, I think he'd have gladly avoided them like he has since we arrived.

Looking at the men before me, I can tell instantly that they're filthy rich and arrogant as hell about it. Hell, the second I met their gazes as we walked towards them they all zeroed in on my breasts, staring shamelessly.

It was disrespectful, not only to me but to Dean.

I'm not the only woman they've been disrespectful to either. They've spoken crudely about the other women around them as if they're sexual objects and not actual human beings. It's disgusting and if it weren't for the fact Dean had to play nice, and I didn't want to embarrass him, I'd have walked away from them all.

The CEO of their company introduces himself to me while Dean stands a few feet to the side, speaking to another gentleman. We were originally standing together, but the man pulled Dean aside to have a quiet word.

Thankfully they didn't move too far, but still, I wish I was next to Dean and not in front of this sleaze-ball.

"Hello, Miss Lola. It's a pleasure to meet such a beautiful woman. I'm Jordan Wallace II, CEO and one of the top ten millionaire bachelors in the U.K," he states proudly, going as far as to place a kiss on each of my cheeks. When he pauses a minute too long, I start to feel uncomfortable, so I pull away, forcing a smile.

I take another step back, putting some much-needed personal space between us. He seems like the sort of man who thinks that introducing himself the way he did will get him what he wants. I'm not going to feed his ego by pretending to find him remotely interesting.

"Right. Nice meeting you," I mutter before turning to walk towards Dean. I pause, finding him still chatting away, and sigh sadly.

Jordan Wallace II, III or whatever, takes my distraction as a means to step in front of me, blocking my view of Dean. I want to growl and kick him in the shin for being so rude.

"Would you like a drink?" he asks, and I shake my head, holding up my full flute of champagne.

My eyes widen in disgust as he blatantly stares at my breasts, his eyes filled with a sickening lust as he readjusts his junk.

I cringe when I see his obvious erection. *Did he just manoeuvre that so it stood out? Ew, that's so freaking gross!*

He catches me off guard while I'm still staring at his junk in horror and my cheeks burn, but not for the reasons he's most likely conjuring up.

Crap, this is embarrassing.

He ignores the disgust and horror on my face and takes my junk glance as an invitation to step into my personal space. Thankfully, before he can get too close, Pagan shows up, stepping between us with a big grin on her face.

"Lola, Jordan," she greets, looking at him with distaste. I don't even care why because at that moment, I want to kiss her.

"Pagan," he mutters staring at her like he wishes he could make her disappear.

"Hi, how you doing?" I ask, enthusiastically "Tonight has been amazing." I try to keep my voice bright as I move away from Jordan, ignoring the way his eyes narrow.

"Oh, it's been a great night, I agree. Don't you think, Jordan?" she asks him, smiling tightly.

"Yeah," he says, not interested.

"Anyway… I came over for a reason, Lola. I need a huge favour from you. Can you come help me in the kitchen? We've had to get new champagne flutes since some waiter dropped the crate and ended up smashing the three boxes we had left. We need help getting them out," she says, her eyes pleading.

"Oh no! I'm glad you've got replacements," I tell her sincerely.

I really should thank that waiter. Maybe even tip him for having the perfect timing.

"Yeah, we had some spares in the barn."

"Okay, well point me in the right direction." I smile, eager to get out of here.

We manage to move away from Jordan, his presence long forgotten. We don't even bother saying goodbye or even acknowledge him. Once we're out of earshot, I turn to her, sagging with relief.

"Thank you so much. You've just saved my life," I say dramatically.

"It's my pleasure. I saw him eye fucking you from over there." She points across the room to where she must have been standing before she came over. "I thought I'd rescue you from the pervert whilst Dean is occupied. I swear, that mooch is only talking to Dean so Mr Pervert could make a move on you. I've seen it before. Jordan gives me the creeps. He tried it on with me last year, but Sid intervened, thank God. And I'm pretty sure a woman in the bathroom was just talking about him, warning her friend to stay away from him. Make sure you do the same," she tells me, her nose scrunched up in disgust.

She doesn't have to tell me twice. I plan on staying as far away as possible.

"Oh, I plan to. He gives me the heebie-jeebies." I shudder. "Anyway, where do you need me?"

She giggles, trying to look innocent. "It was just a tactic to get you away from him."

"Good one." I laugh, but then a thought occurs to me. "So there's no issue with the champagne flutes?"

"Oh yeah, the bloody idiot is going to have them taken out of his pay cheque," she seethes.

"I can help if you want me to. I have nothing else to do, and it would be good to get away from everyone for a bit."

I don't want her to think I'm not enjoying myself because I am, but the crowd is becoming too much for me.

"C'mon then, let's get you to work," she says, not looking offended in the slightest.

An hour passes by quickly, and when there's no sign of Grandpa, I start to get worried. He should have been by hours ago to collect the keys for Dean's place. His flight isn't even long; it's twenty minutes at the most, and according to the flight plan he gave me, there were no delays. He hasn't even called or texted, which isn't like him.

"Is everything okay?" Dean asks as I look down at my phone.

"Yeah, I was just checking Grandpa's flight and if he's called," I explain.

"He hasn't called?" Someone walks up to him, asking about his P.I business. "Excuse me for a second," he tells the bloke. His jaw ticks, looking pissed at being interrupted.

"No, it's fine. I'm going to go outside and call him, see where he is," I tell him, moving to leave.

He grabs my arm, stopping me and stepping closer. "I'll come with you," he offers.

I look behind him at the man waiting impatiently to talk to him, and sigh. "It's fine, really. You need to mingle. I'll only be a few minutes, and then I'll come back in and find you. Okay?" He looks torn, so I lean up on my toes and kiss him. "I'll be fine. Five minutes top."

"Okay, but don't be long," he warns before kissing me quickly.

"Promise." I smile.

I walk through the crowds of people, heading for the entrance. Getting there takes a little longer than I expect and when I step outside, I groan, wishing I'd used my brain to bring a coat along with me. The night air is cold, and I shiver, my teeth chattering. "Jesus," I mutter, my hot breath puffing out in front of me.

When rubbing my arms doesn't keep me warm, I begin to walk, needing to keep the blood flowing as I dial my grandpa's number.

When I look up and realise I've reached the back of the marquee, I stop walking and start to pace instead. The music is quieter here, the area darker since there are only a few lanterns hanging from posts. My grandpa answers suddenly, making me jump.

"Hello, this is Dwayne Lawson," he greets all business like.

"Hi Grandpa, it's Lola. I was just wondering where you are? I thought you'd be here by now," I say, worry lacing my tone. It's not like he could've headed straight to Dean's because he needed to come here first to get the keys. And I know he wouldn't miss a chance at seeing me, not with everything that's happened.

"Lola, I'm sorry, doll. I got held up in a meeting and won't be able to make it until tomorrow. Is everything okay?" he asks, sounding distracted.

"Yeah, I was just worried. I've been waiting for you."

"I'm sorry doll. How did your meeting go?"

Although I know he's genuinely interested, he doesn't seem like he's fully with the conversation.

"She said yes." I grin down the phone, not able to hide the happiness in my voice. My grandpa knew how much I wanted this to work out, and I'm over the moon that it has.

"I'm so happy for you. I've managed to look over everything the estate agency gave you, and you're getting a pretty neat deal there. I'll have everything ready for you and Brooke to sign by the time I get there tomorrow."

"I'm really excited. Thank you for doing this for me. What time are you coming tomorrow? Do you need me to pick you up?"

"No, no, it's fine. I've still got the loan car booked, so I'll meet you at Mark and Lily's. My flight leaves at twelve…," he says, trailing off.

"Is everything okay? You sound distracted," I ask, biting my bottom lip.

Someone approaches me from behind. I can hear their clothes rustling in the wind and their heavy footsteps. Not worried because it's most likely Dean wondering where I am, I don't bother to turn around.

"Everything is fine. It's just been a long day. I'll see you tomorrow, honey. Love you," he says, and again, he sounds like he's in the middle of something. He almost sounds sad.

"Love you too," I tell him.

"Okay, see you tomorrow, doll. Night," he says with more enthusiasm before ending the call. I don't even have time to say goodbye, and I look down at my phone, wondering what the hell is going on.

Needing to talk to Dean about the weird conversation, I turn around, opening my mouth to say something. Instead of Dean, I find Jordan.

My heart rate picks up, and my feet freeze to the ground. My palms begin to sweat as I take in his wobbly stature. He's holding a glass of whisky in one hand, the liquid sloshing over the sides as he takes a step towards me. I don't move quickly enough because before I know it, he's close enough for me to smell the alcohol on his breath and I dry heave, literally.

"Well, well, well. Look who I've found." He grins, looking like he found a million quid. When he takes another step closer, I take one back.

IF I COULD WISH IT ALL AWAY

But it only makes him move closer, invading my personal space.

He's so close. So horribly close.

The alcohol on his breath blows across my face, and I look away, giving him the time to step even closer, his shirt rubbing against my chest. My pulse picks up, and everything in my head screams at me to run, but my feet are still frozen to the ground. Fear is coursing through my body, and I know nothing good is going to come out of him being here.

Snapping out of it, I go to take a step back, but he snakes a hand around my waist, roughly pulling me against his chest. Instinctively, I reach out, palms up, to push him away, but his hold on me is too strong.

When he leans in to me, I think he's going to kiss me, so I move my head to the side to dodge his advance, still struggling to get free. He uses my dismissal as a challenge and starts kissing my neck, licking and biting until bile rises in my throat and I have to swallow it back down.

"No! No! Get off me," I cry, trying to push him away as I tremble with fear.

"Feel how hard I am for you. Can you feel it?" he slurs. "I bet you're wet for me too," he purrs in my ear, and I gag again, trying to push him away.

My chest is rising and falling, working towards a panic attack. No matter how hard I try to control my breathing, nothing works.

If I get lost in a panic attack, I'll either pass out or be sick, and both will end up leaving me vulnerable.

My boobs are already bulging out of my dress because of how hard and heavy my breathing is. That's all the vulnerability I can take at the moment. I just want to get away, to find Dean.

"Let me go now. Please," I beg, trying to sound confident, but it only comes out weak and pathetic.

Struggling only causes his grip to tighten, nearly cutting off my circulation as my panic increases. I try to wrench free from his hold again, but he's too strong, even for someone who is clearly drunk.

What is it with me letting men having this control? Why do I find myself in these situations? Am I cursed?

He pushes his erection into my belly whilst keeping up with his assault on my neck no matter how hard I try to wiggle free. Vomit rises in my throat, and I swallow it back down, tasting like acid.

No! I'm not going to let this happen, I scream inwardly, adrenaline pumping through my veins. Knowing it's now or never, I stamp down hard on his foot, making sure to use the heel of my stilettos. He screams in pain and before he has a chance to recover, I bring my knee up to his groin.

I'm momentarily stunned as he falls to the ground holding his junk, proud that I made him crumble to the floor, screaming in agony. Taking the opportunity to run away, I move, but I don't get far. My split second of hesitation was a second too long, and he manages to recover quicker than I expected, reaching out and grabbing my ankle. I fall to the floor and face-plants in the dirt, my head hitting something hard and rough.

Not letting myself register the pain, knowing it won't do me any good, I scream as loud as I can. I call Dean's name out, begging him to come help me, and when that doesn't work, I simply scream for help.

My throat feels raw and dry, though I don't let it stop me as I keep trying to scurry away from him on my stomach

If I can get closer to the marquee, then someone will hear me.

Jordan pulls at the end of my dress, and I look down, my eyes connecting with his. I gasp, my eyes widening with fear when I see the dead, predatory look in his. He looks like he's out for blood reminding me of Jack Torrance from *The Shining*.

He tugs harder on my dress when I keep kicking out at him and manages to pull it down a little. I stop struggling, not wanting to aid him in removing it. Wiggling is only going to make it easier for him, and I'm not going down without a fight. Not this time. Not again.

He manages to get on top of me, placing his legs on either side of me. He kneels over my legs, pressing them together with his thighs so I can't kick him, and a frustrated sob escapes me. I can't move, not with him trapping me beneath him, his hands pinning my wrists in a tight grip.

I scream out as he reaches for me with his free hand, an evil sneer on his face as he rips my dress, right between my breasts. I hear him moan and start to undo the buckle on his belt frantically, his breathing ragged. I begin to thrash harder this time, ignoring his erection pressing against my stomach.

With each move I make, he moans and rubs against me, acting like it's some sort of sick foreplay.

I try everything I can think of to get him off me, to stop this from happening, but no matter how hard I try, I can't get free of men like him.

"Please, let me go. Get off me." Frustrated sobs break free as I beg, tears falling down my cheeks.

"You're a cock tease, dressed like a fucking slut. You're nothing but a one-night fuck and baby, I promise I'll make it feel *real* good," he snarls, hovering his lips over my mouth.

I pull away, thrashing my head from side to side, wailing for someone to come help me. And for the first time I realise I'm fighting back; no matter what happens now, at least I know I tried. With Rick I never got the chance to fight back, never had that strength, but now I am, and a little hope sparks inside me as adrenaline pumps through my body.

My punching and scratching doesn't even faze him or slow him down.

IF I COULD WISH IT ALL AWAY

It's like I'm not even there; I'm just a mere object getting in the way of what he wants, and he'll tear me limb from limb to get it.

Closing my eyes, I pray for someone to hear my cries, to come and help me but I never once give up trying to fight.

I gasp for air when Jordan's weight is lifted off me, a relieved sob breaking free.

My prayers have been answered.

I'm pulled into a warm embrace, but the fear inside me is manifested so deep I don't know left from right. I begin to scream, my ears ringing from the sound, and instinctively try to break free again. They only hold me tighter, and I'm about to fight back harder when I suck in a lungful of air. Everything stops and I instantly relax into the person holding me when I recognise who it is.

My body sags and a roaring sob breaks free. My voice is hoarse, but it doesn't stop me from begging for Dean, needing him so much.

"Dean! Stop! Stop!" Lily shouts, and the sound echoes through her chest. "Dean, it's Lola. She needs you."

"Dean, Lola needs you," someone from close by shouts. I swear it was Pagan, but she's not here. Is she?

My eyes are closed, too scared to open them only to find out that I'm not safe and this was all a figment of my imagination. I don't want to open my eyes and find Jordan still on top of me, attacking me.

A cold shudder runs through me, and I bury closer to the person holding me.

I'm pulled away from the soothing arms, and for a second I cry out in fear, scared of what's going to happen, but then I'm in familiar arms. Dean sets me in his lap and time stops because it's him. It's really him.

I'd recognise his woodsy scent anywhere, and I cry out with relief, burying my face in his neck and breathing him in.

He rubs his hands up and down my back, soothing me and reminding me that everything is okay, that I'm safe and the police are on their way. He keeps apologising although I'm unsure why. He didn't do anything, but I'm too shaken up to voice that out loud.

I don't know how much time has passed; it could have been hours or minutes before the police arrived. A chair was brought out, and Dean sat me in it, wrapping me up in his suit jacket. Lily and Pagan sat by my side, comforting me. Dean only left my side when a police officer asked to talk to him. I don't know what they're talking about; I've been in and out since everything happened, not really with it. But now that everything around me is beginning to focus, I listen to what they're talking about.

"I know this is a difficult time, but we need to know if Miss Lawson was sexually assaulted," a male officer asks Dean. I watch as Dean's entire body stiffens the second the officer voices his concern and the air around us thickens, the atmosphere tense.

Dean clears his throat. "I… I don't know," he croaks out, and my stomach sinks. I shouldn't have worn this dress. I should have just stayed at home. Would Dean still want me now that he knows how much of a disaster I am. That I'm a magnet for bad men?

"I'm so sorry. This is all my fault. I shouldn't have dressed like this. He said I was a slut and that I wanted it, but Dean, I promise you I didn't. I told him no. I kept telling him no," I rush out, explaining everything in a panicked voice. "I came out here to ring my grandpa because I hadn't heard from him and when I heard footsteps, I just thought it was you. I got off the phone with Grandpa, and he was there, Dean. I swear, I never encouraged him or led him on, I swear," I cry. "I'm so sorry, Dean. Please believe me. I didn't mean for this to happen to me again."

Pagan shoots up from her seat, and I can feel her eyes burning into me. I duck my head in embarrassment. She probably wants me far away from her brother now. I wouldn't blame her.

Another sob breaks free as Dean steps forward, taking Pagan's seat next to me.

"Mom, what does she mean, *again*?" I hear Pagan ask, and my stomach even lower at how sad she sounds. "Mom! Dad! Someone tell me what the fuck is going on. Please. Who would hurt her?" she cries, sobbing herself.

"Oh, sweetie, come here," Mark says, bringing his daughter into his arms. My chest aches, longing for my own parents to comfort me.

"Lola, look at me," Dean says, gently taking my chin and turning me to face him. His jaw is clenched, and I know he's finding it hard to keep his emotions in check so he doesn't scare me.

"I'm sorry," I whisper, needing him to know that I never meant any of this.

"None of this is your fault, love. What Rick and Jordan did to you isn't on you. It's on them. They're sick fucking bastards. I'm so fucking sorry I wasn't here for you. I should have been here. I should have *protected you* like I promised I would. I'll never forgive myself, but I hope that one day you can, even if I don't deserve it. I love you so much, and I'm so fucking sorry," he says, sounding broken. "And by no means of the imagination do you look like a slut. You, my love, look exquisite and dazzlingly beautiful. Please don't let what that prick said get to you.

You're stronger than that," he says, believing it, and I give him a watery smile.

"The police need to speak you," Lily interrupts quietly, gently placing her cold hand against my cheek before stepping away, giving us privacy.

"Thanks Mom," he replies before she gets too far, giving the usually well-put-together woman a small smile. He turns back to me, taking my hands in his and for the first time, I notice his cracked knuckles caked in dry blood. "Before you talk to the officers, I need to know something." He swallows and I move my attention away from his knuckles, concentrating on his pained expression.

"What?" I whisper, my voice hoarse.

"Did he…? Did he…? God, were you *sexually assaulted*?" He looks close to breaking.

"No," I answer, knowing that's what could have happened had he not saved me. More tears fall, hating myself for being in the situation in the first place. If I had just stayed closer to the entrance then maybe none of this would have happened. God, there's a lot of 'what ifs', but I know deep down if I had done something differently, we wouldn't be here right now.

"I'm so fucking sorry," he rasps, pulling me into his arms.

My heart hurts watching this strong, confident, self-assured man break in front of me. I try to wrap my head around the fact he's apologised once again, like this is his fault somehow when it's not. I'm the one who dressed in next to nothing, showing off my assets. I shouldn't have worn something so revealing.

"Dean, you have nothing to be sorry for. I shouldn't have dressed like this, revealing so much skin. I'm the one who's sorry," I tell him, crying softly. Dean wipes away more tears, but I fall head first into his arms, needing him.

"No, baby, no! Should a young girl who is out clubbing with her friends wear an outfit that covers all of her body just so she doesn't get attacked? Or should she be able to wear what she wants?" he asks, rubbing my cheek.

"Wear what she wants, but Dean—"

"No! Don't do this to yourself. Women should be able to wear what they want, how they want without having rapists use what they wear as an excuse for what they do. They do what they do because of power, whether or not you're wearing something revealing. They're monsters. You could wear a bikini, and it doesn't give him the right to attack you," he tells me, his words splitting my heart wide open.

"It wasn't my fault," I sob, falling into his chest as the realisation hits me. I'm not naive to think it was actually my fault, but Dean confirming it helps.

"Shhh, it's okay. It's okay, baby," he soothes. "C'mon, let's go talk to the cops so we can get home."

I nod in agreement and take his hand, letting him lead me over to where the police officers are waiting to talk to me.

I tell the police everything about what happened tonight, from when I left the tent to the last moment I remember before I blacked out—not literally, but mentally.

From what I strained to hear of Dean's statement earlier, he had found me with my dress torn, revealing my corset, and Jordan in the middle of unbuckling his trousers and pinning me down.

Dean had been looking for me, thinking I'd come back into the marquee, but when he couldn't find me, he went to walk outside again. When he reached the front entrance, he overheard a woman saying she swore she could hear someone screaming.

After tonight, I'll fight to my death before I let another man hurt me like this. If tonight has taught me anything, it's that I don't need to be the victim. I'm not going to let this become who I am, *change* who I am. I want to be strong, to be the person Dean deserves me to be, but most of all, who *I* deserve to be. Tonight, I was saved just in time, and I'll always be thankful to Dean for that, but I need to learn how to fight back better, fight back harder.

Being sexually assaulted by a man I once thought I loved was hard, to the point of breaking, but the thought of being raped by a man I didn't even know, any man, would have completely ruined me. It would have shattered me in a way that there'd be no recovering from. Not that what Rick did was okay, it wasn't, but… God, I can't even think about this anymore. I just want to forget this ever happened.

One good thing did come out of tonight, and that was finding out I'm strong enough to fight back. I believe knowing that will give me more confidence with life and help me move on.

Chapter Twenty-Two

It's three in the morning by the time we get back home and, although I'm exhausted, I'm too alert to even contemplate going to sleep.

I kick my shoes off as we enter and sluggishly drop my bag before turning to follow Dean into our bedroom.

He's hardly said two words since the police took my statement and it's beginning to alarm me. He's keeping his anger in check, and although I know he'd never hurt me, I'm still fretting.

"Are you mad at me?" I ask, standing at the edge of my bed. I clutch the ends of his suit jacket in the palms of my hands, making a fist over the material.

He takes in a ragged breath, gripping the edge of the dresser before slowly turning, watching me standing there drowning in his suit jacket with tears pouring down my cheeks. His eyes soften, and he takes a step towards me.

"Lola, I could never be mad at you. I'm mad at myself." He sighs, running a frustrated hand through his hair. "I just want to go smash his face in, but I can't, and it's killing me." He pauses. "I'm worried about you too. You've come so far, and then this happens. I should never have let you go out there alone. I'm going to see to it that the prick gets jail time, even though he deserves a lot more done to him. I'll stamp his name and company through the mud. The bastard stood there and had the nerve to tell me, and everyone else there, that you asked for it," he growls, getting angry. "We could all hear you screaming. I'll never be able to get those screams out of my head. I can still hear you, and it breaks my fucking heart knowing I wasn't there for you."

"What are you talking about, Dean? If it hadn't been for you, it could have been a lot worse. He could have… could have…." I pause, shaking my head. Saying it out loud will make it real, and I don't even want to acknowledge what *could* have happenen.

Dean steps forward, wrapping his arms around me and pulling me against his chest. I go willingly, leaning my head on his chest.

"C'mon, let's get into bed. It's been a long night," he says, then steps back and starts undressing. I nod, pulling his jacket off, but when I look down at my ripped dress, I freeze. My eyes take in the corset, and they water, thinking about my plans for tonight. Dean was meant to be the one to take this off me. I can't end the night with Jordan being the last person to touch me, to be the one who got to see me in this. Not when it was meant for Dean, the man I love. No one gets to see me like this, but Dean, and Jordan took that away.

I've come too far to fall back into my old ways.

"Are you okay?" he asks, and all I can do is nod, unsure of how to approach the subject of what I want. But I need him desperately. "Are you going to get ready for bed?" he asks, eyeing me softly, wearing only his boxer briefs.

"I can't," I whisper.

Walking back over to me he pulls me into his arms, and I sigh, feeling content.

"Why, baby?" he asks.

"I don't want to end the night with him being my last memory, of him being the one to try and get this dress off me. I want it to be you. I *need* it to be you, Dean. I had this surprise all set up for you for when we got back, and he ruined it, Dean. He ruined it." Tears start to fall again. I hate myself for being so weak, but tonight *was* meant to be a step forward for me. I was going to seduce Dean with my new undergarments and make love to him, show him how much I love him.

Dean's hand goes to the zipper on the back of my gown, and for a second my body tenses, but the feel of his cool fingers running along my spine relaxes me instead.

I trust Dean, and trust him to know what I want and need. I know he can make me forget about tonight's incident just from his soothing words and by holding me, but I need him to erase his touch. To erase everything that tonight resurfaced, reminding me of my time with Rick.

It's selfish of me to take this from him, but I need it. I need *him*. I've never needed anyone in my entire life the way I need Dean. And I want to finish today, *tonight*, on a high. I want it to end as a dream, not a nightmare.

The second the zip lowers to the middle of my back, the dress falls helplessly to the floor in a puddle.

He takes a step back, his eyes widening as a small puff of air slips through his gaping mouth. I blush as he slowly, ever so slowly, takes in my appearance from head to toe, taking his sweet time.

I'm still shocked and a little unnerved by the fact I'm actually standing here wearing a tight corset, lace knickers, and garters.

But the minute I bravely look up into his eyes, all those nerves and shyness are thrown out of the window. He's looking at me like he's a teenager and I just flashed him some boob for the first time. I feel sexy and although this seduction malarkey isn't going quite as planned... this is better. With my new-found confidence, I take a few steps towards him, putting an extra bit of sway into my walk.

"Lola, I want you, but we can't do this tonight," he chokes out, not looking away from my attire. "Fuck! I shouldn't even be thinking about this, not with everything that happened." He leans down, kissing me.

I shiver, unable to control my body's response to him or his words. I can feel the wetness between my thighs, just from him speaking in a low husky voice.

Lifting up on my tiptoes, my lips a breath away from his ear, I palm his erection through his boxers.

"This is all for you, Dean. I want you to take it off me. You own me, all of me, and I need you. I need you to help erase his touch. I love you. I'm yours, forever," I whisper, nipping at his earlobe.

And I mean every word. I know after everything that happened tonight I should wait, but I need to erase Jordan's touch, and Dean is the only person who can do that for me. It's only his touch that I want, that I need. His eyes darken, hunger evident, and to drive him wilder, I press my breasts against his bare chest.

"Fuck, you drive me crazy," he rasps, lowering to his knees. Kissing below my navel, he runs his tongue down my pubic bone, over my knickers. I throw my head back, moaning.

His teeth scrape down my thighs, pulling my stockings between them and rolling the fabric down my leg. I lose my mind watching him pay the same attention to my other leg, my core tightening, ready for him.

"I want you to strip me naked, and to feel your skin against mine. Make love to me, Dean. Please," I beg.

"Fuck! I don't know whether to fuck you with this on or strip it off." His hands run over my corset as he captures my lips with a kiss.

"Please." I pull away, arching my neck to give him access.

"I'll give you anything you want. Anything," he whispers, and I wrap my arms around his neck, kissing him softly.

"Anything?" I run my finger down his chest, feeling each ridge of muscle.

"Anything," he agrees, untying the strings on my corset. The rush is intoxicating, shocks of pleasure coursing through my body, and I beg him for more.

"Patience," he scolds me hoarsely.

In no time he has me standing in only my lace knickers, my body aching for a release only he can give me. I'll die if he doesn't touch me soon. My legs threaten to buckle beneath me, and Dean takes notice, picking me up and placing me in the middle of the bed, helping me shuffle to the top.

He pulls my nipple into his mouth, sucking deep until I'm calling out his name. His other hand moves to pay attention to my other breast, squeezing and pinching, the sensation running all the way to my clit.

"You're so fucking sexy when you moan like that," he whispers after letting my nipple go with a pop.

His gaze dips down to my breasts, looking at the red marks he's put there with a wild expression as my breath comes out in sharp pants.

It was becoming hard to concentrate, especially when his hand started lowering, moving between my legs until his fingers were running through my heat.

"Yes, more," I moan, bucking my hips.

"God, if you only knew how good you feel."

His dick twitches, throbbing against my thigh, and I reach down, circling my palm around him and squeezing. "Not as good as you," I murmur, pumping him.

"I can't wait. I need you," he groans and peels my hand from around his dick, taking it in his own hand and pumping once, twice before guiding it to my entrance.

God, I love it when he's inside me.

His eyes are glazed over, glistening with lust as they lock on mine, watching my reaction as he slowly enters me. The tension that had been building since he removed my dress was about to explode, my body damn near release.

His thrusts are slow, his dick coated with my arousal, bringing me closer and closer to exploding. And the second his mouth closes over my nipple, tugging it between his teeth, I shatter into a thousand pieces.

"Yes," I cry out, my body arching and my nails digging into his shoulders as my sex quivers around him.

"Jesus," he whispers, looking down at me with darkened eyes, licking his lower lip. "Do you trust me?" he asks, and I catch my breath, looking up at him in puzzlement.

"With my life," I answer straight away.

"Turn over and get up on your knees for me," he whispers against my lips and my body tenses. He notices, pulling back to look down at me in confusion. "Are you okay?"

"I...," I start, breathing through my panic. "The last time I was in this position was when...."

Realisation dawns in his eyes and they soften as he kisses me. "I promise I'll never hurt you, and if you don't want to then we won't," he says, and I nod, trusting him. "If you're uncomfortable at any time, tell me or if you can't speak, tap the bed three times, and I'll stop, okay?" he says, and I nod again. "Words love."

"Yes, just… just don't hurt me," I plead.

"Never, I promise," he whispers against my lips, capturing me in a breathless kiss, and my sex clenches.

He helps me turn around onto my knees, as I rest down on my elbows. He growls low, deep in his throat and it excites me, already feeling wetness coating my sex.

My eyes water as he poises his dick at my entrance, caressing my lower back lovingly. He rubs his erection through my wetness, coating his dick before entering in one smooth stroke and I throw my head back, the sensation so much more.

"Oh, wow," I cry out, never knowing it could feel like this. He's deeper, hitting that spot with each thrust and my walls start to tighten all over again.

His hands move to my hips, guiding me up and down on his cock. He moves slowly at first before picking up speed, each one driving me crazy.

"You're so hot, so tight," he growls, slamming inside me and I cry out, pleasure rolling through my belly.

"Please," I beg, not knowing what for.

"You want me to make you come?" he asks and God, his words have my sex clenching around him, to the point I nearly orgasm.

"Yesss," I hiss, moving back, slamming myself harder on his dick. I don't know when it happened, but it's not him fucking me anymore—I'm fucking him. It's an experience I'll never forget.

"Fuck, you're sexy," he growls, tapping the globes of my ass and I moan, tightening around him.

His hands on my hips snake around to my front, grabbing my full breasts in each hand, pulling me up a little so he has better access to squeeze and tug at my nipples torturously.

"Yessss," I cry out, slamming back down on him with each thrust.

"Come," he growls into my ear, dropping one hand down between my legs, his fingers strumming my clit, and the touch has me flying over the edge.

I scream, my throat hoarse, and I tense as pleasure courses through my entire body. It's nothing like my other orgasms; they paled in comparison. This one is more powerful, more intense and seems to go on forever.

Dean growls, low and husky in my ear. Lifting my hips up and down his dick, he follows me over the edge, his own orgasm overriding his body.

His breaths come in and out sharply, and his hands dig into my waist as he spills his seed inside me. His dick pulses and I inwardly curse, feeling his arousal dripping out of me, running down my thighs.

"Fuck," I whisper, realising he's not wearing a condom, again.

"I just did that, love," he teases, kissing my cheek.

"No, not that." I giggle.

"What is it, baby?" Pulling out of me and realising himself, he stills. "Shit."

I don't know why but his reaction upsets me, like he's ashamed to have released his seed inside me.

"We didn't use protection earlier either. I forgot to say something because you kept distracting me," I tell him quietly, moving from under him so I can grab my robe.

I leave Dean frozen on the bed while I rush to the loo to clean myself up. My eyes water as I pray he doesn't think I've done this on purpose.

Slowly, I walk back into the room, and Dean has moved to the edge of the bed and is now wearing boxers. The minute he sees me he jumps off the bed and comes over to me.

"Baby, I'm so fucking sorry. I'm clean, I swear. I'd never put you at risk like that. I've never had unprotected sex before, ever, but I do have regular check-ups," he explains and it occurs to me why he's so upset. He's not upset with me; he's upset at the prospect of hurting me.

Silly man!

"I know that, and I trust you," I tell him. "I was more concerned about the other part, the pregnancy part. Oh, and also, I'm clean. I got tested at the hospital on the way here…." I stop, not wanting to dredge up bad memories.

He looks down at me, opening his mouth, but whatever he's about to say is lost, and he shakes his head, frowning.

"What? What's wrong?" I ask, wondering if he thinks I'm lying or something.

He looks torn whether to say it or not, but in the end, he gives in sighing. "Would it be so bad?" he asks, confusing me.

"Huh? Getting an STD?"

"No! You know, carrying my baby? I'm not saying we should start trying, but there's already a chance now that you are, and if we *are* lucky enough to have made a life together, would it be so bad? With me as the dad, I mean," he says, seeming shy about asking.

My heart thumps against my chest as I stare at him, wondering if he's serious or not. Having a child is a lifetime commitment and knowing Dean wants that sends excitement rushing through me. My heart fills with love and happiness, but dread fills me when I realise why we can't.

IF I COULD WISH IT ALL AWAY

"Dean, I love you. I love you more than my own life, and there's nothing I'd love more than to make a family with you," I tell him, smiling sadly.

"I'm sensing a but," he says, looking saddened already, and it breaks my heart.

"*But* what kind of person... hell, what kind of mother would I be to bring a child into my world, where I'm constantly looking over my shoulder in fear? I want it all with you, Dean, all of it. I want to get married, buy a house, and have kids. I couldn't ask for a better person to be with than with you. You're the only one I've ever seen a future with. I love you, and you'd make a fantastic father. But what if he finds me and I'm pregnant? He could—" I choke up, not able to form those words. I don't even know if there's a life growing inside me, but already the thought of him harming our child sickens me.

"He'll never find you, I swear. We're going to stop him before anything happens. I love you so much, Lola."

"I love you too," I repeat, and together we move to the bed, lying down and facing each other.

"What will we do if you are?" he whispers.

"Buy every parenting book there is from Brooke," I tell him seriously before we both burst out laughing.

"I love you so much Lola, and I know I keep saying it but I really do." He pulls me into his arms.

"You can tell me as many times as you want." I smile. Every time I hear him say those three words, my stomach flips and butterflies flutter inside my stomach. "And I love you more, handsome," I say, a loud, obnoxious yawn escaping me.

He chuckles, kissing my temple. "Go to sleep, baby. We've got a long day tomorrow."

Gah, don't remind me.

"Night," I yawn.

"Night, baby," he whispers, pulling me closer.

Chapter Twenty-Three

The next morning I'm rushing around the cabin trying to get ready to meet Grandpa at Lily and Mark's.

Dean and I slept in until eleven. It's now quarter past twelve, and I still can't find my damn clutch anywhere. We're running late as it is.

"Did you see where I put my handbag last night, Dean? I can't find it, and I need my phone. The police said they'd call to update me on what's happening," I rush out, throwing the sofa cushions everywhere.

"Yeah, baby. It's where you left it," he tells me, and I turn around, giving him a dry look.

"And where is that?" I ask sarcastically, hand on hip.

"On the floor by the front door where you chucked it."

Well shit, I did chuck it by the door when we came in last night. I growl, frustrated when I find it where he said it was. "Are you ready to go?" I snap, but there's no heat in my tone.

"Babe, I've been ready for the past hour." He laughs, jumping back when I go to punch his arm; playfully of course.

"If they ask why we're late, I'm blaming you," I tell him, sticking my tongue out at him.

When we finally arrive at the Salvatores, Mark and Lily are standing on the front steps. They both come over to greet us, giving me a warm hug and a kiss. I don't miss the way their eyes run over me, checking that I'm okay.

"How are you feeling today?" Lily asks, her face full of pain and worry.

"I'm surprisingly okay, all things considered. The police haven't gotten in touch yet. I think I'll feel better once I know what's going on. I'm really sorry for ruining last night. I hope I haven't destroyed any future business for you," I say, feeling guilty.

Lily gives me a sharp look, shaking her head disapprovingly. "Look here, doll, we would rather lose our business than do business with people

IF I COULD WISH IT ALL AWAY

like that. We only care about you. We're concerned about you and feel terrible that this happened. I just wish we knew what he was like before."

"What do you mean?" I ask, looking at her and Mark for an answer.

"Well, as soon as he got arrested, everyone started talking. It wasn't the first time he's done this to someone," Mark explains softly, wary of my reaction.

A part of me had already considered this, but hearing it and thinking it are two different things. I feel sick to my stomach. This world can be so evil.

"Oh," I whisper, my heart hurting for those women who didn't get away.

"Let's just try to enjoy the day," Dean says, giving his mom and dad a pointed look.

They both nod, seeming apologetic. "Are you excited to see your grandpa?" Lily asks, changing the subject.

"Yes." My voice is full of excitement and happiness, and Lily laughs at my enthusiasm. She opens her mouth to say something when we're interrupted by my phone ringing.

"Oh, this might be the police. I should get it," I say, looking down at the unknown caller flashing on my screen. I move back outside, sitting down on the step to get a little privacy, although Dean follows a few steps behind me.

"Hello," I answer politely.

"Hi, this is Detective Robson. I'm calling for a Miss Lawson." His voice is deep and smooth. I barely remember the man I gave my statement to last night, but his voice does sound vaguely familiar.

"Hello, Detective Robson. It's Lola here."

"I'm just ringing to inform you that Mr Wallace was charged this morning with attempted sexual assault and battery. According to our records, this isn't the first incident with him. There's another report claiming he assaulted a woman, but the charges never stuck due to lack of evidence. In this case, we have enough evidence and witnesses to confirm your allegation. It won't be going to court, as he pleaded guilty earlier this morning, which means he will get jail time, though he will get a shorter sentence than what he would have if he had gone to court. Are there any questions that you want to ask me before I go?" he asks, sounding curt and straight to the point.

I pause, shocked. I didn't think he'd plead guilty. I honestly believed it would be dragged through the courts since Jordan was telling everyone who would listen last night that I gave him consent.

I'm in complete and utter shock, and I can't help but wonder who got him to change his mind. It's possible that his lawyer told him he'd get a longer sentence if he fought the allegation. We do have a solid case; even the officer from last night said that.

"Miss Lawson?" Detective Robson calls, and I shake my head, snapping out of it.

"Sorry. Um… no, no questions. Thank you," I say numbly, still in shock.

"That's my job, Miss Lawson. I'm just glad we were able to take him off the streets before he could hurt anyone else," he says sincerely.

"Me too," I whisper, realising what this all truly means. He won't be able to hurt anyone ever again. My mind goes to Rick and what this signifies. Would getting him arrested and sent to jail be as easy as Jordan?

I shake my head, concentrating on the phone call, missing half of what Detective Robson says.

"Have a good day, and if you ever need anything, please just ring the station and ask for me. If I'm not there then leave a message for me and I'll get back to you as soon as I can," he offers, which I find remarkably kind.

"Thank you. Goodbye, Detective Robson," I say, still in a daze.

I hear him end the call, the line going dead, but I still don't move. I'm just so relieved I'll never have to see Jordan again.

I am worried about the media. Due to his position, the newspapers are going to be all over this and I don't want my name to be leaked. It will be like sending a neon flashing sign to Rick that says I'm here.

Dean said that they had to respect my privacy due to the nature of the incident, but you never know with reporters these days. I haven't even looked on the Internet or at the newspapers this morning, and I'm not going to. I'd rather not know.

"What did he say?" Dean asks, wrapping his arms around me as he sits behind me, his legs either side of me.

I lean back, soaking in his warmth, and place my hands over his that are crossed in front of me.

"Jordan pleaded guilty. There was too much evidence against him. What your parents were saying was true. Detective Robson confirmed it. He said this wasn't the first accusation made against him." I sigh, saddened about the women who haven't received justice.

"I can't believe he's gotten away with this before. I'm glad he's going to jail," he growls. "How do you feel now?"

The question makes me wonder if he's thinking of Rick. I know how desperate he is for me to go to the police and, if I'm honest, a part of me wants to.

"Honestly? I'm more shocked than anything. I can't believe he actually admitted to it. I really believed that he'd drag this through the courts, pleading his innocence. I'm just glad he can't hurt anyone else."

"I know you did, baby, but you really need to have more faith in the justice system. I'm glad they've charged him. He deserves everything he has coming to him," he seethes.

"Was it the police, doll?" Lily asks, walking out with Mark.

"Yeah, he's been charged this morning. He pleaded guilty," I inform them, still going over Dean's last words about trusting the justice system.

"Wow, I thought he was going to fight tooth and nail. Guess I was wrong," she says, looking dumbfounded.

"Me too. I really thought he'd turn everything around on me."

"I wish the fucker couldn't afford shower gel," she blurts out, and my mouth gapes open in shock before I burst out laughing, everyone joining me.

"Lily." I giggle.

"Ew, Mom," Dean moans, yet a chuckle slips free.

Mark just shakes his head, amused. "C'mon, let's get the kettle on. Your grandpa called me, letting me know he was on his way over. It's why we came out. He'll be here soon."

"I could kill for a coffee," I whine dramatically as Dean helps me up off the step.

"Are you sure that's wise?" he whispers in my ear as we walk in and I look over my shoulder at him, confused. His eyes flicker to my midsection before pulling me back against his chest, his hands rubbing my stomach.

My eyes widen with realisation. "Or tea. Yeah, I can do tea," I shout to Lily and Mark in the kitchen, making Dean laugh as we follow them.

"Where's Pagan and Sid?" Dean asks, seeming more relaxed after the officer's phone call.

Lily fills the kettle and turns it on before turning to face her son. "Sid offered to help Pagan sort everything out at the marquee," she says, looking at me before averting her gaze.

What was that look about?

"I thought she hired cleaners?" Dean says, looking through the fridge for food.

"Stop bloody messing. I'll make you some lunch when Dwayne gets here. And the catering company were meant to clean everything up last night, but we sent everyone home when… well, you know when," she says, waving him off, and her earlier look makes sense. She didn't want to bring it all back up in front of me.

Guilt gnaws at me. "Does she need any help?" I ask, ready to go down there.

"Oh no! We called a cleaning company this morning. Sid and Pagan are basically supervising and getting all the donations boxed up and sent to buyers."

"Are you sure? That sounds like a lot of work," I ask again, biting my bottom lip.

"Dwayne's here," Mark shouts from the other room. My eyes meet Dean's, and a wide grin spreads across my face before I rush through the house, excited to see Grandpa.

As I rush outside, I bounce on the top step, waiting for him to pull up.

Dean said Mark filled Grandpa in on last night's events for which I'm thankful. I don't think my heart could handle telling him more bad news. It's just one less thing to deal with, and by the look on my grandpa's face, I can tell it's going to be a long day. His salt-and-pepper hair looks a mess, like he's run his hands through it too many times.

The car barely comes to a stop before I'm jumping down the steps and running over. He's just getting out of the car when I reach him so when I barrel into him, he falls back a step, catching me.

Bringing my face into the crook of his neck, I breathe him in, and a tear falls from my eye right before I break down, my body trembling with sobs. Grandpa holds me, running his hand up and down my back, letting me get it all out.

Guilt hits me painfully. He's the only blood relative I have left, and I pushed him away. The fear of him having to face Rick's wrath if he ever found out, made it easier, but doing so cost me my grandpa, and I've missed him so bloody much.

"Hush child. Everything is going to be okay," he says hoarsely, sounding choked up.

"I've missed you so much," I cry, holding him tighter.

"I've missed you too, doll." He kisses my temple before pulling away and looking down at me with a sad expression. "Let's go inside. We need to talk."

My stomach sinks and I nod, knowing I need to hear what he has to say. Dean pulls me into his side as Grandpa greets Mark and Lily with pleasantries.

"You okay?" Dean whispers, looking down at me.

"Yeah. I just have a bad feeling about this. He sounded off on the phone last night, like he was distracted," I tell him, having forgotten to mention it last night.

"I'm not going anywhere, love. I'll be here," he promises, taking my hand. I squeeze his gently and together we walk in.

We gather at the dining room table and, like the last time I was here, it feels formal and uncomfortable. It doesn't help that Mark and Grandpa hovered in the doorway whispering to one another before they sat down. It's clear that Mark has already been filled in on whatever Grandpa needs to tell me. It must be bad if he's told someone else before me.

Lily walks in holding a tray of coffee and cups of teas, and I give her a grateful smile as I take my tea, needing it to calm me down.

My eyes drift to my grandpa again, surprised at how pale and shaken he looks. He's barely been able to keep eye contact with me, and I hate it. I don't know what's going on or what's running through his head and it's driving me nuts.

"Who's going to feed Hunter and Dolly?" I ask Dean, needing to say something, anything to keep myself from being sucked into the tension of the room. "Maybe we should go feed them?"

"Matt's going to clean them out today. Don't worry about the horses. He works Sundays to earn money." He smiles, and I nod, remembering him mentioning it before.

"That's good. I mean, they won't starve, and Matt gets money. To spend," I babble nervously.

Dean chuckles, placing his hand on my thigh. "Calm down, love. It's going to be okay," he tells me, looking me straight in the eye. I just nod, hoping he's right.

"Lola, did you want to talk somewhere private, or can I talk in front of everyone?" Grandpa asks, and I turn from Dean to stare at him.

"No, they can stay," I tell him, gulping.

I pick at my thumbs under the table, but Dean feels the movement, and he takes my hand in his.

"You know when we last spoke I said Patrick was on his last warning?" Grandpa asks, and I nod, not seeing where this is going. I thought something bad had happened but if this is him telling me he's fired Rick, then isn't that a good thing?

"Well, the day you called me, I went down to his office to see if he had closed a case he'd been assigned and I found him drinking hard liquor. That was the last straw. There are no rules really for drinking—we all have a glass of scotch now and again—but he was so drunk he could barely stay focused. I gave him his last warning and told him he wouldn't get another chance. One more incident and he was gone," he says, pulling his hair roughly before looking at me. Pain and guilt paint his face and my stomach twists.

"That's a good thing right? You're one step closer to firing him," I say, looking between Dean and Grandpa, needing someone to explain.

"He took a few days off to get his shit together. While he was off, I took over the Salvatore accounts and made sure his assistant knew. When he arrived back, he stormed into the office demanding why I'd taken his biggest client. It ended up in a heated discussion, and Lola, God, I'm so sorry," he says, sounding broken. My eyes fill with tears, but I still don't understand what's going on.

"It's okay, Grandpa. Whatever it is, it's fine," I assure him, needing him to be the strong man I know.

"I pride myself in my work, Lola. I'm a lawyer. But he got me so worked up. I was already struggling not to throw him out of my office window, so when he kept demanding why, I explained I didn't want him fucking up a family friend's account. I explained the Salvatores had been life-long friends and that I didn't want him coming here and embarrassing me and my firm."

I shake my head, wondering where he's going with this. So far, everything seems fine. Rick didn't attack him, and he doesn't know where I am, so I'm unsure why he seems so torn up over this.

"Grandpa, I don't understand. You got him off the case and one incident away from been fired."

"Lola," Dean says gently. When I turn to face him, he looks sad, although his jaw is clenched.

"What am I not clueing in on?" I demand, looking around the table. The only other person who seems oblivious is Lily.

"I think he knows you're here," Grandpa whispers and I gasp, sliding my chair back and jumping up. My hands are shaking, as I glance around the room, like I'm waiting for him to pop out from somewhere.

"How?" I ask hoarsely, moving back when Dean tries to comfort me.

"Please sit down," Grandpa asks gently, looking pained.

"Tell me!" I yell, throwing my hands up. "Please."

"When I was explaining who the Salvatores were, he got a calculating look in his eyes. He asked if I'd spoken to you, and my suspicions were confirmed," he explains.

I relax, sitting back in the chair as he takes a breather. "So it's only a guess? He might not even know I'm here?"

"No. He definitely knows you're here. I denied talking to you, but then he said Sally said you called. He kicked off, causing a mess of the office, and I had to get him removed from the building. After I returned from dealing with security and the police, Sally had already taken the Salvatore case file. I've not seen her since, but I'm assuming she knows she's fired," he says, running a hand across his face. "Last night when you called, I was in the middle of reading a report on Rick. I've had someone keeping close tabs on him since you first called me, but somehow, last night, he evaded them in a DIY store. We haven't been able to find his whereabouts since."

"What does that mean?" I ask dumbly.

"It means that whatever he has planned, you're involved. I'm so fucking sorry, doll. You were safer pushing me away, not calling me. All I've done is put you in danger," he says, his eyes watering.

"Grandpa," I whisper, shaking my head. "None of this is your fault. What about Sally? If she's helping him, maybe she can tell you where he is," I offer, picking at straws.

Lily's phone beeps and she sends us an apologetic look before checking it.

"We tried that. She wasn't at her flat. We tried her mom's place, and she wasn't there either. We have no idea where she is," he says and my stomach sinks, instantly thinking of the worst.

"Maybe they've run away together?" Dean adds.

That's actually a good point.

"Yeah, Sally did hint a few times they were together," I say, hope rising in my chest.

"Maybe, but I don't want to risk your safety," Grandpa says, taking a sip of his tea.

"I'm going to put some food on. Sid and Pagan are on their way," Lily announces as she stands to leave.

"Make extras. Me and Lola didn't eat breakfast," Dean announces to the whole table. I blush at the look my grandpa gives me.

"I'll get to you two later," he says, giving Dean a look that would have most men cowering in their boots. "But first I want to talk about what your next move is. After what happened last night, I don't think going to the police with what we have is wise. From what I read up on about this Jordan Wallace, he has money and is used to getting away with shit. If we go to the police now, as much as what you're reporting is true, it could possibly get him out of charges or a lower sentence," he says.

"But he pleaded guilty," I tell him, confused.

"It doesn't matter. He could say he was coerced," he says sadly.

"That's bullshit," Dean growls.

"You know how the law works, and how defence lawyers can twist everything. If she suddenly goes in, reporting two assaults, then they'll think it's a cry for attention or whatever bullshit they can come up with. We have the hospital records and managed to get CTV footage of you at the hospital," Grandpa says, and I gasp.

"What?"

"Yeah." He winces. "I'm sorry, doll. I did tell you I was going to dig into everything, make sure we had enough evidence."

"So what do we do?" I ask, feeling shaken.

"I know you're scared, but I think we need to wait and see what Rick does. It's obvious he's obsessed with you and that he isn't letting you go. I believe we can find a cop who will take a statement without pressing charges against Rick just yet. After that, we can file for a restraining order. You'll also need to sign a form to release your medical records. But until Rick makes another move, I don't think we have much to go on," he says. "I feel really awful, doll, and I'm sorry I've caused all of this. He'd have no idea you were here if it weren't for me."

"Grandpa." I sigh, getting up and moving around the table to him. "This isn't your fault. In a way, I think this is a good thing. I'm fed of up of being scared, of looking over my shoulder all the time. I knew he was going to find me eventually, but at least I'm somewhat stronger now," I tell him, hoping that's the truth as I wrap my arms around his neck.

Anyone can say they can do something, but the minute they're faced with the reality, everything changes.

I'm still unsure whether I'm okay with talking to the police about Rick, but if it means getting him out my life, then I'll be sure. I need to do this, not just for everyone around me but for myself. I need to.

"Okay, I'll do it," I whisper, kissing his cheek.

He leans into me, kissing my arms wrapped around him. "Good girl." I roll my eyes, feeling like a two-year-old. "Now, about you two...," he starts, and I groan, moving back around to Dean just as the twins walk in.

"Ah, are we in time for the 'don't mess with my granddaughter' speech?" Pagan asks excitedly, rushing over to my grandpa and hugging him.

"Yes, you are." He chuckles before narrowing his eyes on Dean. "Are you going to marry her?" he demands.

"Grandpa!" I yell, covering my face with embarrassment.

"I need to know, Lola, shush. The men are going to talk now," he says, and I narrow my eyes on him, making him gulp. "So?" he asks, looking back to Dean.

"Yes, I am. And we're going to have a family, buy a house, and live happily ever after," Dean says, answering everything my grandpa was bound to ask.

"Will you take care of her?" Grandpa demands, sitting back in his chair as Lily walks out with food. Mark chuckles before looking at his son, waiting for an answer.

"I'd die for her. I'll take care of her, worship her and never take her for granted," Dean answers, not looking affected whatsoever.

Sid makes a whipping noise, laughing.

I roll my eyes.

Pagan giggles.

Grandpa shakes his head.

IF I COULD WISH IT ALL AWAY

And Mark snorts at Sid.

"Good lad. Don't wait long to put a ring on my girl's finger. Her mother will be dancing in heaven knowing you two kids are together," he says, and my eyes water.

"We're not kids," I snap, trying not to sound affected.

Grandpa rolls his eyes. "You'll always be my baby girl."

"*Mom*. Food!" Sid shouts, and we burst out laughing.

"I'm not a little girl," I mumble, pouting, and Dean chuckles.

"One last thing. Do you love her?" Grandpa asks, and my eyes widen, wishing he'd shut up.

"With all my heart," Dean answers immediately, turning towards me. My eyes get lost in his gaze, and I smile longingly at him.

Leaning forward, a wide grin on his lips, he kisses me. It's not a quick kiss; it's deep, passionate and full of heat, and I'm close to reaching out and pulling him closer. I'm also pretty sure I moan.

When he pulls away, I'm breathing heavily. In a daze, I turn in my seat, finding everyone's eyes on us, grinning. I didn't even notice Lily walk back in with plates of food and I blush furiously, annoyed that Dean makes me lose my mind.

So I do the only rational thing a woman can do.

I kick him in the shin.

"Fuck! What was that for?" he asks, a small grin on his face.

"You know damn well what for," I snap. "You couldn't have kissed me like that when, say, we *weren't* surrounded by family?"

Everyone bursts out laughing, and after a few seconds, I follow, shaking my head at everyone. The minute I do, Dean is on me, kissing me once again. I readily submit, getting lost in the kiss.

Damn this man and his charm.

Chapter Twenty-Four

The following day, I pick Grandpa up from Lily and Mark's, since he stayed there instead of at Dean's, and drive us over to Brooke's Books.

He wanted to meet my new friend—like I'm in nursery—and the person who inspired me to start up my own business.

Plus, I get to show him the shop I'm purchasing. I managed to talk the estate agent into meeting me today so I could show grandpa around and they happily agreed, although I won't be getting the keys for another few days since the contracts are still going through.

We enter the store to find Brooke up a ladder, grabbing a book for an older lady who is waiting patiently.

Hearing the door, Brooke turns, a smile lighting up her face. She holds her hand up, gesturing for me to wait.

"You can go sit down on the sofa Miss Bellingham, and I'll make you a nice cup of tea in a minute, okay?" she asks the old lady who nods, pleased. Turning, Brooke rushes over, a frown on her face. "Oh my God, Lola. I heard about Saturday night. I'm so sorry I haven't called. I've been at the hospital and didn't find out until this morning. I wish I was there," she says apologetically, pulling me in for a hug.

Brooke couldn't make it Saturday night because her neighbour had an accident. In a way, I'm kind of glad she wasn't there. It could have been her.

"I'm fine. I promise," I assure her as we pull apart. "The police called yesterday and said he pleaded guilty, admitting all charges, so he'll be going to prison," I inform her. "How is your neighbour?"

"Thank God." She sighs, looking relieved. "She's had to have hip surgery. She fell down the stairs and because her son was out of town, she was on her own. I heard the fall and rushed round. Luckily, the ambulance got there quickly," she explains.

"Oh God." I wince, feeling sorry for the old lady.

"Who's this?" she asks, looking at my grandpa, a bright smile on her face.

I open my mouth to introduce them but, ever the gentlemen, Grandpa steps forward, holding his hand out.

"I'm Dwayne, Lola's grandpa. It's a pleasure to meet you. I've heard so many good things about you," he tells her, shaking her hand, and Brooke blushes at his compliment.

She beams up at him, making me smile. I can already tell Grandpa likes her.

With the amount of money I have, he's always been wary of the people who come into my life, and he drilled it into my head since I was a teenager to be careful of who to trust. But you only have to meet Brooke once and you know you could trust her with your life. She's a genuinely nice, caring person.

"I'm Brooke, Lola's friend," she says, giving the unnecessary introduction. "It's nice to finally meet you too, Dwayne. Lola speaks highly of you. Would you like a cup of tea or coffee?" she offers.

"We can't stay," I tell her sadly. "I'm going to show Grandpa around the shop, and then we're going out for dinner. Do you want to join us?" I ask her, hoping she says yes.

"I would love to, but I've got so much stuff to sort through. With the shop being closed yesterday, I'm a little behind. Maybe we can catch up another time?" I nod. "You're going to love the store," she says to my grandpa, who smiles in return. "Her ideas are brilliant. You've got an amazing granddaughter. She's going to be very successful," Brooke states proudly, and I blush at her compliment.

"She sure is." Grandpa grins, eyeing Brooke with a new-found fondness.

"Right, we better get going. The estate agent is waiting for us next door. Are you sure you can't come?" I pout.

She chuckles, shaking her head. "I wish I could. I really do, but I'm needed here."

I sigh dramatically. "Okay, I'll speak to you later," I huff out, pulling her in for a hug.

"See you soon. And I'm really am glad you're okay," she whispers into my neck. She pulls back, giving me a smile before turning and approaching my grandpa. His eyes widen when she pulls him in for a hug, pecking him on the cheek before stepping back. "It was nice meeting you, Dwayne. Don't be a stranger," she tells him sincerely.

"You too, Brooke," he smiles, warmly. "C'mon then, doll. Show me this store you've been raving about."

I grin, excited as I pull him out of the door.

"I'm so glad you liked it," I gush, taking my seat in the restaurant.

"I really am proud of you," he says, sitting across from me.

Looking over the menu I feel his eyes on me, and it's not the first time I've caught him staring at me. I know he has something on his mind, but it's like he's reluctant to bring it up—or dare I say... shy.

"Spill," I say, not taking my eyes off the menu.

He chuckles nervously, taking a sip of his water. "You're just like your mother and grandma. They always knew when I had something to say," he mutters.

I laugh. "That's because it's written all over your face."

"Right, yeah, well," he sputters, shaking his head. "I just wanted to talk to you about a few things whilst I had you to myself."

My head snaps up "Um, okay," I murmur, worried.

"Yeah, about Dean. Are you sure about your relationship? With everything that happened with Rick, do you think you're ready?" he asks, reasonably.

"Grandpa, Dean would never hurt me," I tell him softly.

His eyes widen. "No! I don't mean in that way. I know the boy would never hurt you. He's been smitten with you since before you were out of nappies." I cringe. "I'm just worried this is all too much for you."

"I love him. I've never been so sure of anything in my life. And I understand your concerns, I really do, because I had the same ones. Everything happened pretty quickly. But this is what I want, Grandpa. Dean is what I want."

"So there's no chance you'll open up your business back in Carlisle and come back home?" he asks, looking sad.

"Oh, Grandpa. My life is here now, with Dean. I can't leave. Once everything with Rick is dealt with, I promise to come and visit you, all the time."

"I'm just going to miss you," he says, looking down at the table.

"Couldn't you move here?" I ask shyly.

He snaps his head up, looking at me wide-eyed. "You'd want that?"

"Of course I would. You're my grandpa, my family," I tell him, my voice kind of high-pitched.

"I'll think about it," he says and opens his mouth, ready to ask something else, but stops himself, looking so sad it breaks my heart.

"Grandpa, whatever it is, just come out and say it."

"I really do wish you'd stop doing that," he scolds, shaking his head.

"It's not my fault. You've got that look, the one that says you don't know how to say what you need to. You've only ever had it with me, Mom and Grandma." I giggle.

"Figures," he says, rolling his eyes. "There's no easy way of saying this, so I'm just going to say it. I need to head home. I know I said I'd be staying for a week, and I hate to leave you when you need me the most, but with everything going on, I need to get back. I also have to meet up with the private investigators I hired to track down Rick. I can't get in touch with them," he says quickly, and my heart sinks.

"But you just got here."

"I know, doll, but I really do need to get back. Anything could happen, and I pretty much left everyone in the lurch. If I'm honest, I don't trust Rick, and I want to do some of my own searches," he admits.

"I understand," I tell him, and he sags with relief. I realise then how hard this must be for him, especially with everything that happened to me Saturday night. "When do you leave?" I ask, hoping I can still spend another day with him.

"As soon as we get back," he answers regretfully.

"Oh!"

"I promise I'll be back as soon as I can, doll. I won't be gone for very long."

My eyes water and I nod, wishing all this mess would go away. "Okay. Do we have time to order or shall we get going?"

"We've got time for food," he tells me, reaching out for my hand.

We go quiet, looking over our menus, and I can't help but feel his loss already. I hate he has to leave so soon.

But now that I know he's willing to think about moving here, maybe I can convince him into saying yes.

With that in mind, I cheer up, enjoying the last few hours with him before he has to leave.

We make our way back to Lily and Mark's, and as usual, they're both waiting for us as we get out the car. I know straight away he's already informed them of his plans and my heart aches. I really don't want him to go, but I understand why he has to.

"You know?" I whisper to Lily, leaving Grandpa to get his case.

"Yeah, he told us last night after you left. How are you feeling?"

"I'm going to miss him, but I understand why he has to leave. I just wish he didn't have to go."

"I know, doll. It won't be forever, and then he can visit whenever he wants to." She smiles.

"I'm going to talk him into moving here. He's been talking about retiring for a while, and he's said he'll think about it," I tell her, smiling wider.

Her eyes widen. "Oh my, I never thought I'd see the day. Well, fingers crossed."

I can't tell if she really believes he will or not; her expression is blank. "Yeah," I say absently.

Dean chooses that moment to pull up, looking ragged. I step away from Lily, walking over to him.

"Hey, what's wrong?" he asks, getting out of the car.

"Grandpa's leaving," I tell him, my eyes watering.

"When?" he asks, scrunching his eyes up.

"Now," I answer sadly.

"Oh, Lola, he'll be back. Did he say why he was leaving so soon? I presumed he was staying for the week."

"He needs to sort out some stuff, and he doesn't trust Rick. I understand why he's going, but I'm going to miss him. I pushed him away for so long, always making excuses as to why I couldn't go around for dinner. I could never let him see the bruises. And now that I don't have to hide and can finally spend time with him, he has to leave. Because of me…. because of Rick," I say, feeling my eyes begin to water.

"Let him do what he's gotta do. I think he blames himself for what happened to you and feels it's his responsibility to make sure Rick doesn't get away with it. He loves you. He hates that you were hurt and he didn't even know. It's his way of making everything better," he explains gently.

"I just don't want him to get hurt. Who knows what Rick will do." I bite my bottom lip; just thinking about it is making me nervous.

"I'm going to be fine," Grandpa says, sneaking up behind me.

I jump, turning around to face him and as a lone tear slips free. "Please be safe," I plead.

"My darling girl, you have nothing to worry about. Now come give me some love," he demands, holding his arms out to me.

I don't need asking twice; I'm in his arms in seconds, holding him tight, more tears spilling free.

"Promise me you'll come back."

"I promise," he whispers, emotion clogged in his throat.

"Good," I choke out, and when he tries to pull back, I hold him tighter, struggling to let him go.

"C'mon, Lola, I won't be gone forever, just a week or two," he tells me, and I feel Dean walk up behind me, pulling me against his chest. I let him, looking helplessly at my grandpa.

IF I COULD WISH IT ALL AWAY

"Okay. Call me when you get there."

"I will," he says, kissing my forehead. I close my eyes, savouring his touch. "Look after my girl," he warns Dean, looking over my head.

I'd giggle if I weren't so torn up about him leaving. Mark and Lily walk over, saying their goodbyes.

"Keep me updated," Mark says, and Grandpa nods sharply.

"Look after her," he says, like I'm not standing right here. But I can't deny the way my heart warms at how concerned he is about me.

"Goodbye, doll," he says, giving me one last kiss.

"Goodbye, Grandpa," I murmur, my throat tight.

He throws his case into the passenger seat before walking around to the driver's side. He gives me one last look, a small smile on his face, before getting in the car.

Dean's arms tighten around me when my legs threaten to give way. My grandpa drives away and, for some reason, it feels like it's the last time I'm going to see him.

I turn around, hiding my face against Dean's chest, struggling to not let any tears fall. Dean holds me close, resting his chin on the top of my head.

"Mom, I'm going to get Lola back," he says, his chest rumbling beneath me.

"Okay, dear. We're here if you need us," Lily says softly, and I hear her and Mark walk away.

"C'mon, let's get you back," he says.

I nod, following him over to the car. "How was your day?" I ask as he gets in, starting the engine.

"Okay."

My brows scrunch together, looking over at him. His hands are clenched around the steering wheel, his posture stiff.

I presumed his absence today was because he wanted to give Grandpa and me some time alone together but seeing his reaction to my question, I'm starting to think it's something else entirely.

"Is everything okay? You seem to be stressing over something," I say, turning in my seat as we pull up outside the cabin.

He sighs, shutting off the engine and turning towards me. "I just…," he starts but then pauses, shaking his head. "It's nothing, just work-related shit."

"Don't lie to me," I order softly, shaking my head. I'm actually disappointed in him. I didn't think he'd evade the question, brushing it off like it's nothing.

He curses, looking at me with a guilty expression. "Fuck, you're right, and I'm sorry. I just…. Please don't be mad at me."

"Why would I get mad at you?" I ask slowly, cursing when rain starts to fall.

"I've been looking into Rick, long before your grandpa said he was going to do it. I've also had someone keeping tabs on him, but we lost track of him the same day as your grandpa and haven't been able to pick him up since. It's like he's vanished from thin air."

I bite my lip, looking at him, wondering how I can word what I need to say. Instead of overanalysing it, I just say it.

"I'm not mad. If anything, I already had my suspicions. I knew you weren't going to move on like nothing happened. It's not who you are, so I'm not mad. I think it's kind of you, but Dean, you can't put all this pressure on yourself. I hate that I'm putting you through so much stress," I admit, reaching for his hand.

Placing his own hand on mine, he gives me a gentle squeeze.

"No! Don't ever think that. You're not putting any stress on me, love, I promise. I'm just pissed. I'm pissed and angry that no matter what I seem to do, I can't keep you safe," he says, running a frustrated hand through his hair.

Now I understand his distant behaviour. He's still blaming himself for what happened to me Saturday.

"You can't keep doing this to yourself," I whisper, moving to straddle him. I struggle at first, and Dean has to push the seat back, making more room.

"What are you doing?" he asks, huskily.

"Proving I'm not broken… well, not anymore. You see, I have this amazing man in my life who has been putting all my broken pieces together and no matter what life throws at me, I know I can get through it. And why you may ask? Because of you. I love you, Dean, and you can't control everything that happens. But you should know that you save me in the important ways, never forget that," I tell him, leaning down and capturing his lips in a kiss.

"I… I don't know what to say," he croaks, his eyes filled with emotion.

"Say that you love me," I whisper, grinding myself down on him.

He grins, his eyes darkening. "I love you, with all my heart." He grips my hips tightly.

"Tell me you want to make love to me," I demand against his lips before kissing the corner of his mouth.

"Oh, I'm going to make love to you." He nods, opening his door. I squeal when he pulls us out into the rain, laughing when he starts running towards the door.

He stops when he reaches it, rain pelting down on us, soaking us.

IF I COULD WISH IT ALL AWAY

"Tell me you love me," he demands, repeating my earlier words.

"I love you." I grin, and he takes me inside, showing me just how much he loves me.

Chapter Twenty-Five

A storm is coming and it's going to tear all our lives apart.

Chapter Twenty-Six

"I can't believe how well this has turned out. I was positive they wouldn't be able to knock that wall out," I tell Brooke, sliding down to the floor in my new store.

"I know. I'm so excited." She grins, taking a seat on the floor next to me.

We watch the builders take measurements in the back room.

After getting the keys a few weeks back, Brooke and I have gone crazy with the decor for the shop. And since I chose the same wild colour theme Brooke has next door, picking furniture has been so much freaking fun. The craziest we've gone is what the builders are measuring for right now, and that is joining our stores together.

At the back of our shops, there is a storage room, so we've asked the builders to knock the wall down and join the two rooms. We didn't even think it would be possible, but we were lucky.

The store opening is in another eight weeks, but Brooke's Books may not be reopened for a further three due to some equipment and safety checks.

"What time is Pagan coming?"

"Any minute," I answer, biting my lip.

"How do you think she's going to react?"

"I'm not sure." I shrug, playing it off, but inside, I'm worried.

Pagan wouldn't take my money for organising our store opening, so today I'm going to surprise her with something much better than payment. Something huge... and it's definitely going to change her life.

I've bought the store across the street, and I'm going to let her use it to start her own business, the one she's planned all along.

I know she's not going to just take it from me, so I'm hoping a little persuading and a sweet deal will change her mind.

I'm seriously nervous about it, worried it will push her into doing something she's not ready for.

"Hey, we're done for the day. We'll get a start on it once we have the correct materials," the young builder says, checking Brooke out.

"Thank you so much," I tell them all, getting up. Pagan chooses that moment to walk in.

"Hey," she greets in a sing-song voice. Her eyes shoot up, lingering on the builders as they make their way out. Once they're gone, she looks at me with wide eyes. "Why didn't you tell me you had hot builders working for you?"

"Um...."

"Um?" she repeats before drawing back, flabbergasted. "You're supposed to hook a single girl up," she pouts, and I laugh at her expression.

"Stop drooling over my workmen," I tease.

"Don't flaunt them in my face then," she tells me, her voice high-pitched. "So, what did you need to show me?"

Brooke stands, grinning from ear to ear. "Something... *big*." She grins, emphasising the last word.

Pagan's eyes light up like a Christmas tree as she starts rubbing her hands together.

"Please tell me it's one of those men and that they're coming back to strip."

I snort unlady-like. "No, you pervert. C'mon, I'll show you."

"Okay... weird," she mutters, her eyes scanning the room.

"Not in here." I laugh, pulling her towards the entrance and out of the store. I lock up, and we head over to the shop across the road.

As I open up the door, I pick up more junk mail and newspapers, throwing them on the pile I stacked up the last time I was here.

"Please don't tell me you've bought another store," she groans, but it's meaningless since she's smiling. "I really think you should slow down." She tries to come off serious, but she starts giggling.

"Shut up." I laugh.

"You'll be the mayor next, owning every piece of land in this town," she continues, and we all begin to giggle.

"I'll forget that comment, you hussy," I scold playfully. "Yes, I've bought this place, but it's not for me."

"Then who the hell is it bloody for?" she asks, confused.

"Well, there's a woman I know who wants to start her own business, but she doesn't have the funds to do it. I'm going to make her a deal she can't refuse so she can start it," I explain.

"Aw, Lola, that's an incredibly kind thing for you to do," she gushes, all playfulness gone.

My lips form into a smirk. She has no idea I'm talking about her. This is better than I imagined it would be.

"Thank you," I say, struggling not to laugh.

"What do you think of the space?" Brooke asks, being sly.

"Oh, I think it's great. I swear I'd love a place like this one day. Whoever this is for is seriously lucky. I'd kill for this," she says, nodding as she eyes the store.

"Well, that's a good job. I was worried for a second there that things were about to get awkward." I sigh, sagging my shoulders for effect.

"Huh?" Pagan murmurs, looking between us confused. It's so adorable I have to chuckle. "Why do I feel like I've just lost ten minutes of my life and in that time missed a conversation?"

I giggle, stepping forward. "It's yours."

She stands there, her mouth falling open into an O shape. It makes me giggle harder.

"Say something," Brooke demands, no longer able to hold in her excitement.

Pagan shakes her head, looking utterly gobsmacked, her eyes watering. "You're joking, right?"

Her words have me sobering and walking up to her, placing my hands on her shoulders. "Everyone deserves to live their dream. I want to do this for you. You've done so much for me, and this is my way of repaying you."

Her chin wobbles, causing my own eyes to water. "I can't afford to start a business or to rent this place, though," she tells me, still looking stunned and a little out of it.

"Ah, well, this is where the 'deal you can't refuse' comes in. But first!" I grin and rush over to my bag, grabbing the envelope of cheques. Her eyes widen when I hand them to her, and her hands shake as she flicks through them, reading each one and who they're from. Her parents, Dean, Grandpa, Sid, Brooke and I have all given her something towards starting up. Although Brooke's and Sid's weren't much, it all added up to a nice amount.

"I can't believe you've done all of this for me. It's too much," she chokes out, tears falling from her eyes.

"It's not. Not for what we all get in return. We get to see you live your dream."

"But I can't pay you back, Lola," she whispers, looking at me.

"Those are gifts," I say, gesturing to the cheques in her hand.

"I can't do this. I won't be able to afford a place like this, and there are so many expenses—"

"Stop! This is the deal. After you're all started and open, you can have three months to get settled. After that, you can give me affordable monthly payments to buy this place. And before you start saying you can't afford it, you will. I won't be charging full price."

"Why?" she asks, seeming dumbfounded.

"Because I knew you wouldn't accept this as a gift. And if you're anything like Brooke and me, then you'll want to achieve this on your own. You'll want it to be all yours. There's no shame in accepting help, Pagan. If you had gone to a bank to start up, then you'd have to pay back the loan with more interest. You won't—"

Pagan charges into me, knocking the breath out of me. Her arms wrap around my neck and pull me in for a hug, squeezing tightly until I'm wheezing for air.

"Thank you," she whispers, her tears falling on my bare shoulder. "All of you… just… thank you."

"It's our pleasure." I grin, pulling away.

"I don't even know what to say. Thank you seems insufficient compared to what you've done. It's not enough. I feel like there's more I should be saying or doing. It's just… God, this feels like a dream. I'm so overwhelmed right now," she says, wiping under her eyes.

"I know exactly how you're feeling," Brooke says before clearing her throat, and I turn, finding her wiping her own tears away. "She can be really pushy," she says seriously, but her face is full of amusement.

Pagan sputters, laughing before bringing me in for another hug. When we pull apart, an idea occurs to me.

"We should go out and celebrate," I suggest.

"Oh, we could go to The Cavery Inn. Their food is amazing," Brooke moans, making us laugh.

"My treat. To say thank you," Pagan states.

"Let's go, then." I grin before stopping abruptly. "I forgot, these belong to you," I tell Pagan, dropping a set of keys into her palm.

She holds the keys, her hands shaking. She doesn't even blink as she stares down at them. I'm worried she's gone into shock because she's completely frozen, but then her face scrunches up before she abruptly bursts into tears.

"I don't think we should've had that third bottle of wine." I giggle, nearly tripping over my own feet.

The girls giggle at me, trying to hold me up as we enter the bar/club called RJ's.

I still can't believe I let them talk me into getting drunk tonight. Everything was going fine until they broke out the wine. After the third

IF I COULD WISH IT ALL AWAY

glass, I'd already begun to feel lightheaded. I've never gotten drunk before, and I swear the room keeps spinning—or am I the one spinning? I don't know. All I know is that I feel like I'm on cloud nine. My entire body is buzzing, and a new-found confidence flows within me.

"You're not spinning," Pagan laughs.

Shit, I said that out loud.

"Yeah, you did," Brooke calls over Shakira's top hit, 'Hips Don't Lie'.

I groan and lean against the bar. I'm literally squished between the both of them as Pagan goes to order shots. As soon as I hear the word tequila, vomit threatens to rise.

"No, I'll be sick," I moan, my stomach turning. Pagan laughs and orders water for me instead, and I smile, swaying as I give her thumbs-up. I may have stuck my middle finger up at her, I'm not sure. I'm too drunk. "God, I'm so drunk," I whine as we make our way over to a table.

"Me too," Brooke slurs before taking a sip of her wine.

"Me three," Pagan cheers. "I'm opening up my own business," she sing-songs.

We all laugh, and I take in the bar for the first time. It's an upscale place near the town centre. Pagan said it's a normal bar in the day, but at night, it's a little of both, playing club music and sometimes live bands. You can't wear casual clothes to enter either; the dress code strict. I'm glad I decided to go for heels when I woke up this morning instead of my usual dolly shoes.

The furniture is black, or maybe a dark blue? It's hard to tell. The floor is glittery marble, and it shines beautifully against the disco lights.

Hanging from the ceiling are mini chandeliers, each directly over a table. Everything in here looks new. If I owned this, I'd be scared to open it to drunken patrons. The owner is either brave or straight-up crazy.

The song changes to Jennifer Lopez and Pitball's, 'Tonight' and Pagan starts squealing, jumping up and down while throwing her hands in the air. Grabbing onto Brooke and me, she drags us to the dance floor, and I groan. I cannot dance to save my life. A monkey in the zoo has better moves than me. But the second Pagan starts. I don't care anymore. She dances like she has Tourette's or is being attacked by mosquitoes. It almost puts me to shame, and I throw my head back, laughing. I don't hold back when I join her, and neither does Brooke. We all dance like we've just escaped D-block and enjoy every single minute of it.

We're into the sixth song when I suddenly feel cold all over, despite the fact I'm covered in sweat. The hairs on the back of my neck bristle and my legs turn to lead.

"Are you okay?" Brooke asks, seeming to notice the sudden tension in my body.

"Um, yeah," I tell her absently, searching my surroundings. I don't see anything out of the ordinary, and that gives me chills. The place is busier than when we first arrived so the sudden mood change could be because of that, but the sensation of someone watching me doesn't go away.

"You sure?" Pagan asks.

"Yeah. I think I'm ready to home though. Is that okay?"

"Me too. These shoes are killing me," Brooke says, pointing to her high-heeled boots, nearly tipping over in the process.

"Yeah, me three. Let me go to the little girls room, and we can go," Pagan says swiftly before making her way through the crowd to the toilets.

Brooke and I move away from other people dancing and head back over to our.

Another cold chill runs down my spine, and again, I feel eyes watching me. Awareness sobers me a little, and as I scan the sea of faces of those around me, my heart rate picks up.

"Are you sure you're okay?" Brooke asks a couple minutes of watching me shift nervously.

"No," I tell her honestly. The sensation is starting to scare me and each time my skin burns, my heart skips a beat. "You know that feeling you get when you know someone is watching you?" I ask, still scanning the crowd of people. I still don't see anything, but it doesn't stop me from looking.

"Yeah."

"I've been feeling that for a while now, and it's starting to really creep me out. I just want to go home," I tell her, my voice trembling.

"C'mon, let's go and find Pagan. It shouldn't take her this long to go the loo," Brooke says, taking my hand.

We get halfway across the room to the toilets when Pagan materialises out of nowhere. Her face is glowing, a smile splitting across her face as she walks up to us.

"Did you fall down the loo? What took you so long?" Brooke asks, wobbling on her feet.

"I'm going to ignore that comment. I've ordered two taxis for us, so don't get your panties in a twist. I've just met the most charming man ever. He's so gorgeous," she gushes.

"When did you meet him between wiping your doo-dah and flushing the loo?" I laugh when I realise how funny that sounded.

We make our way through the club and step outside into the pouring rain, all three of us squealing and rushing under the hoot they've built for the smoking area.

"We bumped into each other... okay, he bumped into me when I came out of the toilets. He's so dreamy and so unlike any of the other men I've met in my life. They either act like dildos or are just plain immature," she says.

"Seriously? By any chance did he have a friend?" Brooke asks, slurring her words.

"No." Pagan giggles and Brooke groans in disappointment.

A taxi pulls up, calling Brooke's name. We say our goodbyes quickly before watching her run through the rain and into the taxi. We burst out laughing when she falls, sprawling over the back seat before getting up and giving us a sheepish grin, shutting the door.

Just as the taxi drives away, ours pulls up.

Sitting in the taxi, I relax, no longer feeling those eyes burning into me. When I turn to Pagan, she's smiling, grinning from ear to ear as she stares mindlessly out the window.

"C'mon, tell us more about this mystery man. What does he look like?" I ask, because honestly, I'm surprised to see her acting like this over a man.

Dean filled me in on her last relationship which ended badly last year. They'd been dating since they were fifteen, but last year, they broke up after a girl showed up on their doorstep pregnant.

Sleaze bag.

I was glad to hear Dean beat the ever-loving shit out of him. But still, he said Pagan hadn't been serious about a man ever since. And all the dates she forces herself to go out on ends early with her making excuses.

"My God, Lola. He was absolutely gorgeous. A bit older than me, but who cares?" She shrugs. "He has short-cropped brown hair, but long enough for me to run my fingers through it. He's got a strong jaw line, full lips, and I swear, the scar at the corner of his top lip is so incredibly sexy. I could totally picture myself running my tongue over it," she says, causing the taxi driver choke and to swerve the car a little to the right.

Me? I freeze, coiled up so tight it's almost painful.

Rick has brown hair, but so do thousands of other men in the world. So I could be wrong. But Rick also has a scar on his top lip.

He did it the time he threw a glass at me. It ended up hitting the wall and smashing, the glass ricocheting and cutting his lip.

Seeming unaware of my sudden mood change, she carries on.

"He asked for my number. He's gonna call me," she says, grinning excitedly.

I force a smile as my brain tries to process everything. It can't possibly be him. I mean, wouldn't Dean or Grandpa know he was here? Needing to know more, I turn to Pagan.

"What did you say his name was?" I ask, trying to hide the quiver in my voice but failing.

"Oh, best part. He said, and I quote, 'You'll have to wait. It will add to the suspense for when we'll see each other next. And we will. It's only a matter of time.' His voice was so husky." She giggles, jumping in her seat as we pull up to the front entrance of Cabin Lake.

A shiver runs up my spine at her words, feeling they were said directly to me by Rick himself.

"You okay?" she asks when I don't say anything and I turn to face her, nodding. Paying the taxi driver, we both get out and head over to Lily and Mark's, where Pagan has been staying for the past year.

"Thank you for such a good night," I tell her. "I haven't had that much fun in ages."

"Any time, and thank you," she says, her face sobering, eyes softening. "What you've done is unbelievable generous and kind. It was sweet of you, so thank you," she says, her eyes watering.

"Any time." I grin, throwing her words back at her.

"You going to be okay getting back on your own?" she asks, shifting on her feet, and I giggle when I realise she needs to pee.

"Yeah," I tell her, giving her a brief hug before waving goodbye.

I can't wait to get back and shower. Dean said he wouldn't be back until the early hours of the morning, so I'm glad I'll have the chance to wash all of tonight's sweat away.

I haven't spoken to him since this morning, and because of that, I've found myself missing him terribly.

Rounding the corner, turning to the path where my cabin is, a shiver runs up my spine. The feel of a looming danger surfaces. The presence of someone lurking behind me has me pushing forward, pumping my legs to walk faster. Glancing behind me, I squeal. A lone figure looms in the shadows at the corner I just rounded.

I start running, bloody pumping through my veins and I don't stop, not even when my cabin comes into view.

A twig snapping to my left has warning bells ringing in my head, and when I look over my shoulder, the shadowy figure is closer. My pulse quickens, sweat soaking my forehead and the back of my neck.

When I finally reach my door something compels me to take another.
I couldn't have imagined that, could I?

I keep scanning the area, trying to find the shadowy form; anything, really, to prove I'm not losing my mind. I've had a lot to drink, so that could be the reason my imagination is running wild and I'm seeing things that aren't there.

Jesus, it's most likely some tenant having a fag outside their cabin. However, the eerie feeling of someone watching is still there, looming over me, and it's unnerving.

A piercing scream escapes me when two strong hands land on my shoulders. Sheer terror runs through me and I begin to shake uncontrollably.

Stepping forward, I turn and end up tripping over my own feet. My eyes close, ready for the shooting pain to come, but when it doesn't, I open my eyes and notice I'm in Dean's arms.

Dean!

Relaxing, I giggle, feeling stupid for being scared in the first place.

"I'm sorry," I chuckle, feeling my face heat.

"What was that about?" he asks, concern etched into his features, but then he pauses, looking me over and taking in my appearance. He leans in, sniffing the air close to my mouth and I move back, frowning. "Have you been drinking?" His lips twitch with amusement.

"Just a little bit." I giggle, holding my thumb and forefinger close together. "What are you doing back so early?"

He takes my hand, pulling me into the front room and closing the door behind us. "I finished early to surprise you, but you weren't here. I knew you were with Pagan and Brooke, but then Mom called asking if I wanted dinner, explaining you went out to celebrate," he explains, guiding me into the bedroom.

Gently, he starts removing my clothes. When he sets me on the soft mattress, I realise how tired I really am, and I yawn.

"Now are you going to explain what had you so spooked outside?" he asks, kneeling in front of me.

"It's silly." I shrug.

"Try me."

He seems genuinely interested, and I find myself, telling him everything that happened at the club and outside. "So you see, I'm being silly, right?"

He doesn't look so convinced, and I run my finger along his frown lines, hating him being so worried.

"Honestly, it was me being paranoid. I think outside had more to do with what Pagan said to me in the taxi," I tell him absently.

He's grabbing one of his shirts for me to wear to bed when he turns around sharply, eyeing me curiously.

"What did my sister say?" he asks, looking ready to throttle his sister.

"She met some bloke at the club tonight and seemed really smitten over him so I asked her what he looked like...." I rattle off, pausing at the reminder.

"Go on."

"It felt like she was describing Rick to me," I whisper, picturing the scar. The same scar I stared at countless of times just so I didn't have to look into those soulless black eyes of his.

"Did you see him?" Dean asks loudly, and I realise he'd been talking to me. His body is strung tight, looking alert.

"No," I rush out, shaking my head. "Rick has a scar on his top lip, in the corner, and when she described the bloke she met having the same one, I thought it was him. But it's not him, is it? I'm just drunk and being stupid."

I yawn, swaying on the bed as he pulls the shirt over my head, helping me pull my arms through.

"I don't know, baby. I'm going to go have a look around outside. Why don't you get into bed and get some sleep? I'll be back in a bit," he says, but before he can step away, I take his hand in mine, stopping him.

"Stay with me?" I yawn. "I don't want to be on my own."

"Okay, love."

He picks me up, helping me to bed, but before he even gets in, my eyes are closed. The last thing I remember is curling up to him and feeling at home before falling into a deep sleep.

Chapter Twenty-Seven

Eight Weeks Later

The time has come.

Tomorrow is the grand opening of our stores, and I couldn't be more excited. I've never been happier than I am right now.

Dean is the cause for my blissful outlook on life right now. Having him and his family—my family—around me is another huge factor. I just wish my grandpa were here to see it.

But Dean has been my saving grace. He's helped me push all my worry and concerns aside and focus all my attention on life. And I have. Being with him is something else entirely; it's magic in its purest form, and I couldn't bear to live without him. He's helped me through so much, and I'll never forget that.

I've been thinking about other women in my situation, some of whom are going or have gone through a lot worse than me. And knowing there are millions of other women out there encountering this kind of abuse has me wanting to help them.

So I've offered the Women's Aid group my shop for meetings, although we've yet to discuss a time or a day because we'll need to work around each other's schedules. I'll need to know when to close my store for the hour the meetings take place.

I've learnt so much about other victims and what they've been through. I even understand why some of them don't leave. Like me, some are scared of the consequences if they're caught. Some stay because they've been manipulated into distancing themselves and becoming secluded from their friends and family. Others stay because it's the only think they know; it's their norm, and they hold onto what they have, feeling like that's their worth.

If I could go back in time and give the younger, naive me, and many women like me, some advice, I'd tell us we were beautiful and worthy and remind each one of us that life only happens once and not to waste it on someone toxic. I'd tell them promises mean nothing and to only trust people's actions because, after all, actions are worth more than a thousand promises.

Sometimes in life you're dealt with a shitty hand, but it's what you make of it that's important. We deserve a life filled with love and joy, not filled with fear and pain.

"Are you okay?" Lorelei asks, snapping me out of my daydream.

Lorelei is one of my staff members. She's absolutely stunning with her white-blonde hair that hangs down past her waist and her emerald green eyes. She's so shy and timid, and I know there's a story she keeps hidden behind those haunted eyes of her. It's a look that you shouldn't see on someone so young and beautiful.

"Sorry. I'm just feeling a little out of it. Did Jeremy get the last few boxes of books ready?" I ask, mentioning my other staff member who is three years older than Lorelei's twenty-four.

He's more of an outgoing person and has a bubbly, funny and charming personality. He's also incredibly hot. He has a sharp figure, a swimmer's build, and brown eyes to die for. But only if you can get past the pain that fills them.

He might come across as arrogant and cocky, but there's definitely something deeper there, and he just uses all that to hide behind.

"Yeah," she whispers, blushing, and I smiling knowingly. Then I remember what I need to talk to her about, and I pause.

"Hey, Lorelei, can I talk to you for a minute?"

"Yes, of course."

"Dean and I were talking the other night, and we've both agreed on this. There was no pause or hesitation on either side, but we will understand if you don't take up on our offer," I say softly.

"Okay," she says slowly, looking confused and skittish, like she's about to bolt.

"We want to offer you Dean's cabin to live in," I tell her. I lose my smile when she pales, and I begin to feel bad for interfering.

"How did you know?" she whispers and guilt fills my chest.

"Dean. He had to do a background check on all of you," I cringe.

Lorelei, although I don't know why, has been sleeping in a grubby, run-down bed and breakfast. Once he told me, I knew I had to do something. She doesn't belong in a place like that. Anything could happen to her there.

"Is that why you hired me?" she asks, her voice low and filled with hurt. She's breaking my heart.

"No! Not at all. I hired you before he even did the checks. I promise you," I tell her. "Please take it. It's not much. It's a one bedroom cabin over at Cabin Lake, where we live, and it's yours if you want it. You won't be putting anyone out, I promise. It's literally sitting there empty."

"I'm not a charity case," she says defensively, her eyes watering. "I can take care of myself. I don't need anyone."

"No one said you were," I tell her softly. "*That* is why I hired you. You're strength, will and the fire burning inside that kind, sweet heart of yours. It's also why we're offering Dean's place to you."

She wipes her eyes, looking down at her feet. "I can't afford it. I can barely afford where I'm staying now," she whispers, still not looking me in the eye, and that saddens me.

"Lorelei, if I make you a deal, will you at least think it over?" I ask, and she looks at me sceptically. Taking that as a good sign, I continue. "How about we give you two months free rent so you can settle in, get some money behind you. Then after those two months we can arrange a low monthly payment you can afford for rent. Will that help make a decision?"

If she says no I have no idea what I'm going to do.

"I don't know," she says, fidgeting. The fact she hasn't shot me down straight away gives me some hope, so I head straight to plan C.

Emotional blackmail.

"Do you want to feel safe? Do you want stability a home?" I ask sharply, yet keeping my voice as soft as possible. "I know I'm being pushy and I hate it, but I really want the girl I've come to care about a lot to be safe. I want to know she's been looked after."

"Okay." She sighs. "But I'll pay rent?" she asks, and I nod, grinning.

"This is so great. I've already got you a new mattress and bed sheets. Dean's were gross," I ramble, scrunching my nose up.

She giggles, shaking her head at me. She's so used to my outbursts that she doesn't question them anymore. "You're mad. You didn't need to do that. Thank you." She smiles, but then her expression freezes for a second before she loses her smile and her eyes widen. "*How* did you know I'd say yes?"

I shrug. "Dean and I made sure I asked you with a plan A, B, C, and D."

"Really? What was plan D?" she teases.

"Kidnap you." I giggle.

"Lola, Pagan keeps bossing me around," Jeremy blurts out, walking up the stairs to my office. Lorelei jumps, her cheeks reddening and as she seems to fold into herself.

"What are you whining about now?" I ask, trying to come across as stern.

"Pagan. She's having me running around like a headless chicken. 'Do this, Jeremy. Get that for me, Jeremy. Make me a cup of coffee, Jeremy. Bend over and let me spank you, Jeremy'," he says, mimicking Pagan.

"I asked you once. *Once*, Jeremy!" Pagan shouts up, and we all laugh.

Pagan has been working her ass off getting everything ready for tomorrow's opening. With my store, Brooke's and hers, she's had her hands full. We decided to use our opening event to promote Pagan's new business. It will be great PR for her.

"Once is enough. Your dad looked like he was going to kill me," he shouts back down, shuddering before turning back to me. "I'll do anything, *anything* for you as long as I don't have to answer to her a second longer."

I laugh, and a small giggle escapes Lorelei, who has moved farther away from the door where Jeremy is standing.

He turns sharply, apparently just noticing she was in the room. A small smirk falls on his lips, his cocky attitude appearing as he stands straighter, eyeing her up.

"You can boss me around any day of the week." He winks.

Lorelei scrunches her nose up. "Go away, then," she mutters quietly.

"One day, pretty eyes, you'll be begging to boss me around," he tells her cheerfully.

"You can go," I tell Jeremy, letting him off the hook. We've got a long day tomorrow, and I'll need him in a happy mood if I plan on making it through the day.

"Really?"

"Yes, now go before I change my mind." I laugh.

"Jeremy, take the bin bags out before you leave," Pagan shouts, and we all burst out laughing. He groans and shakes his head, muttering curses under his breath before leaving.

"Bye, pretty eyes," he shouts up the stairs, and Lorelei blushes. When I give her a pointed look, she ignores me, playing it off.

"What?"

"Nothing," I tease. "I'm going to finish this, and then I'll take you to get your stuff from the bed and breakfast. You can sit downstairs and take a break."

"I'll help. I like to keep busy."

"There isn't much to do. Why don't you go make sure everything is ready downstairs?"

"Okay. If you need me to do anything else, just shout," she says and walks to the door. Once she's in the doorway, she pauses, turning back to me. "Thank you, Lola. For everything. Can you tell Dean I said thank you too?"

"Of course," I say softly.

IF I COULD WISH IT ALL AWAY

She nods, seeming uncomfortable, and leaves the room, heading down the spiral staircase to the ground floor.

I look around my newly furnished office and sigh with contentment. My stomach is fluttering like mad, nerves turning my stomach over as I think about tomorrow and the future.

I've already got some editing lined up. As soon as my website went live, I had multiple enquiries and have a list of indie authors I'll be working with. I think it helps I have the qualifications because one author mentioned her last editor was someone who seemed to have read a book, found a few mistakes and labelled herself an editor. I don't think people realise the hard work that goes into editing a document. It's not just about finding a simple spelling mistake, but about story flow and grammar, amongst other things.

I was lucky Pagan knew how to set up the website for my new business because I had no idea. It's bizarre seeing my name up there above the shop and on my website, but I'm glad I went with what I did.

I've gone with the nickname my mom would whisper to me when she was alive. She'd use it as a way to comfort me or in a loving way. So when the time came to name the store, I went with 'Lo Lo' and had 'believe, love, live, dream' scrawled underneath in italic bold writing.

The name means a lot to me, as does the store. I'm hoping my parents are looking down on me and are proud.

Stepping around my L-shaped desk, I switch off my luminous purple computer, stacking the files of papers in a pile and putting them aside for when I start work in a few days. With everything going on, I know I won't have time to start anything until the buzz from the store has calmed down, so I've tried to do as much as I can.

I really do love my office. It's the only place in the store that has plain colours. I opted for black furniture, wanting it to come across as sophisticated, and decorated the place with luminous colours. My pen pot is yellow, my stapler green and my hole-puncher sky blue. There are other bits and bobs amongst them but my favourites, apart from my computer are the flower pots Pagan said would look beautiful on my walls. So on small, plain white shelves, different colour flower pots are scattered around the room, all filled with daisies.

I have another straightforward desk behind me against the wall with a printer, fax machine, scanner and other bits I'll need. The filing cabinets are on the far wall in front of me, a sofa on the back wall with a coffee table.

It was originally meant to be open-plan since, before I had the floor-length windows in and a door built at the top of the stairs, it was only separated by single metal bars. But because I'll need the silence to work, I had the renovations built.

Moving to the window, I smile, looking down. Everything is how I pictured it would be. I'm still in shock that we managed to get different coloured desks, computers, mice, and keyboards. We had to paint the bookshelves and special order the sofas from the place Brooke ordered hers from. There are a few table and chairs but not many. I wanted people to be comfortable and relaxed here. All in all, I'm over the moon at how it's all turned out.

Switching the light off I lock up and move downstairs, smiling wide when I see everything is ready for tomorrow. Pagan has made sure there'll be little to do as possible. However, we'll still need to be here nice and early in case we run into any problems.

"I'm all done," Pagan calls as she walks back in the front.

Lorelei turns, noticing me, and smiles. "Me too."

"So we're done. This is really going to happen?"

"It sure is." Pagan grins.

"I've had my store for years, yet I'm nervous as a fat kid on a diet in McDonald's," Brooke says, walking in from where our stores are joined.

We all laugh, and I roll my eyes. "Are you finished?" I ask, my stomach twisting in knots. I swear I'm going to be sick because of all the nerves.

"Yeah. You okay? You look a little pale."

"Yeah, it's just nerves. I'm hoping it goes once I have a sleep." I chuckle.

"Everything is going to be fine. I promise. And it's my job to worry, not yours. It's why you hired me," Pagan reminds me, and I nod.

"Okay. I guess I'll see you all tomorrow." I smile, looking at my best friends. It's so weird calling them that, because they feel like much more to me. Even Lorelei means more to me and I've only known her a few short weeks.

"Do you need a lift back?" Pagan asks.

"No. I need to take Lorelei to get her stuff. She's been looking for a place closer to live, so we offered her Dean's," I lie. I have a feeling Lorelei wouldn't like it if I blurted out where she was staying. She seemed upset enough with Dean and me knowing.

"It's about time. Mom and Dad were worried it would sit empty for years. They'll be pleased to know you'll be living there. It was one of the first cabins built," Pagan informs us.

Lorelei seems to relax and looks a lot better about staying at Dean's. I want to kiss Pagan right then, but then she'll know something is up.

I lock up and turn to Brooke and Pagan, smiling. "I guess I'll see you in the morning." I grin.

"I'll be the one next door," Brooke teases.

"And I'll be across the road." Pagan laughs.

We say our goodbyes, and Lorelei and I head to grab her things. The journey has the nerves in my stomach swirling violently. I don't know why I'm getting myself worked up over tomorrow. I don't understand it, not when I'm this excited.

Nothing could go wrong. We have everything figured out.

Chapter Twenty-Eight

"I'm so proud of you." Dean grins, hugging me to him.

I look over my shoulder at him, smiling giddily. "Everything looks perfect," I tell him, looking around at all the open stalls.

We have a few children's stalls that have face painting, arts and crafts and another stand where you can make your own dreamcatcher. We even got the cancer research charity shop involved, and they've opened up a few stalls outside their shop, filling it with random items. Everything looks amazing and it's all thanks to Pagan.

She managed to get permission to close the street off so we could set up a stage at the end of the road. Sid and his students will be up later, showing off their incredible talent. A bucket will be placed at the side of the stage to raise funds for new music equipment.

"I can't believe Pagan managed to get all this done *and* her own shop."

He presses me tighter against him. "She's a miracle worker, but you all did this together," he says as he eyes where his sister shop is.

She has a few roller banners outside with pictures of previous events and a table between the two banners with leaflets, explaining what she offers.

Speaking of flyers, my eyes scan the crowd for Gill, a woman who has volunteered from the local church to help out. She's handing out fliers and the way she's chatting away, I can tell she's enjoying it.

Dean's phone rings and our blissful moment of peace is interrupted. I knew our solitary wouldn't last long.

"Hello?" Dean answers and as he listens, I watch his body grow tight and his jaw clench. "I'll be there in ten minutes."

"Is everything okay?" I ask, worried about the exchange and how quickly it changed his mood.

"Yeah, but I have to go back to Cabin Lake. Dad just called saying there's a problem he needs me to go see," he tells me, and I narrow my eyes suspiciously. I feel like he's just told me the truth as a lie, like he skirted around what's really happening, but instead of questioning him, I just nod.

"Okay. It's nothing serious, is it?"

"Shouldn't be," he says, forcing a tight-lipped smile.

"Okay, well I'll see you later, then." I smile, not wanting to come across whiny.

"I'll be back as soon as I can, baby, I promise," he says, seeming to relax. He pulls me against his front and kisses me.

I moan against his lips, and I'm breathless by the time he pulls away, gazing down at me with hunger in his eyes.

"I'm proud of you," he whispers. "Now go and have fun."

"I do need to check on Jeremy and Lorelei." I nod and kiss him once more before letting him go. He makes his way through the growing crowd, and I don't move until I lose sight of him.

Sighing, I turn, making my way into the shop, shuffling through the line of people waiting to get a look at the store or a cup of coffee or tea.

My stomach coils the minute I smell coffee beans and fresh-baked goods. I place a hand on my belly and pause, waiting for the nausea to ease.

"Hey, you okay?" Jeremy asks. "Need me to sweep you off your feet?"

"I'll tell Dean you said that." I chuckle, breathing through my nose.

"Please don't. The dude scares me a little."

"A little?" I laugh, remembering the first time Dean and Jeremy met. Jeremy had been his normal, charming self and when he was flirting his way into getting the job, Dean had turned up and put him straight.

Although now that we know Jeremy is a natural flirt, Dean chooses to ignore him. Plus, it's only harmless.

Something tells me if Jeremy were ever to really need to flirt with a girl he actually liked for more than a hookup, he wouldn't know what to do.

"Okay, a lot."

"How is everything going in here?" I eye the tables, a few cups and other things littering them, and I frown.

"Don't worry. We've got it now. One of the volunteers from the church has come in to help with a few other people. The queue is endless so we got behind on the tables."

"It's okay. Did you need me to help?"

"No. No, we got this now," he says, waving me off.

"If I knew it would get this busy I would have hired more people," I murmur.

"Yeah, you'll have to start looking soon. If it keeps up like this, you'll need morning and afternoon staff. Just don't forget who was here first." He winks.

"I'll make a note of it." I chuckle and move to the counter to where Lorelei is running around ragged, the coffee machine steaming behind her.

It seemed like she actually slept last night, for the first time, she turned up without dark shadows under her eyes.

"Hey." She waves, handing over a coffee to someone whilst another lady rings up some books next to her.

"You okay? Do you need...?" I pause, my stomach rolling again, and I cover my mouth with my hand.

"Are you okay? What's wrong?" Lorelei rushes out as she abandons the next customer.

I wave her off, unable to speak, and grab the bottle of water that's offered to me. "Thank you." I gulp it down, then take a smaller sip. "My stomach is in knots. It's probably because I spent the whole night worrying if I had everything done."

"Go get some fresh air. We have everything handled in here, and I'm sure Sid's band and class start performing soon," she reminds me, looking over at the bright coral clock on the wall.

"Yeah, maybe fresh air will do me some good," I tell her absently, still feeling a little off.

"I'll check on you in a little bit."

I nod at Lorelei and make my way out of the store, finding an empty seat. Overhead, clouds start rolling in, and I pray it doesn't start raining. It's not something we planned since it was meant to stay dry all day, but with British weather, you never know what you'll get.

Sid's band is introduced on stage by Pagan, her smile wide and full of fondness for her dear twin brother. You can tell how proud she is by the tone in her voice.

Then he steps up to the mike, the first beat to the melody booming through the speakers before his voice soars through and I'm lost. It's hypnotising, smooth and the song is an original, one of their own. It's soft like a lullaby, right up until the rest of the band joins in, and the beat picks up.

"They're good, aren't they?" Pagan beams from beside me, causing me to jump.

"They're brilliant," I answer honestly, my head swaying side to side with the beat.

"How is everything going? Hey, are you okay? You look a little pale."

"I'm good. I think I'm just sick with nerves. I don't know what's wrong with me today. I think all the excitement has overwhelmed me a little," I admit.

"I know the feeling. I can't believe how many people turned up. I think the adults are having as much fun as the kids." She giggles and we both eye a group of moms getting their faces painted.

"It's been successful. You should be proud. You've done a great job," I tell her, squeezing her hand.

"*We* did a great job," she corrects, and I roll my eyes. The woman has done most of the work. She deserves more than I could ever give her. Secretly, I think she just likes bossing everyone around.

"Yeah, yeah."

She opens her mouth to say something when someone calls her name. She huffs out a breath and rolls her eyes.

"I'm being summoned," she mutters. "I'll check in soon."

"Have fun," I call out, waving. Once she's gone, I slump into the chair, feeling my stomach tighten.

A few hours pass and I'm sitting back down after running round helping to keep things flowing smoothly. Sid and his class are singing B.O.B's 'Airplanes'. Everyone is transfixed, listening to their harmony, the song much slower than the original. Sid is an amazing teacher and the kids clearly love him. Not one has been rude, stuck-up or tried to sabotage the show. They've all looked up to him, hanging on his every word.

My stomach isn't any better, and I'm starting to feel a little light-headed. It started to become worse once the crowd picked up; every step I take, I'm bumping into someone. I'm just glad I've managed this long without having a panic attack. I don't do crowds at all, but large ones like this? Well, my sickness says it all.

I look down at my phone to see if Dean has got back to me, but there's still no word. I've tried calling Lily and Mark but both their phones just ring out.

Needing to call Dean before I lose my mind, I unlock my phone, but before I can dial his number, a light tap on my shoulder distracts me.

Turning around, I see a young boy of around fourteen shifting nervously, his cheeks red.

"Hey there, can I help you?" I ask.

"Are you Miss Lola?" he asks, and I smile wide. He's so adorable, with sandy blonde hair and dark hazel eyes. He's a few inches smaller than I am, wearing the music T-shirt with the school logo and plain denim jeans.

"Yes, that's me. Is everything okay?"

"Miss Pagan, Mr Salvatore's sister said to come and ask you if you could grab the box of leaflets out of her car. She said she would go herself but she's in the middle of talking to some potential clients. But if you'd like, I can go and get them from her car. You can trust me. I'm here with Mr Salvatore. I'm one of his students. My name's Alec. I guess I should have said that first, huh? He said we have to stay and help," he rambles, his face becoming redder. He looks so embarrassed to talk to me, and it's kind of cute.

"Hi Alec." I smile. "If you wait here, I'll grab the keys from my office and then we'll walk round and get them. Is that okay?"

"Yes, that's fine."

"Don't move. I'll be five minutes tops," I warn him, not wanting to get one of Sid's students lost.

"I promise, Miss Lola."

I nod, and walk off, smiling wide as I think what a gentleman he is. Most kids his age would have gone off and done their own thing, no matter what their teacher said, so for him to help and actually look like he wants to be there is respectable.

Outside the store, I try to get through the line of people, but the place seems too crowded. Looking through the window, I notice Lorelei, Jeremy, and a few more volunteers than there were there earlier are all busy serving and clearing up.

Hiring a few more staff members will be the first thing I do tomorrow.

Taking one last look at the crowd of people, I sigh and head around back.

The alley is colder in the shade, and a chill runs up my spine. The darkened sky and brick overhead leaves little light in the small area.

There's a tingle at the back of my neck I sense someone watching me. My stomach twists and the impulse to run is strong. Unlike the other times, I actually feel someone nearby, and it makes my skin crawl.

The nausea I've had on and off all day has returned, but this time, there's an uneasy feeling churning inside my stomach.

Feeling compelled, I look back down the alley and find it empty. That sense of dread hits me hard, and I quicken my pace to the back. My eyes only do a quick scan of the car park since my heart is racing and my mind is screaming at me to run, that danger is lurking.

Rushing over to the back door, I nearly sigh with relief. Grabbing the handle, the voices on the other side give me a sense of safety, and I go to push open the door.

But a sharp pain in the back of my head knocks me to my knees. Before I can register what's happening, a shooting pain in my right arm has me blacking out.

IF I COULD WISH IT ALL AWAY

The last thing I remember is reaching out in front of me, trying to beg for help, but no sound coming out.

Chapter Twenty-Nine

Two Hours Earlier

Dean

The car skids to a stop outside the main cabin where Dad is waiting for me. His face is pinched with worry, and a furious look fills his expression.

When he called me, he only said something bad had happened, that I needed to get home quick and not mention anything to Lola. That said everything. If I couldn't tell her, then it was most likely something to do with her.

I don't wait to turn the car off before I'm jumping out, looking at my dad for answers.

"What's going on, Dad?"

"Your cabin's been ransacked, son. It's a complete mess. I've called the police, but it's whenever they get time to get out here with everything going on in town."

"C'mon, let's see what's missing. It could be kids, Dad. Shit. Lorelei just moved in there," I hiss. That girl has already been through a lot, she doesn't need to feel unsafe, not now.

"Son, it wasn't your old place. It was yours and Lola's."

"C'mon. You drive. I'm gonna call in a favour." Getting in the car, I grab my phone and text Cage.

DEAN: Mate, I need you at Cabin Lake, cabin 24A. Urgent.
CAGE: On my way.

Arriving at the cabin, I only have to step out the car to see what my dad was talking about.

"Did you go in?" I ask.

"No, I called you straight away."

IF I COULD WISH IT ALL AWAY

"Good." I stand in the doorway, my eyes doing a quick sweep of the mess. The place has been turned upside down, my laptop and Lola's Kindle on the floor completely smashed to pieces. Whoever did this did it in anger, in rage. Dread fills my stomach, and I take a seat outside, waiting for Cage and the other officers to come.

"Where's Mom?"

"Back at the cabin worried sick. I told her to stay there with the doors locked until I get back. I didn't want to risk the person still being around."

I nod, running a frustrated hand through my hair. "C'mon, hurry up," I curse, anxiety building inside me.

"Keep it together, son."

"I don't know, Dad. I have a bad feeling about this. Something is telling me to go get Lola."

"Son, she's surrounded by hundreds of people. Nothing is going to happen to her."

I nod, knowing he's right. "Yes."

Nearly two hours later and the police still haven't come out and given me anything. We aren't allowed in there while they take fingerprints and whatnot. I'm just glad Cage and his partner are here because I'm about to lose my shit.

"Cage!" I shout inside the doorway, earning a few glares from some officers. I narrow my eyes, not caring.

Lola has called and texted a few times. I hate that I've ignored her, but I didn't want to have to lie to her again. It's one of the things I promised never to do.

"Hey, Dean. We're almost done, but you can come in."

"About time." He raises his eyebrow at me. "Sorry, I'm just stressed. Did you find anything?"

"Yes but first, has anything gone missing?" he asks.

"No. Not that I could tell from looking in the doorway, anyway. You can see my laptop and Lola's Kindle from here. Whoever broke in wasn't after anything valuable," I say, frustrated.

"We know. I just needed to make sure. I need you to keep it together, but we found something, and it's not going to be easy to hear," he starts and my gut clenches.

"Tell me," I growl.

He gestures for me to follow him and when he walks into mine and Lola's bedroom, a sick I find it hard to keep it together as promised.

He turns to me before I make it fully into the room, trying to block me from seeing something. However, I catch a glimpse of Lola's clothes everywhere, and I look to my dad in horror.

"Calm down," he whispers. My fists clench and I breathe through my nose.

"We've had to bag some lingerie and take it to the lab. Whoever this person was is sick and twisted, and left you a present as such." He winces, and I know what he's trying to say.

I turn around, punching a hole through the door. I don't feel the pain or care I'm getting blood everywhere.

Why didn't I see this fucking coming?

"Is there anyone who would want to hurt you or the other occupant of the house, Dean?"

"Yeah," I croak out, pulling the ends of my hair. "Fuck." My roar echoes around the room and my dad steps forward, ready to restrain me if need be.

I grab my phone and dial Lola's number but it rings out, and I start pacing, cursing.

"What am I missing?" Dad asks.

I curse again, turning to both of them. "It's Rick. Lola's ex is crazy. He beat her, raped her and has punished her for leaving before. It's him. We've been keeping tabs on him, but eight weeks ago we lost all contact, and no one has been able to find him since," I explain.

"Fuck!" Cage curses then takes out his phone before turning to me. "I need a name and description."

I do one better, taking my work phone from my pocket and opening the folder I have on him. The picture of Rick loads first, along with his name, height, address and date of birth. Cage calls it in, walking away a little.

As soon as he does I lose my shit, a primal roar rumbling from my chest when I see the bed, Rick's *present* is soaking into it.

"Oh fuck," Dad says, face pale.

"Call Dwayne," I tell him, trying Lola one more time. "Why isn't she fucking answering?"

"Pagan isn't answering either, son, but it could be because they can't hear their phones."

"No. Something's happened. I can feel it. Cage, see if there are any uniforms close to Diamond Street and get them to check on a Lola Lawson. She's not answering, and neither is my sister or Brooke, her best friend."

"Sid isn't either," Dad informs me.

IF I COULD WISH IT ALL AWAY

Tears of panic surface and I try to lock them down.

"We need to go. Cage, do you have your patrol car?"

"Yeah, why?"

"I need you to get me over there as quick as you can," I tell him, knowing he can break every law to get us there quicker.

He nods and gives orders to the remaining officers. Dad calls Mom, letting her know what's happening and that he'll call if there are any changes.

Half way to Lola's the police radio cackles and my face pales.

"This is dispatch. We need immediate backup over Carnal Street on the car park."

Cage looks over at me, seeing my pale complexion. "Isn't that…?"

"Yeah, it's the car park at the back of Lola's," I whisper as my heart plummets to the ground.

Cage puts his foot down, and I'm thrown back in my seat. Dad's phone rings and he answers, sounding relieved but then I hear, my sister and all hope I had disappears.

"Calm down. We're pulling up now. Everything is going to be okay," he says, but my sister keeps crying on the other end, loud enough for Cage and me to hear.

"C'mon," Cage says as he pulls to a stop.

I'm out first, leaving Dad and Cage behind. Rushing over to the car park that's taped off, I see Pagan with a young lad crying in her arms, looking pale and scared.

What the fuck!

I duck under the tape, and a police officer steps forward, trying to stop me. "Sir, you can't go back there. It's a crime scene."

"Like fuck I can't. Where is she? Is she okay? Lola?" I shout, looking around for her. But if she was here then she would be with my sister, consoling her.

My eyes water at the image of Lola alone and hurt. God, if anything happened to her… I don't know what I'd do.

"Stop!" the officer growls but then steps to the side, seeing someone behind me.

"Dean?" my sister calls out, her voice hollow and filled with pain. I rush over to where she's standing and place my hands on her shoulders. I feel sorry for not asking if she's okay but I only have one person on my mind right now.

"Where is she?" I croak, still scanning the forming crowd.

"Oh God," she says, looking ready to vomit. "There was so much blood, Dean… so much."

"Pagan!" I shout, shaking her, but she keeps crying, falling into Dad's arms when he shows up. Looking down at the young lad, I give him a look, and he sniffles.

"It's my fault. I should have gone with her. Pagan told me to ask Lola to get some leaflets out of her car. I should have gone with her, but she told me to stay where I was, and she'd be back in a minute." He sniffles. "When Pagan came to see where the leaflets were and found out Lola still hadn't come back, we come round to look for her." He takes a deep swallow, choking back a sob. Pagan hears the struggle in his voice and takes him back in her arms, looking at me with red, puffy eyes.

"We walked into the staff room, and the back door was open. We thought she went to get them by herself, but when we stepped outside, there was blood everywhere. She was nowhere to be seen, Dean. I looked everywhere after I called the police," she cries.

"Shush, my darling girl. This isn't your fault," Dad consoles her.

"If I hadn't asked her to get the leaflets, none of this would have happened," she cries, and the boy starts crying harder. My chest aches for them both.

"Hey, kid," I call, trying to soften my voice.

"Yeah?"

"It wasn't your fault, okay. It's not yours either, Pagan. Let me go see what they've found out," I say, needing to do something.

I step over to Cage, giving him a chin lift. "Hey, any news?"

"We have a witness. He's in the back of the ambulance at the moment being treated for some bruises and scrapes."

"What did he see?"

"He was walking his dog when he saw an older man in his mid-thirties carrying a young woman in his arms. He watched as he placed her in the back seat of his car and didn't think anything of it. He just presumed she was asleep or not feeling well, but then he heard the woman screaming. By the time he got there the offender was already in the car. The witness barely made it out of the way in time. He only managed to get the car make and half a number plate. We're running it now and have police out searching for the vehicle's description."

I nod and start pacing. How the fuck has this happened? And why the fuck didn't anyone know he was here? Not only do I have men working on the case but so does Dwayne. Surely one of us should have picked up on him being here.

Everything seems to be fucked up at the moment.

The signs were there he was here. Hell, Lola said she could feel someone watching her. Although I double-checked the area of Cabin Lake twice, I didn't see anything, but I looked into it even further myself.

Then a thought occurs to me. The only thing I didn't check up on was the mystery man Lola said Pagan met.

"Pagan, come here. I need to ask you something."

Fuck!

It all makes sense.

It was Rick watching her at the club, and he followed them home. And if he didn't follow them he could have easily asked Pagan where they lived. I know deep down it's him.

"What's wrong? What did they say?" she asks, walking over with Brooke, who looks just as much of a mess as the rest of us. I glance over her shoulder, watching Dad say something to Sid who is comforting the boy.

"Do you remember the night you, Brooke and Lola went out to celebrate? It was about eight weeks ago now."

She nods, looking confused. "Yeah, why?"

"Lola mentioned you met a man. What she didn't tell you, because she wasn't sure, was that you described her ex-boyfriend to her, the one who was violent. So I need you to remember everything you can about that night and this bloke, because I think she was right about him. Can you remember anything you said or he told you that could help us find out where Lola is?" I ask, crossing my fingers that she has something, anything. Even the smallest thing would be better than nothing right now.

Pagan pales and nods, her body shaking. "Um… I don't really remember much of that night if I'm honest. It was all a blur. I remember giving him my mobile number and mentioning where I lived. He asked who I was out with and I told him. It was general stuff. Normal stuff you'd ask people you just met." She shrugs, but then pales further, gasping. "Oh no! I invited him here today, but I've not seen him. What if it was him and I basically led him right to her? Oh God."

"Fuck!" I roar, knowing my gut was right. Why the fuck didn't I look into it? I should have. It's my job to look into everything, even the smallest things, no matter how pointless they may seem, but it simply didn't cross my mind. I'm going to be kicking myself for a very long time over it.

"I'm so sorry, Dean. I didn't know. If I did, I would have said something to you. I'm so sorry," she chants, and Brooke pulls her into her arms.

"Did he say anything else, Pagan? Think! Did he say where he was staying? What was his name?" Cage asks, stepping in.

I pause, staring at my sister as I wait for her to answer. "Think!" I snap, and my dad sends me a warning look.

"Yes! Yes, he did. He said he was staying locally for business and mentioned having something he needed to collect before heading back home. And his name is Carl Holmes," she tells Cage, not looking at me. She looks to my dad, breaking down. "It was her, wasn't it? It was Lola he needed to collect."

"Yeah, baby," he murmurs, rubbing her back.

"No, that's good. Hopefully, he's dumb enough to use that name. I'm going to call it in," Cage says before stepping away.

I walk in the other direction, taking my own phone out and dialling Darius, one of the men who work for me.

"Hey, man, I need you to do a check on every bed and breakfast, housing, car rental, anything you can find out on a Carl Holmes."

"Is this about that Patrick bloke?"

"Yep."

"Done," he says and hangs up. I turn to my family, watching them all comforting one another and it has me wanting to snap at them. No one deserves to be consoled until Lola is found. I know I'm coming across as an asshole, but she's my life, my everything. Without her, there will be no me.

Lola, I'm coming for you.

Chapter Thirty

Lola

I wake up feeling groggy, my head pounding and my body sore all over. I feel like I've been thrown around and run over a few times.

Trying to sit up is useless; I just fall back down onto a mattress, my hands going to my aching head. Wetness coats my hand and I bring it to my face, a gasp escaping me as I take in the blood. Touching my head again in a panic, I wince at the pain and then it all comes back to me. I was hit when I was outside the back of my store.

"Dean?" I croak, needing him.

"Hey, you're awake," Rick says, and my entire body freezes, my head slowly rising to find him sitting in a wooden chair at the end of the bed.

"Oh God, no!" I say out loud, tears falling from my eyes as I stare at the man who has haunted my nightmares for years and years. The air leaves my lungs, and I struggle to breathe. In a panic, I fall from the bed, landing with a thud on the floor.

"Oh no, you don't," Rick growls and I cry out when he touches me. His arms go beneath my armpits, lifting me and throwing me back against the bed, my head banging on the wooden headboard. I wince, hissing with pain and my hand goes to the back of my head, feeling more blood. I start to struggle when he looms above me, pinning my wrists to the bed.

"Get off me!" I shout, and he grins down at me with a twisted expression.

"My, my, haven't we grown a backbone. But it's no use, Lola. You're mine, and you'll submit to me," he sneers.

"No. No! Get off me. Help!"

"Don't fight me, Lola. You're loose, baby," he snarls, lifting his fist into the air and landing a hard blow to my right cheek. My vision blurs as I'm knocked back onto the mattress. Sobs rack through my body painfully as he climbs off me.

I lift my head, feeling weak, and watch as he passes around the bed, glancing at me every few seconds.

"Did you think you could hide from me forever?"

"Yes," I hiss, not knowing where this insolence is coming from but glad it's there.

"Stupid, stupid Lola. I've warned you so many times. So fucking many. I made you who you are."

"You beat me and raped me!" I yell, managing to pull myself up enough, so I'm sitting against the headboard. Keeping a close eye on him, I do a quick scan of the room, finding the place is a shit hole. The Rick I know was a clean freak; everything has to be pristine and perfect for him. But seeing empty food containers and empty cans of beer around the room surprises me. I've never known him to be this disorganised or even eat takeout food. The nearest he ever got to a takeout was when we ordered from a five-star restaurant.

Rough hands grab my chin, and he forces me to look at him. "I said fucking listen to me, you fucking bitch," he says, and I notice for the first time how ragged and unkempt he is. He has a week's worth of stubble on his jaw, his eyes are bloodshot, and he looks his age for the first time since I've met him.

"Fuck you," I say before spitting in his face. I've never done anything so revolting in my life, but if anyone deserves to be spat on, it's him. Hell, I wouldn't pee on him if he were on fire. For what he's put me through, he deserves a far lot more.

"Sweet, Lola," he taunts, wiping the spit from his face. His voice is eerily calm, and out of everything, that is what has me shaking like a leaf. For the first time since I woke up, I'm actually scared for my life.

He laughs at my expression, clearly seeing he's gotten to me. My anger spikes again, and I narrow my eyes, giving him a defiant look.

"Oh, I'm going to have fun with you."

"Fuck you!" I yell, smacking his hands away, but he just squeezes my cheeks harder. I wince in pain, my eyes fluttering closed for a second before they open again, staring into those lifeless, cold orbs of his.

"Oh, you'll have your chance to fuck me, Lola. All in good time. All in good time. But first, we have to get that fucker off my back."

My eyes widen when realisation dawns on me. "Dean," I whisper.

Rick's face twists into an ugly snarl, the veins in his neck bulging.

"Don't fucking say his name," he growls, and I grin snidely.

"He's going to come for me," I taunt him, wanting him to get riled up, so I have a chance to escape. I cast a quick glance at the door once again; if he moves to the other side of the bed, I'll have a chance of getting to it.

"No, he's not."

IF I COULD WISH IT ALL AWAY

"He will because he loves me and I love him," I spit, getting in his face, but it only makes him angrier.

"Then I'll enjoy killing him in front of you. I'll cut him piece by piece and make you watch," he mocks.

I can feel the blood draining from my face, and a hoarse cry escapes me. "Leave him alone," I yell, and he laughs, shaking his head. He shoves my head back, gripping my jaw so hard I'll definitely have bruises.

"Why are you doing this?" I ask, grateful for him moving off the bed. Maybe if I can distract him long enough, I can make my move.

"Why?" He laughs. "I'm doing this because you're mine. You belong to me. *This* ends when I say it ends. You don't get to walk away from *me*. No one walks away from me," he roars, punching his chest.

"So this is all about your ego?" I scoff.

"Nobody takes what's mine."

"I'm not yours!" I scream, tears falling from my eyes. The anger that has been simmering below the surface for years begins to build. I've never hated anyone the way I hate Rick.

"Yes, you are!" he roars back, smashing the dressing table mirror, shattering it. "You let him put his hands on you. You let him touch what's mine," he rants, shaking his head as he paces the floor. "When will you learn? When will you get it through that thick skull of yours that you belong to me?"

"I'm not yours," I yell on a hoarse cry. He's lost the plot, and I don't think he's thinking straight, if he ever did. I've never, not once in all the years I've been with him, seen him like this. It's unnerving, and I tremble with fear, praying I don't show it. "You beat me. You raped me. You even cheated on me," I with a forced chuckle. "But what you could never do was destroy me, Rick. You can't destroy what's not yours. I gave my heart to Dean long before you and I'll love him long after you're forgotten. Let me go. Just let me go," I plead, my strong facade wavering.

He scoffs, looking at me like I'm the ridiculous one. "You loved every second of it, Lola."

I watch as he paces the length of the room again. Just when I'm about to make a move, he turns, watching me. His expression has changed, his eyes softening somewhat and coming across friendlier as he gives me a warm, apologetic smile. But I know Rick. It's not real, and whatever he's playing at, I'm not going to fall for it. And the fact his mood just went from psycho to Mr Tumble in two-point-four seconds proves he's lost his marbles.

"I'm sorry, sweetheart. So fucking sorry. I know I can be demanding and a little controlling at times, but I only mean well. It doesn't have to be like this. We're good together. If you could meet me halfway, listen when I speak and respect my needs, we could work. I can change. You can change," he says softly, and my eyes widen in horror.

He's twisted.

"How did you know where I was?"

"Your grandpa basically told me, but it was Sally who got the information for me." He grins but then frowns, muttering under his breath. "Why would you make me come here and flaunt *him* in my face?"

I look at him in confusion. "Who? Dean?"

"Yes," he growls, anger surfacing but he pushes it down, a smile lighting up his once handsome face. Now it's just ugly. His soul and heart are ugly, and no looks could ever make it any different.

"You've been watching us?" I gasp, my hands shaking.

"Of course I have. I had to watch as he put his hands on you, his mouth." He shakes his head, his hands balling into fists. "It's okay. I understand."

"Understand what?"

"Why you were there. He was forcing you. It's what you think you like, but you only like it with me," he says, and my eyes widen, a cold shiver running up my spine.

He's delusional.

When he moves closer to the bed and sits on the edge, I flinch, scooting away. It works in my favour too, because now I'm closer the door.

"I just want to hold you," he says calmly. It's like he's in a parallel universe, one where everything is perfect, and he hasn't just kidnapped me and knocked me out.

My mind screams to play him, and I look up at him sharply.

"You've got blood all over you." My voice is as soft as I can force it to be, earning me that 'got you' gleam in his eyes.

"Let me go wash up. Then can we talk? We can work out how to make you better. We'll need to move away because your grandpa will try breaking us up. He doesn't think you're good enough for me."

I want to scoff, but instead, I force a smile and nod.

He rises from the bed, looking like he wants to touch me but thinks better of it. I gulp, adrenaline pumping through me as I pray my plan works.

The minute he reaches the bathroom, his back to me, I get up and run for the door. I cry out in frustration when I find it locked, and by the time I get the latch undone, he's on me. He rips me back by my hair, a scream tearing from my throat before he hits me, smacking my face against the door.

My breathing comes out in one gush of air, and I fall limply against him as everything around me spins.

"Where the fuck do you think you're going?" he snarls in my ear.

"Let me go," I choke out pathetically.

"Over my dead body. I knew I couldn't trust you. Fucking knew it. You want it to be this way, then you've got your wish. Because if I can't have you, no one will."

His words come out harsh and dread seeps into my bones, knowing I've pushed him too far.

"No," I whisper, ready to plead, but a sharp stinging sensation jabs into my leg, and everything goes black, darkness filling me once again.

Chapter Thirty-One

Dean

We're all sitting in Lola's store, waiting to hear something back about where she is. We have every police officer available and my PI's working the case, yet no one has come back with a damn thing. It's been over an hour, and I'm tearing the walls down with worry.

Another thing worrying me is Dwayne. No one can get in touch with him or find out what PI firm he used to see if they have any leads that could help us find Lola.

"Have you tried Dwayne again?" I ask my dad.

"He's not answering. No one is picking up at the office either," he informs me, looking concerned himself.

"We'll get in touch with him," Mom says as she sits down next to Dad with a fresh cup of coffee. I watch her hands shake. It's been hard for her to keep it in check since she got here. She broke down when she first arrived and has tried her hardest since to keep it together, for my sake more than anyone else's.

Pagan is on the other sofa, curled up to Sid who looks worried for his twin. The young lad, who I found out is called Alec, was picked up by his mom and dad an hour ago. I felt bad, deciding to go visit him and check he's okay after I get Lola home. I'm going to regret a lot of shit I've done today, but at the moment I can't seem to concentrate on anything other than finding her.

I've logged into my hard drive from Lola's computer and tried looking for something myself, but without my work database, I'm pretty much a sitting duck.

"Does anyone want anything to eat or drink?" Brooke asks, Lorelei by her side, ready to take orders.

Everyone shakes their head, and she sits back down. I notice Lorelei doesn't. Instead, she moves back over to the counter, cleaning the surfaces

IF I COULD WISH IT ALL AWAY

once again. I think she's worried about Lola like the rest of us are, but something more is bothering her, and it's killing me not having the head space to help her. When Lola finds out I ignored her new friend's pain, she's going to kill me.

I chuckle, but it's dry, and everyone snaps their gazes my way, looking at me like I've lost my mind. Maybe I have.

"What's funny?" Mom asks, trying to make conversation.

"Lola. She's going to kick my ass when she finds out some of the shit I've done and said today." I chuckle, but it quickly turns into a pained sob. I drop my head into my hands, pulling at my hair.

"It's going to be okay. If anyone can find her, it's you," Mom says, coming to sit next to me. The sofa I'm on is empty since everyone has pretty much given me a wide birth.

"Is it really?" I ask, turning my face to the side to look at her. "Because I feel fucking useless sitting here when I could be out there doing something."

"Yeah, you could waste petrol driving around. You could look for her and lose signal or something and end up missing a vital call. You're doing what you know is best. Until you have something to go on, there's no point in getting yourself worked up over 'what if'. I know in my heart everything is going to be okay," Mom says, and I wish I had the same optimism.

As if God heard my mom and my prayers, my phone rings, Darius's number flashing on the screen. I snatch it off the coffee table.

"Where is she?" I bark into the phone.

"I've got a positive description of Carl Holmes. He's at a bed and breakfast near the school grounds. You know the old Travelodge on Springel Road?"

"Yeah, I've driven past there a few times. Are you sure?" I ask, already getting up and waving Cage to follow. I take a piece of paper off the side and quickly jot the address down.

"Yeah. I called the reception, and an older lady answered. I explained what was happening and she said he signed out ten minutes ago. I'm on my way already. There has to be something there to give us a clue," he says, and my heart pounds.

We might not know where she is, but it's one step closer than we were before.

"I'll see you there," I tell him and hang up.

I quickly inform Cage what Darius said, and his eyes widen. "I'll take you. C'mon."

"Mom, Dad, keep trying Dwayne," I shout, not waiting around for a reply. I'm already out the door and getting into the patrol car. "Darius is meeting us there."

Cage turns to me, smiling. "I know Darius. Good bloke. Just wish he'd come join us." He chuckles, and I grunt.

"He'd rather be hung. He hates been told what to do by me. It's why I let him run his own cases. He also likes not having a code to go by."

Fifteen minutes later we're pulling into the bed and breakfast, next to Darius's car.

Darius is walking out of a room, shaking his head and muttering something to one of the officers next to him. The officer nods and rushes off to his vehicle.

"Dean, man, I think you should step aside on this one and let me and the cops deal with it," Darius warns, and I rear back in shock. He's not the sort of person to tell someone to step back. It's why he never wanted to be a cop.

"Fuck you, mate. I'm going in there," I snap, then barge in. He calls my name, but I ignore him. The second I step inside, I come to a sudden stop. Cage bumps into me as I stand paralysed.

"Holy shit," Cage hisses.

My stomach drops and any hope I had of Lola being okay leaves me. The blouse she wore this morning is torn up and thrown on a rumpled bed, covered in blood.

Clenching my hands into fists, I take another step, kicking food cartons and beer cans out of the way.

"How the fuck didn't we know he was this close?" I hiss, pulling at the ends of my hair. I'm ready to blow, my anger building to the point of no return.

"I've no idea. But it's not everything," Darius says, gesturing me to follow him over to the desk on the far wall. On the desk are piles of photos of Lola and me.

"He's been following us for fucking weeks. These were taken three weeks ago," I say, pointing to the picture of me, Lola and my parents going out for something to eat.

"Fuck, he's obsessed," Cage curses, shifting some of the pictures with a pen. He moves the top lot to reveal a bunch of close-up photos of Lola. He took pictures of my woman, my Lola. There have to be hundreds of different pictures.

"Have you called someone in to get these fingerprinted?" I ask, looking over my shoulder.

"I asked the officer who met me here to grab some shit," Darius confirms. "Maria, the owner, has CCTV footage. I'm going over there now. Do you want to tag along?"

"Yeah, I'm coming," I tell him, my voice hard.

IF I COULD WISH IT ALL AWAY

"Has anyone radioed anything in?" My eyes catch the bloodied blouse on the bed, and my heart squeezes painfully. If I keep thinking about her hurt, it's going to break me.

"No. Nothing. We have a search going for the vehicle. We're hoping to pick it up soon."

I follow Darius into the main reception, nodding at the scared, young-looking girl sitting behind the counter.

"Maria's expecting you. She told me to tell you to go down the hall and take the second door on the left."

My legs feel like jelly because I have no idea what I'm about to see on the camera. I already know she's hurt, but seeing it is going destroy me. The empty, powerless feeling is strong, and a sense of unworthiness, of being unable to protect her is worming its way around my heart.

The door is open, and we walk in, surrounded by screens and computer equipment. Maria turns, hearing us approach, and gives us a grim smile.

"I've found the time he turned up. You can watch this screen here, and it will play through. If you fast-forward half an hour, you'll see when they leave," she says, stepping back to let Darius take charge of the computer. He presses some buttons, and the screen Maria pointed to earlier shows a car pulling up.

"Pause it a minute. Let me call the plate in," Cage says and starts pressing buttons on his phone. I stand there, waiting impatiently as I turn back to the screen. Darius glances at me, seeing my unease, and presses play.

My blood boils as Rick steps out of the car. I'd recognise his mug anywhere; after all, I did my homework on the sick fuck.

He walks around to the passenger side of the car and lifts an unconscious Lola out. My heart sinks seeing her hair and face matted with blood.

"Fuck! Fuck! Fuck!" I growl, and Maria looks at me sharply before taking another step back. "Fast-forward it."

Darius nods, rushing through the video until movement at their door has him hitting play. The door seems to open a little before slamming shut, and we all look at each other with wide eyes.

"She made a getaway. My stupid girl," I murmur, my eyes never once leaving the screen.

Not long after, the door opens and Rick steps out. This time he's holding a bag and my eyebrows rise. He throws it into the boot before making his way back inside. My heart pumps like crazy, and I lean in closer, not wanting to miss a single detail.

I need to find her.

Fury simmers its way through my veins as he walks back out with an unconscious Lola. This time she looks worse for wear, her body covered in blood in various places.

Darius pauses on her, zooming in so we can see what's going on better. "Fuck," he growls.

Lola is only in her bra, cuts and bruises marring her pale, silky skin. My fists clench and unclench as fiery anger burns inside me and takes root, growing, festering and taking over my entire body.

Maria must sense what's about to happen because she rushes out the room, a small squeak leaving her.

I pick up the empty chair next to Darius and swing it, smashing it against the door.

She's hurt, and she needs me. I've never been so vulnerable than I am at this moment. I've never felt this level of anger or fatigued incapability before, and it's burning through me.

Next, I move the trolley with cups, kettle and other shit on. I launch it across the room, smashing a few computer screens on the left wall, and I hear Maria scream.

Darius and Cage reach for me, pinning my arms behind my back as I struggle, screaming at the top of my lungs like a mad man.

"I'm going to fucking kill him. I'll fucking kill him!" I roar, wishing he were in front of me right now so I could tear his fucking throat out.

She fucking needs me.

She fucking needs me, and I'm in here, watching her hurt on a fucking computer screen, and I can't do anything to help her.

I try shoving off Cage, to get free. I need to get this anger out. I need to do something, anything to get my woman back.

"You need to get it together, bro," Darius hisses in my ear. I knock my head back, hitting him in the nose. He grunts, cursing, but doesn't let go.

"Don't make me fucking arrest you, Dean. You've got a girl to find and a sick fuck to catch. Oh, and you'll be paying for the fucking damages you've just cost the nice lady," Cage demands.

I sag against them and nod, letting them know I've got it together. They let me go, and I step forward, breathing hard.

"Fuck, get it together," I curse to myself, and I hear one of the lads grunt behind me. I ignore it since I deserve more than their shit.

Darius starts moving shit to get to the computer he was on. He's not clicking away for long before he's mumbling something to Cage.

"He's heading west. Do you want to start heading that way, or do you want to wait around?" Cage asks.

"We'll go. I can't just stand around," I tell him, beginning to feel everything all at once.

"I'll wait here. There are a few bits of paper and receipts in the room that I want to check over. I'll catch up to you and ring if I find out anything," Darius says.

"Okay. Be quick. It's clear he's not concerned about hurting her and the longer she's in his care, the riskier it will be. He could…." Cage pauses, glancing at me briefly before looking back to Darius. He doesn't want to voice the fact that Rick could kill Lola.

Maria steps back into the room with a uniformed police officer. He hands Darius a few things, and I turn away, focusing on Maria.

"I'm really sorry about the damages, and for scaring you," I whisper.

"It's fine, dear. I really do hope you find your wife," she tells me, and I don't bother correcting her because Lola will be my wife. When this is all over and she's in my arms, we're getting married the first chance we get. I can't live my life without her.

"Thank you. Here's my card. Call me or email the address at the bottom. I'll send you a check…. In fact, forget it. I'll be in touch in a couple days. I'll have one of my men organise to have a new, top-of-the-line security system put in."

I squeeze her shoulder gently, showing her my gratitude for not pressing charges, and turn to Cage, giving him a chin lift.

Darius gives me a nod as we leave and I check my phone, making sure no one else has tried to call me.

A few messages from Mom, Dad, and a couple of men who work for my company, but nothing with information on Lola. I give Dad a quick text, letting him know what's happened, leaving out a few details. He'll end up coming down here, but with Rick knowing where they are and what they all look like I don't want to risk their safety.

Getting in the car, I run a frustrated hand through my hair and turn to Cage. "We need to find her."

He glances my way as he starts his car, pity filling his eyes. "We will, mate. We will."

We've been driving west for twenty minutes when my phone breaks through my thoughts. I've not been able to stop thinking about where he would take her. It's not back to Carlisle because he would have headed north.

Darius's name flashes and I slide my finger across the screen. "Have you found her?"

"It's a long shot, but I think we have a lead. We found a business card for a Tim Rowland for Gateway Housing. I've called him, and he confirmed a Carl Holmes was a client. But get this—he only looked at one house, one time. The only reason Tim remembered him was because he thought he was sketchy, but it seems Rick thought of everything. He produced a business card for Lawson Law, using his alias's name."

"Where?" I ask impatiently. I know he's trying to explain, not wanting me to get my hopes up, but anything at the moment is better than nothing.

"You know the old derelict house up on Haricot Hill?"

"Yeah. Isn't that knocked down though?"

"No. Apparently the council said it couldn't be, something to do with legislations. Our guy never got back in touch with Tim, but if that is where he's taking her, then he won't even need a key."

"We'll check it out. Head our way just in case," I tell him, itching to get off the phone.

"Okay. Keep in touch," he says before ending the call.

I turn to Cage. "We need to go to the old derelict house up on Haricot Hill. Darius seems to think he's taken her there since he went to look at it through an estate agency."

Cage nods, taking the next right. He turns to me quickly before looking back at the road. "That's what? Half an hour away, a little more?"

"Yeah." I nod, looking at my phone. "And they're over an hour ahead of us. And that's if they're even there," I curse.

"No. I think Darius is on to something. Think about it. He was heading west, and the cameras on Falcon Road picked the car up. It's in the same direction," he says and picks up speed, ignoring the honking horns blasting.

"Go," I tell him, not caring how we get there as long as we get there. Cage grunts but does as I say, turning his sirens on.

Chapter Thirty-Two

Lola

My eyes feel too heavy to open, and my back hurts badly. It feels like pieces of metal are sticking into me, cutting me.

I hiss in pain when I move and realise I'm on a bed. There's no mattress, the springs digging into me. I still and take inventory of my injuries, noticing for the first time that my top half is bare. I'm no longer wearing the blouse from earlier, and I have no idea what happened to it. The next thing I pick up is the tight rope burning the skin around my wrists, the texture rough and unpleasant.

My eyes open in a panic, taking in my surroundings. I'm no longer in the bed and breakfast I woke up in before.

Rick isn't in the room. Taking a chance, I pull on the rope with no luck.

Another scan of the room has me wary. The place is dark, but there's a small lamp with a broken shade by the door, the light so dim it seems pointless to have it on. My eyes pause on a dark figure in the room, the back of my neck tingling in awareness.

Is that Rick?

Has he been watching me this whole time?

When I don't see any movement, I strain my eyes for a further look, but for all I know, it could be a pile of rubbish.

Trying to sit up, the bed springs squeak, and I cry out when a broken one cuts into my back. The warm blood trickles down my back, and my eyes water further.

Someone find me, please!

Someone has to have noticed I'm gone. I don't know what time it is, but it's dark outside. Dean must be going out of his mind.

Oh my God, Dean!

Tears spring to my eyes when I picture his handsome face, his gorgeous eyes and think of his loving nature. All I want to do, more than anything in this world, is have his arms around me one more time. If tonight is the night that Rick kills me, then that would be my dying wish.

I love him more than my heart can handle sometimes, and although it sounds like I'm giving up, I'm not going down without a fight. I can't. I'll fight for Dean, for us and our future.

If you have one, a cruel voice snickers inside my head.

No, this can't be the end of us.

I struggle to sit up again, this time manoeuvring myself so I'm at a weird angle, my head bent forward and my body farther up the bed. I cry out when another spring digs into me, scraping along my skin.

Hearing footsteps, I shiver. Fear courses through my body, and no matter how I try to get free it doesn't happen. The nearer he gets the more I panic, frustrated tears falling down my cheeks.

Please, no. Please get me out of this alive.

The footsteps stop outside the door, the light coming from under it blocked by his looming form. I choke back a sob, petrified.

Back at the hotel I may have been quick to shoot my mouth off, but it didn't stop me from feeling terrified or scared.

Everything seems to happen in slow motion as Rick pushes the door open, standing stock-still in the doorway. I want to cower back on the bed, cover my body up, but I can't. More tears fall when I realise just how vulnerable I am right now.

He steps into the room, the light casting an eerie shadow across his face and making him look even more intimidating and terrifying.

"Well, hello, sleepy head," he drawls as he takes a step into the room. I pull at the rope once more and a slow, small smirk appears on his lips. "Ah, I bet you're wondering why you're tied up."

"Actually, no. I'm wondering why you haven't killed me yet," I snap and he laughs, throwing his head back.

"I thought it was best to tie you up this time round. I didn't want you to make the same mistake twice. We wouldn't want to get me angry now, would we, Lola?"

He walks slowly over to the bed when I don't answer, sliding his finger between my breasts, his pupils dilating. My skin crawls from his touch, and I try to move away.

"God, I've missed you. I've missed you so fucking much. You're mine. You've been mine since the day I laid eyes on you. You'll always be mine, and if you think of running again, I will kill you." He says it so simply, like we're having a normal conversation. There's no sentiment in his tone and, apart from the desire written across his face, his eyes are dead, void of any emotion.

I shake my head, afraid I'll crack if I speak. A sob is already threatening to break out, and I don't know how long I can keep it together. I look towards the door he's left open briefly and wonder if I can get him to untie these ropes. My strength is waning, so if I'm going to make a move it has to be now, before he does anymore damage to my already-broken body.

"Yes, Lola. *Mine*. And if you don't obey, I'll kill your grandpa first. If you still don't listen, I'll kill that prick who thinks he can take you away from me and then his whole family. If that doesn't give you any incentive, I'll kill you. No one gets to have what's mine."

A sob breaks free, his words finally snapping me. I'd rather be dead than spend another day with this monster, but I will if it will protect those I love, and he knows that. He knows I'll never risk my grandpa—he's threatened me with him before—but now I have more people to protect.

More tears fall, and I look up to him, cringing. "Okay. Okay. I'll do anything you want me to as long as you leave them alone," I plead, just as a plan forms in my head.

He grins wide, looking at me like he's just won the lottery. I want to puke and punch him in the face. I've never hated anyone as much as I do him. It's a hate that's rooted deep in my heart, one that will never fade in time.

"Good girl," he says, and it literally has me throwing up in my mouth. I feel like I've just sold my soul to the devil, but then, I already did that years ago.

Dean has your soul. He had it first.

Tears form from the words my inner conscience screams at me. It gives me the strength I need to get through this, to try to pull this plan off even if it means taking a chance that he might kill me.

"I'll show you how great we are together. I'll prove to you that I'm the only one who loves you. No one could love you like I do. And I brought you a present to prove that." The fact he said he's *brought* me a present and not *bought* me a present, doesn't pass my notice. He points to the corner of the room, to where the dark shadow is looming on the floor, and I pick up a wheezing sound coming from that direction.

My eyes widen, and I struggle on the bed. "You promised you wouldn't hurt them!" I yell, tears forming.

He scoffs, rolling his eyes. "I did. That, my pretty, is Sally." He chuckles and my eyes widen further.

"Sally?" I croak out, not understanding what's going on. I thought he and Sally were working together or were *together*. But now he has her on the floor, obviously hurt if the noises coming from her are any indication.

"Yeah." He shrugs. "Stupid bitch. She actually believed I wanted her, that we were going to be together."

He rolls his eyes again and walks over to her. He kicks her motionless form, and I wince, crying for her when a pained noise escapes her.

"Stop."

"Why? She came here thinking I was coming to get revenge for you leaving me for another man," he sneers. "Like anyone would leave *me* for another man. But she turned up to the bed and breakfast. How she fucking found me I have no clue, but she did so I used her to get information on you and your little friends. She even went into the bookshop you frequent so much, gasbagging to the owner." He laughs, and I struggle to breathe. He must have been watching us for weeks.

The weekend when Pagan, Brooke and I went out celebrating comes to mind, and I know without having to ask that it was him that night. I wasn't going mad, and I wasn't paranoid. It was him.

"Why?" I croak out, although I have no idea what I'm asking him to explain.

"Because she wants me and would do anything for me. But then she found out I was planning on taking you and fleeing the country. She found our passports and plane tickets. She went crazy possessive and threatened to tell you everything. She wanted to hurt you, baby. I shut her up. I told her you were it for me and that you were the only woman I loved, but she still wouldn't listen. So, I knocked her out. I've kept her down all week, drugging her, the same way I drugged you." He laughs. "I did it for you. This is all for you."

He gestures around the room, snickering, and my heart jolts in my chest.

"You're going to get caught. Just let her go. You don't need her or need to hurt her. We can go," I tell him, my eyes almost pleading. As much as I dislike Sally and know she was planning on hurting me, I still don't want him to do anything else to her.

"No. She needs to learn, and you are still owed a lesson. So she gets to watch me do whatever the fuck I want to you. But don't worry, you'll enjoy it. If she gets the hint I don't want her after that, I'll let her go. If not, well…."

"You'll get caught and go to prison. You'll have to look over your shoulder for the rest of your life if you hurt her," I rush out, wishing I could wipe the tears blurring my vision.

"Why would I get arrested?" he asks, looking down at me confused.

My eyes widen a fraction as I stare at the man in front of me. He truly is demented. He's acting like this is normal, that no one can touch him. He has no remorse for what he's doing.

"You've kidnapped me, kidnapped Sally and drugged her. I dread to think what else you've done to her. You won't be able to get away with this," I say, swallowing back bile before continuing. "We won't be able to have a future. If you stop this now, let us go, we can sort everything out so you won't get into trouble. Then we won't have to worry."

"No. I've got a plan, Lola. We're moving out of the country. We'll be away from everyone who has gotten between us. We can start fresh. You won't have to worry about anything."

The dead look leaves his eyes as he steps forward, his face lighting up with hope. I play along, knowing I need him to believe I'm going to obey, that I won't fight back anymore.

"So let's go," I say, hoping I don't give myself away. I try to lighten my face but I'm so sore and bruised it hurts. "Untie me and we can go."

He looks at me, seeming confused, before suspicion glares back at me. "I'm not going to fall for that. Do you think I'm stupid? I went to Oxford!" he yells, and I wince, my face crumbling somewhat.

"No, I don't. I promised I wouldn't fight anymore. I told you I'd do what you wanted as long as you left them alone. I don't want them hurt. The quicker we leave, the farther we are away from them. I thought that's what you wanted?" I ask, giving him an innocent expression. When his face relaxes, I sigh, inwardly.

I feel sick pretending, and for even being nice to him. I know it's for my own safety, but having him near me makes me want to scrub my body raw and rip his eyes out all at once. But I need to do this to get away. I'll do anything and if that means playing nice, touching him and going as far as to think I want him, then I will. It's my only chance.

"I do. Say you're mine. Promise you won't run from me, and I'll untie you."

"And then we can leave?" I ask hopefully. Maybe I won't need to touch him after all. If we're upstairs, I can push him down or find a weapon of some sort before he clicks on to what I'm doing.

"No. Then I'm going to wake that bitch up and fuck you. She needs to learn who I belong to," he snaps, and my stomach twists as I silently gag.

I plaster a smile on my face even though I want to cringe, to cry out and shift on the bed.

"Then untie me. We can do whatever you want, but these ropes are really hurting me. You said you wanted to prove you changed, so prove it," I plead, forcing a pout.

He grins, and I can see what he's thinking all over his face. He really does believe he has me where he wants me. And although I know I'm putting everyone's life at risk by doing this, I still have to take a chance. I'm just hoping they understand when they find out. I'm also praying I'm successful so no harm ever comes to them.

"You try something, anything, I'll make you regret it," he promises, and I nod, forcing a smile.

He hesitates for a few seconds before leaning over me and loosening the rope. The second they're free, I pull them down in front of me, rubbing the ache. I ignore the blood around them because I know if I don't, I'll move to soon and I'll never be able to get away.

Rick just swats my hands away. I hiss out in pain, but I have no time to do anything as he grabs me, lifting me off the bed and placing me on the hardwood floor. Although I'm happy the springs are no longer cutting into me, I can't help but panic. I was planning on using the rope on him, manipulating him into giving me some power to prove he's telling me the truth about changing.

When he kisses me, it takes everything inside me not to throw up in his mouth or bite his lip off. Instead, I kiss him back, knowing I need to play this right or it could end badly. I wrap my legs around him and nudge him to the side. He plays along, too lost in the kiss to notice the change in position. I'm straddling him, and as much as it pains me to kiss him, I have to.

Having him right where I want him, I pin his arms above him, deepening the kiss as he moans into my mouth. My body is screaming for me to pull away, but my head is telling me I need to time it just right.

Three, two, one...

His eyes close as I roll my hips down on him, cringing when I feel his hardness beneath me. With controlled movements, I bring my knee up at the same time as I make it look like I'm leaning more over him. His hands are on my hips now, rubbing up and down my sides almost painfully. I try to control the flashbacks wanting to be free. He must sense my hesitation because he opens his eyes, smirking at me. I reach up, practically balancing on my knee, and cup his face. With strength I didn't realise I possessed, I knee him in his groin at the same time I dig my thumbs into his eyes as hard as they can go. He howls in pain, throwing me across the room.

As much as I want to stand and watch as he curls up in pain, I don't have a lot of time, so I take the opening. I run past Sally's unconscious body, wishing I didn't have to leave her but I'm no good to her if I don't get some help.

The house is old and big, with rows of doors scattered down the long hallway. With adrenaline pumping through my body, I turn left, moving in the direction I swore I heard Rick coming from earlier. At the end of the hall, a set of stairs comes into view, and I move, seeing a door directly in front,

I'm halfway down when I hear him coming, his roar echoing around the empty house. I squeal, taking two stairs at a time, managing to get to the bottom when he jumps on me. I slam to the floor with a thud, his heavy weight on top of me.

"Stop!"

"You fucking slut!" he roars. He swings me around so he's facing me, still pinning me down with his body on mine.

With my blood pumping, I kick out, screaming. I scratch, punch, bite any body part I can reach to stop him from hurting me once again. He still manages to undo my trousers and another scream escapes me.

"No! No!"

Looking into his bloody eye, his other one bloodshot, I slap him across the face and turn my head while he's distracted, sinking my teeth into his hand that is currently pinning me to the floor.

My strength wavers a little but I fight past it, needing to do something, anything.

He raises his hand into the air, ready to punch me once more, when Sally comes out of nowhere, jumping on his back. He falls to the side and she bangs his head with something in her hand. A bottle? I'm not sure. I'm frozen, momentarily distracted by her appearance.

"Run, you silly fucking bitch!" she screams, and I wince, seeing her face for the first time. One eye is completely swollen shut, the rest red and blue.

Snapping out of it, I get to my feet, unlatching the front door. I throw it open, stepping out into the pouring rain just as I hear wood splintering behind me.

I turn, seeing Sally lying, dazed, surrounded by splinters of wood and dry wall. Rick is advancing on her, and I know if we have any chance of surviving I need to get help.

I run towards the car, cursing when I find it locked. Not having much time, I head for the woods.

I'm thankful he didn't take my socks off me, the soggy twigs cutting into the balls of my feet. The twigs snap and rain drenches me, spraying in my face, but I don't let it stop me. I keep running, ignoring the pain in my body.

A loud scream from the house echoes into the night before it suddenly cuts off. I cry out, and my footing slows slightly. A part of me wants to go back, to see if Sally is okay, but then I hear him.

"Lola. You can run, but you can't hide!" he roars.

Panic surges inside me and I run as fast as my feet will carry me.

Chapter Thirty-Three

Dean

We've been breaking all the speed limits since Darius called us with a possible location.

"Stop here!" I yell and Cage brakes suddenly, sending me forward into the dashboard.

"What?" he says, looking around for possible threats.

"We need to go by foot so he doesn't hear us approach. If he knows we're here, he could scare and do something to her," I explain, jumping out of the car into the pouring rain. Lightning strikes above us and my heart aches. I can't help but think of Lola and how much she hates storms.

"Bro, calm the fuck down. I get she's your missus and shit, but we have to be clever about this. I don't need you going off on one so get it together," he snaps, and I nod, starting forward. He steps up beside me, both of us pulling our hoods over our heads to block the rain out.

I growl, frustrated with myself and the way I'm behaving. I was a cop for fucking years, a PI a lot longer. I should have learnt how to keep my shit together by now.

As we near the house, everything goes blank, all of my training goes out the window, and I turn to Cage for answers.

"It doesn't look like he's at the back of the house, but we should split up anyway," he says as I move closer to hear him. I see the light on upstairs, and my eyes flicker to the front door, wanting to rush in there and get her.

I'm surprised to find the door wide open, a lone figure outside on the doorstep. I barely give Cage a glance. My heart is pounding and my chest is tightening, a sob working its way up my throat. I rush over to the motionless figure and see blonde hair, a cry ripping from my throat as my chest squeezes painfully.

"Lola," I choke out and skid to a stop, falling to my knees. The

IF I COULD WISH IT ALL AWAY

muddy, wet ground soaks in my jeans, but I ignore it. I take her still body, turning her gently around, and gasp.

It's not Lola.

"What the fuck?" I ask.

"I'm calling 999. Fuck, I'm sorry mate," Cage says and I shake my head.

"It's not Lola," I rush out, laying the beaten and blooded woman down on the floor. She begins to stir and panic fuses through my body. I lean forward so she can see my face, but she's pretty beaten up. "Was Lola Lawson here? A girl with blonde hair?" I ask loudly.

She begins to move again but when she opens her mouth, only a painful gasp escapes. Rain splatters across her face and I look around for shelter. Cage is still on the phone, explaining where we are to the paramedics. The urge to leave and look for Lola is strong but I can't leave the woman in front of me alone.

Who is she? And why the fuck has Rick hurt her?

"Please, do you know where she is?" I ask again, my voice breaking.

Her hand moves slowly, and I sit up straighter. Her index finger points, but her body convulses and she drops her hand so it's pointing to the inside of the house.

"Fuck!" I curse. If he knows we're here…. I need to get to her. "Cage, watch her," I hiss and move. He goes to protest and I hear the word 'backup', but I ignore him and run into the house. "Holy fuck," I whisper. Just inside the door is thin drywall with rows of wooden panels. Someone went through it if the damage is anything to go by. It's a mess, and spots of blood can be seen.

I follow the hall down to a kitchen and shake my head. The place is a fucking tip and unstable. I'm surprised it's even on the market. Nothing seems salvageable. Walking through the door on the other side of the kitchen, I come to the living area. The room is empty, so I rush forward, coming back to the entrance. Cage is still seeing to the unconscious woman outside, but this time they're on the porch, out of the rain.

I take the stairs two at a time, desperate to get to Lola. The long hallway is lined with doors, and I frustrated growl escapes me. Moving quickly, I throw each one open, seeing each room bare. When I get to the one at the end by another set of stairs, there's a light on. The door is already open, and my heart sinks when I take in the room. An old spring bed is in the centre, rope tied to the bars. Looking closer, I notice a patch of blood and what I can only presume is urine. It smells.

"Fucking hell," I mutter and move out before I gag..

Running back downstairs I head straight to the woman and Cage. I'm panicking, needing to know where she is. I can't help but feel powerless.

The anxious and hopeless feeling consumes me, and I'm seconds away from breaking. How could I have let this happen to her? I promised to protect her, told her I'd never let Rick hurt her again, and yet he has. I've failed her, and there's no going back from that. If—no, *when* I find Lola—I'm going to do everything in my power to make it up to her.

"Has she said anything?" I ask Cage, who shakes his head just as the woman mumbles.

"What did you say?" he asks gently, leaning down to hear her better.

"Wuh," she moans.

"What?" I ask urgently. If she weren't broken and pretty banged up, I'd be shaking her for the information she holds.

"W-woos," she mumbles under her breath, and I look to Cage, wondering if he understood.

"I think she means there," he says, pointing to the woods behind him, and my eyes widen.

Just then a high-pitched scream echoes through the trees and my back straightens, terror seeping into my bones.

Not thinking, I run in the direction of her screams.

"Dean, get back here!" Cage roars. I ignore him and keep running, needing to get to her. He's hurting her, and she needs me. There is no fucking way I'm waiting around for the police to come.

I shove the branches away and wipe the rain pelting down on my face and getting into my eyes. I pump my legs faster and time seems to stop. It's like I'm in a dream, when you're running towards or away from something and your legs are working overtime but you don't get anywhere, and everything around you slows.

When another scream pierces the air, I change direction, praying I get to her before he hurts her any more.

Chapter Thirty-Four

Lola

Branches smack into my face as I run, cutting into my cheeks, arms, and legs. I can't even think about my feet or the excruciating pain that comes every time they hit the rough ground. I never know what I'm going to step on and every time it's a stone, a branch, or a stinger, I want to curl up in a ball and cry.

Rick calls my name, his threats cutting into me like a thousand knives. I want scream, but I don't want to give him any indication as to where I am.

Thunder rumbles making me jump. I take another left, trying to get him off my path.

"Lola!" he roars, and he sounds closer. A panicked squeak leaves me as I jump over another fallen tree trunk, landing with a thud. I'm grateful it's just mud on the other side because I don't know how much longer my feet are going to hold up. I'm already slowing. I feel weak, defenceless, and there's nothing I can do about it. My eyes catch a bush not far from where I am, and I run, moving in that direction.

I don't bother looking around as I crouch down, crawling into the bush to hide. I'm cold, my body shivering as I curl my knees up into my chest, wanting to look as small as possible.

"You can't run forever, Lola. I'll fucking find you," Rick shouts, and I jump, his voice sounding close, too close.

I pat around the dirt to find something to use as a weapon, pausing on a thick, wet stick. I grip it, ready to bring it to my chest when I hear him. His footsteps sound close and I peep through the bush, a frightened gasp threatening to escape when I see him. I'm still shivering, and when he stops nearby, I stop breathing altogether, afraid he's found me. But all he does is bend down, putting his hands on his knees as he takes in steady breaths.

Then he moves forward, leaving me behind. Once he's out of sight, I crawl out of the bush and run in the direction we originally came from, hoping he doesn't double back when he realises I'm not wherever he's heading.

Looking over my shoulder, to check he isn't following, I lose my footing and fall. A scream bubbles up my throat as I roll down a hill. The ground cuts into my skin and it feels like I'm on fire.

My head slams into a rock when I hit the bottom, coming to a sudden stop. I whimper, feeling dazed, and when I try to sit up, everything spins and a wave of nausea hits me.

Branches cracking and the sound of dirt sliding gains my attention, and I turn to find Rick barrelling down the hill, gaining on me.

I scream, my voice loud and hoarse. In a panic, I get up on wobbly feet and grab the stick I found earlier, gripping it as tightly as I can in my shaky hands.

I step back, slowly as he comes to a stop at the bottom. My body trembles and with a shaky hand, I wipe away the wet dirt-caked strands of hair from my face.

"Don't come near me," I warn, holding the stick up.

He throws his head back, laughing before locking his gaze on mine. "You really don't get it, you stupid fucking bitch. There is nowhere you can go that I won't find you."

"I hate you!" I scream. "You've ruined my life."

"You're coming with me!" he yells over the rain. When I see him take a step forward, I take another back.

"Fuck you. I'm not going anywhere with you. Why can't you just leave me alone? I'm not yours, and I never will be. When will you get that through your thick head?" I scream.

"No, we belong together," he shouts.

"No, I belong to Dean. I have ever since I can remember, long before I even knew you existed. You don't hold a candle to him."

"If I can't have you then no one will!" he roars, and my body trembles as he pulls a knife from his back pocket. His face is lethal, murderous, and I know I won't be surviving this.

"No," I cry and hold the stick up higher, wishing I had something thicker, bigger to hit him with. It's heavy in my hands, and my arms begin to shake, my strength weakening with each passing second.

"You make me so hard when you're frightened." He laughs, and I gag, crying.

"You're sick," I hiss.

He laughs again before his face turns cold, a deadly look in his eyes. I don't even have a second of warning before he's charging at me. I scream again, as loud as my sore voice will let me, and step backwards.

Before I can turn away, he's on me, knocking the wind out of my chest and pushing me to the ground. I lose the stick as dirt fills my mouth and stones, stingers and twigs cut at my chest.

"Get over here," he snaps, dragging me backwards, and I kick out.

He turns me so he's straddling me, and I kick out, trying to wiggle backwards but only managing to get so far before he has me pinned, immobile. He pressed the knife against my throat.

I gasp, my eyes widening with fear. When he presses it harder, piercing my skin, I go stock-still, tears falling from my eyes.

All I can think about at that moment is how I'll never see Dean again, how we're never going to have a family or get married. I'm never going to see my grandpa or spend time with him or the rest of the Salvatores. My heart breaks and the pain is excruciating, worse than anything Rick has ever done to me before. This is by far the worst feeling I've ever had to endure; I can feel my insides pulling apart, the pain unbearable. He's taken so much from me, more than just ripping away my identification and resolve.

"Don't do this," I beg, trying not to move.

He can't take my life. I won't let him.

He sits up, removing one hand from my wrists and sliding it between my breasts before cupping one, squeezing it until I whelp in pain. His touch is rough, hard, and bile rises in my throat as I close my eyes, trying to fight off the flashbacks ready to surface. The night he last raped me, the worst night of my life, comes to mind and my eyes snap open, forcing the images out.

"That's it. You finally get it. I can do whatever the hell I want to you, and it's about time you learn. You're never leaving me, never. You don't get a fucking choice," he sneers, his lips curling as he tries to smirk down at me.

I choke back a sob when his hands move down to undo my jeans again, but then I realise he's no longer holding a knife to my throat. Since my hands are already above my head, I move them farther, feeling the ground for the stick. More tears fall as I have to lie there and let him touch me, defile me.

Since I'm soaked through, my jeans are hard to remove, and he can't get them past my hips. It gives me enough time to find what I was searching for. When the rough, bark is in my grip again, my heart hammers inside my chest.

Rick grunts, apparently frustrated with my jeans before he gives up and tries to shove his hand down my pants. I scream out, and he startles before his eyes widen for a split second. It's all I need. I swing the stick down, knocking him in the back of the head. He falls to the side, his hand still inside my jeans. I rip it out, shoving him off me before scrambling away from him, needing to move.

I've never felt so weak before, my whole body like jelly. I turn, crawling on my hands and knees to get away from him.

"No!" I scream when he grabs my ankle, dragging me back. He tugs harder, and my arms collapse beneath me, my head hitting another rock.

My vision blurs, spots blinking in front of me as I try to focus. For a split second, I forget where I am and what I'm doing on the ground soaking wet.

I cry out when he grabs me by the hair, pulling back so my face is brought up against his. He leans down, his mouth at my ear. "You're going to fucking pay for that," he hisses, right before a hot burning sensations tears through the skin on my back. I scream out, arching away from the pain, but it only causes him to press further.

"Please! Please don't do this," I beg, my voice weak.

"Beg, bitch. Beg. It just makes me harder for you." He chuckles and, to prove a point, presses his hardness against my ass. I throw up all over the forest ground, dirt sticking to the saliva stringing from my mouth. I cry out, humiliated.

He turns me around, slamming my back against the ground before slapping me across the pain. The wet sting radiates through my cheek, the soreness overwhelming.

Kicking out, I manage to take him by surprise and push him away a little, enough for me to grab the stick again. I swing at his arm this time, and the knife sails through the air, landing a few feet away from us as he roars in pain.

He moves again, and I can see the indecision on his face on whether or not he should get the knife. With that split second, I kick out again, knocking him back. He lands on his back, sounding winded.

I get up, screaming for help before running. He runs after me and grabs the back of my jeans. My body is turned and shoved violently against the tree as I continue to scream out.

"Shut the fuck up!" he shouts, and I wince in pain when he grabs my cheeks, squeezing them. "I'm going to make you pay for everything—for leaving me, for letting another man touch you, and for defying me. I'm going to make you wish you were never born."

I'm knocked to the ground when he lands a punch to the side of my head.

"Stop! Please, stop," I beg, holding my hand out to him as I kneel on the ground.

"Never, you fucking bitch," he screams and walks towards the knife.

IF I COULD WISH IT ALL AWAY

In a panic, I head to the stick, making a grab for it.

"Oh no, you don't!" he shouts, forgetting the knife and heading towards me. I don't know what makes me do it or how I find the energy, but with a hoarse cry, I run towards him, swinging the stick behind my back. When he nears, I bring it forward hitting him in the shoulder. He falls to his knees, and I bring it back up, ready to hit him across the head. It's something I've dreamt of doing since he started beating me, but when he grabs the stick and pulls it out of my grip, I scream, letting go and pummelling him with my bare hands instead. I smack him as hard as I can, anywhere I can reach. Rick's unfazed and slaps both my hands away before pushing me in the chest, knocking me back a few steps before I land on my ass.

He moves quickly and before I know it he has his hands around my throat, squeezing the life out of me.

Everything happens in slow motion after that. I fight, clawing at his wrists to loosen his hold, but he keeps a firm grip, squeezing tighter. His face reddens and as I blink through the rain, I notice the look in his eyes, one I've seen from him before. My whole life flashes before me, and I fall back to the ground, the fight leaving.

Knowing this is the end, I close my eyes and picture Dean's handsome face. I smile—at least I think I do—when I see him clearly, his handsome face smiling down at me while he makes love to me. He laughs and kisses my neck, which makes me giggle, and tells me he loves me.

The grip around my neck tightens.

I tell Dean I love him, whispering the words out loud and wishing he were here to hear them. I hope he knows how much I love him, and I wish that somehow, somewhere along the line, he finds happiness and love once again. Someone like Dean deserves to be loved, to have the greatest love there is.

White dots cover my vision, and for a split second, I think I'm dead, the pressure on my neck suddenly gone.

I thought going to heaven would be peaceful, pain free, and that my parents would be there waiting for me, but all I see is blackness before my mind goes blank and everything around me stills, the silence deafening.

Chapter Thirty-Five

Dean

It feels like I'm putting more distance between Lola and me the farther into the woods I run. Her screams still echo, but it feels like the trees and wind are mocking me, not wanting me to find her. I feel like I'm close, yet so far away and it's killing me, eating me up inside.

I yell in frustration and turn to a broken trail, seeing footprints squelched into the mud. Another scream has me picking up speed. Her scream…. It's filled with pain and fear, and I feel useless, like I'm running round in circles with no hope of ever reaching her in time.

The air is suddenly silent and my heart pounds, a new scary feeling taking route. I pause for a second, trying to hear something, anything, but there's nothing but silence. I groan, running my hands through my hair as I look around. A broken trail not far from where I'm standing catches my attention, and I move towards it, my eyes widening when I see a large amount of dirt disturbed near a bank.

I stop at the top, my eyes widening in horror when I see Lola's motionless body lying there on the floor. I wait, watching her chest for any signs of life, but I don't see any.

My heart rate spikes and movement from the corner of my eye gains my attention. Turning my head in the direction of her feet, I find Rick. He's kneeling there, pulling her jeans down. They're by her ankles now, and I see red. My eyes cloud over and my mind goes blank. The only thing that registers is revenge, and I fly down the bank, my feet barely touching the ground on the way down.

Rick doesn't hear me come down, too occupied with what he's doing. But when I get to the bottom, rage burns through me and I growl. He hears me, his eyes widening when he sees the look on my face. Slowly he gets up, a small smirk on his lips.

"She loved it," he taunts, and I charge. Bending at the waist, I shove my shoulder in his chest and rush forward, keeping him in my grip until I

IF I COULD WISH IT ALL AWAY

see the tree. I move back at the last second so only Rick slams into it. He grunts, his face scrunching in pain as he struggles to breathe. I don't give him time to recover, landing blows to the face one after another until he catches his bearings and starts hitting me back.

He pushes me, and I fall back a few steps before standing strong and going at him again.

"She's fucking mine!" he roars, punching me in the stomach.

"She's her own fucking person, but she's *my* woman. And you've hurt her," I growl, kneeing him in the stomach. He coughs, falling back on his ass.

I step forward, standing over him. He smirks, his mouth full of blood. "Yeah, but can you fuck her like I can and make her love it?"

Without thinking of the consequences, I lift my booted foot and stamp down on the side of his head. He's instantly out cold, but I don't care, kicking him in the ribs over and over until I see Lola's motionless body.

I stumble backwards, my eyes widening as I struggle to get to her. My legs shake, a strangled sob breaking from my chest as I kneel on the floor next to her.

"I'm so sorry," I choke out, wiping her wet hair from her face. The intake of breath I hear when I touch her is visible and I start shaking.

My fingers find her neck, searching for her pulse at the same time I grab my phone, dialling Cage. Her pulse is weak, and I scramble for ideas of what to do.

Her body is bruised and torn up; I don't want to move her and cause further injury.

"I'm in the fucking woods, where are you?" Cage shouts.

"You need to get here quick. She's in bad condition. Tell them to drive down the lane and take the first dirt road on the left. I can see it from here," I shout.

"On it," he says before whispering to someone.

"Who's that?"

"I've got a paramedic with me. Where's Rick?" he asks, his tone hesitant.

"Knocked the fuck out," I growl, not wanting to think about that sick fuck. If I do, I can't promise I won't go back there and finish what I started.

"Shout so I can hear you. I need to know where you are," he says, sounding out of breath.

I mute my phone, set it on loudspeaker and start shouting.

"Over here!" I roar, shining my phone and waving it around.

"I'm close. I can hear, so keep shouting," he tells me and I yell louder before bending down. I quickly take off my jacket and jumper and place them over Lola, keeping her warm as I cradle her head in my lap.

I kiss her forehead, soothing her hair when I hear Cage nearby.

"I'm over here," I shout to Cage and wave my phone around. When he comes into view, I sigh with relief.

"Fuck! Oh, fuck," Cage growls, ripping the jacket off his body and covering Lola with it too. The paramedic moves quickly, kneeling down next to Lola and working on her. He grabs his handheld radio and calls it in.

"We're here," a voice says over the radio, and sure enough, a light from the ambulance shines on us.

"Where's Rick?" Cage rushes out. In a daze, I look at him.

"Over there," I growl, looking at his motionless body.

A foiled blanket is taken out of the bag the paramedic has. He takes the coats off Lola, replacing them with the blanket. Another medic rushes out, and the one kneeling next to Lola speaks up.

"There's another unconscious over there," he tells her, and my head snaps up.

"You move to even check on that sorry piece of shit and I will have you fired. She needs to go to hospital, now. The police can deal with him," I snap, giving them a deadly look.

They both startle and nod. The woman bends down, sliding a yellow board under Lola. She still hasn't moved, and the ache in my chest only intensifies.

"The police are coming down here in a few minutes. They're gonna wait until the ambulance pulls out so they don't block us in," Cage says as he walks back. I look over my shoulder and growl when I see Rick is awake. Barely but still, the urge to go over there and knock him out again is undeniably strong. The fucker doesn't deserve to live.

I don't leave Lola as they carry her over to the ambulance, sliding her in on a bed. I sit at the back, watching helplessly as they set her up to machines, checking her vitals and whatnot. The second her heartbeat, although faint, comes through the speakers, I break. A sob tears from my throat and I drop my head, my hands cupping her feet as I cry.

"I love you so much," I sob, not caring if the paramedics think I'm crazy.

I nearly lost my woman tonight.

I could have lost her.

But from here on out, I plan to do everything I can to protect her. Starting with getting that piece of filth to prison.

Chapter Thirty-Six

Lola

What is that God-awful beeping sound?

And why does my body feel light, pain-free and warm? I don't get it. The last thing I remember is the darkness, the tight hand gripping my throat.

At least, I think that's what happened, I'm not sure. Everything seems foggy, like a dream drifting in and out of realms.

Turning, my eyes burn from the bright light, and I shield them with my hands. The light seems to lessen and when I open my eyes, I gasp.

Spinning in a circle, I smile, feeling the warmth on my face. I'm in our meadow. Mine and Dean's, and it's heavenly.

Bright-coloured flowers blossom from the ground, the grass greener than I've ever seen it, and dandelions float in the air like mist around me. The place is unreal. Even the trees look taller, brighter, and the feeling of happiness and love consumes me.

This is heaven. It has to be.

"Not quite," my mother's voice muses, and I spin around so fast I nearly fall over.

"Mom?" I croak, looking and finding it's really her. She's standing in the meadow not far from where I am, Dad by her side. "Dad?"

"It's us, doll," he whispers, his voice choked up.

I run through the flowers and throw my arms around them, a sob breaking free. They smell just like I remembered, but they look different. They look healthy, care-free and happy.

"I've missed you so much. I hate that you're gone, that you're not there," I choke out and pull away, wanting to look at my parents' faces again. My mom's hair looks longer, shinier, and I smile when she smiles at me, running her fingers through my own. I glance to my dad and my eyes water when I find his green ones, like mine, staring down at me. "What am I doing here? Am I dead? Please don't leave me, not again," I cry and fall to my knees. The ground softens and I choke back a gasp, finding a blanket of pillows beneath me instead.

As if reading my mind, my mom sits down, reaching for my hand. "You're in between. You're neither dead nor alive. Anything you want, or think of, or need will appear to your heart's content."

"But how? How are you here?" I ask, looking at them. "God, I love you and miss you so much."

I'm still in shock, in awe, and I can't keep my eyes off them. My dad takes my other hand, and together we sit in a circle, holding each other.

"LoLo, we don't have a lot of time," Mom whispers sadly.

"No! You can't leave me. Not again," I tell them vehemently, shaking my head.

"We love you and miss you every day, sweet girl, but now is not your time," Dad says, squeezing my hand.

"What do you mean?" I ask, wiping my tears.

"You have to wake up. You need to. Your life isn't meant to be over. You've still got so much to achieve and give," Mom finishes.

"No, please no. I can't leave you. Can you come with me?" I cry, begging them. Tears fill their eyes as they look at me and I feel small, like the eleven-year-old girl I was when I lost them.

"We've never really left you, my girl. We've always been watching over you. We've watched you fight and pull through so much, and you can do it again this time. You're strong, Lola, and we're so proud of you."

"But Dad, I let him do those things."

He shakes his head sadly. "No, girl, you didn't. You are strong, fierce and when you love, you give it your all, but you were so lost. You were still mourning us, and Dean and his family," he tells me.

I gasp. "Dean. Will I see him again?" I cry.

"You need to wake up. He's waiting for you. He's going out of his mind with worry."

"I don't know how. I don't know how to live without you. It's been sixteen years and every day it's like the day I lost you. I should have been with you. I should have died that day. I've messed up my life. I let you down. I let Grandma down and everyone else," I sob, falling into my mother's arms when she holds them out for me.

"You could never let us down. We couldn't be prouder of the woman you've become, and seeing you these past few months has made us the happiest we've ever been. Seeing you happy, living your life, it's more than we could ever wish for. You need to live on. You need to grow old, marry Dean and have children," Mom whispers.

She runs her fingers through my hair, my head in her lap as Dad keeps a hold of my hand.

IF I COULD WISH IT ALL AWAY

"You may have lost who you were, but baby, we could never be disappointed in you. It took some strength for you to fight back, to find yourself and move forward. You're an amazing woman, but you really do need to wake up now, baby."

"But I don't want to leave you," I say, holding onto Dad's hand tighter and snuggling closer to Mom.

"When your time comes, we will be here waiting for you. We love you. Don't ever forget that."

My eyes grow heavy and I begin to panic.

"I love you. Please don't leave me," I beg, trying to cling to them as much as I can.

"Never forget we're watching over you," Mom sobs and I choke back my own, my eyes growing tired.

"No!" I scream as everything around me once again turns bright, too bright, before dropping into complete darkness.

Chapter Thirty-Five

Lola

I become aware of voices and my head screams in protest. It sounds like they're shouting, whoever it is, but they're only probably whispering. With my eyes closed, I try to get a feel for where I am and become aware of something in my hand, uncomfortable and foreign.

A familiar beeping sound echoes in my ears and my mind tries to remember where I've heard that before.

Before I figure it out, the two people who were whispering become clear and I strain to hear.

"Why isn't she waking up? It's been fourteen hours," Dean says and my heart picks up, beating wildly.

He's here.

He's really here.

And then I remember why I'm so desperate for him to be here. It all comes flooding back. Rick kidnapped me, beat me, and chased me through the woods and… and I don't remember. Why don't I remember?

"It's perfectly normal, Mr Salvatore. Miss Lawson has suffered a horrific ordeal. Her body needs time to heal. She's suffering from a severe concussion, so her mind needs time to adjust to the trauma it's taken. I promise she'll wake up when she's ready."

I tune the voices out and try to remember what happened. When it comes back to me, my eyes snap open, and I gasp.

The first thing I see when I'm able to focus is Dean. He's standing at the end of the bed, looking tired and worn out. His jaw has a shadow from where he hasn't changed and when I look closer, I notice blood covering his shirt.

I panic, thinking he's hurt, but when I try to move, everything in me becomes painful. I lie still, feeling out of breath.

"Dean," I croak out, then wince in pain. My throat hurts, feeling raw and dry.

IF I COULD WISH IT ALL AWAY

"Holy fuck," Dean gasps, looking in shock. He snaps out of it and comes rushing to my side, taking my hand gently in his, careful not to touch the wires sticking out of my hand. "Lola, baby, thank heavens you're awake. I thought I'd lost you. I'm so fucking sorry," he tells me hoarsely. "I love you."

"Water," I whisper.

He nods, worry marring his features. He leans over, pouring me a glass from the jug by my bedside before coming back to me, placing the straw at my lips. The water stings at first before it soothes the dryness and pain. The feeling has my head throbbing and my chest restricting painfully.

"Small sips, Lola," the man from before says, and I turn my head. The doctor eyes me, taking notes as he looks at the machine.

Knowing I don't have much time before he starts asking me a bunch of questions, I turn back to Dean with sad eyes.

"None of.... This isn't your fault. He would have come eventually," I whisper, my voice hoarse. Then my eyes widen when I remember Sally, hearing her screams inside my head.

"What is it, baby? Are you hurting?" he asks panicked. The doctor hears and comes to my side.

"Sally? What... what happened?"

He looks at me sadly, and I can see in his eyes that this isn't good. My eyes water and I pray it's not true.

"She died. Cage tried everything, but her injuries were too much," he whispers, and I choke back a sob wincing when the pain in my throat worsens.

"What about Rick? Did he get away?" I sniffle and go to wipe my nose but the second my hand touches my skin, I cry out.

"Careful. Try not move for me, Lola," the doctor instructs as he moves around me.

My panicked eyes move to Dean's and he rushes to comfort me. "He's in prison. He'll never touch you again. He won't be seeing daylight ever again."

I sag against the bed, not realising until then how much I needed to hear those words. Broken sobs escape me and Dean curses. He tries to comfort me but with my body bruised and battered, there's hardly anywhere for him to touch.

"Shhh, it's okay, baby. I promise everything is going to be okay."

I choke back another sob and turn to face Dean, letting the tears fall down my cheeks this time. "You don't understand. I had to do things. Things I didn't want to do but needed to. You'll hate me forever. I don't even remember how I got here or if he...." I start to cry, shaking my head.

Dean's eyes widen, and he leans forward. "Talk to me," he says gently, and it breaks my heart.

"I made him think he won so I could escape. I kissed him, sat on him, made him believe I was going to—" I start, but end up choking on my words.

"Hey, you did what you had to do, Lola. Don't get upset. You wouldn't have escaped."

"I would have gone through with it," I choke out, and he looks taken aback. "He threatened you, Grandpa and your family. I couldn't let him hurt you."

"Fuck, Lola, you're killing me. Please, it's over. We can get through this, I swear. He can't hurt you again."

"Did he…? Did he rape me?" I ask and again, the doctor takes notice. I want to snap at him to give us some privacy.

"No, baby. I found you. Darius had found the lead, and we followed it, finding Sally first. I chased you through the woods and found you unconscious on the floor. I thought you were dead."

I stare at him, my tears falling harder. "I love you so much. I'm so sorry for what I did." And I am. At the time I didn't think, but now that I'm looking back on it, I cheated on him. I betrayed him for the monster.

"What for?" he asks, and his eyebrows do that cute thing they do when he gets confused. It's adorable, and I realise I might not have gotten to see that again had he not followed us in those woods.

"For what I did with him."

"You survived. I'll help you through that nightmare, baby, but you have nothing to apologise for. I'm not going anywhere. I love you, more than life itself." He smiles, running a finger gently over the top of my hand.

"I saw my parents," I blurt out, my eyes widening when I realise I did. I saw them, I felt them, smelt them.

"What?" He looks to the doctor worriedly. "Love, your parents are dead."

"I know. But I saw them. They… I don't know," I say, suddenly feeling embarrassed.

"I'm sorry to interrupt, but I need to check you over."

"Am I okay?" I ask the annoying doctor before turning to Dean who tightens his lips.

"He wouldn't tell me anything because I'm not a blood relative. He just said you were stable," he tells me, hostility in his tone.

"I'm sorry but the hospital rules state—"

"Tell me, am I okay?" I remember every hit, every kick, and punch, and if I'm honest, I'm kind of worried about the pain in my throat.

"Am I okay to talk freely?" he asks, and I roll my eyes. Well, I would if I could open one properly.

"Yes."

"You've suffered bruising to your left ribs. You have a severe concussion, which we would like to observe overnight, and lacerations to your front and back. We're concerned about the bumps to your head, but from the tests we've been able to do, you should be okay within a few days or so. The blood vessels in your eyes have burst so your eyes will be bloodshot for a few weeks, if not longer but should heal back to normal. You'll need to see your medical practitioner about your throat. You have bruises from where you were strangled, which you can see clearly. I'm sure you can feel a lot of pain. That's the swollen trachea, but it's only mild and should heal in a few days at the most. You'll most likely suffer from earache and some neck pain."

"Is that serious?"

"It's not one hundred percent, but we're certain you didn't pass out from the strangulation but from shock. Had it been from the strangulation, you and I would be having this conversation on paper and the vessels in your neck would have burst. You're a very lucky woman," he says, and I want to scoff. How is any of this lucky?

"So when can I go home?" I ask. I hate hospitals, ever since my parents died.

"We want to monitor you overnight now that you're awake, but there's also something I'd like to talk to you about. Are you sure you wouldn't like some privacy?" he asks, his eyes flickering to Dean. I can feel Dean's annoyance from here, and I shake my head at the doctor.

"He stays."

He nods and takes the clipboard, looking it over. "We did some tests while you were sleeping and before we could give you any X-rays. The bloods came back with a positive for pregnancy," he says and I stare at him, wondering if I heard him right.

It can't be possible.

Not after everything I've been through. There's no way my—our baby—survived. My heart aches and I turn to Dean, tears falling down my cheeks.

"Is it okay?" I choke out, and the doctor gives me a sad smile.

"With trauma like yours, it's hard to tell. I'm going to get the ultrasound so we can check out the baby, okay?"

I nod, feeling numb as I turn back to Dean who is sitting there stock-still. His eyes haven't left where the doctor was standing, and I move my hand, snapping him out of it. He looks at me, his eyes wild and glassed over.

"We're going to have a baby," he says, breaking the intense silence. I want to have the same enthusiasm, but the possibility the baby hasn't survived is all I can think about.

"What if... she or he...?" I stop, my words shaking as more tears fall.

"We can't think like that, baby. If something has happened, then we'll get through it. We can try again. I love you, Lola, and I'm going to spend the rest of my life with you."

God, I wish these tears would stop falling.

He grabs a tissue when he sees me hesitate to wipe them away, not wanting to cause anymore pain. He wipes my face gently, and I relax, my eyes closing.

"You're going to be a daddy," I whisper.

"And you're going to be one hot mom." He grins, and I give him a watery smile, placing my hand over my stomach.

"I don't feel so hot. I nearly lost you and *our* baby. I really thought I'd never see you again. You were all I could think about, and when I thought I was going to die, it killed me. I didn't want to lose you but knowing now that there was a chance—that there *is* a chance—I could lose our baby... I don't know what I'll do," I whisper, feeling broken.

"I'm not going anywhere. I'm here. I just wish I was there for you when you really needed me."

"You're always there for me." I smile as the doctor walks back in, pushing a machine. A nurse walks in behind him and gives us a bright smile of her own.

"You've got quite the crowd waiting to see you." She gives Dean a soft look. "This one hasn't left your side since they brought you in."

"It does seem you have people patiently waiting for you, so hopefully this will be quick," the doctor says. "This will feel cold on your belly for a minute."

He holds a tube of gel and very gently pulls my gown up to reveal my belly, keeping my lower half covered with the blanket.

I welcome the coolness and watch in a daze as both the nurse and doctor fuss around with the machine. The nurse dims the lights before moving to stand behind the doctor.

"This is a probe. It will help me see if the baby is okay and project a picture on the ultrasound," he says, but I'm too transfixed on the screen, although I can't see it. I'm hoping if I stare long enough he'll turn it for me.

I jump when he sets the probe against my gel-covered stomach and starts pressing it in. I can't even feel the pain because all of a sudden, a *thump, thump, thump* sound echoes around the room.

"That's your heartbeat," the doctors says, not bothering to look my way.

He starts muttering under his breath, moving the device lower, pressing it at different angles before a new sound comes through the speakers and I gasp.

I know.

My watery eyes shoot to Dean to find him with the same wondrous expression.

"Is that my baby?" I choke out, and the doctor turns this time to address me.

"It is. You have a very healthy baby. I'm just going to do some measurements and make sure everything is okay first.

I nod and cry out when he turns the screen. On there is a half-moon of black, the rest static of black and white. When he points to the middle, my eyes focus on that, watching the movement there with vast fascination.

"That there is your baby's heartbeat. Here, you can see the head," he starts, pointing out the different parts.

Dean's hand grips mine tighter, but I don't care. I'm just glad we're here, that the baby is alive and we're still together.

We wait for the doctor to finish up before I turn to him, my words coming out in a breath. "Do you know the sex or how far along I am?"

"You're around ten weeks. I can't tell the sex, but you'll find out at your twenty-five-week scan. Everything seems to appear normal but to be sure, I'd like you to have weekly check-ups until we're certain. I know you've got visitors waiting to come in and see you, but I do advise you keep it brief. You need rest, Lola, and if you're okay to leave in the morning, you'll be released. Any questions before I leave?" he asks.

"Could I have a picture?" I ask, shyly.

"Yes." He smiles and clicks a few times on the machine before leaving. He returns moments later with a picture, and I grin, staring down at the beautiful image.

"Remember, not too long."

I ignore the doctor, I don't even hear him leave.

"I'll go and get your family but before, I'd like to talk to you about something," the nurse says, and my attention snaps to her. "Another doctor will be in to see you later. With what you went through, we offer some help and support. Will that be okay with you?"

I nod and smile. She pats the bed once before leaving, going to get our family.

I turn to Dean, my eyes widening when I see his head in his hands, staring at the floor.

Chapter Thirty-Eight

Dean

"Dean," Lola whispers and I look up with tears falling down my face. I can't believe it. It didn't feel real before. I was trying to stay positive because she had already been through too much. I thought this conversation would be ending differently, that we would have lost our baby, our first child.

I can't speak, can only stare at the scan picture she holds in her fragile, cut-up hands. The past twenty-four hours have been a nightmare for me, and it's all playing in my mind. The only time I remember it could have been worse is when I see her chest, watching it rise and fall with each breath she takes. The second I look at her broken body, it's just another reminder that she was still hurt, no matter the outcome.

But seeing and hearing our baby, the life we've made growing inside her, it's too much. I'm overwhelmed, and it's all building up.

"You don't want this?" she whispers, and my head snaps up. "It's okay. I'm scared too, but we can do this. I know we can."

"Are you kidding me, Lola? This is the best news since the moment you came back into my life. I'm just overwhelmed right now. We have a baby on the way. And yeah, that scares me, but what scares me the most is that I couldn't look after you. I couldn't protect you. I could have lost you because of that. I know you're alive, but you're still hurt, and this could have turned out a lot different," I tell her, wanting her to understand.

"Dean, this isn't your fault. You can't beat yourself up for something *he* did to me. If it weren't for you, I'd have nothing to live for. Nothing." she sighs, then looks up at me through her eyelashes. "When I was… asleep, when I saw Mom and Dad, they told me I had to come back, that I had so much to live for. I felt broken having to leave them, but I knew I had you waiting for me, that I needed you. So I'm not going to let what happened come between us. I love you. I love you so much it hurts. It's over. It's finally over. We can be whoever we want to be, go wherever we want to go and not have to worry about him."

I stare at her in awe before pushing back my chair and grabbing the box from my jacket the medic hung on the back of the chair. The nurse wasn't lying when she said I hadn't left her side. I saw my parents briefly before moving into her room. She frowns at first, and it's cute, but her eyes soon widen when I kneel down next to her, my head reaching the top of the bed. I feel like a dwarf, and this isn't exactly the way I hoped this would be going, but here goes nothing.

"I was going to do this yesterday after the store opening, but I think now is the right time," I tell her and hold up the purple velvet box. I watch as her eyes fill with tears and I crack, my throat tightening.

"Dean," she gasps, covering her mouth.

"I love you so much, and I'll love you more tomorrow and a trillion times more in years to come. I've never wanted to spend my life with anyone, not the way I do you. I want to share all the good times, the bad times and even the hard times with you. I want to share everything with you, make a life with you. Lola Lawson, will you do me the honour of becoming my wife?"

I begin to feel nervous when her body starts to shake and she stares at me through tear-filled eyes, saying nothing. I can't take it, and I'm about to open my mouth, to beg her, when she nods.

My chest squeezes and the nerves I hadn't realised I had disappear. Standing straight, I lean over and kiss her forehead gently.

"Yes, yes, yes, yes. I love you, Dean," she cries, and I smile big, pulling the ring out of the box and pushing it on her finger, mindful of her cuts.

I chuckle as she stares at the ring, bringing it closer to her face, but she doesn't hear me.

"It's the most beautiful ring I've ever seen," she whispers. I stare down at the white gold band that has a pink diamond in the centre with four tiny diamonds surrounding it and my chest swells with pride, seeing it there. It reflects the light, and I smile.

"I love it," she whispers. "I love you."

"I love you too Miss Soon-To-Be-Salvatore." I grin, and she laughs, leaning in to kiss me. I kiss her back, savouring her lips and moaning, but a knock on the door has us pulling apart.

Turning to the door, Mom, Dad, Pagan, Sid and Brooke pile into the room. I notice Lola is quick to grab the tissue I handed her earlier to wipe her face, wincing in pain when she does.

"You okay?" I whisper, and she nods, turning to gaze at everyone in the room.

They all look tired, but I knew they wouldn't go home for anybody. Once they get a good look at Lola, Mom, Brooke and Pagan start crying and Dad and Sid curse, Sid pulling at the ends of his hair.

I can tell Mom, Pagan and Brooke haven't stopped crying. Fuck, my sister looks seconds away from collapsing. I know they're all shocked; none of them saw her when she was brought in, so I know it's unsettling. Fuck, I've been in here for twelve hours, and I'm still not used to it. She's been through the ringer.

Mom's the first to step forward, but then a booming voice echoes down the hallway, making Lola jump before she realises who it is.

"Where is she? Where's my grandbaby!" he shouts, sounding seconds away from cracking before he's in the doorway, his expression distraught and concerned.

I watch with concern as he says nothing, his eyes landing on Lola and giving nothing away. He walks over like it's been practiced and stands there, staring down at her. Everyone in the room must be thinking the same thing as me because Dad goes to take a step towards Dwayne, but then Dwayne does the unexpected. He breaks down on his granddaughter, his face cracking and lowering as he falls to the floor, taking her hand.

"She's okay. My grandbaby is okay," he says before standing up and staring down at her. "You can't leave me, young lady. Ever. I die before you, not you before me. I won't have it. I can't. What did he do?" he croaks hoarsely, seeing her injuries for the first time.

Lola's face crumbles as she begins to sob again, shaking her head as she takes her granddad's hand.

"I'm fine, Grandpa. And I can prove it, I promise. Dean and I, we have some good news, news that will make you forget what happened," she whispers, looking around the room. They all stare at us, confused.

"I doubt that, my sweet girl," he chokes out.

I notice Lola slip her left hand under the blanket before looking at me, asking permission. I give her an encouraging nod, knowing they all need this good news. Plus, I'm bouncing off the walls ready to tell someone that not only am I going to be marrying the woman of my dreams, but I'm having a baby with her too.

"We're pregnant," she blurts out. The room goes completely silent, so silent you could hear a pin drop.

When no one moves, she waves around the scan picture, wincing when she does. I take it off her chuckling, and all of a sudden my mom is on Lola, my dad next along with everyone else.

"Your mother will be looking down on you with a huge grin on her face. She'd be dancing in the heavens knowing her wish has come true. This is everything she ever wanted for you. Your happiness meant more to her than anything else. I'm so happy for you two. And I'm so glad you're okay. You gave me quite the scare," Mom says, wiping her eyes.

"Lily," Lola sobs and I reach out, taking her hand.

"I didn't mean to upset you," Mom whispers.

"No, no! These are happy tears. I love you so much, and I'm so thankful to you for raising the man I love to be the man he is. Without him, I wouldn't be here. I don't know where I'd be. And now we get to spend the rest of our lives with each other." Lola sniffles before she falls into heavy sobs.

"Calm, love. The baby," I soothe and listen as she slowly calms down.

"Wait, is the baby okay?" she asks, going awfully pale.

"Yes mom. They did an ultrasound to check."

"I'm going to be a nanny," she whispers and falls into my arms, hugging me.

"I'm so proud of you, my sweet girl. I'll be a great-granddaddy," Dwayne whispers hoarsely, and I realise he's been standing there staring at his granddaughter in awe since we shared the news.

"Does this mean you'll retire and come move over here?" she asks him, and tears fill his eyes.

"I'd love to," he chokes out. "Not the retiring part though. I've got years left in me."

We all laugh and, one by one, everyone says their own congratulations. They also wish her a speedy recovery, each one looking worried. But when it comes to my sister's turn, I sigh, knowing she's blaming herself.

"I'm so sorry. All this is my fault." Pagan sniffles.

"Huh?"

"Dean didn't tell you?" Pagan asks, looking at me.

"No, he didn't," Lola answers warily, looking at me. I frown. Everyone else in the room has gone deadly silent.

"The man I met at the bar—"

"Was Rick, but how does that make this your fault?" Lola asks softly.

"You knew?" Pagan gasps.

"Not at first. He was watching me for a long time, Pagan. None of this is your fault anymore than it is mine. We didn't ask for this. None of us did."

"I love you," Pagan says and bravely, but gently, leans in to hug Lola. "But if you turn into a bridezilla I'll arrange your wedding without you." She laughs through tears.

I could kill my sister. We were waiting to share that next.

"How?" Lola asks, stunned, shaking her head.

"What?" Mom asks, stepping forward.

"We're getting married. I asked Lola, and she said yes." I grin, and my mother looks ready to pass out. She starts crying, throwing herself at my dad who is wearing a huge grin of his own.

"Let's go back to how Pagan knew," Lola says, shaking her head as she ignores everyone's second round of congratulations and cheers.

"Lola, you've been hiding your damn left hand since we all walked in," Pagan reveals, smirking, and everyone laughs.

Lola pulls her hand out, showing her ring off proudly and I smile, watching her glow with happiness despite the ordeal she's been through.

"But…." Lola starts, looking at me.

"She already knew. She helped me with the size and style. She also helped me set everything up down at the lake. I was going to take you out on the boat to a new spot I found. We had the candles and blankets all set up waiting for us to arrive," I tell her, smiling.

"It sounds perfect," she whispers, staring up at me in awe.

"This is perfect. You're perfect. I love you, Miss Soon-To-Be-Salvatore."

She grins. "I love you too, but are you going to call me that until you have me down the aisle?"

"Sure am." I grin, leaning down to kiss her.

Epilogue

Part One
Lola

Dean and I are sitting at a round table full of family and friends at another fundraising event, this one organised solely by Pagan.

Once she heard the full story of my life with Rick, she wanted to help other women like me, so she pulled this fundraiser together to raise money for shelters and other supporting networks that help women and children.

I have already donated a large sum of money because if it weren't for Julie, my Women's Aid support worker, and the group she signed me up for, I would have never fully moved on from the torture Rick put me through. With their help, my family's, and Dean's, I've managed to move forward. The only thing to remind me of the time I spent with Rick is the nightmares I have from the last attack. I still blamed myself for what happened to Sally but with Rick in prison, serving life, it made me feel better that she was getting justice.

The group has helped me so much. At first I was uncomfortable listening to their stories, hearing their heartache made it hard not to lose it. They were all going through so much. But once the fourth or fifth session started, I began to feel more comfortable and managed to talk about what happened to me, and the day I was kidnapped.

Everything since that day has been a whirlwind. Just days after leaving the hospital, Pagan started organising our wedding, and in months we were walking down the aisle. We only invited close friends and family, wanting to keep it low-key and private. It was the perfect day, and one of the best days of my life.

My gown had been custom-made so it covered the small bump comfortably and I had Brooke and Pagan as bridesmaids. Dean had Sid as best man and Darius and Cage as groomsmen. After the hospital, I came to know the two well and thanked them for saving my life.

But what made that day for me, apart from promising my love to Dean in front of our family and friends, were the speeches.

God, I can remember it like it was yesterday. I don't think I'll ever forget those words for as long as I shall live.

I laugh at Dean, leaning in to kiss him when Lily stands up, clinking her champagne flute with her fork.

Everyone goes silent, and we turn, smiling at the beautiful woman. Confusion fills my features, and I look to Dean for an explanation. We've already done the speeches, so I'm puzzled as to what is going in.

"I need everyone's attention," she sings across the marquee. "Nearly nineteen years ago my best friend, Cece and I made up a wedding box. We imagined what it would be like for our two children to be married, to unite us as a family rather than friends. We made an oath that day, already seeing that our children were destined to be together, and promised each other that if anything happened to one of us, we would read a letter out on their child's wedding day. So when Lola and Dean announced they were getting married, I dug out the box, looking for that very letter."

I gasp, silently sobbing into the tissue Dean handed me when Lily first started. I wasn't expecting this, especially when she pulls out a crumpled letter.

"To my darling Lo Lo. If Lily is reading you this on your wedding day, then it means I'm not longer with you, and that pains me more than you'll ever know. But I want you to know that, even through death, I'll never leave your side. Death couldn't keep me away from you or your special day.

"Lily and I are both sitting here crying as we write down the words we may never be able to speak, so hopefully I get this right and not babble my way through.

"I want to tell you how beautiful you look. I know this because there is no way you couldn't be the most beautiful bride I've ever seen.

"I want to wish you all the happiness in the world and remind you that no matter how much life throws at you, you are strong, you are loved, and you are cherished. Dean will guide you through, and if you're not marrying Dean, well, this is really awkward. But I can't see you marrying anyone else. It's destined, my child.

"Dean, please take care of my girl. Treat her with kindness, with gentleness, and love and cherish her. She may be strong but deep inside that girl she has a heart that can be easily broken. She cares about the world, the people in it, and I don't think that will ever change. She needs you just as much as you need her, and I wish you both a long and happy life together. I couldn't wish for a better son-in-law.

"Take care of each other and your father. I bet he's weeping right

now, looking at you and thinking everything I'm thinking. But if he's somehow not there with you, then he's next to me, looking down on you.

"It saddens me to know I won't be the one who gets to dress her only daughter on her wedding day, watch as she walks down the aisle, takes her first dance as a married woman or to meet my first grandbaby in the future. I wish I could be there for all those things but I can't. But I know Lily will be, and that makes me content. I couldn't wish for another mother for you.

"I love you, my darling Lo Lo, always. You are the miracle your father and I wished for, and we love you with everything we have.

"Be happy, be strong, be loved.

"Congratulations, Mr and Mrs Salvatore. If I got the wrong name… awkward! Hopefully, Lily Tillie uses that beautiful mind of hers and changes the name somehow.

"Love you always, Mom."

I snap out of my daze, finding tears in my eyes. Dean gives me a worried glance, taking my hand, but I shake my head, giving him a bright smile.

That letter is now framed in my bedroom, above my dressing table so I can see it every day. It was the best wedding gift I could have ever received, and I'll thank my mom every day for thinking of doing such a beautiful thing.

I'll also be doing the same thing for my son or daughter, knowing that life can change in a split second.

Pagan calls my name, and I shake my head, forgetting I was due to be called on stage to give a speech. Getting up, I give Dean a quick peck on the lips before letting him give baby bean a kiss. Everyone chuckles, watching the grown man smitten with my baby bump. He doesn't care, and neither do I. I love him, and he loves me, and together we love our miracle baby much more.

The walk to the stage is more of a waddle, and I curse my backache as I stand in front of the mic, greeting Pagan with a kiss on the cheek.

My back has been giving me grief for the past few days, but the doctor said it's due to the extra weight I'm carrying. Unfortunately, I'm not due for another two weeks, so I have to suffer through until then. Rushing around today hasn't helped any. In fact, it's made it worse.

"I would like to start with a huge thank you to everyone who has supported and donated tonight. Your money will save a life, save women and children who are affected by domestic violence.

"Some of you may know that this course is very personal to me, so on behalf of Women's Aid and from all the women this money will help…

thank you. Thank you so much," I say, a sharp pain causing me to take in a deep breath.

"This money will help two hundred and twenty organisations with more than three hundred local life-saving services to women and children. The Women's Aid campaign not only helps survivors but they also raise awareness, encourage healthy relationships and help build a better future where domestic violence is no longer tolerated. They help hundreds and thousands of women a year, and your money and help bring more awareness to make that happen. So thank you.

"But I'd like to give a personal thanks to… Dean!" I scream out.

The pain in my abdomen comes on suddenly, sharp and tight. A chair scrapes back in the distance, but I'm too busy staring widely down at the water trickling between my legs.

I've just peed myself in front of hundreds of people.

Then water gushes out from between my legs and I gasp. "Dean, I think we need to go to the hospital," I breathe out, staring at him as he makes his way across the hall to the stage. "My waters just broke."

Everyone in the room stands, cheering, but I want to yell at them. This sucks monkey balls, the pain excruciating.

Dean makes it to me just as another wave of pain hits me in the stomach and I bend forward, screaming.

"Fuck! C'mon, baby, let's get you to the car." He wraps my arm around his neck at the same time my grandpa meets me, taking my other side.

We've formed a crowd by the time we make it outside. Lily, Mark, Pagan, and Brooke are all standing by the car Sid is sitting in, ready to take me. They all look excited, big grins on their faces. If it weren't for the fact I was about to push out a baby the size of a watermelon, I guess I would be too.

"Owwww!" I scream. "Dean, make it stop."

"Baby, I can't. Bean was going to be born sooner or later. I can't take the pain away." He helps me into the car, getting in beside me.

"You promised me. You promised nothing would ever hurt me again," I moan, clutching my stomach. "You lied. Why couldn't you get pregnant?"

Dean laughs and shuts the door behind him, telling everyone he'll see him at the hospital. Luckily we've got the hospital bag already in the car, having packed it a few weeks ago.

Epilogue

Part Two

Dean

"I've got to get back in there. She's ready to push. Not long." I grin excitedly at everyone in the waiting room. They all cheer for me as I run back into the delivery room where Lola glares at me.

"Where have you been?" she snaps. Her face is bright red from pushing, and I instantly feel bad. We've been here four hours, and for the past hour, she's been pushing.

"I can see the head," the midwife says, and both Lola and I forget her question. Not that she didn't already know where I was; I told her twice before I left. But because she's had so much gas and air, she's high as a kite and doesn't know her left or right. It's been hilarious to watch, but seeing her in pain? Not so much.

"Push. One more push, Lola. You can do this," the midwife encourages, and I stand next to Lola, taking her hand and letting her squeeze me to death.

Lola grounds her chin into her shoulder, pushing through her next contraction, and my world stops. There's so much commotion going on around the room, but when I hear our baby crying, nothing else matters.

I look down to Lola and her eyes meet mine, hers filled with tears and shining with happiness.

Our baby is passed over to Lola, the midwife smiling. "Congratulations, Mrs Salvatore. You have a baby girl."

I gasp, looking down at the tiny little human wiggling to get free of the blanket the midwives have given her. I reach out, taking her tiny hand with my finger, and smile, my own eyes filling with tears.

"Perfect," I whisper, looking down at my two girls.

Lola looks up at me with a watery smile. "You're both perfect," she whispers before looking down at our daughter. "Welcome to the world, Ms

Cece Lily Salvatore."

Lola's name has been passed down to each generation, but when we were deciding names, she agreed to start a new tradition, opting for her mom's name and my mom's as a middle name. Her mom would have liked it. If she were a boy, we were going to call him Nathaniel Jerry Salvatore.

But looking down at my precious daughter, I know we picked out the perfect name for her.

"Hey, my beautiful baby girl. Mommy and Daddy are here. I promise you with all my heart that I'm going to love and protect you and your mother for as long as I love. I love you so much already," I choke out, leaning down to give my daughter a kiss. Instead of pulling away, I turn to Lola, taking her mouth in a soft kiss before deepening it, needing to show her how much I love her and for giving me such a truly precious gift.

When we both pull away, we're breathless. Cece is crying between us and we giggle. "We'll have to start getting used to that."

Lola chuckles, kissing me again. "Never."

"I love you, Mrs Salvatore, with all my heart. Thank you for giving me your heart, your soul, and your mind. You've given me the world," I tell her, my eyes watering once again.

"Oh, Dean." She sighs. "Thank you. Thank you for loving me, for giving me life and something to live for. And thank you for our daughter. I love you more than words could ever describe," she says, and I lean down, bringing her in for another kiss.

THE END

Author Note

As some of you may know, this book has been re-written. When I first wrote, *If I Could I'd Wish It All Away*, I never expected for people to actually read my book, let alone like my work.

But you did.

Yes, I still had some bad reviews and yes, the book was unedited. It was only edited through a friend, but as a beginner, I couldn't afford a legit editor. All the money profited was given to Women's Aid, and I'll be leaving a link below for you to donate, if you wish. The point is, you guys understood where I was coming from with the story, and that means a lot to me.

What a lot of you don't know is that the story was originally *my* story about my life. And when I shared it with an author friend, she told me to publish it, to get it out there, but for me, it was too personal. I couldn't share that with you, the struggles, the pain and the torment of wishing it was all over.

So I changed names and the majority of the story line, and fiddled around with other scenarios concerning the domestic violence. Some parts are still true to the original version, especially the part where I received help from the Women's Aid group. Without them I would never have found the confidence to press charges, to leave my ex, or to move forward. He'd taken so much from me already. And even to this day, I still suffer with anxiety amongst other things. And although every day is a struggle, and another fight, it's worth it. It's worth more than I could ever describe and for the first time, *I* felt in control.

I'd never be where I am today if I was still with him, and Women's Aid, are to thank for that. They helped me so much and I'll never be able to thank the support worker who helped me enough.

I hope women who have been or are currently in a relationship like Lola and Rick's will step forward and get help. Life is not meant to be lived in fear. You deserve to be happy, to be loved and cherished. You deserve someone who would rather cut off their own arm than raise a hand to you.

YOU ARE WORTH MORE.

Here is the website for women's aid, where you can get in touch with a support worker, donate, and find more information about the organisation.

https://www.womensaid.org.uk/

Printed in Great Britain
by Amazon